GUARDIAN OF THE SUNSHINE BRIDE

AUSTIN REHL

AUTHOR'S NOTE

Dear Reader,

I realize this is a commitment of your time and attention. That means a great deal to me. Especially since this is my debut novel. This story, and those that will follow in the series, are based on stories I created for my daughters, Riley, Allison, and Elayna. It is to them that this book is dedicated.

"Rehl Sisters Forever!"

I finally turned those bedtime stories into a novel. The story arc will last through a number of books. It will be exciting!

Thank you for reading.

Sincerely,

Austin Rehl

Like a seed of the spring flower,
She was carried on the wind.
From sunlit shores to frozen lakes,
An Empire she would mend.

Attributed to Emperor Heathron Dol Lassimer, Third Age

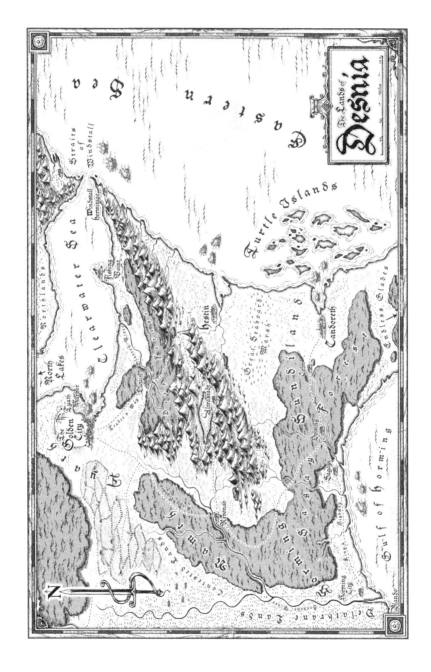

SAFE PASSAGE

"Get in the boat Jared," Arabella commanded.

The little boy stood shivering on the wind-lashed shore of the Clearwater Sea in mid-winter. Snow covered the ground, and ice formed along the shore as well. The wind was bitter cold. Nine-year-old Jared DeTorre crossed his arms over his cloak and shook his head in defiance.

He replied in a light, frightened voice, "If we try to cross, we are going to die," he said, his teeth chattering as he clutched a little threadbare blanket around his shoulders with one hand. His other hand held a dagger. It glinted in the moonlight.

"There is no food at home," his twelve-year-old sister said, "Seth will help you pull the oars, and I will steer the boat toward the light."

Seth, whose crystal blue eyes stared out from a gaunt face, nodded and waved for his twin to climb aboard as he shivered just as violently as Jared. It was the only way most people could tell the boys apart.

"You can't see the light," Jared insisted. He looked across the dark, stormy sea, at the waves heaving in the wind. How could Arabella possibly navigate her way in this weather? "We'll die..."

he whispered, then shouted it over the sound of the wind. "We'll die!"

"No we won't. The Windstall Hermitage has food, and warmth. We can make it," Arabella pleaded with him.

Jared suddenly felt the weight of the dagger. It was so large in his palm, and heavy, as if it might pull him down into the earth. His father had given it to him just three days before.

Jared leveled his eyes at his sister's once more. "It is a long way across the sea. Mother and Father would not want us to go."

"Mother and Father are dead," Arabella said coldly. "Mother and Father are dead, Jared," she said again, but this time there was warmth in her voice too, as she reminded her little brother of what he already knew. "Besides, you and Seth always said you wanted to be Sīhalt Guardians. Now is your chance!"

Jared shook his head. "I won't," he said.

"But we can't do it without you. Please…" Arabella held onto the boat as it tossed against her hand.

A sudden lash of wind almost pushed Jared into the sea. He resisted, stepping back and gathering himself. "Father told me to protect you. I won't let you die," he said, his high-pitched voice piercing the wind.

Arabella's features hardened until they were like bones licked clean, shining under the stars. She looked suddenly fierce, and pointed to Seth. "Look at him! He needs food! If we wait, we will all die. We will starve, or freeze, or…" she trailed off, as if hesitant about what she would say next. "Or the snow bears will come again."

"You said you wouldn't say that… You said you wouldn't do that anymore!" Jared shouted, gazing over each shoulder with intense fear. It was common for his imagination to take Arabella's warnings and make the threats they warned against come to life with paralyzing clarity. The white bears held more fear for Jared than winter, or famine — in fact, they held more fear for Jared than most things, even a stormy sea.

2

"I'm not trying to scare you, Jared…" But he didn't hear her. He heard the wind. He heard the roar. He felt the heat of the long scars he still carried of one of those beasts' giant claws carving into his back. It had happened on a hunt that had gone wrong. The bear had ripped his flesh and held him under the water, until his father had rescued him. "…I'm telling you the truth!" Arabella's voice drifted through the haze — he heard it now. "I am leaving, and I need you, I want you to come with us."

Arabella turned, impatient now, and waded further into the icy water. Jared watched her use all her strength to push the boat ahead of her, away from land, away from him. The holes in her leather boots invited the freezing slush to soak her feet, but she did not stop.

Jared panicked. "Arabella!" he called after her.

She turned around, her dark, inquisitive eyes wide within a storm of black hair that blew and twisted in the wind.

"What?" Her lips were cracked and blue, her cheeks burned by the cold air, but she was beautiful to Jared.

He said nothing.

"I love you," she said, "but I will leave you if you do not get on the boat." Behind her, Seth sat hunched within the boat. He clung to the oars, his thin arms spread wide.

Jared stood frozen, knowing this was a moment that could decide forever.

"If you help Seth, we might make it," she said.

Jared turned this over in his mind, eyes wide with panic, lips slightly parted. Then he tucked his dagger in his belt, and sprang up over the side, joining his sister and brother.

Arabella shoved the boat free of the ice and climbed in.

"Pull!" she cried over the sound of the water.

The little boys did their best to fight against the heaving waves. Jared rowed with a madness born of survival instinct. He would not give up! His fingers froze to the wooden oar as the wet spray solidified in the wintery blast. Still he rowed to the cadence of Arabella's cries. "Pull!" she shouted, again and again. Sometimes the oar would unexpectedly come out of the water as the little craft rose on a swell. Jared would be thrown about, but each time he would right himself and try again.

Only the worthiest of sailors would dare to cross the Straits of Windstall in a rowboat, and especially during winter. Only the desperate would do it at night. The mountains on the north and south of the Straits channeled the wind through the narrow passage. The shallows were treacherous for any vessel, filled with boulders that had dropped from the shouldering mountain faces. But the children of Elmar and Marine DeTorre were taught to endure — and so they rowed. Arabella used the rudder to correct for the weakness on Seth's side. He did not have the strength to row as hard or as often as Jared. Waves crashed in, pouring over the rails of the little boat—hands, cheeks, feet froze icy cold. They seemed to be making no progress at all. How much longer could they survive at sea? Jared wondered if he had already died, and was serving his sentence to the Dark One of death.

"I see the light! I see the light!" Arabella finally cried as she squinted into the storm before them.

Jared dipped his oar into the Clearwater Sea and pulled all the harder. He closed his eyes and kept his head bowed as he strained against the oar.

Thank you Abbath, he prayed silently. *Thank you.*

They were finally within sight of the Windstall Hermitage. The tall black towers rose into the night, staring out to sea with faint glowing windows of warmth. As they approached the land, another crushing wave tossed the little boat skyward. Jared felt the air cut into his cheeks, then nothing at all. He was weightless. He was spinning, and the storm danced around him. Next he felt the cold crush engulf him, and the dull, chill sounds of the waves. The rowboat had capsized and was shattered by another pounding wave. An explosion of wood floated among the sharp rocks.

"Jared! Seth!"

Arabella was able to stand up and keep her head above water. She fought to grab her brothers and pull them to the shallows. Jared could not speak he was so cold. He shivered violently. Once pulled out of the water, like newborn lambs they staggered on shaking legs, walking toward the towering doors of Windstall Hermitage.

Three small children looked up at the iron-bounded doors. Arabella was not tall enough to reach the metal ring set in the door as a knocker to announce their arrival. Instead the girl lifted her fist and began to pound on the frozen doors.

Jared huddled close to Seth. Their lips were blue and their clothing was crusted with ice.

Jared listened with his keen ears to see if anyone within would respond to Arabella's feeble knocking.

From deep within the Hermitage, Jared caught the words of a man who sounded strong, but tired.

"Who might it be on a winter's night like this? Probably more beggars suffering from the Plague. I will turn them away. We cannot have more sickness within our walls, we have buried enough of our brothers already."

Then Jared heard another voice, resonant and kind.

"Give them this food, before you send them on their way. Tell them they may sleep in the portico to stay out of the wind."

"Yes, Master Tove," the first voice answered.

The great doors began to open. Jared, so cold now, shivering violently, strained to see through the crack. There was a fireplace, the glow of it flickered around the room. He craved to sit by that fire, to feel it's warmth.

"Please..." Arabella managed to say, "let us in."

With the door fully open now, a man emerged dressed in all black with silver patterns stitched into his jacket. A black cloak clung to a tall, wiry frame, and the firelight glinted from the edge of a thin sword strapped to his hip. Jared stopped shivering, and just stared at it. The swords matched the craftsmanship of his own dagger. This was a Sīhalt Guardian.

The man saw him looking, and stared at him. Jared looked away.

"It's a Sīhalt Guardian!" Seth hissed in his ear.

The man appeared surprised to see the three small frozen figures before him. "Come see, Master Tove," he said beckoning an older man who after several ponderous steps joined him at the door. The old man was also dressed in black, and he knelt down to gaze more clearly into their frozen faces. He smelled of mulled cider and spices, Jared thought.

"Now how did you three come to arrive here, little ones?" he asked in a high, cracked voice. Hazel eyes stared out of a thousand wrinkles, and his grey moustache stuck out at different angles.

Arabella, who was shivering less than her brothers, composed herself. "These are my brothers," she said determinedly, "and they will go through anything to become Sīhalt Guardians."

"I can see that," he said, raising wiry eyebrows. A faint smile drew up the corners of his mouth. Then, looking at Jared, he frowned again and said, "Where are your parents, child?"

Jared took a step forward, finding the courage to speak through teeth that were so cold they no longer chattered. He clung to the dagger for strength, and was so hungry he could cry. In a weak voice he struggled to make himself heard.

"We rowed our father's boat across the Straits of Windstall tonight, Lord Sīhalt. Our father is dead from the Sickness, and so is our mother. But we are not sick. You said you buried your brothers. Let us join you. We will grow strong and serve you well. We are not sick, only cold and hungry."

Jared looked at the freshly baked bread the other man held in his hands. The older man looked at the younger man and raised an eyebrow.

"How did you hear Master Tove say that we have buried our

brothers?" the Guardian asked the boy. "The doors were shut when we spoke."

"I listened," Jared replied, "I can see and hear things from far away."

"What were we speaking of before that? Did you hear anything else?" the Sīhalt asked.

"Just before our boat was smashed, I heard your voices on the wind..."

"Tell them whatever you heard, Jared. It's okay, you will not be in trouble," Arabella said.

Jared looked up at both of the men wearing black. They seemed like men he could trust.

"You helped to arrange a marriage for a little princess in Candoreth, didn't you?" Jared said.

"Remarkable," the younger man muttered, then looked around outside to see if anyone else was there.

"Come in children, come in," Master Tove said, and placed a strong, warm hand on Jared's back as he ushered them in to Windstall Hermitage.

CHALICE OF PAIN

Ten years later....

The Sīhalt Guardians wore their wavy hair long, pulled back and tied at the neck. It lifted under the gentle motion of the horses, as they rode through the sparsely-settled grasslands of the western lands of Desnia. They galloped toward a low sun, and its golden glow filtered through swaying leaves and onto the same angular features and raven hair the brothers had inherited from their parents. Both young men were tall and lithe, moving with the graceful precision of the saber-toothed snowcats that prowled around the mountains of their home in Adisfall far to the north. They looked identical except for the color of their eyes. Seth's shone the same ice-blue as their grandfather's, while Jared's were a softer storm gray.

"How long has it been now since we have seen Arabella?" Jared asked, his voice clear and deep.

"It has been too long. Her baby is no longer an infant. He is already walking and talking now," Seth said

"What did you think of the last report she sent?" Jared asked, squinting into the sun and scanning the trail ahead. Satisfied he turned in his saddle and glanced behind.

"Arabella has been working on that peace treaty with the Delathranes for the last few years. She said the clans were beginning to coalesce around the leader of Clan Razewell, and that worried her."

Jared's face hardened. "I hope we can sort things out. Master Tove said I am supposed to transport a princess from Candoreth to Tyath. I have to be down south within a month to do my background work."

"Delivering a precious package?" Seth raised an eyebrow.

"Don't laugh. It pays well and escorting a Daughter of the Realm is an honor."

Seth shook his head and smirked, before leaning over one side of his saddle, and then the other, to stretch his tired back. "Whatever you say, brother. After we are done here, I will be going back to the Hermitage for some much-needed rest. We have been on the road for two years now."

"As soon as we can track down this Delathrane discontent, we will all be happier. I hope Arabella has a stew pot on the fire. I'm famished," Jared said.

Seth nodded.

"I know cattle have been known to wander, but King Raldric would be a fool to let the treaty go to waste by border raiding. That is the same Delathrane king we visited last time we were in the Grasslands, isn't it?"

"It isn't like Arabella to get this concerned about small things. She sounded scared in her letter. I wish we could have come sooner," Jared said. "She seemed so urgent in her report."

"I'm sure everything is just fine. Maybe she has found a beautiful princess she can't wait for you to meet," Seth offered.

Jared sighed with displeasure. "Yes, she doesn't hesitate to let me know she thinks it's time for me to settle down and begin a family..."

"Big sisters are like that," Seth said, laughing. "Anyway, if you take the brunt of it, she will leave me alone for a couple more years!"

Jared squinted at the horizon. "Do you see a shadow above those trees in the distance?"

"Rely on your eyes, Jared. You are the Sensor, not I," said Seth, gazing off in the direction his brother had indicated.

Jared looked again, evaluating the skyline in the far distance. He tipped his nose to the wind and Scented the air.

"I Scent smoke," Jared said, "far off. And not from a small fire!"

"Something bigger? A raid?"

The brothers exchanged a look of alarm.

"Callas!" Jared hissed, and their horses, Tamed by the trainers at the Windstall stables, galloped swiftly ahead. Jared's black mount charged forward the quickest. Seth was right behind him on his white mare, and both of them felt an icy jolt of fear begin to spread along their spines. Together they rode toward the farmstead that Arabella called home.

We should have come sooner, Jared thought.

The farmstead was torn apart. Not one wooden beam stood atop another among the buildings that made up the walled stockade. Plumes of smoke roiled like ghosts from the thatched roof of the barn, disappearing into a cold, clear blue sky. The gates had been forced open, and all the livestock was gone, while the door of the little cottage swung sideways on one hinge. Not a living soul could be seen in the wreckage.

The brothers ran towards the broken buildings and called for their sister.

"Arabella!" Jared called.

No one answered. Only the creaking of the off-angle door gave any response to their calls.

"The Delathranes were here just hours ago!" Seth confirmed as he stooped, studying the tracks in the dust.

"Arabella was right. They are asking for war," Jared said.

Seth looked around, hoping to find a clue as to where his sister was. "Arabella is smart and fearless—what would she have done?"

"A young mother running with a child? What chance did they have to escape?" Jared shook his head and passed his hands over his face.

"She is not here, so she has been taken, or she is hiding. Quick, let's ride to the river bank. We might be able to read more of the tracks outside the fence," Seth said.

"Arabella! Arabella!" they cried, as they rode their horses through the tall grass near the river, calling until their voices were hoarse from the effort.

Jared held up his hand at one point, and Seth remained silent while Jared turned his head to one side and listened intently.

Jared picked up the low tone, like a spring peeper calling from a brook in the forest, "Help...help...help..." she called weakly.

The brothers dismounted and ran to the side of their sister.

"What have they done to you?" Jared said, when he saw Arabella lying on the ground.

They knelt beside Arabella in the blood-stained grass beside the river road. There were signs of an intense fight. The grass was matted and trampled, as if a tornado has touched the spot. The blood on the grass was not all her own. Three Delathrane warriors lay dead nearby. There was no sign of the child she had defended so bravely.

While Seth searched for medicine in the saddle bags that might help the young mother, Arabella shook with a thousand small tremors. Jared cradled her head in his hands and leaned over to kiss her forehead.

"I'm sorry, Arabella. I'm sorry, I'm sorry," he repeated over and over. She was in shock from the wound to her skull. The bones around her left ear shifted under Jared's fingers as he held her.

11

She looked up at Jared, still clutching the small kitchen knife in her hand. Her lips moved, trying to speak.

"What is it?" Jared asked through his tears. "What is it, sister?" He leaned over her, bending close to listen.

"They took Tand," she breathed out in a whisper so faint even Jared struggled to hear. "They took my baby…to make him…a chalice." She spoke the last words so faintly Jared could not be sure he understood. Arabella frowned at this last, the corners of her mouth turning slightly downturned in a look of despair.

Jared was uncertain if he had heard the words correctly.

Make him a chalice? Jared recalled.

The words made no sense. Was it the delirium speaking? He rocked his sister gently.

"Who did this, Arabella? Who has taken Tand?" he said.

"Raldric," she managed to say.

Her trembling hands closed over Jared's arm.

"I have an infusion of jade cress for her!" Seth offered, handing the packet of healing herbs to Jared.

Arabella let out a long, soft moan. Her fingers spread apart, her neck and legs going rigid as she struggled to breathe. Her brows knitted and then began to relax with each short gasp. Finally, her face relaxed.

"She is gone," Seth said.

Jared smoothed her black hair, turning her face so he could not see the injury that had taken her life. He ran his hand gently over Arabella's eyes to close them. She was beautiful, even in death.

It had been Arabella, as a girl of twelve winters, who had held Jared and Seth tight that first lonely night their parents died. She had given Seth and Jared the last of the food. She took their childish dreams of becoming Sīhalt Guardians seriously enough to make the voyage to Windstall Hermitage and pound on those frozen doors with her small fist. Jared never forgot the bravery of his sister.

The savagery that had taken her from him sparked a cold anger that began to burn within his heart. As Jared held Arabella in his arms, a flash of the last image he had of his father played over in his mind as well. Moments before the Sickness took him, Elmar DeTorre had held his eldest son's face in his weakening hands and asked the small boy:

"You will protect your sister and brother? Promise me!" His demand was followed by a coughing fit so severe it obscured whatever else he might have said. The father pressed his finest possession into the hands of the nine-year-old Jared — a dagger forged at Windstall.

"You are the man of the house now. You must protect your sister and brother."

I have failed you, Father. Jared said to himself.

The brothers wrapped Arabella in a linen cloth. They gathered stones from the river bed and stacked the rocks reverently in a pile to cover her remains. In the silence that followed, they washed their faces, and hands in the clear running water.

When they had finished Jared looked into a calm pool of water. He drew the knife his father had given him. The silvery blade gleamed sharper than the coldest wind he had ever felt on his face.

Jared removed his black Sīhalt Guardian cloak. The silver thread of the stitching glinted on each side. He began at the right side of his forehead and began cutting his hair in fistfuls, then he carefully shaved close to the skin, looking at his reflection in the still waters. The pale skin of his scalp contrasted with the tanned skin of his face. His black hair fell onto the surface of the water, disturbing the mirror image.

"You are not to blame for her death," Seth said, shaking his head in disagreement in the act of Sīhalt mortification. "We could not have known Arabella and her family would be attacked. Should I shave my head in shame as well? Now is not the time to feel sorry for yourself. I feel anger, not shame! We must follow the trail of these barbarians and make them pay."

"You think I don't feel anger?" Jared said, his fists clenched tightly, an animal growl escaping his lips. "I could have defended her. If we had left a day earlier — she tried to warn us!"

"Let's go now. We can at least rescue our sister's son!" Seth said.

"King Raldric did this," Jared said. "We know where to find him."

"How do you know it was him?"

"She whispered it to me before she died. She said Raldric took her son and 'made him a chalice, or chattel, I am not sure."

"If the trail leads to King Raldric's encampment, there is no peace treaty for me," Seth said.

"Master Tove forbids us to act as assassins without his approval. We should ride back and report this to him. When we swore to honor the ancient laws, we gave up our right to seek our own justice," Jared said, his hands and voice trembling.

"You swore to protect our sister first!" Seth said, pointing to the dagger. "The ten-fold law applies."

With that, Jared nodded and replaced the hood of his cloak. He looked like the shadow of a death angel. Determination now chiseled into his young, bereft face.

"The war band headed west," he said, looking toward the setting sun. "Let's ride."

BRIDAL NEGOTIATIONS

Queen Renata rolled her eyes at her stepdaughter.

"Kathleen, he is waiting in your father's study right now," she said. "You will not keep an Imperial magistrate waiting, no matter what your hair looks like."

Kathleen tried to smooth her hair down on the sides where the wind had teased it out in wild, wispy strands.

"I look like the sea-witch from Elayna's puppet show!" Kathleen protested, while passing her hand again and again over her red hair. She paused to look at a mirror in the hall. She noted the contrast of her visage with that of the queen's. Kathleen was all curly red hair, pale skin, and a few freckles. The queen's skin was flawless and sleek. She had the ebony complexion and wide dark eyes common in the kingdom of Hestin.

Her stepmother took a deep breath. "Kathleen, this is it. Here is your future." The queen placed her hand on the heavy door.

"I hope this doesn't turn out to be my prison," Kathleen replied.

"Let's hope not," she said with a trace of understanding. Then Renata pushed the heavy door open.

The Imperial magistrate looked up from the map he was perusing. He lifted a well-used handkerchief to his nose and wiped it ever so gently. He then inhaled through the still-somewhat-clogged nostrils and made an obstructed sucking noise.

"Your Majesty," he said in a strong nasal tone.

He swallowed and continued, "I am Imperial Magistrate Dirm Uppenslaw."

The magistrate's lisp only added to the difficulty in listening to him speak. Kathleen forgot about her hair. She managed not to let her disgust show on her face. She was a princess of House Dal Sundi, after all. One glance at her stepmother, however, made her want to laugh out loud. The look on the queen's face was one of unschooled revulsion. Her opinion of the man was thinly veiled with a grimace-like smile.

"And this must be lovely Princess Kathleen Dal Sundi?" the magistrate said with a lisp. Kathleen thought his nose might drip on the floor.

Kathleen nodded with a polite smile. Then the man reached out and took Kathleen's hand, pressed it to his lips, and kissed it. She only moved to wipe the back of her hand on her dress when the magistrate turned to speak to the queen again.

"Your Majesty, I have come to negotiate the nuptials," he said to the queen.

Kathleen wondered why the magistrate would not just speak to her. *Negotiate the nuptials? Am I a cow at the farmer's fair?* Kathleen thought.

"I assume the king will be joining us?" the magistrate asked.

Queen Renata moved and gestured out the window.

"He will arrive shortly," she said.

Dirm drew some parchment out of his case and laid it on the table. The lettering was exquisite. Kathleen saw the beauty of the loops and flourishes attached to the even-handed script. Her eyes skipped over the legal jargon and moved down to the lines that mattered most.

Whereas the Princess Kathleen DeLunt Dal Sundi, of her own free will and choice, doth herby affirm acceptance of betrothal to Prince Heathron Dol Lassimer of the Imperial family, with marriage to be held no later than Midsummer's Day of the four hundred and fiftieth year of the reign of the Imperial law...

Kathleen knew her upcoming marriage to Heathron Dol Lassimer was not an established fact. To the Candoreth court's surprise, the prince had not turned away from the marital contract formed over eleven years before, when Kathleen was only six years of age.

It is my duty.

She looked out the window at the sun-drenched beaches of her home. She loved the palm trees and the waves. She loved the sounds of the sea birds circling overhead. She would miss it all.

Kathleen had read about the cold north. She spoke to merchants that said rivers as wide as their harbor would freeze solid. The only ice Kathleen had ever seen was enjoyed on special occasions when she had chips of it in a sweet tea during hot summer days. She couldn't imagine a harbor full of ice.

Dirm Uppenslaw sneezed loudly. He held a hanky near his nose and sniffled. Wiping the sweat from his brow, he looked at the fly buzzing around the room and murmured, turning to his assistant, "Flies at this time of year." He shook his head and drew the corners of his mouth back.

"What a dirty swamp," he said, leaning over the documents.

Magistrate Uppenslaw spoke in a low tone, but enough that Kathleen could hear him. She was glad her father had not heard him speak of Candoreth in such a way. It was hard to tell what Lukald might do to a man who insulted his kingdom.

"You must arrive by midsummer," Dirm said, listing the articles one by one. "You must, by sunset of the summer solstice, be presented to the Gates of the Golden City. Once at Tyath, your champion may request that the gates be opened to you. You must be accompanied by a herald to declare your house colors and crest. As you know, you must arrive with at least fifty horsemen in your retinue."

Kathleen was growing sick of his 'you must this, and you must that.' The servants entered with the emblems of House Dal Sundi, large silken flags emblazoned with the House emblem—a passion flower in full bloom. Dirm stamped each one with the Imperial seal.

"These will be your tokens at the gate," Dirm said. Kathleen nodded and handed them to one of the nearby clerks.

"And your signature will be needed here, here and here," indicated Chief Magistrate Uppenslaw.

As he spoke, he almost sneezed again. He managed to keep it under control by raising his eyebrows and placing a finger firmly against his upper lip. Kathleen evaluated him again. *What a strange worm of a man*, she thought.

She dipped the pen in the ink and paused. Kathleen felt willing to do her duty for her country. She knew how much her people needed the bonds of matrimony with the Capital city. They had not recovered from the effects of the Plague, even though fewer cases were seen every year. Her marriage could help open markets for trade in the northern cities. If the pirates could be repelled, all the families who relied on shipping and farming and textiles could prosper. If she did her duty, her father might even get out of debt.

Without her marriage to the Imperial family, her people would continue to suffer. Her father could even be deposed. They were counting on her—all of them.

"I hoped my father would be here when I signed," Kathleen said.

Queen Renata looked around. She seemed surprised to see King Lukald was still not in the room.

She pursed her lips and said, "Where is he?"

The clerks and lawyers who had entered the room shook their heads. They didn't know either.

"I will be leaving at first light, Your Highness," Dirm said. "I've got to get out of this infernal heat. Perhaps take the road back north through the mountains. Maybe it will be cooler." A bead of sweat rolled down his pale forehead. "At any rate, we shouldn't delay," he said in his snotty voice.

He reached for the handkerchief, and Kathleen looked away. Even though she had known this day would arrive, this wasn't how she imagined it. It felt forced.

She signed the first place, then dipped the pen again and signed the next. A voice boomed from the hallway.

"That's my little girl!" King Lukald said.

He strode into the room with wide confident steps and hugged Kathleen. A few drops of ink from the pen dripped on the parchment, much to Dirm's displeasure. A clerk began dabbing it immediately. The king paid him no mind. He held Kathleen by the shoulders and looked into her eyes.

"Are you sure you're ready for this, Kathleen? Are you sure?"

Kathleen knew the opportunity for a marriage such as this would not come again. It felt like a chore that was in need of completion, and Kathleen was not a person to shrink from a job that needed doing.

"I'm seventeen, Father," Kathleen said. "I'm even looking forward to making the final plans for the wedding procession."

She looked into her father's eyes and blinked back some tears. She needed to be strong for him.

"I will personally witness this contract and take it to the Imperial Registrar myself," Dirm said with his strong nasal emphasis.

Kathleen wondered to herself why it was that so many academics, accountants and clergy often spoke in that same irritating tone. She preferred a manlier voice like her father's.

"Of course she is ready, Lukald," Renata said. "She has waited her whole life for this." The queen swept in to hold her husband's face in her hands, keeping him from seeing the emotion Kathleen was struggling to control.

"Every young lady wants to marry royalty. I did." The queen gave King Lukald a kiss on the cheek and turned him toward the table.

"Kathleen just needs to sign at the bottom of both copies, and the contract with the Empire is binding. We will do our part and they will do theirs," she said.

The king slowly nodded his assent.

"The day has finally come!" he said.

Kathleen wasn't sure if he spoke of the relief that would come to him in this political bargain, or the sadness in seeing his daughter leave. She hoped it was a little of both.

Her father leaned over and signed the contract with a sigh. He turned to Kathleen and hugged her.

"My little girl is all grown up."

Kathleen felt the strength of her father's embrace.

King Lukald handed her the ink stylus, and Kathleen wrote her name below his. She gave her signature a little flourish—her penmanship included a delicate design that invoked the passion flower as a subscript to her name. This would be the last legal documents wherein her last name was Dal Sundi. She signed in her best handwriting:

Kathleen DeLunt Dal Sundi

Magistrate Uppenslaw slid a copy of the document toward King Lukald. "This is for you, Your Majesty," he said, and tucked the other copy carefully into his case.

"Congratulation to House Dal Sundi." He bowed toward those gathered in the room. "Best wishes, Princess. I expect to see you before the Longest Day of Summer," Dirm said.

Then the man brought out a ring. It was golden and encrusted with diamonds along the thin band. The central mount held a gem that perfectly reflected the light streaming in the window.

"As a representative for Prince Dol Lassimer, I, Dirm Uppenslaw, place this engagement ring on your finger."

As beautiful as the ring was, she felt like recoiling from his

GUARDIAN OF THE SUNSHINE BRIDE

touch. Kathleen wondered why it was that men were always congratulated in marriage and women were given 'best wishes.' She hoped she wouldn't need them.

"She will leave soon," King Lukald affirmed. "There will be plenty of time for traveling, merry-making, and feasting. Kathleen will arrive a week before midsummer, I would guess."

Kathleen looked forward to seeing cities and towns that were new to her. For all her adventuring, it had mainly been on the water, among the islands of the coasts or riding horses in the hills above Candoreth.

Who would not want to spend the better part of a season attending parties and feasts in one's honor? It would all be culminated in a grand ceremony at the Great Golden Cathedral. She and Heathron would be married and form a new union, joining Sundiland to the empire by a renewed marriage for the coming generations. It was what her parents had wanted all those years ago.

"Perhaps you will appreciate a portrait of our Prince Dol Lassimer," Magistrate Uppenslaw said. He handed a likeness to Kathleen. She looked at it closely while the queen and the royal lawyers discussed details of the engagement contract with the magistrate. Kathleen wasn't listening closely but looked intently at the painting instead.

Kathleen turned back the portrait in the light, allowing the dimension of the dried paint to give her a better sense of his features. It had been so long since they had met. They were only children then.

Would he be kind? she thought. *Would he be as handsome as the artists had made him?*

He was certainly wealthy—all the Imperial princes were.

Can I love him?

Kathleen wasn't sure.

Before leaving the room, the magistrate turned and said, "Also, the empire has taken the liberty of hiring a Sīhalt Guardian for the princess during her journey northward. The roads have not been as safe of late."

"But we already have a Sīhalt for House Dal Sundi," King Lukald protested. "Sīhalt Girdy Frast is like family. He will go with Kathleen during the wedding procession."

Dirm turned to the king with a look of derision.

"You may send whomever you like with the princess, but your man won't be the Prime. Our man will. His name is Jared DeTorre. He should arrive soon. No need to worry, we're paying him, not you. Read the contract!" The magistrate turned his back to the king and held up the case, waving it in the air as he left the room.

King Lukald was red in the face. He seemed to be realizing for the first time that he was giving up more than just his daughter in this deal with the Empire. The magistrate was gone, leaving behind only the open door and the copy of the signed marriage contract.

DREAM OF LOVE

"**B**ecause I am tired of being lied to," Prince Heathron Dol Lassimer said.

He took a deep breath and centered his hand back on the mat. He felt sick at the suggestion his father had made.

"You are willing to throw away your Marriage Day for the no-name girl from Sundiland?" the Emperor asked.

"I wasn't the one who made the agreement, Father," Heathron managed to say as he held the Hare Caught in a Snare pose. His legs pointed upward as he lifted one hand and held it out to the side, balancing his entire body on one arm.

Emperor Kade Dol Lassimer placed his hands on his knees and leaned forward in his wheeled chair, trying to look at his son while upside down.

The Emperor sighed.

"I could just *command* you to break the betrothal. We made those arrangements with King Lukald and his wife before the Plague, before the financial ruin of the whole city of Candoreth."

Heathron noticed his father's sigh. The Emperor only did that when he felt strongly about something. Those who failed to notice this habit had made grave errors while negotiating with the Empire.

The prince held the pose a moment longer out of determination. His sandy blond hair fell downward, hiding his brown eyes. He finally allowed his body to relax as he rolled onto his back and then gracefully stood before the Emperor.

"It is not Kathleen's fault the Plague struck. Nor is it her fault the Candoreth treasury was drained. If she keeps her part in the bargain, I will keep mine," Heathron said.

The Emperor sighed again deeply.

"House Dal Sundi was not the only one to suffer when the Plague came through."

The emperor gestured toward his useless legs under the blanket on his lap.

"For all your ability, you amaze me at your lack of political acumen. You have the noble houses eating out of your hand! Among all my potential heirs, you have succeeded me. Can you even remember the details of that distant arrangement with the little red-haired girl?"

"I remember her like it was yesterday, Father," Heathron said. His eyes filled with a faraway mist in that moment, so much so that he failed to notice the servant in front of him proffering a towel. When he came to, he took it and wiped the sweat from his brow.

Emperor Dol Lassimer shook his head.

"You should just marry a noble daughter of a prominent family here in Tyath. Jessica Turlin, for example, would be happy to accept your attention."

Prince Heathron's upper lip quivered at the mention of Jessica's name.

"That girl is strikingly beautiful!" his father said.

"And manipulative to no end!" Heathron added.

"She is just doing her duty and seeking the best outcome for her House. They are all expected to do so," the Emperor said.

Heathron thought of the years he had known Jessica Turlin. She had been vicious to him when they were children. It was not until he had risen from obscurity, and gained a real possibility at ruling Tyath some day, that she had become all smiles and niceties. Heathron had no doubt that were he to fall from grace, she would turn on him again. Jessica Turlin was a viper in a silk dress.

"If Kathleen refuses me or fails to show up by midsummer, I will choose another bride. However, I will not simply discard her."

"What if I were to grant you greater lands and titles while I yet live?" Emperor Dol Lassimer suggested, rising slightly in his chair in hope. Heathron began shaking his head, but his father continued, "I would be willing to throw in the northwestern Marches as part of your personal inheritance. That includes all the settlements along the river—on both sides."

"Would you like to know what I want most of all, Father?" Heathron asked.

Emperor Kade Dol Lassimer paused and considered the question.

"What is it you want most, my son? I will happily give it to you if I can," he said.

"I want a chance at love! True love. I am tired of the intrigue among the ladies at the Imperial court. I love our nation, and I will do my duty to lead, but I grow weary of the back-stabbing nature of the nobility. It has been my greatest defense to tell them I am already betrothed to a girl in Candoreth, a girl they cannot easily malign." Heathron lowered his voice, realizing he bordered on disrespect to his father.

The Emperor stroked his beard and considered his son's words carefully.

"You want love? Yet you are willing to bring your unsuspecting bride to this Golden City, full of intrigue?"

"As my wife, I will protect her. At least I know she comes without ulterior motives."

25

The older man laughed at Heathron's words. It had the tone of good-humored amusement. He motioned for his son to come closer and clapped the prince on the shoulder as he spoke into his ear.

"They all come with ulterior motives, son. All a woman really wants is security—then everything else!"

He laughed again at his own joke.

"Fair enough, Heathron," Emperor Dol Lassimer said. "I will support you in your childlike faith. We will pursue the contract with Candoreth as we first established."

"I already have," Heathorn admitted. "Magistrate Uppenslaw should be in Candoreth signing the documents as we speak."

"What!" The Emperor furrowed his brow, then he began to smile. "Well done, my son. A future Emperor should go grasp what he wants and make it his own! I am glad you didn't wait."

"You think I am a fool?" Heathron had not prepared himself to have his father agree with him. The Emperor's sudden willingness to acquiesce threw Heathron off balance. It left him wondering what his father's next move might be.

"When I was young, I made decisions based on love. This world could use more of that—for however long the love might last."

"You think I am making a mistake?"

"You are a better man than I am, Heathron," Kade said. "I will not hinder you in this decision, but do not expect me to expend a great effort. I will not send a military escort to bring Princess Dal Sundi here. Her father must do that."

"What about sending the navy to escort her here safely to our harbor?"

"You know the dangers of the sea between Tyath and Candoreth. The pirates have grown thick as wave grass in the coastal waters. I will not risk our ships either."

"The roads are very dangerous in these times, especially far from the capital. I would go there myself if the law allowed it," Heathron said.

"You are the groom. You must remain here in Tyath," Emperor Kade said.

"I hired a Sīhalt Guardian from the Windstall Hermitage to escort her," Heathron said.

"Short of an elite regiment, a Sīhalt is probably the best you can do. We have reports the Delathranes are restless," Kade said. "Good luck, my boy."

The chair-bound emperor saluted his favored son as a servant turned his chair around and pushed him from the room.

Heathron felt relief flood over him. He had not relished the idea of telling his father what he had done. It had gone better than he had hoped. On one hand, he still had his mother to contend with--on the other hand, it appeared he might remain free of Jessica Turlin.

SWORDS OF JUSTICE

L ittle Cedric tried to tighten the rags he wore about his waist, but gave up. The thin belt woven through slits in the loincloth refused to be cinched any tighter. It still hung loosely around his bony hips.

"Cedric, quit scratching yourself. It makes me think you have fleas again," King Raldric said.

The little boy cowered, ready for whatever might be thrown in his direction.

"Cedric, we don't want to see anymore of your scrawny hide," the Meat Witch said with a laugh. "Now if you were a strong, handsome, young warrior, that might be different!"

Azrah's position in the clan allowed her to speak at will. All the other people who mocked Cedric did so only after following King Raldric's lead.

Little Cedric hated her for it.

She should respect my father like all the others, he thought.

For the thousandth time, he promised himself that he would break her jaw if she ever ran her mouth when he was the leader of Clan Razewell, Meat Witch or not.

Cedric pretended to ignore her as he set the carved game

pieces, made of light and dark wood, back on the board. He played against himself, since no one would play *Chendris* with him anymore. He had already beaten them all—many times. They might mock him, but they were no match for him in a game of strategy.

"He might reach manhood yet. He has survived eleven winters so far," King Raldric said, eying him while slouching in his seat. "He just doesn't look like it."

A few of the warriors chuckled hesitantly, not sure if Raldric intended for that to be funny.

The chieftain-king had the glassy look of someone caught in the dreams. Cedric saw his father use the powder more and more often since meeting with the *Handri* noblemen at the Golden City.

Cedric looked at his arms, scrawny and bruised as they usually were. He failed to put on weight like his peers, and he often coughed and was slow to heal from any blow he sustained. At least when King Raldric was inhaling the smoke of dream leaves, he was beaten less often.

"Only the scowls on his face and his knack for *Chendris* reveal any kind of fire that he is my son," King Raldric said, looking at him with a grin. Cedric watched out of one eye as he set the pieces carefully in battle array against each other.

"Are you angry, Little Cedric?" the king asked.

Cedric scowled.

King Raldric laughed.

"He does look like me when he does that! Doesn't he?" the king said.

Cedric treasured the compliment. His father was the man he most wanted to emulate.

Cedric twisted his face into his best rendition of rage and indignation. He held his small knife out in front of himself. The barbarian king laughed loudly, stirring the rest of the warriors in the tent to laughter as well.

"Look at his face. If he were not so pale as a *Handri*, he would look like me! I make that face in battle, do I not?" King Raldric laughed, pointing at the little boy crouched in the corner, growling like an animal.

"Be careful, he is known to bite!" King Raldric said to the laughter of the Clan leaders that lounged about the haze of the enormous royal tent. The air smelled of smoke from dream leaves and the *Handri* farm they had burned. They dragged the spoils of their conquest back to their encampment on the Great Grasslands.

Cedric knew that his father and the other warriors would be drunk today in celebration as well. It was a relatively safe place for him. Cedric preferred the occasional backhand from his father to the certain torment he received from the other children outside the royal tent. He stayed close to the king, watching and listening, trying to be invisible when possible.

The setting sun still slanted through the tent flap when the people began to call for their leader. Cedric heard the yells and whoops of excitement among the people. King Raldric looked up and took another sip from his newest cup. He held it like a trophy and wiped his mouth with the backside of his other hand. The delicate chalice had a thin braid that wrapped around the king's knuckles. The rim of bone, not yet polished smooth, still held some of the coloring of the blood that had fed it earlier that day. He held the thing easily in one hand and swirled his drink beneath his nose, savoring the smell. The plaited hair on the little vessel was still attached to the tiny skull that had been lifted with it. Delathrane runes were newly carved alone the edge.

A messenger boy arrived and knelt before the king.

"My king, the *Handri* have sent messengers to our encampment. They are coming on horses," said the boy.

"How many?" asked Raldric.

"Only two, my king," the boy said.

King Raldric looked around at his warriors, smiled, and raised the cup filled with drink.

"They come to talk. That is all the *Handri* do these days, talk, talk, talk. Since the Serpent God struck the Empire with the Great Sickness, they have had no stomach for war. Let us see what these Sīhalt Guardians have to say this time. Perhaps they will bring even more gifts to try and buy our friendship for the Empire," King Raldric said.

The barbarians laughed and cheered their king, who settled back onto his throne, taking another sip.

Cedric watched from the corner of the tent, where the shadows hid his thin form. He crouched on the hides that covered the ground around the backside of the throne. He wanted to see how his father would deal with the *Handri* emissaries.

"Is it not dangerous to allow them here, so soon after our raid into their lands?" a warrior asked, before adding, "I do not think it wise."

King Raldric placed his arm around the shoulder of the concerned warrior. The gesture of friendship was swiftly followed by King Raldric holding a dagger at the man's throat, the tip pressing into the flesh. Cedric could see a drop of blood begin its pathway down the man's neck.

"I can take care of myself and my own," King Raldric growled.

The warrior nodded slightly—otherwise, he held perfectly still.

"You have fought with me in many battles. Do not let our friendship cloud your judgement. You are not Chieftain, and I have not smoked as many dream leaves as you think."

King Raldric then sheathed his dagger as quickly as it had been produced.

Cedric, watching from the corner, felt so proud of his father.

The flap of the royal tent was pulled aside. The commotion told Cedric the Sīhalt Guardians had arrived.

Two men of equal height stooped down to enter the tent. They stood taller than any of the warriors. Only King Raldric could have looked them in the eye. Cedric shifted to get a better look at the visitors. He often wondered how the weak *Handri* people had pushed the fearless Delathranes away from the ocean, out of the mountains, and finally to the grasslands they now inhabited. Cedric had never met a free *Handri*—he considered how easily he might defeat them if he were king.

Cedric had expected the men to look weak, but these Sīhalt Guardians looked strong. They carried swords at their sides and daggers in their belts. They wore high leather riding boots and thin black cloaks that almost reached the ground.

Cedric wondered at the meaning of the emblems on their clothing. It was a curved stick, crossed by a sword. Their skin was pale like Cedric's, and one of the men had ice blue eyes and long black hair pulled away from his face. A silver clasp held the hair at the back of his neck. Cedric briefly imagined himself cutting the hair of the blue-eyed Guardian and stealing the silver ornament. The other Guardian wore a deep hood. Cedric could only see the lower portion of his face.

"Welcome, Guardians," King Raldric said, his hand gesturing in a sweep that took in the whole of the throne tent. "Do you have word for me from the Golden City?"

Cedric crouched on the floor, watching the two Sīhalt Guardians. The blue-eyed one scanned the area, almost as if he were counting the people in the tent, taking note of their posture and position. Cedric drew his feet under him and grasped the leg of a table, pulling himself closer.

"King Raldric, we have word for you," the hooded one said. Cedric noticed a tremor in the man's voice. "But it is not from the Golden Cit—"

"Take off your hood when you speak! I will see the face of my guest," Raldric said, interrupting the Sīhalt.

The man paused and slowly removed his hood. A smooth, freshly-shaven scalp gleamed in the torchlight along with eyes that were gray in color, but rimmed in red, as if the man had been crying.

"You have no hair, Guardian!" King Raldric laughed. "Are you taking on the Delathrane ways?" He laughed and gestured to the warrior at his side. "A few tattoos will make you a better warrior." The drunk barbarian warrior smiled and patted the swirling patterns on his scalp.

The Sīhalt Guardian did not laugh. He did not even smile politely.

"We stopped along the way and saw a farm that was ravished," the bald Guardian said, the emotion in his voice more apparent.

"Our cattle had strayed across the river. The *Handri* did not want to give them back! You would have done the same in my situation," Raldric said proudly.

The Guardian stood tall and stared at the barbarian king. His bald head tilted as if considering the words of the king.

"King Raldric, you and your men took a small child from a woman along the river," he said softly. "We have come to get him back."

"I cannot remember every slave we take. We have captured many. You cannot expect me to know of what you speak!"

Cedric crawled closer. He was intrigued. His short life had been a string of abuses, often given without much warning. He had learned to read the faces and body language of those around him. Cedric learned to cower even from the hand he did not see coming, anticipating its strike. Cedric saw the blue-eyed Sīhalt was not relaxed, and there was something in the manner of this bald one that had made him feel on edge. Cedric watched and listened.

"This woman fought bravely before she was killed. At least three of your men were killed by her."

A murmur of recognition arose among some of the men. A few nodded and grinned.

"Ah yes, she fought like a panther. Was that woman your lover? If so, you are a brave man!" King Raldric laughed and sipped the dark liquor more calculatedly this time from his bone goblet.

"She was our sister. We have come to ransom her son," the man said darkly.

"I cannot give you the child," the king said. "But allow me to offer you a drink."

My father is not afraid of them, Cedric thought, his heart thudding with excitement—or was it fear? He clung around the edge of the wall, watching closely.

King Raldric began to laugh again.

"Have a drink with us, Sīhalt. We can put our differences with the Empire behind us and drink together as comrades."

There was a pause, and the room filled with a powerful tension.

Cedric watched as the bald Guardian's hand crept ever so slightly toward the hilt of his sword. Then, he took a step forward. Had his father noticed this?

In that moment, Little Cedric leaped up from the floor, in between his father and the Guardian, grabbing his knife. "Father, he is going to attack y—!" he screamed. But before the last word had even left his mouth, he felt a hot pain burst across one side of his face. His head was rattled and his vision went black for a second or two, until he found himself sprawled on the fur-covered floor

He raised his head to see his father, King Raldric, standing over him. He had slapped Cedric with an open palm, sending the small boy spinning away.

"Nonsense!" the king said, rubbing his hand. "The Sīhalt Guardian is going to have a drink with us!"

Cedric looked up from the floor at the glowering Sīhalt Guardian. The man had jumped back as Cedric sprang, and now he was baring his teeth at the king, but Raldric ignored the danger.

"I will give you some drink, Guardian. Only a little though-- *Handri* can't hold their liquor the way the People of the Serpent do." The king motioned for Cedric to rise. "Give our guest a drink, Cedric," he said with a knowing smile.

Cedric reached to take the small cup from his father's hand. The freshness of the recent scraping of the skull was still evident despite the Delathrane runes carved into the surface. Cedric accepted the small vessel full of the dark liquor and carried it to the Sīhalt standing before him.

"Here is my newest cup—it is little, but very pretty. Do you like it?" the king said.

Cedric noticed the man's eyes widened in strange recognition and his hand quivered as he reached for the small chalice. Cedric hesitated, seeing anger, not fear, in the Guardian's face. The man took the chalice from Cedric. Then the Guardian turned the chalice and poured its contents on the floor at Cedric's feet before placing the little cup carefully inside his cloak. Cedric barely had time to dive to the floor as blades came out.

The throne tent erupted in shouts and screams. Cedric cried out as he watched the Sīhalt Guardian lunge and plunge his sword multiple times through his father. Warriors, too late to save their king, leapt from their seats to grab weapons. They fought the Guardians.

The blue-eyed Guardian held his ground, protecting the flank of the bald one. Cedric crawled out from beneath the chair. He climbed onto his father's lap. King Raldric held two hands against the wound in his chest. His breathing was short, and he winced with every breath. Cedric sobbed and placed his pale hands over that of his father's and tried to apply even more pressure to staunch the bleeding.

The rest of the tent was complete chaos. The whirling devils, those Guardians dressed in black, kicked and punched and stabbed. When they didn't strike with the blade, they struck with an open hand or a fist, breaking bones, blinding eyes.

King Raldric gasped for air and looked into the large eyes of his son. Cedric felt the rise and fall of his father's chest slowing. The man that had always stood so tall was unable to rise from his throne. In Cedric's mind, King Raldric would always remain a mountain of muscle and determination. But now, here, the king had closed his eyes, and his breathing was slowing. Cedric dared to do that which he had always dreamed of doing. He laid his head on his father's chest and hugged him tightly. "I love you, father," he said. "Don't leave me." Then came the last words Cedric would ever hear his father say.

"Get away from me, you filthy mutt," King Raldric said, and weakly pushed Cedric away. As much as those words hurt, the thought of losing his father filled Cedric with terror. Without his father alive, how would Cedric live? His father's blood now covered half of his face. Cedric screamed for the Meat Witch.

"Come Heal Father!" The boy yelled. But the Meat Witch was nowhere in sight. All that Cedric could see were flashing blades and fallen forms of Delathranes in the throne tent. More and more warriors streamed to the fight. The sides of the tent were ripped open by knives as more of the people, including women and youths, surrounded the throne tent and pressed upon the Sīhalt Guardians, desperate to bring them down.

The blue-eyed one struggled to maintain his feet. "To the horses!" the bald one yelled. "To the horses!"

The battle was fierce, and Cedric could barely see what was happening. The Sihalt were surrounded!

Cedric heard what sounded like an angry lion. A hole opened up in the middle of the violent throng. The People of the Serpent began to fall back! They trampled each other in an attempt to run away. Cedric could not believe what he was seeing. Just two men were making the Delathrane warriors flee? Where was their courage? He clutched his knife and scurried among the legs of the crowd. He was the only one moving in the direction of the fight!

Cedric was stepped on and kicked, but he struggled to find the Sīhalts he would kill. When the torchlight finally fell on the scene, Cedric saw two demons dressed in black. The floor inside the enormous tent could hardly be seen for the bodies and discarded weapons that littered the ground. The bald Guardian stood panting like a wolf that had finally killed the entire flock. The other seemed to hold him upright.

Cedric saw his chance. He crawled close and lashed out with his knife and struck the demon behind his knee. He was rewarded with the sight of blood, and in the same instant, the feel of steel.

At first it didn't hurt. Cedric saw the Guardian's blade, but didn't quite comprehend what it would do to him. The thin profile of the blade swept in a graceful arc, as quick as a dragonfly on the wing, leaving his face divided as neatly as a loaf of bread cut in two. Dropping his knife again, Cedric writhed back to the floor, grasping his face, trying to hold it together in some way. Then the pain came. He screamed in the darkness.

FLIGHT OF THE FEARLESS

Darkness had fallen. Seth was able to run, but Jared hobbled toward their horses. The wound to the back of his knee made him grit his teeth with each painful step, his leg swinging awkwardly as he moved. Seth's cheek was streaked with blood from the gash below his eye, and the People of the Serpent were not giving up. Jared whistled for Steed, and the stallion whinnied in reply. Nothing would keep the horse from coming to him now.

The war cries of another band of warriors rode into the encampment. Jared hobbled faster. The war band encircled the burning royal tent, looking for the enemy. They took aim and began to shoot arrows when they spotted the Sīhalt Guardians running for cover. Some of the Delathranes even resorted to rocks and sticks. Jared's cloak crackled, its protective properties activated with the impact of a stone. He ran and slid beneath a wagon in the enclosure. Hearing Steed approach, Jared climbed up the side of the wagon. He jumped into the air and managed to land on the back of the horse. Feeling for the stirrups, Jared turned Steed with his heels.

"Go, Jared, I will catch up!" Seth said. He sprinted in the direction of a sturdy corral that held his white mare.

Jared urged his mighty black stallion through the darkness that now surrounded him. He heard the soft sound of arrows passing harmlessly by. He could hear the curses and hoofbeats of his pursuers fade into the distance. The Delathrane horses were almost like ponies. They were no match for the Windstall stallion when it came to speed and stamina.

Jared felt for the pouch beneath his cloak. It bulged slightly with its contents. Jared had gathered the remains of his sister's son. However, he could not shake the numbness he felt or the image of the Delathrane boy lying on the ground in the tent.

I murdered him. I massacred those people, he thought.

He had killed the boy, for what? Was he wrong to defend his home, his family, himself?

I'm no different than those who murdered Arabella.

Jared rode back to the river and crossed back over to the site of Arabella's resting place. Jared uncovered the body of his sister and placed her across the horse's back. He would take her to be properly buried at Windstall Hermitage.

He waited for Seth, listening in the night for any sound of footsteps or hooves. The wild dogs howled in the darkness. Jared could see their eyes gleaming as they approached the site of Arabella's burial. They could small death on the air, and they were hungry.

A large one approached, hackles bristling.

"Be gone," Jared said quietly, knowing the keen ears of the wild dog would hear him. "I am in no mood to deal with your kind this night. I have killed enough beasts for one evening." The wilds dog sniffed the ground and, sensing no fear in this man, led the pack away into the undergrowth.

Jared waited for Seth all night, but as the light began to grow in the eastern sky, Jared mounted his horse and rode toward Windstall Hermitage, hoping to meet his brother there.

INFECTION OF REVENGE

Back in the Delathrane encampment, Clan Razewell was still in commotion from the massacre they had suffered the night before. During it all, a small boy with a mangled face gradually regained consciousness. Now the blistering pain came back. Cedric choked on his own congealed blood. His divided face had swollen. He could not manage a word. He struggled to breathe or turn his head toward the form of A'hald, his father's First warrior. The tattooed man squatted by Cedric and set down his axe. He looked him over and huffed. Cedric fought for vision against the blood that oozed from his forehead. He saw the First warrior walk to the form of King Raldric, slumped on his throne. The First warrior leaned close to his father, feeling with his cheek for any air passing by the king's lips. The boy cringed inside when he saw A'hald lift his father from the throne and drop him to the earth.

I will kill you for that! Cedric thought, in the silent recesses of his mind.

The Meat Witch hummed and moved among the Delathranes that had not yet died. Cedric could hear her wooden beads clinking as she made her way among the dead or dying. She walked among the fallen, feeling for a pulse, listening for breath. Those that still lived were given a small dose of Healing at the hands of the Meat Witch. Cedric could hear the gurgling of his own breath. The pain made him wish he had joined his father in death. He tried to call for help, but his voice sounded like air being blown through water. The bubbles sounded louder than the words.

"Little Cedric still lives," he heard the Meat Witch say as she leaned over him.

Cedric felt the tendrils of warmth as the Meat Witch chanted while laying hands on both halves of his face.

The pain increased. Cedric cried out.

A'hald intervened.

"That is enough. He won't amount to much anyway. Drag him to the corner of the tent. Save your strength for those that make our people stronger."

A'zrah removed her hands and looked at the wound again.

"I mended the largest vessels, but he still might die from infection. There is horse manure here," A'zrah said.

He lay in a fevered coma for weeks. Luckily he was not the only one who was sick. No one would have made an extra effort for Little Cedric. However, an old woman, tasked with caring for the wounded, passed by at times and poured a bit of soup down his throat or placed a moistened cloth across his heated brow. Cedric shivered from cold and burned with heat. He lost track of time, but remained alive.

There were times that he was slightly lucid. He caught snatches of conversation here and there. Most of the words dealt with the needs of the people after the Guardian attack. Many of the best warriors that had been in the encampment that evening died. A'hald sent out emissaries asking for reinforcements from surrounding clans. They came, swearing allegiance to the new Chief of Clan Razewell.

A'hald found no challengers to his role as the new leader of

Clan Razewell. Leading the central clan gave him a strong claim on the leadership of all the Delathranes.

Tears rolled down Cedric's face as he listened. He knew the throne belonged to him! Yet even in this near-death state, little Cedric provided amusement to the People of the Serpent. He became something of an oddity as he lay in the corner of the tent, taking one breath in, one breath out. All the other people had either recovered or died, but not Little Cedric. He breathed laboriously, and the people began to place bets on whether or not he would live to see another week, another day.

"I can't believe he hasn't died yet. If he makes it to the new moon, you must Heal him completely," A'hald said.

Cedric heard the new Chief and grabbed on to the statement with the strength of a man in fear of drowning. To the new moon. He would live!

Each new moon came and went, and still no hand of Healing was offered. Cedric felt the cold of winter approach. He kept fighting to survive. He had long since transitioned from feeling sorry for himself. In his lucid moments he began to plan revenge.

They will bow to me, or I will destroy them all, he swore to himself.

He used the time lying on the floor in his father's tent to nurse his hatred of the Meat Witch, the Sīhalt Guardians, of all the *Handri* that could not be trusted.

"If he lives, he will have a massive scar. I have never seen a wound quite like that. Look at it ooze," A'zrah said. "I will need to save up some reserves for this one."

"Why did you help him in the first place?" a newly sworn warrior asked.

"It was a crazy day. I did what I could for everyone," the Meat Witch responded. Her manner was one of someone who gave a gift worth nothing.

They should've saved my father.

Cedric knew if King Raldric were still alive, the warriors

GUARDIAN OF THE SUNSHINE BRIDE

wouldn't be sitting around. They would be avenging themselves on the false Guardians who attacked them, while his father offered them a friendly drink.

RELUCTANT PROTECTOR

J ared lifted his head from the cold, white stone of the altar in front of him. He tilted the hilt of his *impla* so that he might more deeply kneel to pray. Jared closed his eyes tightly. He placed his hands on the well-worn stone altar. Over centuries the edges had been made perfectly smooth by the hands of the devoted. The cavernous sanctuary seemed to Jared to be the tomb he deserved. The smoke of incense hung in the air.

Jared looked down at his callused hands. The iron and proteins dried to a dark brown and found every crevice of his skin. The blood was not his own. His fingernails were darkened around each edge by the lives he had unjustly taken. No one else could see it—he had scrubbed his hands clean, but his eyes still saw the stains. Jared knelt, bare-footed on the floor, dressed in a white linen robe. He heard the quiet approach of Master Tove.

Jared passed his hands through the air in the motions of infinity, wafting the smoke toward his mouth and nose, breathing deeply, the wide sleeves of his white robe like the wings of a dove.

"Yes Master?" he said, and rose to his feet.

They bowed towards the four points of the compass before Jared and Master Tove left the dimly-lit Sanctuary of Mediation.

"Jared, you have an assignment," Master Tove said.

Jared's heart sank. A knot of loathing rose in his throat. His head involuntarily began to shake from side to side.

"I already have a mission. I must find my brother," Jared said to Master Tove.

"You seek revenge for his death."

"I am sure he still lives!" Jared exclaimed.

"You must not focus on Seth's disappearance. The Sīhalt Order needs you to perform as the Guardian you were trained to be."

"I have waited for Seth long enough. He has not arrived. I plan to travel south and west and search for him, even if I must travel the to the Western Sea," Jared said.

"You have a duty to perform!" Master Tove spoke forcefully. "You are a man in the strength of your youth, fully trained. You have accepted a commission to escort a Daughter of the Realm. You must serve, not seek your own desires. It is only through service that you might gain the wisdom and restraint needed to function again as a true Sīhalt Guardian."

The words bit deep into Jared's heart.

"You believe me to no longer be worthy?" he asked.

"No amount of searching or killing will bring your brother back. It did not serve your sister either."

Jared bit his lip and glanced over at the newest grave in the Windstall cemetery. At least he knew where Arabella could be found.

"Then can I not stay here and complete Sandu?" Jared asked, looking in shame at the floor.

Master Tove shook his head.

"You will not take your own life with my blessing," Master Tove said.

"I brought death upon those I love most. I brought them into danger and I was unable to protect them," Jared said.

"Our newest initiates look at you with awe. Those boys watch your every footstep in the gardens, every bite you take at meal time. They all want to be like you." Master Tove turned and gestured toward a line of boys who were waiting for their morning meal.

"I am no longer worthy of their admiration," he said under his breath. "I only ask their forgiveness. I am a failed Guardian," Jared said.

"It is not their forgiveness that you must obtain," Master Tove said gently.

"You are right, Master. I beg your forgiveness. You welcomed us into your walls as starving orphans. I have failed you as well." A quick hiss was heard, and Jared had the sharp tip of his *impla* sword pressed to his own neck. If only this Master would give the word, he would turn his blade upon his own throat and end his dark existence.

Like lightning, Jared heard the pristine ring of Master Tove's sword contact his own and lift the tip safely away.

"Put away your sword, my son. It is not my forgiveness you must seek either, but your own. Are you still willing to obey my commands?"

Jared slid the thin sword back into the sheath at his side. He raised his storm-gray eyes to look into the kind face of his master. Jared noticed the lines of age that creased Tove's face. His hair was now mostly white.

"I have an urgent message from Prince Heathron of House Dol Lassimer." He held out a small cylinder made of wood, carved with the icons of the Imperial House. The thing was completely coated in wax. The Fox and Acorn insignia had been impressed at each end.

Jared opened the seals slowly. Removing the parchment and holding it up to the light, Jared began to read:

Lord Sīhalt,
Our family has relied on the Sīhalt Order in the past.
I hope to be able to do so again.
I do not know what may be the cause of your delay.

However, I wish to provide details concerning the protection of my bride during the wedding procession.

Please meet with me in Tyath on your journey southward.

In Order and Peace,

Prince Heathron Dol Lassimer

Jared shook his head and handed the parchment to his master.

"I have no interest in babysitting a princess on the way to her marriage. I wish this assignment could be given to one of the others," Jared said.

"No one is more prepared than you, Jared," Master Tove said earnestly.

Jared passed his hands through his black hair, now starting to grow back. It reached the base of his neck.

"Jared, do you remember the day we first met?" Tove asked.

Jared looked at Master Tove and blinked.

"Yes. I..." Jared corrected himself. "We were freezing and starving, but Seth and I trusted Arabella to save us."

"We opened the door and saw the three of you. I was so worried about the people already within our walls that I almost closed the door. Do you know what made me invite the three of you in, even during the height of the Plague?"

"I always thought it was because you knew I was a Sensor. I was able to tell you what you had said before you opened the door. Only someone with exceptional senses could have done that."

"That was only part of the reason."

Jared waited for Master Tove to continue.

"I looked down at your sister Arabella, and she said, 'These are my brothers, and they will go through anything to become Sīhalt Guardians.' She believed in both of you, even at that young age. It made me believe as well. The difficult road was beginning, not ending, at our door, and yet there she stood: half-starved, mostly frozen, holding the hands of two little boys. If she were alive today, she would still believe in you."

"I remember, Master," Jared said solemnly.

Master Tove reached down and grasped Jared by the hands, holding the small scroll to Jared's chest. They stood eye to eye.

"Serve House Dol Lassimer in this assignment and regain the strength I know you possess," Master Tove said.

"Is this a command, Master?" Jared asked.

"You are like a son to me. I ask it as a loving father would ask his child."

Jared took a deep breath.

"May I have your blessing to search for Seth after I complete this Imperial wedding procession?"

"Do your duty in this assignment, then I will bless your efforts to discover the truth regarding Seth," Master Tove said.

"I will go to the prince immediately," Jared said.

They embraced and walked toward the dining hall to join the others at breakfast.

SWORN TO PROTECT

J ared rode toward the gates of the Golden City, his face hidden by the black hood of his riding cloak drawn over his head. Silver tracings of crossed Swords and Staves visible on each side. His ever-present sword and dagger at his belt. He rode slowly, scanning the land and forms about him. Jared had been to the capital city a few times during his training, but this was the first time he arrived for an assignment.

"Good morning, Lord Sīhalt," a stout peasant said with respect and placed the back of his callused hand to his forehead in salute. Jared looked down from his mount and nodded in return.

"A good morning to you as well, Master Farmer," Jared said.

The man pushed a cart laden with the golden amaranth grain seeds.

Since it was planting time, the fields of Tyath were full of peasants of all ages plowing, planting, and tending the little round seeds of the amaranth grain that fed the population during the long winters.

As Jared rode, other men saluted. Mothers pointed him out to their children, young men stood a little taller, and older girls whispered to each other, adjusted their aprons, and looked in his direction. Jared felt pleased that the common people of the Golden City still had such a high esteem of his Sīhalt Guardian Order. He wanted to be worthy of that respect.

One whole section of the fields approaching the city was planted with stone instead of grain. Thousands of grave markers, row upon row, stood out against the green shoots of early spring grass. If one did not know the history of the Plague that had struck all of Desnia ten years ago, it might have seemed foolish to devote so much level agriculture land to a cemetery. The City of Tyath had suffered greatly. A third of the population had died that year. Those who had lived through the devastation knew that the bodies needed to be disposed of quickly. They buried the dead in the expansive fields surrounding the Capital city. The land would certainly lay fallow, for a generation anyway—there were fewer mouths to feed, and fewer farmers to work the ground.

The grave stones gleamed with the same golden glow of the walls and buildings of Tyath. Jared wondered if perhaps some of the homes within the city had be torn down, the blocks being used to memorialize the dead.

The City Guards stood at attention as Jared approached the famous gates. "How may we be of service to you, Lord Sīhalt?" the ranking officer asked, his eyes looking straight forward with his chin lifted in formal posture.

"I have come to speak with Prince Heathron Dol Lassimer," Jared replied in a deep, even tone.

"Do you know the way, Lord Sīhalt, or would you like me to provide an escort to the Imperial grounds? It is a fortunate day whenever a Sīhalt visits our city," the Captain of the Guard said. He held himself in a rigid stance of attention.

The stone walls of the city were enormous, and standing close to them, they obscured all but the tallest spires of the Imperial Cathedral and Keep within.

"Thank you, Captain…"

"Bastion, my lord. Captain Jarek Bastion at your service, and my men as well, sir." The man stood even more erect than before.

"That won't be necessary, Captain Bastion. I know the way."

The captain saluted crisply, and his men followed his lead.

Jared continued on his way—he could hear the captain speak to his men.

"That is a real Sīhalt Guardian! You saw the Sword and Staves on his cloak? Take a good look, Guards, because there are not many of them remaining."

The line of soldiers watched him until he turned the corner.

Jared avoided the main Market street, with its chanting vendors and trading merchants. He smiled a tight-lipped smile beneath his hood.

Am I a true Sīhalt? he thought.

Deciding to avoid as many people as possible, Jared turned into a narrow way that led behind a stone wall of a private garden. The wealthy merchants in this quarter of Tyath maintained gardens walled off from the public. The ivy climbed over the private walls and twisted along the stone arches along the narrow side street. The cobblestones were washed clean, and banners bearing the Fox and Acorn herald of their Imperial House Dol Lassimer were hung between the buildings on each side. Even the raked gravel of the catch trench in the middle of the side street was free from debris. The city was still very clean, at least in this neighborhood.

A few noblemen and moneychangers quietly acknowledged his passing by stopping and raising their gilded walking canes.

Jared nodded as he rode Steed slowly along the street.

He finally rode into an elegant central courtyard and dismounted. A steward, dressed in the livery of the Imperial house, closed the gate to the courtyard. Jared noticed the six guards hidden among the ornamental evergreens but gave no sign that he had seen them. They probably carried crossbows. He allowed them to believe they blended in with their surroundings —other men would have missed them.

The horse snorted. "I know, old boy," Jared whispered to Steed. The animal had eyes and ears almost as good as his own.

Jared kept riding, looking straight ahead. He dismounted, and another steward reached for Steed's reins as they approached. The massive horse pranced sideways, tossing his head slightly to avoid his grasp. Jared clicked his tongue a few times, and the stallion calmed down and allowed himself to be led away.

A tall, lithe man stood at the top of the steps leading to the main entrance. He wore his sandy-colored hair in a manner that matched his riding boots. It appeared windblown. The man wore a hunting shirt made of leather, embossed with the crest of house Dol Lassimer. It was a fox and acorn motif. Jared saw the man lift his open hand in welcome as he descended the stairs, his brown eyes pulled tight at the corners by a sincere smile. The smile contrasted with the fierceness of his angular jaw line. Encircling his forehead, he wore an ornate band of glinting metal.

"Lord Sīhalt, I welcome you to the Golden City! How was your journey?" he said.

Although they had never met, Jared knew this was the son of the Emperor, Prince Heathron Dol Lassimer. He was surprised at the prince's open, friendly demeanor.

"I apologize for not being more prepared for your arrival. I did not expect you so soon, but I am pleased to welcome you today."

Jared knelt and placed his palm over his chest in a show of respect. "I am at your service, Prince Lassimer," he said.

Heathron took the last few steps to meet Jared and clapped him on the shoulder. "They say a Sīhalt Guardian will readily kneel for even the lowliest urchin he is sworn to protect, but never bow by force, not even to an emperor. Is that true, Lord Sīhalt?" Heathron asked.

"Our custom is as you say, Your Highness. We will serve faithfully those to whom we are sworn, but bow only to God," Jared said, his posture erect as he now stood before the prince. He then stepped forward and accepted the hand Heathron offered him in friendship.

"Thank you for coming. I am very anxious to have my new bride here soon." Jared nodded and removed the hood he had worn since before entering the city.

The prince took note of Jared's features.

"You can't be any older than I am," he said, looking unimpressed with the guardian before him. "I told my messenger that I wanted a man with experience. I want a warrior that can accomplish this job," Heathron said. "Are you sure you are up for this commission?"

"I am following my master's counsel in being here," Jared said, striving not to betray his true feelings.

"You mean, there no other Guardians, then? More experienced?" the prince asked.

Jared breathed in long and hard, but he said nothing.

"Are you prepared for a long journey with a young princess as your charge? My father tells me you will have to travel through wilderness, villages and cities from here to the southern realm. Will the princess be safe?" Heathron asked, his face suddenly awash with innocence, but then hardened as if conscious he needed to show authority.

Jared, however, looked sharply at Heathron, his gray eyes flashing.

"My skills need not be questioned. I will protect my charge, prince," he said in a low voice.

Suddenly aware of the powerful tension, Prince Heathron's eyes widened a little before he raised his palms slightly and smiled dumbly. "Er, I meant no disrespect, Lord Sīhalt." The prince smiled again, friendly as before. "I would go myself if law and tradition allowed it! We have little time to prepare. You will be traveling to Candoreth before you know it. Let us go in and discuss the details."

FETCHING

Prince Heathron Dol Lassimer had the bearing of a man who learned early to tread carefully among the egos and entanglements that enmeshed the capital city of Tyath.

"I may not be the smartest or the most experienced Imperial prince," Heathron explained to Jared as they sat in his library. "I have half-brothers, nephews, uncles, and cousins that are older than me. They all have varying levels of power within the Imperial family. But this wedding is my chance to forge a stronger alliance—just as father tells me—and to strengthen the Imperial ties to a vassal state." He paused then, as if this was something he understood much less than he was trying to project. "There is a whole web of legal contracts that allow tax money to flow into the Imperial treasury—it's really quite interesting. None of the contracts used to be so valued as the marital contracts with the outer realms. A proper wedding to a Daughter of the Fealty and a princess from one of the surrounding kingdoms could bring a young prince a real chance at leadership in the Imperial power structure," he explained.

"I hear that the southernmost kingdom at Candoreth, and its

surrounding lands, have been overlooked for years," Jared said in agreement.

The prince nodded. "When the Plague swept the whole continent of Desnia, our capital city was in chaos just like all the others. The Imperial family in Tyath suddenly paid little attention to the vassal realms further away. We had to stop the losses within our own walls first," Heathron said.

"It is impossible to seek prosperity when your very survival is at risk. Even in the far north, my home in Adisfall was struck by the Plague. The Windstall Hermitage had victims during those years as well," Jared said.

Prince Heathron nodded with enthusiasm.

"Some fled to other kingdoms in the hope of survival. That didn't work. Some say it helped the sickness spread faster. So many people died. The Luzian priests were there to care for the sick and orphaned. They taught us that the Talented ones brought the curse upon us by trying to circumvent Abboth's will," Heathron said.

"It didn't take long for the Academy in Tyath to be shut down. Are there any Talented schools remaining open anywhere?" Jared asked.

Prince Heathron shook his head.

"They brought ruin upon us," he said. "They can't be allowed to do that."

"There were some Healers that saved people. Some even died trying to help the weakest victims. The people seem to have forgotten that," Jared said.

"The people were afraid. They wanted answers."

"Is a Talented person safe in Tyath these days?" Jared asked.

"We finally have implemented ways to deal justly with the Talented folk. They don't hold the same status they once had, but they can't be killed without a royal decree either," Heathron said. "They are welcome as long as they abide by the rules."

"You have learned your craft well, Prince Dol Lassimer. That was a very diplomatic way of putting it. I hope it hasn't all been turned over to the Luzian Church. Their Great Cathedral was built with the magic of Talented Builders during the Second Age. They are still benefiting from the ancient ways those Talented people followed."

"With all the problems we had here in Tyath, during the aftermath of the Great Plague, many don't like to remember the truth of our history. Most believe that all agreements that existed beforehand should be void. I guess tragedy makes you evaluate your priorities. My father doesn't think I should keep the promise with the princess in Candoreth. However, I still remember the days we spent together as children. I fell in love with her." The prince smiled at the memory. "I know I was just a child then, but I remember walking hand in hand with her. She was so kind and genuine to me. I remember her green eyes, easy laugh, and hair the color of a red sunset. She seemed like an angel to me. No one has treated me with so much honest kindness since," Heathron said.

"The experiences of our childhood can be formative," Jared agreed.

"If any part of that angel I remember has remained with Princess Dal Sundi as she has grown, I want a chance to be with her again."

Jared considered the prince's words. Being familiar with the history of House Dol Lassimer, he understood the machinations that happened between the rival branches of the Imperial family, mixed with the influences of the Luzian Church. The internal competition for wealth and power led many a young boy to die early in his crib, or an old man to breathe his last breath with a pillow over his face. As cunning and ruthless as these men could be in their struggle for superiority, the women of House Dol Lassimer, and many aspiring noble houses, were drivers of much of the conflict. They sought to manipulate any opportunity for their gain. Often their very survival depended on it. It was said that the only woman an Imperial Prince could trust was his mother, as long as his father was already dead. A sincere and loving marriage would surely be a treasure in the Golden City.

Prince Heathron laid a small book of poetry on the table.

"Have you ever loved or been loved, Lord Sīhalt?" Heathron asked.

"From parents, you mean?"

"I mean loved by a woman. Has a girl ever stolen your heart?"

Jared lowered his eyes but pinned back his shoulders at the same time. "My training was constant from early childhood. I spent time studying under the Sīhalt Masters. I am familiar with the great love stories of history. Literature and history were part of my education, but I am afraid I am more practiced in the martial arts than those of love, Prince Heathron."

"Well, I love love," Prince Heathron said, and all of a sudden the vain authority he had worked hard to generate drained away like raindrops landing on sand. He became misty-eyed, tender… weak, Jared thought.

The door opened, and the clerks came shuffling in. They were standing close by each other like a flock of ducks, scribbling their notes and nodding importantly. One magistrate, dressed in gold-trimmed robes, kept touching his nose and sniffling importantly.

Jared noticed the man was favoring the right nostril. Jared could hear the subtle difference in sound. At times like these, his gift as a Sensor could be a curse.

He could use a vapor of blue satinwood each morning... to help him break his habit of dream powder.

A quick look at the man's glassy eyes told him for sure.

Yes, dream powder.

The chief magistrate in the gold-trimmed robe acknowledged Jared with a nod of his head. The man appeared full of himself. He spoke up in his forced nasal tone.

"We are hiring you to escort Princess Kathleen DeLunt Dal

Sundi here to the Golden City. Law and tradition stipulate that her wedding procession must arrive here at the gates of Tyath. After being announced and welcomed, she must enter the gate anytime after the sun has reached its zenith on Midsummer's Day. She has been told all of this. There is a timeframe in which Princess Kathleen must arrive. Imperial marriages take place during the Festival of Longest Day."

Heathron looked furtively at the Guardian. "Lord Sīhalt, does that all make sense?" he asked.

Jared nodded in understanding.

"She will need to be accompanied by a retinue of horsemen as she approaches the gate. I expect her father, King Lukald, to ensure those requirements are met," the chief magistrate added.

The prince scanned the document in front of him and listened as the chief magistrate quoted from it. "The law reads that the princess must lead a company of at least fifty horsemen in battle array to the city gates." He paused and then added, "That should not be too difficult for King Lukald to arrange, even in his weak financial condition. So, 'after making merry with music and feasting, the bride will approach the walls of the city and be announced by her Herald, and present the endorsed banners of her house. Whereupon a Captain of the City Guard, doing his duty, will open the gates and receive the princess into Imperial protection."

Heathron nodded, smiling at the document before him. He looked up with eyes shining with excitement.

Jared wondered how a man could be at once so astute in the political realities of Tyath, but also appear as a boy smitten by the beauty of his first love. It softened Jared momentarily, who was surprised by the feeling.

"Have you heard what she is like, Lord Sīhalt?" Heathron asked.

"You mean the Princess Dal Sundi, my lord?" Jared said.

"I do hope she is as beautiful. I remember her freckles. We were just children. Women with freckles can really go either way when they grow up, can't they? I mean, I am sure she turned into a beautiful woman, but have you heard? Among your Sīhalt spy network, I mean."

"We usually do not employ our secretive Sīhalt spy network to check up on the development of local beauties," Jared said, one corner of his lips curving up into a smile. He went on, "But before coming here, I do recall reading a report that referred to the princess as 'fetching' in one of them."

"Fetching? That's good, right?" Heathron nodded, looking to the Sīhalt Guardian and then to the few clerks still in the room.

"Well, he did not say she was 'as radiant as the naked sun, rising from the sapphire sea, with molten drops of golden rays dancing to eternity...' but I am sure she will be beautiful," said one of the younger clerks.

"Speak not of nakedness, clerk, when discussing my bride. I don't care if you are quoting the poet Zahan."

"Yes, Your Highness," he said and placed his fist to his head. "I just saw the book. I meant no disrespect."

"Besides, the words of Zahan likely will not do her justice." The prince smiled again at the Sīhalt. "Bring her here safely, my friend," he said, placing his hands on Jared's shoulders, eyes leveled—it was as if they had known each other for years.

Jared was reminded of what a fool a man could turn into when he was in love. He commended himself for never having allowed his heart to be taken.

"I will," Jared said simply.

Heathron beamed. "Now that you work for me as a Guardian and counselor, is there any advice you would give me before you go? Anything I am missing?" he asked.

Jared was surprised at the question. Rarely did a young ruler see fit to ask for advice. Instead, they would abdicate responsibility for their choices and leave others to clean up the mess. He found himself more impressed with this prince the longer they interacted.

"Your plan seems sound, Prince Lassimer. You have estimated sufficient time for the wedding procession to wind its way without being rushed. Scouts should be able ride ahead and prepare each settlement or city for the necessary festivities. I agree that a water route up the coast would not be wise."

The prince nodded, listening intently.

"Our informants say the Delathrane barbarians remain divided. Over land will be the safest way for your bride to travel. For all their destructive tendencies, the barbarians spend more of their energy attacking each other. No chieftain has been able to unite the clans since the Empire defeated them at Dumal Wells a generation ago. Their population has increased. We are not sure by what craft they were able to avoid the worst of the plague, but they are no longer as timid, and their raiding has had an uptick. Barring a union among the clans, there should not be a force large enough east of the Great River to endanger your bride if she is going to have a military escort."

"Then I pray for tranquility, Lord Sīhalt," Heathron said.

"I swear to bring your betrothed to the gates of this city by the summer solstice, or die in the effort to do so, Prince Lassimer."

"I believe you," Heathron said, looking directly into the fierce eyes of the Sīhalt Guardian. "I believe you."

"I am comforted that you believe the plan is sound. Is there anything else?" Heathron asked.

"Yes," Jared said, leaning close to the prince's ear. "Remove your chief magistrate from his position."

Heathron looked at Jared in surprise.

"Terminate Magistrate Uppenslaw? Whatever for?" he said quietly.

"He's addicted to dream powder." The prince just blinked. "My prince, you can't trust a man using that powder," Jared said.

Heathron didn't know what to say, but he nodded in understanding and then lowered his voice. "That may be complicated," he said quietly, "but thank you."

Jared gathered his notes and left the meeting to prepare for the journey to the warm coasts of Sundiland.

CAPITAL SPIES

irm opened the door after a quiet series of taps. Lord Balfoest entered, his skeletal frame towering over the magistrate. "So how was your trip to Candoreth?" he said in a slow, knowing tone.

Dirm wondered how Lord Balfoest already knew of his recent return from the South.

Does the man have spies in every corner of Tyath?

"I am not at all happy in that southern swamp. They had flies, already. At least I wasn't required to travel with the princess during her procession," Dirm said.

The tall nobleman drew one corner of his mouth up, a partial grin.

"My niece, Larissa, is a friend of hers. I asked if the girl had any proclivities for sorcery. Larissa wasn't sure, but I wonder if the Dal Sundi girl inherited her mother's...abilities."

Dirm recoiled at the notion. "Is she Cursed?" he asked.

"I don't know, but she plans to be married into House Dol Lassimer by mid-summer."

Dirm's eyes widened, and he pursed his lips.

"The prince doesn't know the risk?"

"He is so love-struck he will not see reason," Balfoest said. "But I believe there may be another explanation "

Dirm raised his eyebrows in interest. "I won't stand for our Golden City to be defiled by that Cursed girl."

"Perhaps our clever prince knows exactly what he is doing. He already has the confidence of Admiral Hale, and he has promised to build up the Tyathian Navy. A wife that could help in that endeavor would be most valuable. He would to pretend to love her for that reason alone. Do not underestimate Heathron."

"How does this change our plans?" asked Dirm.

"Not in the least. We will have the barbarians in place to harass and slow the wedding procession at every turn. I offered a reward to King Raldric if he could bring the Princess Dal Sundi to me. I believe his successor is just as interested."

"Where will I find this leader of the savages?"

"You will meet and negotiate with the Chieftain-king of Clan Razewell. Find him in the contested lands." Lord Balfoest said.

A greedy smile grew on Dirm's face as he dabbed his nose again with a personalized handkerchief, sniffing as he did so.

"Ah yes, the Delathranes. Better to have it done with in the wilds of the road. We don't need a massacre on the city square," Dirm said.

"We are not going to kill her, Dirm. We need to test her first. If she inherited her mother's ability with sorcery, we will make our decision then," Balfoest said, irritation growing with his explanation.

"We don't want a witch roaming free in Tyath," Dirm said.

"If she fails to meet her obligations at midsummer, she won't be married to House Dol Lassimer. Prince Heathron will simply be forced to choose another bride. We want Kathleen Dal Sundi here on our terms, not as our future Empress," Lord Balfoest said.

"Won't King Lukald declare war and try to rescue his daughter?"

"I have associates along the southern coast who have agreed to attack the city of Candoreth when I give the word. She will be trapped here. Poor little thing. If it is true that the girl is able to use the old ways, the...Talents..." Lord Balfoest said. He smiled deviously.

Dirm blinked as understanding dawned. He felt torn between the duties to his faith and his own desires.

"We can all use more dream powder," Dirm agreed, licking his lips and sniffling. "I will make sure it happens as you say, my lord."

"She's the bleeding bait that will lead the wolves to her door. If you are the one to succeed in destroying her chances of marrying the prince, you will be rewarded as we agreed. If you fail, you won't need to worry about Abboth smiting you. I'll do it myself," Lord Balfoest said.

Dirm began to quiver at the thought. The thought of reward gave him reason to hide his hands behind his back as they began to shake. Dirm hated himself for his weakness.

The girl should be eliminated, he thought.

The insufferable blasphemer, Lord Balfoest, turned to leave. Dirm frowned at the skinny man's back as he retreated from the room.

Dirm immediately found himself considering how he might win the prize! He despised Lord Balfoest for the power he held over him. Dirm dreamed of a retirement in the countryside filled with dream powder. The idea held such sway over him. He knew he would do anything Lord Balfoest asked.

Luckily, his secretive master had left a memento of their meeting. Dirm picked up the small bag and knew immediately what he must do. After telling his guards he would not accept visitors for the rest of the day, he detached the round pipe-like handle of the knife and arranged the powder into neat lines. He covered the delicate blade with the power and drew his long sleeve up, exposing his upper arm. He began to slice into his skin. He felt a warmth cloud his mind as the powder blended with his blood. He no longer felt the painful longing. With his mind now clear, he snorted the remaining contents up his nose. Then he fell back on his bed, trapped in the exquisite nightmares of his addiction.

RISK WORTH TAKING

The Princess Kathleen DeLunt Dal Sundi tiptoed into Elayna's room and stood for a moment, watching her little sister sleep. The little girl reminded Kathleen of herself when she was a child. The six-year-old lay snuggled up in her blankets, her pale, freckled face framed by the curly red hair they both inherited from their parents. Kathleen knew she would miss the excitement Elayna brought into her life, the little kisses on her cheeks and the spontaneous flowers her hands would offer as a gift. Kathleen leaned over and whispered in her ear.

"Laaaaynie, do you want to see the turtles? Let's go see the turtles, Laynie."

The little girl moved and stretched a bit. She finally opened her bright green eyes and blinked slowly. Elayna raised her eyebrows.

"Hi, Katie. Did you say turtles?" she asked, with interest rising in her voice. "Can we go today?"

Kathleen nodded and pulled the covers back. "We sure can," she said, "And I'm having Samuel set the sailboat ready so that we can sail out to Turtle Island and stay all night too."

Elayna squealed with joy and jumped up from the bed. She ran around the room, singing a song repeating over and over. "We are going to see the sea turtles!"

As she danced around the room in her nightgown, the morning sun backlit Elayna's skinny arms and legs. Kathleen laughed with pleasure at the sight of her little sister's antics.

Queen Renata suddenly appeared at the door of Elayna's bed chamber. Her black hair was pulled tight against her head, smoothed to perfection. She raised an arched eyebrow, revealing more of the golden eyeshadow she favored.

"Sam told me what you planned to do," she said.

Her lips were full and broad, and when she smiled, although she didn't look happy, she displayed two rows of immaculate teeth. The tone of her skin was just as dark as her hair and glowed in the morning light. Kathleen wondered how her stepmother managed to always look so refined.

Kathleen turned to the servant Samuel, and his guilty face pleaded for forgiveness.

"I was asked directly by my queen, Your Highness," he began to say.

"You don't need to explain yourself, Sam. You answer to me, not Princess Kathleen," Renata said.

The elegant woman looked at the two disheveled girls and shook her head subtly.

"I insist that you stay within the walls of Candoreth. It isn't safe to go wandering," Queen Renata said.

"Renata, I know exactly where we are going. I've been there every year since I was a child," Kathleen said.

"Well, you are not a child anymore, and we have a lot of plans that depend on your upcoming marriage. So you can't go to the islands today, let alone spend the night there!"

Kathleen wrinkled her brow, trying to understand why Queen Renata thought she could tell her what to do.

"My parents would have never let me go sailing along the

barrier islands. Besides, your Sīhalt Guardian Prime will be here any day."

Kathleen fumed.

"In Candoreth we do things a little differently than in your homeland," Kathleen said. "I will be taking Elayna to see the sea turtles today. Sīhalt Girdy will go with us for protection. We will stay only one night."

"You can't risk it, Kathleen," Renata insisted.

"By next year this time, I will be suffering through a long winter in Tyath. Who knows how long it might be before I will see my little sister again? So, by your leave, should the new Prime happen to appear while I am gone, he may rest here until I return!"

Queen Renata's eyes widened at the forceful retort from Kathleen. Little Elayna must have sensed the tension in the room, because she stepped closer to Kathleen and put her arms around her waist.

"You should begin thinking of others, instead of just yourself," the queen said.

"Renata, I recognize that Father needs me to marry well. Let me have a day with my sister. Then I will deal with the final details of the wedding procession."

"You cannot plan a royal wedding procession in a matter of days! These things can take months to plan, Kathleen. You will be out on the road in a carriage for many days, traveling from city to village to town. There is the matter of food and festivities. Your attire! I don't mean to overstep, but I fear you have done little to prepare."

"Well, I have not had a mother to help me prepare..." she said archly.

Queen Renata stiffened a little. There was a moment of silence.

"Your Highness," Samuel interrupted, hoping to diffuse the tension, "the wedding procession is traveling over land to Tyath because of increasing sightings of pirates on the Eastern Sea. Most of the navy is being used to escort the merchant ships through the few sea lanes that are still open. The pirates drift ever closer to the barrier islands. I fear it is very dangerous."

Next, Elayna's high-pitched voice rose highest.

"Do we still get to see the turtles today?"

Kathleen turned to the little girl and smiled warmly. "Girdy will keep us safe. We'll keep close to the inner coasts—that way we shouldn't have any problems."

"You are taking a foolish risk with your life," Renata said.

"We can't make every decision based on fear, Renata. If we can't live the life we want, what is the worth of living at all?" Kathleen said.

The queen looked at her stepdaughter. Kathleen kept her face a placid shield of decorum. She would give her no expression to read.

"Girdy is not as young as he once was," Renata said finally.

Kathleen ignored her. What right did she have to force her to stay within the city walls like a prisoner? She might be getting married, but in Kathleen's mind, no one would take her freedom.

"Samuel, go ahead and get my sailboat ready, will you?" Kathleen said.

"Yes, my lady," Samuel replied, and scuttled away.

Queen Renata shook her head and clicked her tongue in warning. "You are making a mistake."

"Then on my head be it," Kathleen said, before hitching up her dress and turning to glide away.

TURTLES AND DOLPHINS

The day came with all the glory of an ocean sunrise. The breeze swept out to the sea as Samuel and another servant waited beside the little sailboat, beached on the bright sand. They already had the mast in place, and Kathleen gazed at its white sail with the Dal Sundi crest, making little cracks of sounds as it flapped in the wind.

Perfect weather, she thought, then turned her eyes to the coast. On a clear day such as this, one could see the Turtle Islands in the distance, hazy and idyllic. They would make good time on the water. They probably wouldn't even need to row. The foaming surf from the previous night had swept the beach clean, meaning the only footprints were those of her own and Samuel's. She reached the boat and saw the other servant carrying a dry bag of supplies. He moved ponderously through the sand and placed it on the edge of the boat.

"For you, Princess." He looked a little cautious, hesitant. "But I must remind you that Queen Renata thinks this isn't a good idea."

Kathleen's petal-soft face creased with annoyance as she stared at the servant.

"And that is not your place to remind me, is it?" she said.

"Besides, I am fully aware of the queen's feelings. It's not my fault she's trapped in the palace and is scared of everything. I will be quite okay, thank you."

"Forgive me, Princess.... Dreadfully sorry, Princess." The servant's face went a little white with fear, as if suddenly realizing the mistake he had made in speaking out of turn. "I didn't mean to offend. I'm sorry, honestly I am!"

He bowed and slipped away backwards, Kathleen watching him disappear back up the beach.

"Princess!" came another voice, this one cracked and gravelly but rich all the same. It was the voice of the old Sīhalt Guardian, Girdy Frast, and Kathleen turned to see him waving to her and Elayna, his white beard and black cloak blowing sideways in the wind as he approached. He smiled, his blue eyes staring out from beneath a hundred wrinkles—it was a smile that always let Kathleen know she was loved.

"Good morning, Girdy!" Kathleen said as she gave the stout old man a hug.

"Good morning, my princesses," Girdy replied, his voice even heavier now, like carriage wheels on river stone. It was a voice of deep and confident strength. Kathleen could not remember her father's father, but she had always imagined him to have been like Girdy: old, benevolent, but fiercely protective.

"So, Laynie, we're going to see the turtles?" Girdy asked.

Like the sun which rose higher to its zenith, Elayna's whirlwind of energy since dawn had not abated. The little girl held a thin stick in her hand and twirled it about as she danced across the sand. She stopped to draw a quick picture in it, then danced onward, circling the sailboat.

"That's right, Girdy," she said with excitement, "and maybe you could do the wedding dance with me. Katie is getting married, you know."

Girdy laughed as he coiled the rope and placed their bags in the boat.

"So I hear! She is all grown up now. It seems like just yesterday she was dancing around like you."

"Be careful with that stick, Laynie. You could poke yourself in the eye," said Samuel now, who stood on the edge of the boat and was twisting some rope in his hands. It had been his job to prepare the boat.

The little girl was now using the stick to kick up small amounts of wet sand, flinging it into the air as she danced.

"I'll be careful, Sam," Elayna said in her high-pitched voice. Then she stopped dancing around and pointed the stick at him. "This is my sword to fight the pirates! Don't you know?"

She jumped toward him, then veered off, giggling, twirling and dancing again.

Girdy shook his head. "We don't want to see any pirates on this trip. And we certainly don't want to fight any. Your Highness, we will keep to the inner islands, just in case."

Kathleen nodded. She knew that Girdy only used her title when he was serious about his role as protector, or in the presence of the public. Otherwise he just called her by her given name.

"Thank you, Girdy," she said. "This is the only day that will work for me to take Elayna to the turtle islands. It may be my last chance."

Girdy placed an old hand on Kathleen's shoulder. "Considering the season and Queen Renata's schedule, you are lucky to have found a day to spare," he said.

"You have no idea!"

He smiled at her, and Kathleen saw his look of grandfatherly understanding. Kathleen stepped into the sailboat and held her hand out to Elayna to help the little girl climb over the wooden sides. Girdy lifted the stern, allowing the surf to raise the bow a little with the next wave before he shoved it forward and climbed in himself.

Samuel, who had now hopped down, waved from the beach,

and Elayna stood with her wind-tossed hair blowing and yelled to Samuel. "Don't forget to feed my goldfish!"

Once the boat had begun to move through the waves, Kathleen held the tiller firm against the wind blowing across the sprit rig sail. It was a simple rig—the trapezoidal canvas was held tight with a simple line holding the diagonal shaft upward to the right corner. The red pennant at the tip of the mast stood straight out toward the leeward side of the little sailboat. It was another beautiful blue-sky day off the coast of Candoreth, with widely scattered puffy clouds punctuating the horizon. Kathleen smiled at Elayna.

"Who is that up there?" Elayna said, pointing to the bluffs that overlooked the beach.

Girdy squinted at the dark figure that stood high above them. Kathleen shielded her eyes to look back at the land and saw a man standing proudly on the bluff overlooking the water. He wore all black, and his cloak rippled quickly about his legs.

"That," Girdy said, his voice strained somehow, "is your new Sīhalt Guardian."

Kathleen stared up at him. Even from this distance she could see by his straight spine and powerful stance that he was younger than Girdy. There was an energy that clung to him, an energy forged with the same hallmarks of the other Sīhalt Guardian next to her: full of strength, confidence, devotion—but free of the warmth that Girdy possessed. She wondered if this was something Girdy had only cultivated in his later years, away from the order. Still, she couldn't imagine the intimidating-looking figure in the distance ever possessing anything other than duty. It made a little shiver run up her spine.

"What do you know of him, Girdy?" Kathleen asked.

He sighed and then said, "I have not maintained regular contact with Master Tove for years. I will inquire when we return. But you can be sure, as a Guardian, that he will protect you to the death." There was a note of caution in his voice, she noticed then, as if he too read something that he didn't like.

"I see," she said, and fell silent. But when she looked back at the bluff, the Sīhalt Guardian was no longer there.

"When are we going to be there, Kathleen?" Elayna complained, shouting louder than was needed for Kathleen to hear her over the slap of the waves against the wooden hull. It snapped Kathleen's attention away, watching her sister point excitedly toward the dolphins that surfaced to breathe. No matter how many times the smooth gray dorsal fins cut the surface of the water, Elayna would either cheer and point to them in the distance or quietly place her finger to her lips, shivering with excitement. Kathleen imagined she had been the same way as a child when she first got close to the dolphins. She wished their mother was still alive to see them now.

Later, they set up camp on the nearest turtle island, waiting for the moonlight that would allow them to see the mother turtles make their way onto the sand and up to the edge of the dunes to lay their eggs. They played in the surf and then ate a small dinner Kathleen had prepared. Kathleen made sure a sand ring surrounded their small campfire that flickered on the beach. There was no need to have a fire beacon as the sun began to set, as they did not want to confuse the turtles or be seen by any other ships on the water.

She thought she heard voices at one point but was not sure if it was the palm trees being blown by the wind. Kathleen went to look for Elayna and found her playing with sticks and little pieces of salt grass, her hair tossed in free winding twists and tangled locks of soft, light red hair.

"Look what I made, Katie!" she exclaimed. "It's a mother and baby dolphin—just like the ones we saw today."

Kathleen was astounded by the delicate grass shaped to a familiar curve— even a dorsal fin was woven into a fine resemblance. The twisted grass and sticks were placed in such way to mimic the beauty of what they had seen earlier in the morning. Even the sand was arranged in perfect waves "This is so beautiful, Laynie. You captured them perfectly!"

Kathleen wondered if Elayna had the gift of Art. She wouldn't be surprised. In a few more years they might be sure. Kathleen held Elayna close. She snuggled next to her sister despite the warmth of the sand under their feet and the comfortable ocean breeze.

"I will miss you when you go to get married," Elayna whispered.

The moon rose and began to illuminate the dunes, their tufts of grass swaying in concert with the incoming waves.

"I will miss you too. You will have to come and visit me," Kathleen said with a smile. Elayna shook her head without looking up at Kathleen.

"I heard that it gets really cold there. I like the warm places," Elayna said.

"I suppose I will just have to visit you right here in Candoreth then," Kathleen said, smiling.

Girdy sat close to the fire, his old, lined face glowing warmly. He stood and began to hum a familiar tune. Elayna recognized it as the Sīhalt Guardian wedding music, and she clapped her hands in excitement. She ran to Girdy and curtsied. Girdy circled Elayna with a profound look on his face. Then he winked with a twinkle in his eye and brought out a flower to tuck in her hair.

Kathleen joined in the tune and pounded a hollow piece of driftwood like a drum. Girdy pranced and stepped with the crispness of a new groom. Elayna stepped onto his feet and, holding her hands in his, Girdy followed the intricate steps, turning this way and that, to Elayna's delight. Kathleen remembered when Girdy used to dance with her when she was a little girl. She smiled in the firelight and looked up at the stars overhead. She would miss this.

After dinner Elayna fell asleep on Kathleen's lap as they looked out over the waves. The moon was high now, and Girdy spoke with Kathleen about the wedding procession route and the traditions of the north. She watched him speak, his face illuminated in the firelight, and thought of how good and kind he had always been to her. Girdy was the stability she needed when she had lost her mother and her father had been withdrawn and cold. Girdy, the Sīhalt, was both her protector and friend. She leaned her head on his shoulder and placed her smooth hand in his wrinkled one.

"You have grown so quickly," he said.

"The years pass no matter how much we want them to remain still," Kathleen agreed, surprising even herself with how mature she sounded.

They waited and waited, and Kathleen was almost falling asleep when, bobbing on the waves in the distance, she opened her eyes and spotted solid shapes turning to dark, fluid forms with rounded heads.

"Look, Elayna! Look! Here they come!" Kathleen sprang up and whispered to her sleeping sister in excitement. By the light of moon, the sea turtles came. They pushed further toward the beach. Elayna woke back up and climbed into Kathleen's lap to see better.

"You girls enjoy the show. I will get things ready for bed," Girdy said, and made his way back to the camp a short distance away.

Kathleen pointed out the hundreds of bobbing forms in the waves as they swam toward shore. Elayna drew in an excited breath as the first of the great sea turtles pulled herself through the surf and finally onto the dry sand. The turtle nosed about at the edge off the dunes then began to use her flippers to slowly whisk away the sand to make a hole beside the dune. Finally, she positioned herself and deposited her many white eggs into the hole. Kathleen felt the wonder she remembered as a child the first time Girdy had brought her to see the turtles.

The beach was covered with their large, delicate shells. They shuffled onto the beach to nest and finally headed back to sea again.

Elayna turned to Kathleen.

"Do you think they visit the North Sea, Katie?" Elayna asked. "Because if they do, I could send you a turtle message after you move there. I will just tie a scarf around one and you can look for it when it gets up there."

Kathleen smiled at the thought.

"If I find a sea turtle with a scarf, I will know it came from you, Laynie," she said and hugged her little sister tightly. They fell to silence then, watching each turtle disappear as it sank back beneath the waves. The only sound they heard was the soft-lapping shore and the popping of the fire—and neither of them heard the quiet footsteps of the men approaching.

DANGERS AT SEA

Kathleen held Elayna in her arms when a rough hand smelling of fish oil clamped around her face.

She was so surprised she did not even resist initially. Her mind was trying to make sense of the situation. Then came another hand, this one at her neck. The dull, petrifying thought shot into her mind.

Pirates! Kathleen flooded with fear.

Princess Elayna, turning now, scrambling backwards on her elbows in the sand. She began to let out a shrill scream when another form appeared next to her, and Kathleen saw the body of her little sister fly sideways as a man cuffed her in the side of the head.

"Shut it, wretch!"

The little girl lay motionless in the sand.

"I told ye to keep'em quiet!" another voice hissed.

Kathleen's heart was almost thumping out of her chest as she twisted her head to get loose. The hand on her mouth closed tighter even as she dug her fingernails into his skin, drawing blood. It didn't last long. Another hand, achingly strong—pinned her arms to her sides, and her scream came out muffled, no louder than the tender waves. The man pushed her face into the sand and she felt a hot, rancid breath at her neck as a man whispered in her ear.

"Calm down now, missy. I'll slit ye throat if that's what ye need."

He held her there until she finally lost the strength to struggle.

"This is the princess, mates," the man went on. "We've got 'er. Captain Dagger said to keep 'er on the sand, don't let 'er get into the trees, or she'll make trouble in the forest."

Kathleen's cheek was pressed painfully into the hard-packed sand, so hard that the first soft layer above it now pooled around her head and she thought she might suffocate. She felt another hand clamp her hair, pulling up her head momentarily so that she could breathe. She opened her mouth to scream for help, but a strip of damp cloth was shoved in. What could she do now? She needed to get away or call for Girdy. She knew he was close. Her eyes darted like moths around lamplight. Kathleen could still see Elayna lying on the sand. She still had not moved, and she screamed her little sister's name despite the gag.

Had they killed her?

"We got the one we came for, let's go." The man behind her spoke. Another pirate joined in.

"They brought but one guard with'em, Trath. Let's grab the little one too!" he said, pointing to Elayna.

"I don't think we killed the little rat—she might even fetch a few coins," the man said, his voice hoarse and rum-soaked.

Another stout man walked up, his bare feet wide and hairy. "We didn't find the old man. He weren't at the camp. We'll keep an eye out, but there's plenty of us."

Kathleen continued to struggle, but the pirate's grip wrenched her shoulders the more she did so.

Kathleen's thoughts came like daggers. Where was Girdy? Was he dead too? Would he be able to help? Would he realize?

"Better pray ye don't find 'im. Old man or not, that be a Sīhalt

Guardian in the black cloak we saw earlier, and it'll take plenty of us to stop 'im back if he shows up while we have the girls. Leave the little one. Maybe that'll slow 'im down."

The man swore and motioned for the others to help as he hauled Kathleen off her feet, and soon the men were trampling along the beach. Kathleen was slung over the shoulder of the stout one carrying her. She was so light that her slender body bounced painfully. Twisting her neck, she could just make out the dark silhouette of a ship moored in the distance, while two row boats were beached around the sandy point.

By now, the first soft light of the new morning was soaking up to the sky from behind the sea. The dark sails of the pirate ship were drawn up, the three main masts outlined against the softly brightening sky. Kathleen could make out a man wearing a captain's hat, standing on the foredeck, sea glass to his eye. He directed the men on the beach with loud shouts.

Kathleen struggled and twisted, trying to free herself and look behind. She was trying to search for Girdy or Elayna. She felt sick with the realization that Renata had been right. Why didn't she listen to her? She truly believed they were safe.

The pirates kept to the hard-packed sand where the surf rolled in and out. The receding waves left the wet marks, and Kathleen renewed her struggle. The men seemed to carry her easily, but she would slow them if at all possible.

Then she saw a dark streak. A cape flowed out behind him. Sīhalt Girdy rushed from among the palm trees onto the beach in front of them. Shouts rose from the men on the ship. Kathleen's vision was partially obstructed when a few more barefooted men gathered around to protect the prize they had stolen. Others fanned out to flank the oncoming Sīhalt Guardian.

What can one man do against a dozen marauders? she thought with horror.

Kathleen felt astonished at how fast the old Sīhalt moved. Girdy advanced at a sprint without a word. He drew the slender blade he always carried at his hip. Kathleen had known Girdy Sīhalt from her childhood, and although she had seen him practice with the sword countless times, she had always seen the movements as a dance, and nothing more. He moved with the grace she remembered, but for the first time in her life, the man she thought of as gentle and kind was deadly.

Whipping the blade with one hand, Girdy distracted the men positioned in front. They quickly reached for their own weapons, but Girdy had expertly thrown a dagger between them. Before their blades had even cleared of their belts, a knife spun past Kathleen's ear and buried itself in the throat of one who held her. He released her immediately and fell to his knees, pulling at the handle.

"Run Kathleen, run!" Girdy commanded as he closed on the remaining men.

Kathleen spun on her heels and began running back in the direction they had come. The gag in her mouth made it almost impossible to catch her breath. Her nostrils flared as she ran with her arms tied behind her back. Kathleen looked back frantically to see that five of the pirates were already sprawled on the beach, the waves washing their blood in streaks. Girdy stood with his legs apart, rising on the balls of his feet, and danced in a sequence that included a spinning blade punctuated by sweeping kicks and striking fists. Pirates lay sprawled haphazardly on the sand.

Kathleen sprinted, struggling for breath. She looked back again to see Girdy clutching his side as he began running after her. At first he gained on her, but then staggered, almost falling to the sand.

When Kathleen turned to run back and help Girdy, she saw fear in those blue, twinkling eyes. His blood-soaked hands pulled the gag out of her mouth and off of her face. She gasped, sucking in air. Girdy quickly cut the cords at her wrists.

"Get Elayna to the boat," he said while wincing with pain. "I will follow you if I can."

Kathleen nodded.

The pirates could be heard now, yelling and encouraging their comrades. Kathleen sprinted to the dunes where she had last seen Elayna. The little girl was crying out for her and wandering around the camp where they had danced the night before, her eyes wet and glazed from the blow.

"Come on, Elayna!" she yelled, running at full speed. "We need to get to the boat." She grabbed her sister's arm and dragged her at a sprint toward the little sailboat on the beach.

From the rise of the dunes, Kathleen could see Girdy still struggling to make his way to the boat. He clutched his side and seemed to drag that leg as well. The next wave of pirates had almost reached the shore and were planning to run them down before they could launch their sailboat back to Candoreth.

Kathleen pulled harder on Elayna's arm, the girl's feet barely touched the sand as they ran over the last of the dunes back to beach. The wind and the curve of the island was in their favor—if they could make the boat.

"Come on, Girdy!" Kathleen screamed.

She yanked up the stake holding the mooring line and grabbed the breasthook of the little boat and began dragging it to the water. The lightweight wooden hull carved a shallow trench in the wet sand. Elayna mumbled something about Girdy bleeding and the pirates coming, but Kathleen ceased to hear anything more. The pounding of her pulse in her ears covered all else. Kathleen lifted her sister into the boat, shoving it free of the sand as she climbed aboard.

Girdy waded into the surf, up to his waist, blood spiraling outward in the water around him. The waves tugged the red stain back and forth. He dropped his sword over the gunnels. Girdy was halfway in the boat but struggled to make it over the side rail. Kathleen grabbed his clothing to finally pull him the rest of the way inside. It was only then that she saw the seriousness of his injury.

Girdy's white beard was wet, and rivulets of water and blood ran down his neck. His left hand still clutched at the open wound. It started at his navel and ran upward toward his arm pit. Some of his ribs had been severed, and Kathleen thought she saw his vitals as well. He looked pale and faint. Girdy began having torso contractions that left him convulsing on the floor of the boat.

"Hold on, Girdy. I will get you home!" Kathleen said.

She let go of the oars and unfurled the sail. It snapped open with the strong morning breeze. Kathleen slammed the dagger board down, and the little boat responded by stabilizing and responding to the rudder. She tugged on the rope for the downward pull on the boom. Then she trimmed the sail, close hauled to the wind.

The small, elegant boat cut through the waves, and Kathleen looked up to see the pirates running down the beach toward the water behind them. She knew now they would not catch her as long as they stayed out of the deeper water, and ran with the wind. She looked back to Girdy and found him looking at her as he lay curled in the bottom of the boat. He clenched his teeth in pain, but had a look of pride on his face as he watched her sail them home.

"I'm sorry, Your Highness," he managed to say.

MEAT WITCH

S amuel came running down to the docks with the alarm
bells clanging in the harbor tower. The old Sīhalt was
pulled from the boat as Samuel arrived, gasping for
breath.

"Melva is not far behind," he said.

Girdy's breath was shallow now, and he was unconscious. Melva,
the old Healer summoned, moved as fast as she could down the steep
stairways that led to the docks. Her beaded necklaces rattling as she
held on to the railing—she turned and shuffled across the dock
toward the crowd gathering nearby. She paused to take a handful of
food from the bag at her waist and placed it into her mouth, coming
to kneel beside Girdy. She chewed and then placed her hands
directly on the wound, closing her eyes and examining him by touch.

"Can you do anything?" Kathleen said, kneeling over them.

Melva nodded, hands covered in blood, sliding up and down
Girdy's torso. Murmurs rose from the sailors and merchants that
gathered to watch.

"He is old, but I can give him strength," Melva said, breathing
deep incantatory breaths.

Kathleen was pleading now. "Can't you hurry? He is weak."

"That is why I must go slowly, child. I must kindle the flame of physical strength and build it slowly, or I could blow it out forever."

The warning bells were still tolling. A crowd had gathered on the docks. Kathleen saw her father and Queen Renata making their way quickly to the docks as well. Kathleen watched intently as the rise and fall of Girdy's chest became more pronounced. Melva closed her eyes and appeared to strain, humming, leaning forward against an invisible force. The open wound began to close from both ends. The skin began to reach out for the adjacent side, and soft pink tendrils of tissue created a lattice of connective tissue. The color in Girdy's cheek began to return—his lips no longer appeared ashen, and his hair, beard, and fingernails began to grow before their very eyes.

Melva continued to move, and then she began to hum louder. Girdy's breathing got stronger, inhaling and exhaling in time with the Healer's chant as she pushed her hands more firmly against his abdomen. With a sudden gasp, and then a moan, Girdy's eyes opened, and he looked into the sky.

Melva relaxed, appearing exhausted.

Girdy stood up slowly in his blood-soaked tunic. He looked around as a man waking from a dream. His hair now fell almost to his waist, whereas before it had been shoulder-length. His beard had grown longer, and his fingernails looked as if they had not been trimmed in some time. He looked older in some ways, more wrinkled, but also appeared refreshed and seemed to stand without pain.

Girdy kept feeling his side where the torn fabric exposed a newly Healed wound. He sought to make sense of the blood on his clothes and in the boat.

"Kathleen," he murmured in recognition. Then, looking toward Elayna, he fell back to his knees, moaning softly, and hugged the little girl, who remained in shock from the whole scene.

"I'm sorry, little one," he said.

Elayna cried with her head on his shoulder.

The palace guards that accompanied Sam and Melva held the people a few paces back. Some of the sailors among the citizens were heard to whisper and point. Kathleen heard the words "Meat Witch" mixed with profanity, and she looked around to see who would be so vulgar. Was this not a moment of miraculous grace? She did not see who said the derogatory thing but was reminded of her own need to be careful. People with the Talents were rare, and unwelcome, in these times since the plague.

"Give him some of the water," the Healer said in a hoarse voice. "He will be thirsty. And he will need meat to restore his energy."

Kathleen breathed out a sigh of relief. "How many years did he lose during this Healing?" she asked. As an old man, Girdy didn't have many years to spare.

"There were no broken bones to mend, and no infection, but he probably lost at least a couple of years," Melva said. "If he keeps getting himself in that kind of trouble, he will catch up with me." She smiled, but it was laden with exhaustion.

"What happened?" King Lukald said.

"We were attacked by pirates," Kathleen said. "They were moored at the cove of the closest Turtle Island. We barely escaped."

"I will send warships to pursue them!" King Lukald said.

"They already headed out to sea. It was a black ship with a double mast and moved fast. I don't want to put anyone else in danger for my safety," Kathleen said.

"If that is true, you should have considered what I said before you left yesterday," Queen Renata said, her arms folded and mouth drawn to one side.

"They are more brazen than ever," Lukald said.

"I am sorry, Your Majesty. I have failed you this day," Girdy said.

"Old friend, my daughters are safe once again. You have ever been a true and faithful Guardian," King Lukald said. "You are a hero to all of us."

"Princess Kathleen was the hero today, Your Highness. She pulled me into the boat when I had no strength to do it myself, and she rescued Princess Elayna," Girdy said.

The people in the crowd murmured their approval.

"Kathleen, we are counting on you to keep yourself safe. It was foolish to insist on going to the islands at this time. What would we have done if you had been killed?" Queen Renata asked.

"You would have had to find another way to ensure your security, Renata," Kathleen said.

"That was not fair, Katie," King Lukald said. "We all care for you. I thought you wanted to go through with this wedding."

"I do, and I will. But the pirates were not going to kill me. They were trying to capture me," she said.

"How can you be so sure?" Renata asked.

"I heard them say as much," Kathleen said.

"What did they say?" a deep voice asked from behind her. It was the darkly dressed man she had seen on the cliffs, the Guardian. He walked out from the crowd where he had been watching the scene on the docks.

Kathleen stammered, curiously nervous in front of him. "I don't remember the exact words they said, but I think it was, 'We got the one we came for.' One of the pirates was named Trath. I remember that," she said, and waited for the man's reaction.

He gazed into the middle distance for a flicker of a second. "Trath is a fairly common name," he said eventually, "but I will remember that detail. Did you see a name on the ship?"

"I didn't see a name," Kathleen said, "but it lay low on the water and was slim and sleek. It moved quickly when under sail."

"Master Girdy, did you hear the same?" the young Guardian asked, turning to the older man.

Girdy tilted his head, trying to recall the events of the morning. "I don't remember. I was trying to get to Kathleen. I didn't hear any of what they said."

"Your Highness, if there is plot against your life, I will need to be ever ready to protect you," the new Sīhalt Guardian said.

Renata nodded vigorously while raising her impossibly high eyebrows to an even higher arch.

"He is contracted to keep you safe until you are married," the queen said. "Now you have your own personal Sīhalt Guardian. You might as well let him do his job!"

Girdy frowned, and Kathleen realized how Renata's words must have sounded to him.

"We have not even been introduced!" Kathleen said.

"Forgive me, Your Highness. In the urgency of the situation, I forgot my manners." He knelt dramatically and swept a fist to his chest. "I am Jared DeTorre, a Sīhalt Guardian sworn to serve and protect you."

"I already have a Sīhalt Guardian. He has kept me safe since childhood," she said, placing her arm around Girdy's.

"Until today," Renata said.

Kathleen winced at Renata's retort.

"I don't need a shadow to my every step, Lord Sīhalt. When I am within the walls of Candoreth, the royal guards and Sīhalt Girdy are enough," Kathleen replied.

King Lukald spoke up.

"Kathleen, your mother does not mean any disrespect to Girdy. We all love him. He just isn't as young as he once was," he said, gesturing to Girdy's torn clothes and long white beard.

Kathleen hated it when her father referred to Renata as her mother. Her actual mother, Annalise DeLunt, would not have demeaned Girdy—she would not even have criticized him in public. Renata was nothing like her mother.

"But it wasn't his fault," Kathleen cried, incredulous now—how could they treat him like this? Just toss him aside now that he was older. It was with the same ease they were tossing her aside for marriage, she thought to herself bitterly. "There were so many of them. When the pirates attacked, they struck Elayna and tried to carry me off. Girdy fought them just enough so that we could escape. Otherwise we'd be dead. And he risked dying just to defend us!" By now her fists were balled so hard her fingernails pierced the skin of her palms.

"Princess…" Girdy whispered, and tried to calm her with a soft touch on her shoulder.

Melva the Healer, whose stillness and silence at that moment was unsettling to everyone but Kathleen, who found her Talents intriguing, said, "Yes, child, he is lucky to be alive. In a few more moments, I would not have been able to save him. Be thankful for the wind at your back and for what is left of the Candoreth Navy in the harbor. The criminals are becoming bolder."

"Pirates on the seas and brigands in the forest," Queen Renata said, quoting the mantra of those nobles who seemed hesitant to support her father.

Kathleen looked at her stepmother. "My father is doing the best that he can."

The queen stepped closer, extending a hand, which Kathleen backed away from. "Look, it is a long road from Candoreth to Tyath. I'm just worried about you, that's all."

Kathleen brushed back the loose strands of red curls from her eyes and took a measured and determined breath before she said, "I will have Girdy with me on the journey."

King Lukald looked to Sīhalt Girdy.

The wizened old man stared back for a few seconds, then looked down in understanding and spoke softly. "You'll have soldiers of Candoreth to accompany you, and many horsemen."

"But can you not come along as well?"

"You and your sister are both in my charge. I am not as fast as I used to be," Girdy said, smiling weakly. He loved Kathleen like a daughter, and it shone through his tired, yellowed eyes. "I am getting older."

That was enough for her then. She nodded and smiled and threw herself into him. The old Sīhalt Guardian was taken aback by it and lost his breath slightly. "You'll be protected," he whispered as he held her, before speaking more loudly and addressing the man over her shoulder. "Sīhalt Jared DeTorre will be taking my place as your Prime Guardian."

The young Sīhalt Guardian with intense gray eyes waited for her to untangle herself from his predecessor. But Katheleen didn't turn around. She felt everything she loved was being taken away from her.

She wanted to scream.

PEOPLE OF THE SERPENT

W eeks had passed since the Sīhalt Guardians' attack. A'zrah, the Meat Witch, had been wise. She paced herself, offering Healing to the people who would benefit from it most. Most of the wounded had returned to full health by now. Clan Razewell was getting stronger, but the boy Cedric still lay in a fever, drifting in and out of consciousness. Like a piece of fruit that had fallen from the tree and rolled down a rocky cliff, his body lay bruised, shivering.

"Little Cedric certainly is an ugly child, but against the longest odds, he has survived. Will you Heal him?" A'hald said, leaning over the boy's inflamed face to listen to his weak breath. It whistled through the partially exposed windpipe like a stiff breeze passing through a crack in a tree trunk. He looked over the swollen flesh, and now the split in the boy's face was even wider. His tongue was now forked like a snake's, divided like the rest of his face in two halves. Every bit of it struggled to mend itself back together.

Delathrane warriors gathered around the body of the boy, standing back slightly. To them he had become somewhat of a curiosity, transitioning from an object of general derision to what he was now: a symbol, a mascot of resilience and revenge for the Razewell Clan. For them, ever since the attack, he had come to embody Delathrane fortitude.

Warriors from distant Delathrane clans came to pay their respects to the tenacious son of King Raldric. They came in the hope that he would recover.

"He is one of ours, A'zrah," the new King A'hald said to the Meat Witch.

"It will take some time. The poison still spreads throughout his body. He may not survive the Healing."

"And if he does?"

"If he does, the scarring will be horrific."

A'hald crossed his arms and stroked his beard. It was his choice now: either to put the boy out of his misery, or order the Healing and bring him back to life. After a long pause, he gave the order.

"Do it," A'hald commanded.

A'zrah glided over to the table and placed her hands on Cedric's bare chest. They moved softly at first, then harder. And A'hald watched as she closed her eyes, raised her head, and began to chant.

Cedric's eyes fluttered at the Talented touch of the Meat Witch, lying there in his own filth on the floor of his father the dead king's tent. Silence. Eyes watched the ritual, unblinking. Firelight flickered around them all, drawn as if under a spell too.

Meanwhile, down in deep, misty depths, Cedric began to stir. His mind, a cauldron of shadows and smoke, began to clear. And then he heard the voice. Softly at first, faint and whispery, but then more clearly, like a bell ringer approaching in a storm. *A witch's voice?* he asked himself. *Where am I?* He felt a surge of new strength enter him, compelling him. He could hear words of encouragement from other people now too. *Who are they?* his muddled thoughts asked.

Standing around him, the onlookers watched the sleeping,

OF THE SUNSHINE BRIDE

stirring boy. He looked as if he was having a nightmare—his limbs thrashed and his back was arched. The Meat Witch's voice raised to a crescendo. Cedric began to feel strong! He felt his bruises begin to soothe.

And then he opened his eyes. Cedric sorted through the cloudy images in his mind. What had been real, and what had been imagined?

The Sīhalt Guardian did this to me.

Cedric rolled over to his side and felt the weight of his body. He looked up at the smug woman standing over him. She chewed a mouthful of food.

"He's not so bad, A'hald, if you don't look at his face." She raised her eyebrows in consideration. "The thick scar will stay, just as I predicted," she said.

Realizing he was naked, Cedric pulled an Auroch hide blanket across himself. His proportions were somehow different —better.

"How long have I slept?" he asked.

His voice was different as well, deeper. It sounded like his father's voice, and yet his tongue struggled to form the words. It was no longer swollen, but the two halves had healed independently.

"You need to eat. Your father no longer lives," she said, laughing at his modesty. "But you do sound like him. If he were a serpent."

She turned to the crowd. "I did well on him, didn't I?"

He stood slowly, the hide around his shoulders. He towered over the room of gathered Delathrane barbarians. The chieftain's tent had been repaired, and Cedric placed his hand high on the support pole, near the peak. He looked at his arms. They had once been spindly and weak, where now they were muscled and thick. He closed his fist, one finger at a time, and felt the strength in each hand.

So this is what it feels like to be a man.

The Meat Witch continued chattering at him, and he finally turned to focus on what she was saying.

"...You are still a stupid boy, Little Cedric. Just because I gave you almost twelve more winters, you are no warrior until you prove it." She reached up and poked him in the chest, now ripped with strength. "...Don't think you are so big that we cannot still kick you in your ugly face. Inside this big man is still the little boy, scared of his father." The Meat Witch turned to walk away, laughing.

My father is dead because you didn't save him, he thought.

Clarity from the Healing began to dawn on Cedric. His heart pounded. His eyes widened, and he felt a mix of relief and guilt that his father was no longer alive. He felt guilty for surviving his father, and angry at himself and everyone for the relief he felt at knowing he would not be beaten by King Raldric again.

In the shadows of his young mind, Cedric decided to focus on the anger. "Witch!" he called after her.

With a whistling backhand swing of one arm, his great fist slammed into the witch's jaw. He felt the bones give way, and she fell in a heap, grabbing her jaw, trying to hold it in place. There were a few surprised grunts from the warriors in the tent. A few others lay passed out, their fingertips blue with Kabris juice.

"I was not scared of my father, Meat Witch. Just respectful." The woman knelt, bleeding from her open mouth, and caught a few teeth that had broken with the impact. She looked horrified.

"Now who is scared, woman?" Cedric asked harshly. "What a shame you can't heal yourself."

"I Healed you!" she said, her words barely intelligible but her shock evident.

"You should have Healed my father," he said and walked from the room, the crowd parting as he passed.

"He was already dead," she mouthed, but Cedric had already left.

A white scar as wide as three fingers now ran from his hairline, down his face, over his mouth and down to his throat. He had a tongue like a serpent. It was a token of the wound the Sīhalt had given him. He wrapped the hide blanket more tightly around his shoulders, his long black hair contrasting with the red and white fur. He looked again at his strong fully-grown body in amazement. Not even a bruise anywhere. He felt famished.

Cedric approached the nearest cooking fires outside and reached for the meat that was roasting. He ignored the stares of the people gathered in the clearing. Grasping the wooden spit, he lifted it to his mouth and tore a portion of meat from the leg bone. The inner layers were raw and oozed warmth as he chewed. Other than the hunger, Cedric had never felt stronger.

"You struck Azrah!" Cedric recognized the voice of A'hald, his father's First warrior. "I am the leader of Clan Razewell now, and I will see you whipped for your violence to our Meat Witch," A'hald said.

The scrawny boy, who had suffered torment and teasing for years, stood before A'hald—now he was a giant of a man. The ugly face now featured a bright white scar that ran between the dark eyes and split the full lips. Cedric was as pale as he had ever been, but his skin rippled as his natural strength was displayed beneath its surface.

"I will submit to your whipping, King A'hald," Cedric said, trying to deal with the reality of a split tongue. The crowd gathered more tightly in the circle that was forming around them. He chewed nonchalantly on the meat, tearing off another big bite, unconcerned. "If you are willing to accept a challenge from 'Little Cedric' first."

A'hald shifted his feet. He was a man used to situations where personal combat could be instantaneous. Cedric laughed loud, chewing his meat with an open mouth. "I challenge you, Chief A'hald, for the right of leadership."

A few of the warriors snorted, disbelief displayed in their

faces. Who was this young warrior, scarred as he was, to challenge A'hald?

He snapped his teeth together, then flicked his serpent tongue for effect, eyes brightly aflame. No one had ever feared him before. It felt good to him. Cedric appeared insane. He felt elated.

The circle around them expanded in anticipation of the fight. Cedric stood in his bare feet, wrapped in his blanket, and continued to eat. The challenge hung in the chilly spring air.

"I'll just whip you and get this over with," A'hald said with a slight hesitation in his voice.

He grabbed the whip from the hand of one of his men and advanced. Cedric remained near the cooking fire, eating and smiling toward the crowd. A'hald lashed out with the whip.

The stinging tip cut across Cedric's shoulder and face, but the heavy fur blanket protected his back. He didn't even wince.

Now murmurs ran through the gathered crowd. Many were impressed.

"Did you think I would cower?" Cedric bellowed.

Then he let the blanket fall to the muddy ground around the fire, exposing his hulking naked frame. He turned to fully face A'hald.

Cedric looked at the welts rising on his skin and then back at A'hald. "Thank you, A'hald," Cedric spoke through gritted teeth. "I needed to see some welts on my skin. I was beginning to wonder if I was still alive."

The second stinging lash of the whip caught Cedric's bare chest and arm, but he caught the ends of the whip in his hand and held on. He began to pull the whip, hand over hand, and walk toward A'hald.

"However, having felt the lash again this morning, I do not want to be kicked or whipped anymore."

A'hald struggled in vain to pull the whip free. The man looked like a child playing rope-pull with a cave bear.

"'Little Cedric' is tired of being demeaned and spat upon," he said, scanning the surrounding crowd. The people nodded, their faces humbled by Cedric's words.

"You were always a weak little half-wit! Even you father hated you. He was embarrassed of you," A'hald said derisively.

"My father loved me," Cedric protested. "He made me stronger. You and the others were just mean and hateful."

"Your father never believed you would live ten winters. You were just our entertainment. You are a *Handri* half-breed whose mother was a slave. That is why the Meat Witch hesitated to Heal you once the Sīhalt Guardians left. You are not one of us. We kept you alive because we wanted to have more fun with you." A'hald wore a sneer so vicious it did something to Cedric.

The crowd remained silent. The potential truth in the words cut Cedric deeply, but he was used to verbal abuse that cut him daily for as long as he could remember. He had always wondered why he was lighter than the others. He was ashamed of his lack of pigmentation. He knew nothing of his mother—he had no memory of her. The treatment he had suffered all his life began to make sense. He decided it would stop this day.

Cedric yanked hard on the whip still wrapped around A'hald's hand. The man jerked forward. Cedric strode toward him, still holding the spitted meat in his other hand. He drove the sharped wooden spit into A'hald, the half-cooked carcass now bunched at the end protruding from the Chieftan's chest. Cedric quickly looped the whip around his neck, pulling A'hald up to his toes and then lifting his feet off the ground, staring eye to eye. A'hald struggled to dig his fingers under the coil around his neck. His eyes bulged, and his feet kicked frantically.

"My father loved me, A'hald," Cedric said. He leaned down a bit and took another bite of the meat still adorning the dying man's chest. Then Cedric threw the man's body down on the ground like a bundle of wet hides. "Do not call for the Meat Witch to Heal this man," he commanded.

Turning to the people gathered around, he said, "I am Chief of

Clan Razewell now, King of the Delathranes. You allowed the Sīhalt to murder my father and did nothing!" He pointed at the crowd, implicating them with his outstretched hand. "Now we will avenge my father. We will take prisoners and loot from the Handri. When we are strong enough, we will bring down their empire. We will feast ourselves in the great hall at Tyath. The People of the Serpent will rise!"

A warrior in the crowd shouted, "Cedric the Serpent King!" Cedric sought to find the man who had spoken up, but was unable to spot him in the crowd. No one else spoke. Only the heavy breathing could be heard from Cedric, who was no longer a help-less boy within death's grasp. All at once, a cheer rose from the people. "Cedric the Serpent King! Chieftain of Clan Razewell! Victory for our King!"

Young warriors came forward and knelt before Cedric, offering their allegiance. Cedric raised his fists in the air. He felt drunk on this new power, this new vigor of success.

"I have a gift for you, my king," one warrior said. "We kept him alive these weeks while you have slept."

The crowd parted, and another warrior dragged a broken figure to the front. Too frail and beaten, the captive was unable to stand—or was he unwilling? Cedric stared at him, at the matted black hair of the figure at his feet, hanging loose over bruised, broken limbs.

"Look at me," Cedric said.

And then when he did, Cedric's heart thumped, first with fear, then with excitement. His breath caught in his throat, and his muscles grew taut and hard, like constricted coil springs. "You..." he whispered, his voice electrically intense. But it was not as elec-tric as the ice-blue eyes that stared back from the figure looking up him.

This, he knew, was a Sīhalt Guardian.

LOVE IS BEST

Queen Renata Dal Sundi sat reclined near the window of the grand palace parlor in a long blue flowing gown. Her black hair was pulled into a tight braid that wove the small curls into a an intricate pattern. She sat quietly, with a focused look on her face, staring intently at something in the courtyard below.

She raised a finger, and then her voice. "Lukald!" she beckoned over her shoulder. "Why is the Chief Steward moving loaded chests from the treasury? We have a wedding procession to pay for!"

When she turned, Kathleen, who sat on a palm frond carpet reading, could see the easily sparked strain in her features. It filled her with anger. It was when she complained so easily like this that Kathleen was reminded that her stepmother would never replace her real mother. Annalise Dal Sundi would have never spoken to her father in such a tone, she thought proudly over the dull ache of sadness.

Lukald sat with his head in his hands. He looked up at Kathleen with a tired, exasperated face. The queen stood then and rounded on him, hands propped on her waist, her dark eyes flash-

AUSTIN REHL

ing. The perfectly plucked, arched brows framed them beautifully, her black face always possessing that inkling of surprise, even when she was angry. There was no doubt she was a great beauty, and Kathleeen wondered if it was her sternness that enhanced her beauty.

"The noble houses are talking," she said sharply. "They say 'Pirates on the Seas and Brigands in the Forest'. We can't keep paying to fight these raiders without making real headway. We won't have any money of our own left, Lukald." Her charged, hot voice was a mix of anger and fear.

"Well we won't have any money at all if we don't fight them!" Lukald bellowed back at his wife. "We must pay the soldiers. Who else will fight the barbarian raiders all up and down our western frontier? And then we must pay the sailors to keep the sea lanes clear of pirates for trade. What part of this don't you understand?" he added. "Otherwise I will have to pull back…"

"And give up everything your father secured?"

The king said nothing.

For a moment the queen appeared sympathetic, but only for a moment. "Well, I will not live in danger simply because you wasted your fortunes on gaming!" she added, spitting the words out.

Kathleen couldn't stop the short scoff escape her, and the queen's head swiveled around. She leveled her dark eyes at the Princess.

"Yes? Do you have anything to add?" she said, hotly.

"Oh, nothing. Just wondering if perhaps what you're most worried about could be that your wardrobe allowance might be diminished. You do have a talent for spending…"

If Queen Renata's gaze were any sterner, it would have gained physical form and bore through Kathleen like two daggers. She bit her tongue, leveled the deadly glare at Lukald, and then left the room, a couple of maids at her tail. They awkwardly tried to keep up with her along the hall, while also trying to remain unseen.

Lukald and Kathleen watched her until she disappeared around the end of the hall.

The clerks and book keepers had already exited at the first sign of trouble from the queen. The king sighed and smiled weakly at his daughter.

In the five years since King Lukald had married Queen Renata, Kathleen had watched the arguments between them increase. The lower the treasury sank, the less Renata seemed to love Lukald. Kathleen realized, even at seventeen years of age, that some relationships were like that. She did catch herself thinking sympathetically that the struggles in Candoreth had turned out to be more than Renata had bargained for. But then the incursions came as a shock to most people in the realm, and it had affected the lives of many people in much more harrowing ways than in damaging the size of the queen's wardrobe.

"You see my daughter," King Lukald turned to explain, stroking his red beard where streaks of gray accented his chin, "I always said I was more like my grandfather. Some kings are made for peace. Others are made for war. My grandfather expanded our lands and reinforced our southern border all the way to the Endless Glades." He smiled slightly and looked into the distance, out of the tower window. "My father enhanced the Candoreth bureaucracy and instituted an effective trade tax. He improved our streets and libraries. He was a man who knew how to win the peace." He paused then, and all brightness seemed to drain away from his face. "Placing a warrior-king like myself behind him is this kingdom's greatest failure." He bowed his head and Kathleen felt compassion for her father. She clambered up from her knees and went over to his side. "You have been a good king, Father," she protested. "You are in the hearts of the realm."

He smiled again, but it was a weak smile. "No Kathleen, I thirst for risk and battle. Not the reports from clerks and stewards." He muttered. "But what is that worth if you can't pay the men who fight for you? These barbarians have no booty to take, the pirates neither, unless we are taking back what was already ours."

Kathleen admired the strong hands of her father. He could ride, sail a ship, and wield the sword better than men half his age, and he always had loved to take risks—was he right, was that what had led to their ruin?

In more recent years, after the plague, when battle wasn't needed, he spent years at the Churning Fields and the gaming houses allowing sport and dice to give him the thrill he sought. Eventually the costs rose to the amount of a real army, a real navy and now financial ruin was on the horizon.

"Father, the contract we signed will be our salvation. I will be married this summer and you will have the support we need from the Empire."

King Lukald looked like a man who hoped his child would not see the pain behind the smile of a knowing, but loving parent. "You will be quite the bride Kathleen. The Empire may not know what to do with you, though. You are good and kind. But the politics of the capital city are cruel. Stay close to Melva."

"I will, Father." She kissed him on the cheek and decided to leave the room before her step-mother returned. As she walked from the room, Kathleen felt the weight of Candoreth, and the families of all the realm, weigh heavily on her shoulders. If that was how she saved her father, and her realm, who was she to say no? She would do her duty and marry the Prince Dol Lassimer.

When she emerged in the cool air of the courtyard at dusk, she glided under the colonnade and climbed a tree at the center of it, folding her long, delicate limbs as she rested in a nook. The tree's bark was warm and a little rough on her skin, but she liked it. For an hour, as the thick air dissolved into the clarity of night and the darkening sky was sprinkled with hard stars, Kathleen thought of her mother again.

"She is proud of you, you know," came a deep, familiar voice from behind a stone column. Kathleen jolted up, gazing down through the leaves. An old woman approached the tree; it was Melva.

"How do you know what I am thinking, Melva," she asked.

The Healer came to a stop, her hands laced benevolently in front of her. "I have been around a long time, child. Have you looked into the reflecting pool recently?" Kathleen turned and looked into the still water of the courtyard reflecting pool. It stretched under moonlight beside the old woman. When the angle was right, she could see not just the starry sky above her, but her own skinny reflection looking back. "You look just like her, Kathleen," Melva said. Kathleen smiled at herself in the pool and then looked up at Melva.

"I guess you're right, I do look like my mother's painting, kind of," she agreed.

"I was wondering if she would think what I was doing was right," Kathleen explained.

Melva looked back at her for a long moment and said, "Well, it is done now. You are contracted to marry an Imperial prince and drag Old Melva up to the freezing North with you." Melva laughed heartily in a way that let Kathleen know that she would go along if it had to be.

"I…will do my duty, Melva," Kathleen stated seriously.

"Well, I will do my duty too," Melva said, imitating Kathleen's intonation. Kathleen came down from the tree then, her feet landing in a soft thud on the cold flagstones.

"There are a number of reasons to do a thing, Kathleen," she said, vaguely. "And duty is one of them. But it is not the *only* reason to do a thing."

Kathleen thought about this for a moment and said, "I feel like almost everything I do in my life is because of duty."

Melva nodded. "Of course, you are bound to some choices based on duty, and some people…" Melva stopped. Just then the clip of swiftly walking heels sounded on the courtyard flagstones. Queen Renata in her long midnight robe walked by, revealing more leg than was modest. She waved to the guards and they crisply opened the door she approached and she was gone as swiftly as she had come. "...make their decisions based on a hope for a reward." Kathleen could see the wisdom in Melva's words. She could think of many instances when people made decisions based on a prize they wanted to obtain, Renata being among them.

"Some people do what they do out of fear too." Melva motioned to the guards their faces betrayed little but Kathleen knew the entire castle staff was terrified of Renata. There was a reason they had been so crisp and formal in the performance of their responsibilities. No one wanted the wrath of Queen Renata. Even the lowliest stable boy knew to jump when she was near.

"But child, the best is Love." Melva closed her eyes as she said the word almost as if she were savoring her favorite food. "If you do a thing out of love, it is always the sweetest. Love is the best reason to do a thing, so if you have to do your duty, find the love in it and you find happiness too," Kathleen sighed and smiled at her maid.

"Your wisdom never ceases to amaze me, Melva," she said.

"Oh that isn't mine, child, I wish I could claim it." She winked at Kathleen with her cheerful but impossibly wrinkled brown face and whispered, "It was your mother that told me that. She said that the day she married your father."

Kathleen sat down on the stone bench and leaned her head against the wall. Her breath left her suddenly.

"Thank you Mother," she said. Kathleen realized, as Melva shuffled away, that perhaps her Mother had heard her question after all, she just chose an old wrinkled woman to send her the answer.

Kathleen decided to spend some time in her private garden. Her life was changing rapidly and she needed time to clear her mind.

UNWANTED SHADOW

K athleen strode briskly to the private garden, unlocked the gate and closed it softly behind her. A low-scudding cloud passed overhead, and suddenly the moonlight poured down over the garden, illuminating its gentle slope and many citrus trees. Kneeling into the earth, she gathered a bunch of the delicate, sweet-smelling blossoms and held them under her nose. Her eyes closed as she drew a deep breath. She looked around at the gated garden and its high, private walls. The night air hung soft and fragrant. She felt unsettled, as if she was being watched—but she knew that here she could be safe, alone. Here she was not the Daughter of the Realm. In this garden there were no titles, no royal facades.

Kathleen held the blossoms gently in her hand. She looked around to make sure she was alone again. Then she took great care to keep her Talent hidden.

As she had done so many times since that first time, Kathleen lightly touched another cluster of fragrant white blossoms. She set the intention in her mind, then willed the tree to grow. Kathleen felt a tingle up the back of her arm and center at the back of her neck just below the skull. She breathed and concentrated on the blossoms in her hands. She could feel them swell, and continued pulling. Kathleen rubbed gently on the small oranges and expanded her fingers slowly. She smiled as she felt the tree respond and push the newborn fruit to maturity. With her eyes still closed, Kathleen lowered her hand, ever-so-gradually allowing the considerable weight of the fruit to pull on the branch. When she felt a sudden release of two large oranges falling into her hand, she smiled broadly and mouthed the words, "Thank you," and opened her eyes again.

In that instant, she thought she saw some movement in the corner of her eye. It looked like a shadow. A person perhaps?

"Who is it?" she said in a sharp whisper. She looked around. The shadows were still.

Kathleen knew she had left guards at the garden gate, and no one was allowed in the gardens without royal approval. She thought of the stable boy that liked to visit the gardens in his free time. She frowned and took few steps down the path.

Again she thought she caught a glimpse of black boots moving quietly away down a tree aisle, barely disturbing the dust on the path. Kathleen remembered the tall pirate in his knee-high boots standing on the foredeck of that awful black ship. A stoke of fear ran through her.

They could have sent someone to hunt me here in Candoreth, she thought.

Her heart pounded with the thought of the danger. Kathleen decided to move quickly to the gate.

Surely the guards would not have left me alone in the garden if they knew someone was already here!

Kathleen began to panic. *Who is this man?*

She walked faster, struggling to hold the fruit in one hand and her long skirts in the other. Kathleen peered around the formal shrubs that marked the transition between the citrus and nut trees. The uninvited guest to her garden now moved along the far side of the honeyberry bushes. She decided to run. Hiking up her skirts, she sprinted around the row of bushes

Looking to the right just as she was rounding the corner of the shrubs, she saw no one, so she kept running. Her heart pounded in her chest.

I can't call for the guards, or he will know where I am, she realized.

Swinging around to look down a path to the left, Kathleen ran to the right and ran headfirst into the man. The impact made her lose both her oranges. They went rolling on the ground. The stranger put both hands around her waist just to keep her from going headlong onto the garden path.

He wore formal black traveling clothes, accented with silver and black with riding boots to match. Silver details adorned the black fabric of his cape, draped across his muscled shoulders.

"My pardon, Princess Dal Sundi." He took a step back and knelt, then arose holding the oranges she had dropped. "I am at your service," he said slowly as he looked at the ripe fruit.

"You are in my private garden," Kathleen said.

A streak of fear ran through her as she considered what this man might have seen. Did he observe her using her Talent? Had he seen her grow the oranges?

She wanted to grab the fruit and hide the oranges behind her back, but that would have drawn more attention to the strangeness of their existence this time of year. Kathleen prayed he didn't notice.

Now that she stood close to him, she could see the Sīhalt Guardian was handsome. He was well-dressed too, despite still wearing his traveling clothes. She felt like a foolish girl staring at him, then blinked her eyes and recovered.

"How did you get in here, Lord Guardian?" she asked. She wondered why she suddenly felt so hot.

"I climbed the wall," he said, handing her the oranges. His voice was deep and carried an air of seriousness.

"There is a gate. You could have requested entrance," she said, trying to change the subject.

"I needed to know how difficult it might be for an assassin to reach you here inside. I scaled the walls without a problem. It would not do for me to wait at the gate while you were in danger inside the garden walls."

Kathleen wondered if the heat in her cheeks was due to her recent fearful sprint, her embarrassment, or his smile.

She took the oranges back, smiling.

"Forgive me for running into you. I panicked when I thought you were an assassin, a spy, or perhaps just an irritating boy," she said.

"I'm afraid I have been accused of being all three in the past."

Kathleen noticed how fierce his storm gray eyes appeared.

"Which one was the most recent? A spy or an assassin?" she said.

"I accept the compliment," he said, but he didn't smile sincerely at her comment. Kathleen liked people better when they smiled with their eyes too. The man hesitated before answering, and Kathleen thought she detected a flash of pain cross his face.

"A boy, Your Highness. I am afraid I have never outgrown being an irritating boy," he said, the smile now gone, hiding his white teeth behind his perfectly-shaped lips.

Kathleen shook herself and looked away from his lips. She wondered if he lacked a sense of humor. She knew Sīhalt Guardians could be trusted. However, from the width of his shoulders, and the depth of his voice, she thought he certainly had not been an annoying boy in quite a while.

He is handsome, she thought.

"Lord Sīhalt, I must tell you again, I appreciate the seriousness with which you take your commission. However, while we are within the walls of Candoreth, you do not need to be so concerned. I know this place better than you do. While the road to Tyath will have its dangers, I am sure, I do not need, nor desire, your constant vigil. I must be allowed to enjoy the last days in my home city without appearing to be fearful or overshadowed by a Sīhalt Guardian I must stumble over every time I turn around."

"You were looking the other way when you turned the corner. Otherwise you would not have run into me," he said.

"I was just speaking figuratively."

"I am capable of using much more stealth. When I saw you stumble, I wanted to catch you. I didn't want you to fall in the dirt," he explained.

"Thank you, Lord Sīhalt," Kathleen said with a curtsy. She needed to remember her manners, but felt an case in the young warrior's presence that made her flush again.

"I will not promise to distance myself from you. I am sworn to protect you. I cannot do that without being close by your side."

She turned quickly to hide the color rising in her cheeks.

"Okay, have a delicious orange. It's the least I can do for you after goring you like a bull in the arena," Kathleen said.

Accepting the fruit, the Guardian held the orange, obviously considering its importance. "Thank you," he said and tucked the thing inside his cloak.

They left the garden together, and Melva was there to greet Kathleen. The Sīhalt bid farewell and walked along the garden wall to where it bent with the street. He crossed to the other side, and Kathleen noticed that she did not hear the song of his boots on the cobblestones. He moved silently.

"Hello, Guardian," Kathleen said to Melva under her breath as she watched him retreat. "He's almost enough to make a girl wish she were not betrothed." Kathleen smiled to Melva knowingly.

Just then the man in black turned. Before turning the corner, he looked toward Kathleen with a flat stare and blinked, almost as if he had heard her comment. The old woman raised an eyebrow and shook her head at Kathleen with a gapped-tooth grin.

"He couldn't have heard me from this distance, could he?" Kathleen asked.

"Girdy told me the new Sīhalt Guardian is a Sensor, Kathleen. He probably did hear you, even from here."

Kathleen blushed profoundly and lifted a hand to her mouth.

"Well, I am now officially engaged to Prince Heathron Dol Lassimer." Kathleen tried to sound reasoned and practical.

"I know, my lady, but you started it," said Melva, her smile just as big as before.

"Quit laughing at me, Melva. That man is going to be with us during the whole procession!"

"Walk with me, child. I need to talk with you about something," Melva said. Linking arms with Kathleen, she led her down toward the beach.

MELVA'S GIFT

The beach had been swept clean by stronger winds the night before. Seashells were scattered far up toward the dunes. As thy walked, Kathleen spoke of the frustration she felt at Renata's intrusion into her procession planning. Finally, Melva turned the conversation in another direction.

"I asked you to come with me so I could help you. I want to make sure, before you leave for Tyath, that you know how to use your Talent safely."

Kathleen looked at Melva with widened eyes.

"What do you mean?" Kathleen asked.

"Child, I have known you since you were born. I watched you learn to crawl and walk. I thought you might have inherited your mother's gift as a Gardener, even if you need to hide it," she said.

Melva raised the orange Kathleen had hidden in the pocket folds of her dress.

"Enjoying sweet oranges in this month of the year is a clue, though."

"I make sure not to use it in front of anyone," Kathleen said quietly.

"That is wise, especially in these times. You don't want people saying Prince Heathron is marrying a Plant Witch."

"I've kept it a secret as best I can," Kathleen said.

"I have not brought it up, because there was no use in prying. I thought you might come to me and ask, but that's okay that you didn't. People are afraid of the Talented ones these days, child. It is even worse with the people up north in the Golden City. It is good that you keep your abilities to yourself. But what I'm talking about is using the Talent safely."

Kathleen had never considered her ability to be dangerous. She used it to make flowers and fruit.

"I've never felt like being a Green Grower could hurt me."

"Do you feel hungry after using it?"

"I only do little flowers here and there. Sometimes I will perk up a shrub now and again. I use it like a Gardener."

"Do you feel hungry afterward, child?"

"I always feel hungry." Kathleen smiled.

"I'm telling you this so you know what your mother used to do."

"She used her gift often?"

"Not just for pretty flowers, Kathleen," Melva said seriously.

"What do she do?" Kathleen asked.

"Annalise Dal Sundi did her Growing with intention. She put her power into it. You could learn to do the same."

"Father said she planted the orchards and formal gardens around the castle when they were first married," Kathleen said.

"She also grew the wood for most of the Candoreth naval ships. Many of the ships in operation have masts and hulls made from trees grown by your mother," Melva explained.

Kathleen was amazed. She had not considered the implications of her Talent.

"Father doesn't speak of these things with me. How long did that take her?" Kathleen asked, picturing the towering masts on the largest of the ships in the harbor.

"I saw her grow a tree from sapling to maturity in a matter of minutes."

Kathleen looked surprised. "Minutes for a tree of that size!"

"She could even shape them and bend them as they grew. She was the carpenter guild's favorite patron. They used to have images of your mother in the Shipbuilder's Guild hall. She made quite a difference before the plague and the Luzian Church called to eliminate the use of Talents."

"I can't imagine doing that! I do get really hungry afterward, even after only a little bit," Kathleen said.

"It takes patience and practice. Why don't you show me what you can do?" said Melva.

They looked up and down the beach. There was no one to be seen.

Kathleen stooped down and touched the slender green blades of salt grass growing on the beach. She tried to concentrate, but it felt strange using her talent in front of someone else. She had always done it alone and felt self-conscious with the old woman watching.

"Could Mother make plants grow without touching the leaves or stems?" Kathleen asked, feeling a little frustrated and trying to break the silence. She did not want to start humming, but that was what she often felt like doing when she used her gift. A dragonfly circled her ear, and Kathleen waved it away.

"I don't know for sure, child. I'm not a Gardener like you, but I think you have to touch the plant in order for it to work. Your mother always did it that way," Melva explained.

Kathleen allowed her finger to dance along the edge of the blade of grass. She had trouble focusing and broke her concentration to look back up at Melva. Her Talent felt natural to her, but there were a number of natural bodily processes she did not wish to do with an audience.

"How strong is your ability, Kathleen? Did you have to work hard to make this?" Melva asked, holding up the orange.

"It just feels kind of strange with you standing there," she said.

"If you have already weakened yourself, don't push it too hard," Melva said.

"All right, I'll do it," Kathleen said. She took a deep breath and grabbed the tuft of grass by the base.

"Grow!" she said in a commanding voice.

The small tufts of sea grass exploded upward, their color roiling from a pale sea foam to a deep green. The grass had grown so tall she could not reach the top. It even bent over on itself, and the saw-toothed tips reached all the way back down to the sand. It was impressive.

Melva looked up in sudden shock, her mouth falling open slightly. The blades of grass that had been only slightly taller than Kathleen's fist a moment before now stretched above their heads and cast a shadow over them.

"I never saw your mother do it like that, child," said Melva. "But I don't think you are supposed to do it so fast. You could hurt yourself."

Kathleen clutched her bleeding hand.

The old woman shook her head in amazement, the beaded necklaces clinking around her neck.

Kathleen had felt the growth immediately in response to her command. The exhilaration that brought was instantly followed by the pain of a slice of the sea grass cutting through her palm. Then the wave of hunger swept over her.

The tender blades of sea grass, upon maturity, could easily slice through fabric or skin. Kathleen had not had a chance to move her hand back as the grass shot skyward. Now her hand was cut open, and she thought it might need binding to close the slice.

"I did hurt myself, Melva," she said.

Kathleen felt a wave of emotion flow over her. She wanted to cry. It was not the pain of the cut on her hand that brought the tears, but rather the memory of her mother, now dead. All the stresses of the upcoming procession and wedding only added to her tears.

"I wish she were still here with me," Kathleen said. Melva wiped her wet cheeks with the back of her hand as she knelt beside her. She placed her other, wrinkled brown hand on her shoulder.

"She loved you so much, child," Melva said softly. "I never did see a woman so proud of her little girl as she was of you. I never did." Kathleen balled her bleeding hand into a fist and threw her arms around Melva. She hugged the old woman fiercely. Melva blinked back tears of her own. "I know what it is like to lose the ones you love, child. I lost them all on a day like this when I was just a girl."

Kathleen rocked back on her heels and looked at Melva's face. The old woman had brown eyes that were so old they almost appeared blue. Melva's brown face was wrinkled like paper crumpled up many times over. Kathleen knew that Melva had served her mother and grandmother.

It was said she came from the Endless Glades. Some people whispered that Melva was a savage, no better than a Delathrane Meat Witch, but Kathleen never used that term for her. Melva was a Healer, a Red Grower. Her father had mentioned that Melva couldn't even speak the Common Desnian when he first found her, naked and bleeding, huddled under the overhang of the stable during a spring storm many years ago.

Kathleen had never asked Melva about her past. She had always been a permanent fixture in Kathleen's life, like the towers of the castle, the fruit trees in the orchard and the rolling waves of the sea. Even during the plague, Kathleen had taken Melva for granted. Kathleen just assumed that Melva would remain, even when her mother had been taken by the sickness.

Kathleen opened her fingers slowly. Melva looked down at her still-bleeding hand. She examined the gash, and then held the hand closer to take a look. "I'll fix you, child," she said. "We just have to make sure there is no grass caught inside." Melva led Kathleen down to the water and washed her hand. The salt stung and made Kathleen wince, but the wound was clean. Melva took Kathleen's hand in hers and spoke softly. "Kathleen," she said. "First, you have to get your own mind right. If it works the same for Gardeners as it does for Healers, you do not want to be all flustered. 'You can't be angry when you are Healing or Growing,' my mama always said."

Melva wiped a drop of oozing blood away from the wound.

"Your mother was a Healer too?" Kathleen asked.

Melva smiled her gapped-tooth grin. The remaining teeth were a perfect white in contrast to her dark brown skin and wrinkled lips.

"My mama was a Green and Red Grower, child!" she said. Her voice grew happy at the memory. "She was the only one our people ever found that had two Gifts. She taught me how to be a real good Red Grower when I was a girl. She told me not to get too emotional when I was using my Talent or I could burn myself away. My mama said she could talk to the swamp spirits, and some were just Talented people that got too caught up in Growing, Healing, or Building whatever, and they forgot to stop to rest, or eat. They became a Whisper, a Spirit of the Wilderness. Mostly it was the Healers who faded, though. Since they sometimes need to save a life, it's real easy for them to get burned away trying to do too much at one time to save somebody else." Kathleen listened, spellbound. She knew very little of the old woman's history. This conversation opened a whole new understanding.

Melva closed her eyes and said, "Now give me a moment, child." Then she began to hum to herself. Kathleen felt a warmth and a tingle across her palm. The edges of the wound swelled and turned a bit darker, then cleared to a pale pink and began to close. Kathleen resisted the urge to lightly scratch at the cut as it mended from each end. In a few seconds the wound was gone—

no scar remained. Melva stopped humming and opened her eyes. "And that is how it is done. Are you hungry, child?"

Kathleen nodded. She felt so empty. It was as if she had fasted for days. She felt an urgency to eat that surprised her.

"I always get hungry after I do a Healing," Melva chuckled.

"And you did some Growing, for sure." Melva smiled and patted Kathleen's shoulder, looking over at the tallest cluster of sea grass on the dunes.

"I think we have done enough for today," Melva said.

Kathleen rubbed her newly-healed hand.

Melva handed Kathleen a handful of the mix of dried food she always carried. It tasted of savory smoked and salted meat.

"I agree," said Kathleen as she chewed purposefully on the food. She could feel her hunger subside and strength return.

As they walked back arm in arm, Kathleen felt a closeness to Melva that she would never have imagined possible. Melva had transitioned from a caretaker to a friend.

"Tyath is a long way from our home. I am glad to have you with me," Kahtleen said.

"Leaving home is a day a girl will never forget," Melva said.

"Aren't the Endless Glades your home, Melva?" she said.

Melva looked out to the sea, the wind tossing her gray hair away from her face.

"I am from the Southern Reaches. The Glades border it to the north, and my people lived there for many generations." Kathleen had to slow her pace to allow the old woman to walk and not feel rushed. Melva could not move quickly.

"We used the Endless Glades for food. We would hunt and fish there. We gathered fruit, and we would hide there if there was danger," Melva said. "I grew up in the swamps with my brothers and sisters."

"Where are they now?" asked Kathleen.

The maid grew silent and stopped walking altogether. She

looked at Kathleen, and once again she could see faint pain in Melva's face despite the passage of years.

"They're all dead, child. I was youngest, but not by far. I had a brother just one year older than me, and I had two sisters that were twins, and a big brother. They were all killed on the same day. It's a good thing, too, because I would have burned myself out for sure."

Kathleen shook her head at the notion.

"What happened?" she asked.

"I came back from fishing to our home. I thought Father was burning a new area to plant, because I saw the smoke rising big over our home. The closer I got to the village, the more scared I was, because I thought I could hear screams. Then my sister came running to me and knelt down and told me to run back and hide quick. I did, but I kept a lookout when she ran back toward our house. I sat there all day until it started to get dark, and then I sneaked along the path to our home."

Melva stopped speaking and took a deep breath.

"They were all lying around the yard: my mother and father, even my sister that saved me. They were dead, but I tried to Heal them. I tried on each one. I yelled at them just like you did with the grass today. 'Heal!' I said. They were already dead, and I would have been too if even one of them was a little bit alive, because I gave it all I had, and I was just a girl."

"Who did it, Melva? Who killed your family?" Kathleen asked.

Melva looked at Kathleen with those deep black eyes and said, "You know who did it, child. The Delathrane barbarians did."

Kathleen shivered at the thought.

"I saw a picture in one of my father's books, Melva. They look awful." Melva placed her hand over her mouth at the memory.

"Awful is not the word for them, child." She shook her head. "The Delathranes found me with my family, and then they did terrible things to me. I can't remember it all. There are blanks in my memory of those days. Somehow, I came here. All of my people were gone. I do remember your grandfather finding me at the stable and giving me a cloak. I stayed with house Dal Sundi ever since. I will never forget the cruelty of the Delathranes or the kindness of your House."

Kathleen let Melva's story soak in as they walked again back toward the castle. Kathleen felt that perhaps her life was not so bad. She still had a father that loved her and a younger sister she adored. However, Kathleen knew she had a real friend in Melva, too.

BARBAROUS NEGOTIATIONS

As he often did when unoccupied, Chief Magistrate Dirm Uppenslaw had drifted away into the recesses of his mind as he waited for his host to arrive. Dirm's story had been one he was proud of, a swift rise to power forged only by those ambitious enough to resist conscience and do-gooders. Like most of the city's inhabitants, Dirm had been born after the victory at Dumal Wells. He had grown up in relative peace, and then his career had advanced nicely when the Great Plague swept the capital city. Once those that had seniority over him had died of the sickness, it was worth the weeks of miserable contagion and a few superficial scars to consider how he would play his hand next. He had been lucky, he had always thought, though recently he had begun to wonder if he had not been chosen? Dirm preferred to think of himself in this way. Chosen. Those who jousted with him for power — and for the prized position of Chief Magistrate of Tyath — were either taken by the plague or, for those who resisted it, were snuffed out using other means. Only one who was chosen would have navigated a path such as his. The thought made Dirm smile again. He had been clever. It would have been a shame to let the crisis of a generation

GUARDIAN OF THE SUNSHINE BRIDE

go to waste when there was so much opportunity for a young and ambitious man. In those days, no one thought twice of a few extra bodies tossed among the heaps of the dead.

After working himself into the good graces of House Dol Lassimer, Dirm had labored to finally possess the office of Chief Magistrate of Tyath. He couldn't afford to have an Imperial wedding take place between Prince Heathron and Princess Kathleen. He had made promises.

"So you say she is leaving Candoreth and will follow the King's Highway?" Cedric, the Serpent King said, his forked tongue speaking in a lisp. He had entered the chamber with a scroll in his large hands, and presently was rolling it out over a crude wooden table. Once spread, it revealed a map much inferior to those drawn by the imperial cartographers in Tyath, whose drawings inspired beauty in the lands of Desnia, but, for a map drawn by the clumsy hand of a barbarian, it was close enough.

Dirm, blinking several times as he was snapped out of his reverie, straightened and cleared his throat. "Er, yes, that is correct," he replied, moving the rudder of his mind consummately to the reason he was here. He continued, "My Prince said the wedding procession will follow the King's Highway all the way to the narrows along the Great River. It is possible that you could attack them along the towpath here..." The magistrate bent slightly over the table and extended a thin finger to the western portion of the map.

"I will be the one who decides when, where, and if we attack *Handri*," Cedric said.

Dirm shrank back from the map, out of reach of Cedric's hands.

"I see the strategic benefit of attacking when the procession line is stretched out along the river, guards could only be two or three deep on the whole line." The barbarian licked his lips.

"What will your prince give me if I act as his sword *Handri*?" Cedric asked, his huge bulk slouching back in the throne made especially for him. He gave an air of indifference. "Besides, we like the flatlands, and this is already in the foothills of the eastern mountains," he said, pointing to the map.

"Prince Heathron Dol Lassimer is prepared to pay handsomely," Dirm assured him.

"Give me specifics, *Handri*," Cedric said, twirling a half-eaten leg of prairie chicken between his enormous fingers. "Why doesn't the prince just marry a different girl if he doesn't like this one? You *Handri* make no sense."

"I would prefer you not call me *Handri*, King Cedric. I know something of your native tongue, and the term '*Handri*' is not a word to be used with business associates," Dirm said.

The Serpent King laughed. "You call us barbarians. Your people also call us 'savage.' We are the people of the Serpent. I am not your business friend and I will call you what I like, *Handri*." He flicked his tongue out and licked the grease that covered his upper lip.

"You know what makes me happy, *Handri*?" he asked.

Dirm wrinkled his brow in thought for a moment. "I do not know. What makes you happy, Your Majesty?" he said finally.

"Roasted prairie chicken makes me happy." The Serpent King threw the leg bone down and stabbed the table with his knife. "And killing *Handri*!"

The finely dressed informant held his lips in a tight line. He would not show fear—not now.

"What is your price to destroy the Wedding Procession?" asked the magistrate.

"You would have me bid against myself, *Handri*. No, no, perhaps I will take my warriors west over the Great River and leave you *Handri* to your own problems. Maybe the Great Sickness will return this year and all our problems with the Empire will go away. The people of the Serpent will rise again, *Handri*, I promise you."

"Just agree to help disrupt the thing a bit, and you could find yourself in a very advantageous situation. However, the princess must be kept alive and unspoiled," Dirm insisted

"That will cost extra," the Serpent King said.

"You will need to bring enough men. She will be accompanied by a contingent of soldiers from Candoreth."

"We will build the Serpent Mound, and Clan Razewell will lead them. We will have enough warriors."

"Then we will pay you the weight of the princess in gold when she is delivered to me. That will at least ensure that you feed her well in captivity."

"You will place her on the scales in front of me, and I promise not to stuff her with rocks. I will send word when we have her captive. You must offer three hundred horses in payment as well."

"As you wish." Dirm smiled. "That can be arranged, but there is something else you need to know."

Dirm tried unsuccessfully to control a smug grin.

"Why do you smile, *Handri*? Have I made a foolish bid?"

"No, King Cedric, you drive a good bargain, but I have some information that may make this operation more desirable in your eyes."

Cedric waited, saying nothing. His flat stare was one that would unnerve the bravest heart.

"The Sīhalt Guardian escorting the Princess Dal Sundi is none other than the one you call '*Der'Antha*.'"

Cedric froze.

"*Der'Antha* will be protecting the princess?" Cedric said.

The chief magistrate nodded.

Cedric clenched his fists and reached for his knife.

"That will make the job more dangerous. I would ask for more payment, but I will enjoy killing him so much. Is it wrong to be paid for the pleasure?" Cedric laughed like a boy who had played a trick on one of his fellows.

"You have sought him for some time," Dirm said.

"*Der'Antha* has not taken the bait I have laid for him these months since I last saw him. Now I will go to him!" Cedric said.

The barbarian king leaped up and yelled to his men, "We have found *Der'Antha!*"

Dirm thought they might go ahead and kill him too while they were caught up in the excitement of the moment, but a huge hand, driven by a scarred face, slapped him on the back in brutal friendship. The fire in the crazed eyes leaped with demonic gratitude.

"*Handri,*" Cedric said for the last time that evening, "If you speak the truth, you have brought me a great gift. We will build the serpent mound tonight!"

"I have brought other gifts as well," the pale envoy said. He unwrapped a package and displayed the many doses of dream powder before the elated warriors. They readily traded rings and bracelets of silver and gold. Dirm gathered the precious items into a large sack and tied it securely to the saddle of his pack horse. He hated to see dream powder wasted on the ignorant savages, but this wasn't the highest quality powder to begin with. He doubted if the side effects of tainted powder even bothered the Delathranes.

With hoots and howls that resembled the cries of wild animals, the Delathranes began the pounding of drums. Some people ran for woven baskets, while others immediately stuffed their clay pipes with the dream powder and passed them to their families. The dream powder refined in Tyath was much more potent than the dream leaves gathered by a Delathrane warrior on a traditional vision quest.

In the baskets, they carried many handfuls of soil to cover the stones laid out in the shape of a giant serpent swallowing an egg. Small children packed the soil with their bare feet and hands while the older people tended fires to light the area. Delathrane riders rode out from the camp, yelling in excitement, to gather other clans. Dirm knew the Delathranes believed the effigy would unite them and bless them in their ongoing war with the hated

Handri. They would work all night and continue for many days until the undulating earthen mound of the serpent had an egg in its mouth. The egg being the *Handri* empire and all it represented.

"Abboth save us. What have I unleashed?" Dirm said as he rode carefully back to the road that led away from the barbarian encampment. The burning embers from the Delathrane fires rose into the night air along with the whoops and yells of the gathering clans.

LADY ALBODRIS

L arissa Albodis walked into the room with short, quick steps, and arms held wide. Her golden curls framed an angel's face.

"Katie! I heard it is all official. You are going to be married!" Larissa said, with a tone that threatened to break into song. Larissa rushed forward to embrace her and kissed Kathleen on the cheek. "I'm so happy for you," she said. Her light purple gown clung to her voluptuous body. Kathleen sometimes wished she was shaped like Larissa, all curves and softness.

Kathleen exhaled and smiled hesitantly. "I signed my life away!" Kathleen said.

"You are going to love the capital. I take it as my personal responsibility to get you ready. I came prepared too," Larissa said as her servants began bringing in many trunks and armloads of new gowns and accessories.

"We need to arrive in style." Larissa twirled to emphasize the fact that she was, in fact, dressed in style.

"I'll even show you how to fix your makeup."

"I'm not wearing any," Kathleen said.

"Not even a little black for the eyelashes?"

"No, I didn't have time this morning."

"Well, you are lucky. I would kill for my eyes to naturally look that good, but we can all be improved."

"My mother used to say 'even a barn looks better painted,' but she didn't live long enough to show me how to do it," Kathleen explained. "I've always just let my freckles show, and went without it."

"No worries, Kathleen. This is going to be so fun!" Larissa began picking up articles of clothing and holding them up to Kathleen, puzzling over whether they met her approval. She tossed one back and picked up another.

"The journey will be an adventure. Once we get to the Golden City of Tyath, there will be parties and dances every week. You barely have time to recover from one before there is another."

"I'm not always that comfortable in large groups of people," Kathleen said.

"You are going to love the capital." Larissa gestured emphatically with her hands, as she always did when speaking. If she were bound at the wrists, Kathleen suspected Larissa might not be able to speak at all. But that was one of the reasons Kathleen loved her. Larissa always had a cheerful air about her, and it was contagious.

"Have you been on the northern coast this whole time?" Kathleen asked.

Larissa nodded. "My mother insisted that I give the Marquis Eldin Stellat a chance. So she arranged to have me stay at their estate for a few months."

"Did you learn to like the tubers they eat with every meal?" Kathleen asked.

"Oh, the tubers didn't bother me at all. I might have put on a little weight from their traditional diet," Larissa said, examining her form, "but it was his whole family which made the visit kind of strange."

"They didn't like you?"

"They were kind, but different."

"In a bad way?" Kathleen asked.

"Up north, they are very devout in the Luzian Church."

"It isn't all that different from our traditions in the south, is it?" Kathleen asked.

"They don't think Talented people should be free."

"Are you serious?"

Kathleen felt a jolt of emotional pain at her words. Kathleen wondered why so many people could think of using a gift from Abbath as a crime.

"I mean, I don't really care one way or the other. If a Talented person doesn't use their abilities, I don't think they should be locked up," Larissa said.

"I don't either," Kathleen said.

"Anyway, Eldin's mother wanted us to have two chaperones with us at all times, and that was fine, but she treated me like I was the reason they were needed. It is probably because our families don't hold to the Tyathian doctrine. What difference does it make whether we say Abboth or Abbath? Seriously."

"Larissa, why would a caring mother have concerns with you corrupting her little boy?" Kathleen said with a smile.

Larissa laughed with a slightly intentional evil note, then put on the most innocent face possible. "Whatever do you mean, Your Highness?"

"Did he propose? Did he try to kiss you?"

Larissa smiled broadly but shook her head.

"He didn't do much at all without a little coaxing," she said.

"Larissa, you are so forward. No wonder Lady Stellat wanted two chaperones!"

"Well, when you are riding along a beautiful cliff at the seashore, and the sun is setting, and the fat, near-sighted chaperones are a ways off, it would be a shame not to steal a kiss at that moment. Am I right?"

"Whatever you say. I wouldn't know. I've never spent time alone with a man at sunset, or any other time for that matter."

"Speaking of men, I saw a glimpse of Heathron Dol Lassimer when we were in Tyath."

"You did?" Kathleen raised her eyebrows.

"It was from a distance, and the sun was in my eyes, but he is quite the sensation in the capital city."

"Did you not talk with him?"

"No, it was from a distance, but he does know how to ride well. He sits tall in the saddle."

"I have a portrait of him. I got it the day I signed the contract."

"Oh really? Let me see it!" Larissa said. "I haven't seen him up close."

Kathleen unwrapped the small portrait of Prince Dol Lassimer.

"Did he look like this?" Kathleen asked.

"I'm not sure. I hope so." Larissa laughed.

They looked at the likeness given to Kathleen by the Imperial magistrate. The handsome lines of his face and eyes held both young women's interest.

"Nice looking for sure. Do you suppose he raises his eyebrow like that when he smiles?" Larissa asked approvingly, then raised one eyebrow slightly higher than the other.

"I only have one memory of him from our childhood. I remember him being kind and energetic. He had sandy blond hair," Kathleen remembered, "and dark brown eyes, dimples, and a few freckles across the top of his cheeks."

"The women of Tyath say he trains every day in resistance strength techniques. I am told Prince Heathron is very fit because of his training regimen."

"I only remember him as a little boy. He was missing a front tooth at the time."

"Yes, front teeth would be nice. I don't see any freckles in this painting," Larissa said.

"I remember Prince Heathron running with me to the stables."

"That is so cute," Larissa said.

"My feet were windmilling down a grassy slope. I slipped as we rounded a large evergreen tree and tumbled to the ground. Heathron came back for me and asked if I was all right. He held out his hand and offered to help me up. He was so serious. 'You'll be my wife someday' he said. Even as a seven-year-old boy, he said, 'I've got to look out for you.'" Kathleen paused in the memory.

"Your mother was alive then, wasn't she?" Larissa asked.

"Our parents were watching from the veranda, enjoying the spectacle of the children's games. They must have been so secure in the knowledge that the alliance between our families would be prosperous.

"I assume that the prince is informed. I am not sure why he still wants to marry me now."

"Maybe Candoreth has something he wants," Larissa said.

"Our kingdom doesn't have as much to offer him in the way of an alliance. Our economy isn't what it once was."

"Maybe he loves you."

Kathleen considered this for a moment. She bit her lip gently, considering the plausibility.

"How could he love me? He doesn't even know me. We haven't seen each other for almost eleven years. I'm sure he has plenty of girls from noble houses in Tyath that would love to marry into House Dol Lassimer."

Larissa nodded confirmation.

"They aren't shy about saying so either," Larissa admitted.

"He could have decided not to go through with the arrangement," Kathleen said, looking at the image again.

"Well, I don't claim to understand men perfectly, but as a whole, they seem fairly simple to me," Larissa said.

"How so?" Kathleen asked.

"They are motivated by glory, riches, and love," she said with confidence.

"In that order?" Kathleen asked.

"Oh, I don't know, it is probably different for each man."

"What about food? I've heard boys are highly motivated by food," Kathleen said.

"True, we should add food to the list," Larissa agreed.

"Melva told me the other day that my mother used to say duty and fear are also reasons people do some things," Kathleen said.

Larissa paused, considering Kathleen's statement.

"Are you afraid, Kathleen?" she asked.

"Yes, I am afraid. I don't really want to leave Candoreth. I am grateful to be able to help Father and look out for Elayna in some way. The past years have been very difficult for him, and if I were not marrying Prince Dol Lassimer, I wonder what would happen to our realm."

Larissa nodded solemnly.

"Our nation is not doing so well either," she agreed. "The Delathranes are ascendent. It is as if the plague didn't even touch them."

"My father is worried, Larissa. We barely have enough ships to keep the pirates at bay. They keep coming up from the southeast and harassing our merchant vessels."

"Well, I saw fields outside Tyath that have thousands of markers for people that died during the Great Plague. The northern winter added to the devastation. The poorest citizens were just buried in mass graves. You will see the marker stones when you arrive there this summer," Larissa said.

"I am looking forward to seeing the capital for the first time. I always wanted to visit Tyath. It just so happens that the first time I see the famous walls, it will be my new home. As long as I make it there safely."

"I heard a special Guardian was hired to protect you as well."

"Yes. I ran into him in the garden."

"Did he speak with you?"

"No, I mean, I actually ran into him. I almost knocked him over."

"And… is he handsome?"

"Is that all you think about?"

Larissa arched her eyebrow defensively. "Well, I heard he was almost the same age as me, so I thought I would ask."

"He is handsome, I suppose, but kind of strange too. He was following me in the garden and it was…"

"A little disconcerting? Yes, it's meant to be like that. Taking his guarding duties seriously, I see." Larissa gave an approving nod.

"Well, maybe. But just be careful what you say around him. He is a Sensor, I found out. You will meet him tomorrow at the arena during the Farewell Feast."

"Fascinating. Being a Sensor is good. That should help him keep a sharp eye out for any danger."

Kathleen gave Larissa another hug as they moved toward the door. They swept past the royal guards who walked quickly to keep in the correct position in front of and behind them as they moved down the stone hall that linked the stables to the inner courtyard.

"The wedding procession needs to be memorable for all the people along the way, Kathleen. They will talk about it for years to come. Mothers in little hamlets from here to the Golden City will tell their little daughters about the day Princess Kathleen Dal Sundi walked through their main street on the way to her wedding. You'll be such a beautiful bride."

"This isn't about me, Larissa. This procession is for my people," Kathleen said.

"No. This is about you, Kathleen. We are going to make your wedding procession the best the people have seen in a generation, no matter how much Queen Renata wants to pinch coppers."

"It's true, if my wedding doesn't happen by midsummer, there is little else that can save Candoreth," Kathleen agreed.

"I knew there was a reason I wanted to help you with the

procession plans. How often does a girl get to go shopping and look pretty in order to save her nation!" Larissa said.

"That's you, Larissa, always looking on the bright side," Kathleen said.

"Oh, it is going to memorable, I promise."

ARENA PROWESS

"Again!" Across the practice arena, the word rang out from King Lukald.

He was evidently enjoying this.

Jared could see the smile on the regent's face, even hear him say, "We'll put the boy through his paces now," to the men standing near him on the podium.

"If you are going to be the Protector for my daughter, I'd like to see your skills," the red-bearded king proclaimed loudly enough for all of Candoreth to hear.

Some of the men spoke quietly to each other, discussing what they had seen. Jared saw money change hands. Even here, King Lukald couldn't resist a bet.

Jared nodded his head. He could always use more practice. It kept him in good form. He sensed he would be fighting multiple combatants in short order, so he decided to dispense with the cloak and tunic. "A moment, Your Majesty," Jared said as he paused to lay his black formal attire aside for the next bout. The flowing white shirt without a collar allowed the sea breeze to cool the perspiration that had begun with the first short demonstration. Jared's boots disturbed the perfectly raked sand of the area.

He flexed his toes inside his boots, straightened his legs and stretched to reach them. Then he stood tall and turned to one side, then the other, warming the muscles of his torso and shoulders.

"Come on, Guardian, you won't always have an hour to prepare for battle when you are in the wilderness!" the king shouted across the arena. A few of his cohorts chuckled.

Girdy Sīhalt just sat silently on a bench across the arena, watching him. It was for the old Sīhalt Guardian, more than the king, that Jared wished to prove himself. Jared had heard tales of Girdy Sīhalt during his training at the Windstall Hermitage. The old man was a legend for what he had done at Dumal Wells. House Dal Sundi would not even exist if it were not for this old man. Some argued the Empire wouldn't either.

The stories said Girdy Sīhalt singlehandedly defended King Lukald's father from the attack of a Delathrane charge. The bards called it *The Dance on the Serpent's Spine*. Jared doubted the man had actually used an effigy mound of the Delathranes as the high ground to gain strategic advantage, but that battle was the one in which the barbarians were beaten so badly they had only begun raiding in earnest during the past few years. It had taken the barbarians more than sixty years to begin to forget that one. Girdy had been the one to turn the tide of that battle.

Jared nodded to the old man and was pleased to see Girdy's fingers move quickly in the silent sign language of the Sīhalts.

"Welcome to Candoreth, young Guardian," the fingers wove.

This far across the arena, Jared couldn't be sure if the old man was speaking to himself, or testing Jared's eyesight. Perhaps he was seeking to know his level of training.

"Master Girdy, thank you. I am honored to be here." Jared signed the words quickly in the moment before he picked up his sword again. The untrained eye would have missed how his fingers flew.

Girdy Sīhalt nodded subtly and leaned back in his seat along the stone wall. Now Jared knew the old man wasn't talking to himself. Jared stretched his shoulders and legs, loosening the muscles and sinew.

"I'll wager he can't stand against Captain Dur Ruston. Channing is the best Candoreth has to offer when it comes to the broadsword," one of the king's cohorts said. Jared's excellent hearing caught every clear word spoken by those in the stands and on the training benches waiting to spar.

"The princess, your new charge, is like a daughter to me. I will not see her harmed," Girdy signed.

"That is why the prince commissioned me to be the Prime for the journey." Jared responded immediately with his free hand as he continued to prepare for the next round of practice.

"Now three, that should be enough. Certainly the young men of Candoreth can give this Guardian a reason to sweat!" the king shouted. The young soldiers saluted their liege and jogged out onto the sandy ground of the arena to encircle the Sīhalt.

They took up positions around Jared, trying to force him to fight in three different directions. Jared looked up at the sky and noted where the shadows of the walls partially shaded the arena floor. He decided it might be useful to have the sunlight in their eyes while he enjoyed the shade. Jared shifted in that direction, shuffling his feet and testing the reflexes of each of his opponents in turn, moving them toward the shaded ground he wanted.

"I have heard the reports," Girdy began again, nonchalantly seated on the bench, watching the bout.

"Reports of me?" Jared's anger flared quickly as he signed back to the old man. Hero or not, Jared felt it was unjust for the old man to bring up his past.

"Go get him, boys! Make him dance." King Lukald cheered the advancing soldiers.

"No. Reports of incursions, not of you. I am not sure why you are so upset, young man," Girdy signed. Emphasizing Jared's youth in the movement of his fingers.

"And I'm not sure why you are so inquisitive," Jared managed to

respond just before using both hands to defend himself against a hasty offense from the heavier of the three soldiers. The man was breathing heavily in the Candoreth heat. His strikes were strong and fine for an infantryman's needs, but Jared was so much faster and more precise. He knew the man's next move before he made it. Jared, tiring of this unwanted exhibition, ran his blade quickly along that of his opponent's and kicked his opponent's sword hand. The soldier let out a mild curse, more from the embarrassment he would have in the barracks than from any real pain. Jared didn't wait to enjoy the look of surprise on the big man's face but instead turned to face the other two.

"I just want to make sure the princess is safe, that is all," Girdy signed.

"Then why did you let her be taken by the pirates recently?"

Jared knew he was being harsh, but his ire was up and he was in no mood to entertain a gambling king or explain himself to an old man.

"Her blood was not drawn. I brought her back to safety." Girdy's fingers flew in response.

"I heard it was she who brought you back to the safety of the city's harbor, Master Sīhalt," Jared continued. He used his sign language with Girdy the same way he used the blade with the soldiers. He was quick, sharp and cutting.

"It looks as if the Sīhalt fellow has a twitch or a hand cramp. His hand is twitching all over the place," a nobleman in the galley said to Lukald.

"Attack his left hand, boys. He's cramping!" the king yelled from above as he shaded his eyes.

Jared danced away from one, moving in an arc, in such a way as to line up the two attackers. The movements kept him from being flanked now, and Jared could more easily attack in one direction. Then he switched hands with his sword and fought on.

"You know little of the situation. They knew we would be there," Girdy explained.

There was a lull in Jared's footwork as he considered this piece of information. The two soldiers attacked with vigor, much to the pleasure of the group of nobles and the king in the galley.

"An inside source? The military escort may not even be enough," Jared signed.

"I cannot go along. I must stay here in Candoreth with the rest of the House. We don't know who hired the pirates or informed them," Girdy signed with heartfelt pain.

Jared could forgive the old man for his lack of respect to him as Prime. He had spoken out of concern for his loved ones.

"I had loved ones too. I will take her safely to the walls of Tyath," he replied between another quick change of hands on his hilt.

The old Sīhalt Guardian nodded his approval as the two remaining men pressed their attack. The nobles in the galley clamored, sensing an end to the duel and an end to their bets. They yelled in excitement, evidently betting on a couple of Candoreth's own rather than a young Sīhalt Guardian dressed in foreign clothes.

Seeing that he had demonstrated sufficient aptitude to Girdy, Jared attacked with energy. The soldiers fell back a bit, and then Jared took few quick steps in reverse to gain even more distance between himself and his attackers. He withdrew a couple of daggers from his boots and used one in each hand. He expertly flicked them toward his opponents. His timing was expertly calculated, and the heavy, blunted ends of the handles hit each man squarely on the bridge of their noses. They both dropped on the spot, covering their face with their hands.

"What have you done, Master Sīhalt?" the king asked. "This was a sporting duel—we were not out for blood!"

"Have no fear, my king!" Jared shouted up to the king. "These men will be fine. They were struck by the handles of my daggers, not the blades. Other than a couple of black eyes, they will be just fine. I was well within the rules of our sparring to throw them an unexpected attack like this."

The men stopped rolling in the sand and began getting to their feet, some blood sprinkled in the sand at their feet. They handed Jared his daggers.

"We are the best in our regiment, and you seemed to be toying with us," the younger soldier said. "Are all Sīhalt Guardians able to fight like that?"

"He probably would have been able to beat the three of you when he was only twelve years old," Girdy said, walking up to join the men. "Jared was trained from his early childhood at Windstall Hermitage with the Sīhalt Masters." The men stared in admiration. Only the haughty captain of the guard seemed unimpressed.

"I hope you didn't bet against him, Your Majesty," Girdy shouted up to King Lukald as the money was changing hands again among the nobles in the audience.

"Not this time, Girdy!" King Lukald smiled. "I figured if the Imperial Prince hired him, he must be good. After all, you were like Hell wrapped in a cloak when you were younger. I remember!" the king said.

"Perhaps you would be willing to spar with me?" Channing Dur Ruston said to Jared. He smirked at the Guardian with a look that made it clear he placed himself far above the infantry men Jared had bested.

"I am at the service of the princess and her family," Jared said.

"We must have another day of duels tomorrow for the Farewell Festival. The queen, princess and whole royal court will be here. Since you will already be in attendance, why not join in the fun?" Lukald added.

"As you please, Your Majesty," Jared said.

"It's confirmed, then. Captain Dur Ruston and our new Prime will duel with you tomorrow for the pleasure of the court. I might even join in myself!" Lukald said.

There was a general agreement among the small crowd in the arena that afternoon. Jared walked over to recover his tunic and cloak. His thoughts turned to what Girdy had communicated to him.

The pirates knew she would be there.

It was no wonder the old Hero of Dumal Wells had almost died on the island. Jared decided he would try to get to the bottom of this.

VICTORY RIBBON

The red pennants were flying in the brisk air, high above the highest seats in the stadium. A buzz of excitement filled the arena. People of all ages had come to watch a celebration of martial prowess as part of the Farewell Festival for Princess Dal Sundi. Jared watched with interest at the face of Kathleen during the day's spectacle. She had grimaced often at the visage of the bullfight previously. She had attempted to make her face smooth and serene, but Jared had noticed the twitch at the corners of her eyes when the animal fought with all its strength only to be pricked and prodded and finally brought down by the slayer's blade. Technically, it had been a fantastic display of skill, and the Auroch bull had certainly embodied the strength and cunning it was meant to portray. The princess, however, had not enjoyed it. She was likely feeling empathy for the animal.

She does not enjoy seeing suffering. That is good, he thought.

Jared wanted an informed opinion of the young woman. If his mission was to get her to the capital safely, he wanted to know as much as he could about her. She had only looked in his direction a few times during the bouts and, unlike her blond-haired friend, he saw no flirtatious looks or wantonness cast his way by Kathleen.

She does not seem to need all the attention either, or perhaps she does not wish to be married and the festivities hold less excitement for her, he thought.

No matter, Jared decided, he had a job to do and it did not involve determining the wishes of a princess. He would interview the staff of the castle from the kitchen to the stables—he would find out all he could regarding Princess Kathleen DeLunt Dal Sundi.

Looking around, Jared noticed most of the seats were filled with people from all walks of life. Jared accepted that he must do all in his power to assist every aspect of the wedding procession. He would do what he could to give the people a reason to be excited for the union of House Dal Sundi with that of House Dol Lassimer, even if it meant playing the role of arena swordsman.

Captain Channing Dur Ruston took to the center of the arena sand. His bay mare pranced around, nodding to the crowd as they cheered loudly. The captain he had met the previous day was just as haughty as ever.

Clearly the opportunity of a good night's sleep has not brought the man any more wisdom, Jared thought.

"He must have many admirers," Jared said to the lad who had been assigned his Second.

"Captain Dur Ruston is the champion of the Marth duel. He rides his horse like it is part of himself. People call him the Stallion because he is so at ease in the saddle," the boy said.

"That make sense," Jared said wryly. "Did he give himself that nickname?"

Finally, the crowd quieted as the captain raised his sword upward for a dramatic call for silence. Channing's voice rang out clear as a baritone bell.

"Thank you, dear queen, for the opportunity to entertain you," Channing said with a low sweep of his white plumed hat.

"That isn't regulation headwear for a captain in my guard, is it?" asked the king.

"We men of Marth are known to do all things with a bit of a flourish. I meant no disrespect, Your Majesty," he said, bowing low again.

"He has an excellent military record, Your Highness, so we extended forbearance to Captain Dur Ruston," the major said. "We will gladly remove his feathered cap should you find it offensive."

"He can wear his Marthian cap, as long as the captain intends to fight in the Marthian manner, exposed to the waist," the queen said. The queen's ladies tittered, and the captain nodded appreciatively.

"Yes, Your Majesty. I am willing to engage in the Marth duel. It would be my honor. However, my opponent, to whom I have offered the challenge, has the right of accepting or rejecting my selection of weapons, armor, and style of fighting. I would like nothing better than to fight in the manner and custom of my people."

"I accept the challenge and the terms," Jared said loudly.

The crowd, drawn by the drama of the mysterious Sīhalt Guardian and the proud captain of Candoreth, cheered in response.

"As a Sīhalt," Jared began, walking further into the arena, "it is our custom to learn the ways and manners of others."

Jared turned, looking at the crowd of brightly colored costumes of the people who had gathered for entertainment.

"We Sīhalts have no fighting style of our own, but rather a mix of every style we study. I have trained at times in the past in the Marth duel—I will do so again today!"

The crowd cheered again. Jared smiled to himself. He was wiling to do his part. If the people of Candoreth were talking of the festive demonstration at the arena, they would not be talking of the weak treasury or fan the rumors of weakness within House Dal Sundi. Jared told himself he was just doing his part to protect Kathleen.

"Don't you think the captain will be difficult to beat at his own style?" his Second asked, his eyes blinking against the bright sunlight.

Jared whistled, and Steed came running into the arena from one of the tunnels at the end of the oval. The crowd cheered to see the Windstall stallion, mane flowing and hooves kicking up sand as he raced around the perimeter of the area and finally stopped as he approached Jared, snorting and sliding to a stop.

"My horse is better than his," Jared replied with a smile to the boy.

He took the large black horse by the bridle and looked into his intelligent eyes.

"All right, Steed, we have a sword fight planned on horseback. I can handle the ride—are you going to have trouble with that Candorethian mare?"

Jared thought he saw an offended look on Steed's face. The horse often looked offended. Most people learned to steer clear of him.

"I didn't think so," Jared said as he climbed into the saddle.

The crowd clapped and cheered. Jared, due to his refined senses, could hear, among the roar of voices, individuals expressing their own opinions.

"He will tear you to pieces, Sīhalt!"

"Don't be a coward, you should fight on foot in hand-to-hand combat!"

Jared turned an ear toward Princess Dal Sundi. She was watching him with a look of concern on her face. Jared saw her turn to Lady Larissa and say, "Channing Dur Ruston has won this event for the past five years. I hope this Guardian knows what he's getting into."

"My money is on the Marth," Larissa said, eyeing Channing with approval, "but I think the Sīhalt Guardian is up to the challenge."

A dirty little boy in the crowd covered his ears and smiled at the sound of the sharp whinny from the hay mare. He crowded the front rail, leaning as far as he might dare to look into the arena. To his left, Channing Dur Ruston rode up. With a flourish of his cap, he warmly gestured toward Kathleen and inspired the crowds to greater cheering. As Captain of the Guard, Channing had the privilege of wearing the royal livery and a white jacket to designate his role as an officer. Larissa raised an eyebrow as she caught sight of tight leg muscles under his even tighter tan pants.

"Who is going to win, little fellow?" he asked the boy.

"Who wins this day? The Sīhalt Guardian or the captain of Candoreth?" Captain Dur Ruston asked in a voice for the everyone to hear.

The boy looked back and forth at each of the contestants and then back at the princess. The urchin stood tall, without fear. He wiped an eye with a dirty hand and said in a high-pitched voice, "T'aint neither one of you! The man that wins today is the lucky Prince Dol Lassimer, a'cause he's marrying our princess!" The crowd laughed and clapped at the urchin's words. Jared watched as Kathleen nodded to the boy and smiled as she fanned herself with an intricate ivory fan. She directed a servant to reward the boy for his little speech.

Channing stood in his stirrups facing the crowd, waving.

"That little chap is right, Princess," he said with a raised chin, now shading his eyes with the feathered hat. "Heathron Dol Lassimer is the luckiest man I know."

He bowed low, and the princess nodded to him as well. Lady Larissa Albodris sat looking at Channing. She licked her lips as if she were thirsty, but she had a cool drink at her side, so Jared assumed it must have been for the captain.

Channing began stripping himself down to the waist. First removing his hat, he passed it to his attendant. He slowly untied his cravat as he rode slowly along the barrier. His fans clamored for the silken tie. Channing tossed it to a maiden who shrieked with excitement. Those closest to her reached out to touch the fabric, then Channing deliberately tied a ribbon to his left arm.

I hope he isn't coming with us on the procession.

"Is that necessary?" Jared asked his attendant.

"You mean slowly stripping to the waist for the pleasure of the queen and her ladies? No, not required," he said.

"I'd rather get on with it," Jared observed.

Channing removed his shirt and revealed a tanned chest, muscled shoulders and powerful arms. He was now wearing only his tan breeches and broad leather belt with riding boots to his knees. He must have anticipated Jared's acceptance of the challenge to a Marth duel, because it appeared he had already rubbed himself down with oil that made his skin glisten in the sunlight.

Jared rolled his eyes.

You have got to be kidding me, he thought.

"You have to take off your shirt," the attendant said. "You can use the leather armor if you like, but men do not typically use it in this country, only boys."

"Only boys, huh?" Jared confirmed.

He examined the leather armor and decided it wasn't flexible enough to be helpful.

"I'll just go bare-chested like the captain," Jared said and began to take off his black tunic and untuck his white undershirt. The crowd roared when they saw Jared strip to the waist, because they knew he had accepted the captain's challenge to fight in the Marth style. Jared then tied the red ribbon he had been given to his left arm.

Jared rode over to pay respect to the king and queen.

"You are very pale, Master Guardian," the king noted.

"I better beat him quick, or I'm going to have a severe sunburn," Jared replied, looking at his arms and chest. His arms were thick, and when he flexed, the smallest fibers were visible as well as the veins, which stood out against his skin.

"You've been up to the north. The people traditionally cover up a little more there, don't they?" the queen asked.

"I tan just fine when I am in the sun, but I prefer to have my cloak on no matter the weather," Jared said.

"Where did you get those scars?" she asked.

"I haven't won every match I've fought, Your Majesty, but I don't expect to lose today."

"Should I bet on you?" Queen Renata asked.

"Guardian," the little boy in the stands yelled out. "I put all three of my coppers on you!" he said, and winked as if there was some understanding between them.

"Well played, boy. Let's see what Steed and I can do to win you a little money," Jared replied. He was beginning to enjoy this.

Jared turned back to the queen. "Do your duty, or go with your heart? Isn't that always the question?"

He saluted the queen, then turned to salute the princess and her court. For some reason the girl was blushing profoundly and barely looked him in the eye. Her friend, on the other hand, looked as hungry now as she had looked thirsty just a moment before. She didn't look him in the eye for long, but that was because she seemed to linger on his form, her eyes drifting up and down.

Jared saluted and turned Steed away to take up his position in the arena.

His keen ears heard Larissa ask the princess a question as he rode away.

"Can you imagine riding behind him on that saddle, Kathleen?"

"Stop it, Larissa, he can hear you."

Jared shook his head. The women of the southern realms were certainly more likely to speak their minds when it came to men.

Channing Dur Ruston wasted no time in racing his horse toward his opponent. In an effort to catch him off guard, Channing kicked toward Steed's belly with the boot in the stirrup.

Jared made Steed lunge forward and moved out of the path that Channing had taken. Now the horses circled each other at a distance, the riders leaning into the turns as they sought to flank one another. Jared rode with his sword held upward, his left hand holding the reins. Channing swung his sword dramatically, making the sunlight dance along the polished blade. Jared wasn't sure if his style was one to just please the crowd, or intended to intimidate the opponent. It was working for the crowd, not for Jared.

The Sīhalt Guardian used his knees to guide his black horse to a sharp turn. The change in direction now had the riders going in opposite directions. As they passed one another, they struck out with swords ringing, steel on steel. Jared's lighter blade was turned aside when the swords struck, he could feel the strength of the muscled captain through the force of each strike. Jared used a measured technique—he allowed Channing to overcome the force of each blow. Jared used just enough strength to keep himself from being harmed. There was no need to sever the captain's blade either.

The people in the stands cheered and responded to each entanglement. Twice during their rides around the perimeter, the horsemen attempted to gain the advantage, neither of them giving ground.

During the next pass, Channing used the flat of his blade to smack the hindquarters of his opponent's stallion.

"Tell him to leave the horse alone!" yelled the boy in the front row. "That is cheating."

The black horse leaped sideways, almost throwing Jared from the saddle. The crowd responded with awe. Jared fought to regain his balance in the saddle. Channing used the time to close quickly, striking fast with repeated strokes that sought to wound or unhorse the Guardian. Jared could hear the chanting of the crowd in favor of the captain. He could hear the sounds of exertion the man made as he sought to finish him off with a series of attacks. Jared defended from a lower position, somewhat awkward in the way he had slipped from the saddle to place more weight on the one stirrup. He took his time defending himself, allowing his horse to sense the change in balance in order to compensate.

Steed shifted sideways, moving to give more room for Jared to regain his mounted position.

"That a-boy, Steed, hold on." The horse bucked slightly—he wanted to attack the mare, but Jared held him back. The captain turned and swung his sword again, hitting Steed's rump hard with the flat of his heavy sword blade. Jared saw the move.

"This duel is between us, Captain. Don't strike my horse again."

"In battle, I'll take any advantage I can. You are lucky I didn't separate the sinew from bone, the way that horse sidesteps in fear."

Jared knew that Steed would attack the other man and his horse if given enough slack in the reins to do so. The horse, being a Windstall Stallion, was trained to fight alongside its master in kicking, stomping or biting. Jared sought to entertain this day, not kill.

"Easy, Steed," he said.

The horse was breathing hard, and wanted to join the fight. The jeers of the crowd were in his ears.

Jared found himself looking over toward Kathleen again. He heard more snippets of their conversation.

"It looks like the people really are not impressed with this new Guardian of yours," Larissa said to Kathleen. The sun, now at its height, shone down in warm rays. The wind blew gently over the arena and stands, giving a brief respite from the heat.

"They are just great fans of the captain, I think," Kathleen said, acting unconcerned.

The captain had twice struck the Sīhalt's horse and still had not landed a blow on the Guardian. Dur Ruston appeared to be frustrated. Certainly none of his other matches had lasted so long. He gritted his teeth and kicked his spurs into the mare's sides. She jumped and ran along the barrier of the arena, spraying sand with each hoof that struck the ground.

"I think it is about to get interesting," Larissa said with a grin. "Just look at them sweat."

They closed again, and just as before, Channing not only struck out at Jared but used a moment, as the horses moved close to one another, to land another loud smack to Steed's hindquarters. The sound carried to the audience, and there was a recognizable "ohh" as they heard it. Blood began to trickle down the flank of the black horse.

Captain Channing yelled and raised his sword again for another blow.

Jared gave the stallion his rein. Responding to the slackness, the Windstall charger lowered his head toward the ground and swiftly gathered his strength. Jared leaned far back, anticipating what was coming. Steed's back hooves flew up, leaving the ground together and fully clearing the shoulders of the bay mare. The iron-shod hooves connected with the captain's chest, lifting him clear off the saddle. With his sword arm raised, he looked for moment like an angel of vengeance poised in the air, glistening in the sunlight. Then he fell to the dust.

Jared looked at Channing, lying still on the arena floor. His sword landed a few feet away. Jared dismounted.

"I can't breathe," Channing said quietly, not moving.

Jared felt the man's sternum and looked him over carefully. The crowd was silent, wondering if they had witnessed the death of their captain.

Nothing was broken. No blood ran except the deep bruises of two horseshoes stamped into the perfectly tanned chest of the captain of Candoreth—he was just stunned.

Jared took a moment to speak to Channing.

"Some people believe the open horseshoe to be lucky. You have two of them now."

"That horse is a demon," Channing whispered, trying to regain his voice.

"You're lucky my horse only kicked you out to of the saddle. He wanted to kill you."

"I think he did," the captain said.

"You will recover, I am sure of it. Now raise your fist to let the people know you are yet alive."

Jared used his slim blade to cut the red ribbon tied to Channing's arm as the captain raised a fist up from the dust.

The crowd cheered.

Jared helped the captain to his feet. "If you had waited for me to beat you silly, you would have no convenient excuse for your defeat." Jared smiled.

"Thanks for keeping your horse from stomping me into the dirt," the captain said, rubbing his bruised chest and walking gingerly across the arena to pick up his feathered cap.

"I won some money!" the boy in the front row said. "Thank you, mister Sīhalt! Thank you!"

Jared passed the ribbon he had cut from Channing's arm to Kathleen. She accepted it with grace.

Do I detect a hint of humor in those eyes? he thought.

"Well done, Lord Sīhalt," she said, keeping her eye locked on his.

Jared felt a thrill run through him. Was it the excitement of the moment? The rush of victory?

"May I ask, on whom did you place your bet?" he said, returning her gaze respectfully.

"The captain," she said. "Although I am glad to know I am being protected by such a capable Guardian."

Captain Channing walked up, wincing as he touched the newly stamped prints on his chest.

"Don't worry about that, Princess," he said. "Just borrow that horse and I am sure you will ride all the way to the Golden City in safety. You will not even need my men to protect you!"

They all laughed as Kathleen accepted the victory ribbon that Jared tied around her wrist.

GIRDY'S GIFT

When they had a moment alone, Girdy sat down beside Kathleen. He didn't talk but sat in silence.

"What is it, Girdy? I can tell you want to say something," Kathleen began.

The old man didn't look her in the eye. He looked at the ground. It was unlike him.

"You need to do your duty. I understand that," he said.

"What is bothering you?" Kathleen asked as she laced her arm around his.

"Your mother found happiness. I hope you do too," Girdy said.

Kathleen laid her head on the old man's arm and wrapped her arms around him. He smelled faintly of eucalyptus oil and sea salt. She loved this man, her adopted grandfather.

"Girdy, I will miss you too," she said.

He laid a hand on her head.

"I fear the danger on this road will be greater than you expect," Girdy said.

"I'm not afraid of some stuffy noble women in the Imperial palaces, Girdy. I'll just give them a wave of my hand as I go about doing exactly as I wish," Kathleen said.

"I suppose you are not so easy to tame," he said, smoothing her hair gently.

They sat like that for a while, Kathleen enjoying the closeness of the man who had helped raise her. Girdy had always been there for her. He was always the one to look to with a question, or run to if she was in trouble with her parents. He never judged her harshly. She would miss him so much.

A tear formed at the corner of her eye and ran across her cheek, finding a path along the corner of her nose. Kathleen hugged Girdy more tightly and asked, "Girdy, you seemed hesitant with the new Sīhalt Prime for the procession. Why?"

Girdy held her close. "Something is not right about that young man. I do not fully trust him. He is skilled, for sure, but there is a deep melancholy about him. Despite all his talents, that gives me concern. I do not know exactly what happened in his past."

"He is very capable," she said, remembering his performance in the arena.

"I believe he is very dangerous," Girdy replied solemnly.

"Sorry you can't be my Prime on the journey," Kathleen said.

"I will stay here and watch over Elayna. The road is getting more lawless these days. As much as I hate to say it, the pirates would not have captured you for even a moment when I was a younger man. I failed you and Elayna."

"You and father are both are so quick to judge yourselves! You have given us a wonderful and safe childhood. As a child, I never felt afraid of the dark when you were standing guard," Kathleen said.

"I wish I could have done better for you. That is all," he said.

"Not one drop of our blood was spilled," she stated.

"I almost died. Your sister was harmed. It could have gone very badly that night on Turtle Island," Girdy said.

"We made it through," Kathleen said, not knowing what else she could say to show her appreciation to Girdy.

"That is true," Girdy said.

"Are you still going to call me 'Little Kathleen' when I am an Imperial bride?" she asked.

"I'd call you Little Kathleen if you were the empress herself," he said, his white beard hiding a big smile.

Kathleen knew that was true, and loved Girdy all the more for it.

In the distance, a shadow of a man in a black cloak drifted silently away.

UNWANTED PRESENT

"It's all in order, Kathleen," Queen Renata said the next morning.

Renata raised her eyebrows at her own reflection, carefully isolating the lone hair that did not fit within the bounds of the flawlessly groomed arch above her eye. Her maid plucked it with a quick move of her fingers, then Renata turned her head from right to left comparing the result. She seemed somewhat displeased with what she saw. Pushing her maid to the side, she muttered to herself in exasperation. "I'll just use the pencil for that. If you want things done correctly, you have to do them yourself."

Kathleen had given up keeping track of all the ways Renata and her own mother were different. Renata treated Kathleen's private chambers as if they were her own. The queen looked closely in the mirror.

It would be nice if she would look at me when we are talking.

Queen Annalise Dal Sundi had never been one to speak with her back turned to someone, even if she could see them in a reflection. Renata, on the other hand, was facing the audience she adored most: herself.

"I have some ideas for the Farewell Feast music and flowers," Kathleen said, trying to keep the frustration out of her tone. She did not want an argument, but the event did belong to her as the bride. Kathleen wondered why Renata could not content herself with the role of stepmother and simply allow her to celebrate as she wished.

"The food will be delivered in six courses instead of nine, not counting the desserts," Renata explained. "I thought we should have the Royal Players provide the music and help save a few coins for the whole production. They even offered to act out some scenes from your childhood during the feast for the entertainment of the crowd."

"I don't think I want to provide the comedic relief at my own wedding feast," Kathleen said.

"It would all be in your honor," Renata said, as if that made the idea acceptable.

"I'll talk with Sam. The Royal Players can provide the music, but they will need my guidance on what is appropriate material for the feast," Kathleen insisted.

"Good, because I already made sure they were paid to perform, and I have a surprise for you at the feast."

Kathleen paused. Queen Renata had treated the planning of the Farewell Feast as if it were her own, again.

"As far as the flowers go, you probably want the Dal Sundi passion flower too," Renata said. "Don't you ever get tired of those blossoms? I mean, there are so many more options. I think we should go with the light orange Sunlight flowers and drape the tables in deep pink."

"I have red hair, Renata. Orange is the last color I want at my feast. That would look horrible," Kathleen said.

"We have plenty of the orange and pink flowers already, though. I wanted to surprise you, so I ordered enough for the whole dining hall. They will arrive tomorrow afternoon. I didn't want you to feel like you had to Grow them all yourself. That is such a dirty business, dealing in sorcery. You had better hope the prince only finds out about that after you are married," Renata said.

Kathleen clenched her teeth together in anger. She hated that Renata knew about her Talent. The woman always threw it in her face as often as she could.

"You recently bought an orange gown too," Kathleen said flatly, remembering the queen's maid carrying it in the week before.

"Yes, I think it will go nicely with the whole decor." She smiled pleasantly, and one not familiar with the queen would have thought it sincere. Kathleen knew better.

"I will not be wearing pink or orange for my Farewell Feast. I would rather see the great hall with barren wood tables and not a scrap of food than be dressed up in colors to match your new gown," Kathleen said.

"Then what will we do with the flowers I ordered?" the queen asked.

"We will not do anything with them. You can throw them at the feet of the carriage as I leave Candoreth!"

"They were expensive," Renata protested.

"No, Renata, you are expensive. You are the costliest decision my father has ever made."

"How can you say that? You know he has a gambling problem."

"At least gambling brought him some element of happiness," Kathleen said.

She wished she had not said it as soon as the words escaped her lips. Like downy feathers from a broken pillow, words said in haste cannot be retrieved easily. They are carried on the winds and scattered in hard-to-reach places of the mind and heart.

"I love your father," Renata replied.

Now Kathleen turned her back on the queen. She knew it wasn't proper, but she was at her limit.

"Just go. This is my wedding, not yours."

"I just stopped by to give you this letter from Lady Allison Dal Avery. One of your mother's witch-friends, I presume. I promised to give it to you."

Kathleen took the letter from Queen Renata's hand. To Kathleen's surprise, Renata left without another word. The rift between them had grown larger, and at this point, Kathleen felt little desire to try to build a bridge. Once Kathleen was sure that she was alone, she opened the letter. The paper was fine and crisp. She began to read:

Dear Princess Kathleen,

Please burn this letter once you have read it. I would not want my past to endanger your future.

I am writing to you out of love, and hope. As the chosen Daughter of the Fealty, all of our lives are now firmly intertwined with your own. When you were a child, your parents and I were very close friends.

I have watched you grow into a lady and often wondered if you inherited the same Talent as your mother. Do you find yourself drawn to living things? Do fruit and flowers give you a sense of peace? Do you ever find yourself longing to leave the stone walls of the city and be surrounded by nature? If so, you may be feeling the beginnings of the Gift you have been given. No one has been there to teach you.

I, like your mother, am a Gardener or a Green Grower. We attended the Academy together in Tyath as girls. As the only students from Sundiland, we spent a lot of time together during those years. We remained close for the rest of her life. When your mother died, Renata was jealous of the friendship I maintained with your father. She pushed me away, and to keep the peace, I withdrew. I am sorry for that now.

I congratulate you on the finalization of your betrothal to Prince Heathron Dol Lassimer. I really did not believe he would accept our kingdom of Candoreth in marriage. Not because you lack any beauty, for you are truly radiant and good, but because our land has suffered greatly in the recent past.

I am so angry that I am no longer allowed to help Grow the crops for the people. I am not nearly as strong in the Talent as your mother. She was amazing, but everyone should be able to help as their abilities allow. The times are changing rapidly. I remember when those with the Talents were respected by the Church and the State.

Your Highness, even if you do not share in your mother's Gift, will you remember us? In the future, if you sit on the throne in the Golden City, will you offer aid and comfort to the Talented people among your subjects who are displaced? We need you. I dream of a day when the Academy for the Talented is once again available to the young people of Desnia. I believe we can help to face the challenges of our times.

With admiration,

Lady Allison Dal Avery

K athleen read the letter through once more, lingering on the passages that spoke of her mother. Larissa entered the room.

"What was that all about?" Larissa said. "Is the queen trying to tell you how to celebrate your own wedding again?"

Kathleen rolled her eyes. "You have no idea. She did give me this letter from Lady Allison Dal Avery, though."

"Is she asking for favors now that you are on your way to Tyath?"

"I remembered calling her 'Aunt Allison' when I was a small child. She and my mother were good friends. I always wondered why she stopped coming to visit with me. I guess Renata made sure she felt unwelcome."

"Just another reason to not like her. It is probably best in this case though. The woman never married—she's kind of strange. Lady Allison Dal Avery is even rumored to be an unrepentant sorceress."

"You mean a Green Grower?"

"You know what I mean," Larissa said. "In any case, I'd burn that letter."

A FIT OF LAUGHTER

The Farewell Feast would be a success. Larissa succeeded, in the last moment, at getting some flower merchants to sell her all the flowers available. Kathleen considered what it would take for her to grow the flowers herself. Of course that was out of the question. She didn't want to flaunt her Talent. She wondered how long it would take her to grow that many. That kind of Growing was beyond anything she had tried before. The variety of flowers obtained by Larissa, combined with those the queen had already purchased, transformed the Great Hall in the castle into a paradise of blooms of every color. Each centerpiece laid out on the long tables had a large, beautiful passion flower in the center. Kathleen thought of her mother each time she saw the intricate flower. It was more than her House Sigil— it was an emblem of the mother taken so early. Kathleen wished her mother was alive to attend.

"I am so grateful for your help, Larissa. You are amazing," Kathleen said.

"We did it together," she replied as they leaned against each other, arms across each other's shoulders.

Sam moved around, putting the finishing touches on the tables and arrangements.

"You both are wonderful," Sam said. "I could not have kept the other servants as organized and on task like you did. Now go and get yourselves ready for the feast!"

"Sounds good. I'll race you back to our room," Larissa said.

"You mean like we used to do when we were little? I always won. Will you never learn, Larissa?" Kathleen asked with a smile

"That's right, but you won't beat me this time, Your Highness," Larissa said, taking a few steps toward the door.

"I know a shortcut," Kathleen called out.

"You are going to need it," Larissa promised.

It may have been the silliness that comes with exhaustion. Despite being tired from all the preparations, Kathleen found herself sprinting past Larissa toward the door. Larissa turned, trying to make the door as well. She let out a playful scream, and her slippered feet began to churn rapidly on the polished floor.

They were both squealing as the doors slammed open and they tripped and tumbling into the hallway, a tangle of skirts and tresses.

"Stand clear!" came the deep voice from the hall.

Jared DeTorre, the Sīhalt Guardian, leapt into the room, sword drawn. He scanned the room for attackers and placed himself in front of the two young women. "Are either of you injured?" he asked in confusion. "I heard the screams."

The man's voice made Kathleen sit up quickly and brush her hair our of her face. Larissa struggled to right herself and sit up as well.

"We are fine, thank you, Lord Sīhalt," she said. Her face was blushing fiercely.

After verifying there was no immediate threat, he put away his sword and offered a hand to the young women.

"It seems half of the times we've met, you were falling to the ground," he observed.

Kathleen recoiled at the comment.

"Yes, and it seems half the time we've met you were skulking like a shadow to my steps. We were doing just fine without you, sir," she said sharply.

The Guardian blinked, then bowed.

"If you are not in danger, or injured, I will take my leave." He turned and walked away.

"I am sure he meant no offense," Larissa said. "Your Guardian is supposed to be close at hand, isn't he?"

"I'll take my chances in the hallways of my own castle," Kathleen said as she watched the man with the black cape walk away. "He is irritating. I wish he had never arrived here in Candoreth."

The embarrassment took the fun out of the race, so Kathleen and Larissa walked slowly toward the wing of the castle where they could bathe and get dressed for the evening's feast. Melva was there to help them get dressed.

Kathleen chose a blue velvet gown Larissa had helped her pick out the day before. She also wore a necklace of fine pearls and earrings to match. "You have grown to be quite a lady," Melva said. Larissa nodded in agreement. "That complements your form nicely too," she said. "Are you going to be able to dance okay in that?"

"I wasn't planning on dancing very much tonight," Kathleen said. "Now that I'm betrothed, there are few men that would risk a dance with me."

"Your father will want to dance with you one last time before you are married," Melva said.

"Your next dance will be with your husband." Larissa smiled. "You might want to dance with the Sīhalt Guardian too," Larissa said.

Kathleen rolled her eyes and smirked.

"I'm sensing there is something to that comment," Melva observed.

"She told her Sīhalt Guardian to leave her alone," Larissa said.

Melva raised her eyebrows.

"I asked him to just give me some space," Kathleen explained.

"You asked him to quit 'skulking like a shadow' to your steps," Larissa said.

Melva looked at Kathleen.

"Why would you say a thing like that, child?" Melva asked.

"I was irritated."

"And embarrassed," Larissa said.

"We were lying on the floor. We tripped coming out of the Great Hall, and he was right there to see it all."

'Stand clear!' Kathleen imitated Jared's tone and stood with a wide stance as if she held a blade. Both girls burst into laughter.

"No, Lord Guardian, but if you wait until I get my friend off my leg, and pull my dress down, I'd be happy to stand up and greet you properly," Larissa said in a sugar-sweet voice.

Then they both laughed so hard, their sides hurt. Melva watched them with a grin on her face.

"I think you owe him an apology. He was just doing his duty," she said.

"You should have seen Larissa rolling around on the floor like a pig trying to get up!" Kathleen accidentally snorted with her uncontrolled laughter.

Larissa pointed at her, and between giggles managed to say, "You, you are the piggy, Kathleen."

"I'm going now. I will see both of you at the Farewell Feast," Melva said.

She closed the door to the sound of two young women still struggling to control their laughter.

FAREWELL FEAST

rincess Kathleen danced with King Lukald. They both wiped a few tears from their eyes as the Royal Players played the anthem of House Dal Sundi. The king kissed his daughter on the cheek as they danced.

"I will miss you so much," he said.

"I will miss you too, Father," she replied as he twirled her again, then held her close.

Queen Renata oversaw it all with a regal bearing. Her face one of sufferable distain. She evidently did not like the decor or the music Kathleen had chosen.

Kathleen looked at the faces of the people she had grown up with, scattered about the room. Candoreth, having been hit hard by the plague, had raised some of the minor Houses up to fill in the ranks of the deceased among the major Houses. Kathleen didn't know all of them, but she felt they were still her people, and she appreciated the support they showed to her father. She caught the eye of Lady Allison Dal Avery, and the striking woman returned a knowing smile.

"Don't forget us when you reign in the Golden City," her

expression seemed to say. Kathleen promised herself she would not forget the Talented people of Desnia.

Melva and Girdy, two of the few aged faces in the room, danced around together as if they were decades younger. Elayna sat with some of the younger maids, eating and talking.

The new Sīhalt Guardian stood in the dark recesses of the Great Hall where the flames of the torches didn't reach. From his position, Kathleen assumed that he could hear any conversation in the room.

I really should apologize to him, she thought.

She curtsied to her father after the song ended and a round of gentle applause filled the room.

After some time, Kathleen walked over to the Sīhalt Guardian, standing apart, his back against the stone wall. As she approached, she noted how the shadows on his face blended with the darkness, making it look as if he was wearing the black hood of his cloak. He did not look pleased.

She could read his expression, but drew closer, determined to speak her mind. Kathleen wanted to be proper. It would not do to offend the people tasked with protecting her. She had seen that too many times from Renata.

"Lord Sīhalt," she began, "I would like to apologize for being so ungrateful earlier today." He stood still, in the darkness.

She continued: "I know you are tasked with protecting me, and I regret having been so terse. I appreciate your willingness to escort me to Tyath, and I hope that during our journey there we might become better acquainted."

The man remained silent.

"I just wanted to let you know."

Still he did not respond. The moment grew awkward, and then he said softly, "Is that all?"

"Well, yes. I hope you can forgive me for being rude."

"There is nothing to forgive. I want to make something very clear. I did not accept this commission with a willing heart. I only decided to be a Guardian to your procession so that my master would allow me the freedom to pursue my next mission. I do not desire to become better acquainted with you, except to better understand what foolishness a spoiled princess might undertake, so that I might minimize it and keep you alive, despite yourself."

"So in your mind I am no more than a package to be delivered, at a certain place, by a certain day?"

"Whether you live happily ever after beyond Midsummer's Day is no concern of mine."

Kathleen was shocked by the force of his statement. She had not expected him to speak to her this way. It had rarely happened that anyone had spoken to her with such a lack of respect. She opened her mouth, then closed it.

"Well, that makes you nothing more than a high paid courier. I expected a more dignified response from one in your station, Guardian. Your lack of respect is—disheartening. You are my Prime, after all," she finally managed.

Kathleen used his title as a weapon in her response, throwing it out in a tone that told him he didn't measure up.

The Guardian didn't flinch.

"I come from a place where decorum, loyalty and commitment are highly prized. As for my role as your Sīhalt Prime, you will find those virtues in me. But my respect, I give that to those who earn it, Princess."

He used her title in the same way she had used his, and she felt the burn in the truth of his words. She lacked decorum, and it remained one of her fears of living in Tyath. He had seen her rolling around on the floor, after all. She did not want to be seen as a countryside peasant in comparison to the nobility in the capital. As far as commitments and loyalty were concerned, however, she considered herself most capable.

"I am as loyal as anyone to those that I love. Why else do you think I travel north to be married? I am committed to my family, city and my nation," she said passionately.

"But not to your future husband," he said curtly.

Her mind raced trying to think of why this man would say such a thing. It was true that she had doubts about the joy she might truly find in this marriage, but there were other considerations.

"I have heard you make a mockery of the wedding contract. I will have you know that Heathron Dol Lassimer strikes me as a good man. You should strive to be worthy of him."

"More unsolicited advice from my vaunted Guardian," Kathleen replied. "I don't make conversation with those that deliver the mail."

Larissa approached and said the worst thing possible in that moment.

"Kathleen, I can't have you sneaking off into dark corners with strangers. You are betrothed now, remember!"

"I was just leaving to speak with Captain Dur Ruston about the preparations for the morning departure. Good evening, Lady Albodris," Jared said as he excused himself from the situation.

Kathleen turned with a mortified look at Larissa.

"What was that about?" Larissa asked.

Kathleen's response was interrupted by the voice of the Master of Ceremonies.

"Hear ye, hear ye. Queen Renata Dal Sundi has an announcement." He pounded his staff, striking the marble floor with resounding thud, thud, thud.

The queen rose and smoothed her brilliant orange gown.

"Lords and ladies, thank you for coming tonight to celebrate the betrothal of my loving stepdaughter."

She scanned the crowd and, seeing Kathleen, motioned for her to come back to the raised dais where the head table was set. Kathleen and Larissa walked back to front of the Great Hall, nodding to the approving smiles of the people seated along the long tables. The wine was flowing freely, and many of the guests were red-faced with the effects of alcohol. This was usually when

Kathleen preferred to leave a party, but as the bride-to-be, there was no escaping this feast, not until the very end.

"I have coordinated with the Royal Players to have a special performance: a skit to enjoy and remember our beloved princess."

Kathleen sat in her seat but wanted to shrink back from view.

What could she possibly be planning? Kathleen wondered.

With a sweep of her arm, accented by angel sleeves, the queen gestured to the open space between the tables.

"I give you Princess Katie," she said dramatically.

A singer walked to the middle of the floor and began a solo. He sang in a strong voice and began to tell the story of Kathleen's life as he strummed on his lute. What began as a beautiful piece quickly devolved into a comedy. The crowd laughed and clapped when he used an unexpected rhyme and even used some tawdry language. Kathleen looked to her father, hoping to see disapproval on his face, but the king was clearly drunk and clapped and laughed along with the rest. Renata seemed to be enjoying it immensely. She actually looked happy for once. The bard sang of Kathleen's love of horses and sailing, which was all true, but Kathleen dealt with a mix of fury and embarrassment. The singer continued, while actors played out his words:

...And as a girl of just thirteen,
She sailed around the harbor,
In between the merchant ships,
Going to and fro.
The waves were fraught that windy day,
They caught her boat in a foamy spray
Until at last, our bonnie lass
Was thrown to the deck on her bonnie...
Pass! She did over the rails,
But not before her full-rigged sails
Caught the wind and dragged her under the choppy waves.
So what does the Princess of Candoreth do,
Not what I, nor you, would do!

No! She holds on tight to the rope in her hands
As if her feet are on solid sands,
And then begins her famous plight
Within the sailor's and seaman's sight!
She sailed right proudly, like a thing from the deep
We thought she had drowned, not hearing a peep.
Until hand over hand and thumb over thumb,
She climbed back in her boat, all covered in scum!

The people laughed and cheered. Larissa placed a hand on Kathleen's shoulder to comfort her. Kathleen tried to pretend she did not mind being demeaned amid the laughter. She tried to put on a brave face.

She turned to Larissa.

"My Farewell Feast was ruined," she said through the clenched teeth of her attempted smile.

Then an energetic baritone voice drowned out the laughter.

"My dear bard, your talents are great, but they do not measure up to the priceless gift that is our princess!" The bard tried to keep strumming his instrument, but a firm hand quieted the strings. "I have travelled far and wide! I have climbed the mountains and seen the tide on the other side!" His black cape whirled and he stamped his boots in a shuffle to get the crowd's attention. His voice rose and fell with perfect dramatic intonation.

"And let me assure you, my lords and ladies, that we have before us a beauty not seen in Desnia for a generation. Her mother was a woman worthy of veneration!" Jared Sīhalt pointed to Kathleen, extending his hand with a flourish.

Kathleen could not believe what she was seeing. The reserved Sīhalt Guardian spoke with the practiced voice of an actor on stage. He moved like a professional Storyteller and held the audience spellbound. Here and there, around the room, voices piped up. "Here, here!"

The young man, dressed in black, drew his sword and made slashes in the air to punctuate his words. "She comes from people who were quick with the Sword! Her father, his father, and his father too, it's true, have all been willing to face death for Candoreth!"

Now King Lukald chimed in. "Here, here!" he said, raising his glass.

"Our Empire's son has chosen this one." Now he laid a hand gently on Kathleen's shoulder, standing behind her. The people were silent.

"And so, my dear people of Sundiland, know you not that you must stand, and raise your glasses with pride? There is no other like Princess Kathleen Dal Sundi, your Sunshine Bride!"

The people suddenly rose to their feet, cheering and toasting the health and well-being of the princess.

For Kathleen, the darkness that had overcast this special day dispersed like the clouds of a brief summer shower. Jared's actions were like the rays of the sun itself, dispelling the gloom. Kathleen questioned what had made him do it. Especially when he had just been so unforgiving and critical of her.

"That was remarkable," Girdy said, leaning close to whisper in her ear. "Now you have seen another facet of a Sīhalt Guardian at work. He will defend his charge no matter the battlefield."

Kathleen nodded her agreement. "It was impressive."

He must protect the package he will carry, she thought.

Somehow, her bright blue sky seemed tinged again with a bit of gray.

LEAVING CANDORETH

Kathleen looked around the interior of her royal carriage. Melva had her few items placed carefully along one shelf, and Larissa had more things by far, but they were stacked neatly at one end of the carriage. Kathleen climbed onto the high seat atop the carriage and arranged her skirts appropriately.

"You look radiant, child," Melva said.

King Lukald stepped into the carriage and sat down beside his daughter. He patted Kathleen on her knee.

"I have a final gift for you," he said.

King Lukald drew out a silver chain necklace. It had a pendant with a swirling pattern of green, red and white.

"What is it?" Kathleen asked.

"It's a Talent Pendant," Melva said reverently.

"And now it is yours," the king said.

"The design looks like a small green leaf, a little white fang, and a drop of red blood chasing each other."

"The emerald, ruby, and white stone pendants were made for the Talented Ones who attended the Academy of Tyath. This one belonged to your mother," he said.

"It is beautiful." Kathleen turned it over, looking at the other side of the gemstones.

"This would have been given to your mother on the day she first performed as one of the Talented under the supervision of an instructor," Melva explained.

"So all the Growers and Healers have these?" Kathleen asked.

"The Builders used to have them too. That is what the white stone represents," Melva said.

"It's been a long time since a Builder was seen in Desnia, though," Lukald said.

"Well before my time," Melva agreed. "The walls of Tyath were made by Builders, though. Same white stone too," Melva explained, pointing to the pendant. "That is why they shine."

"I will wear it with pride," Kathleen said solemnly before drawing the necklace close to her chest.

"If you wear it, do so discreetly, my child," Melva warned seriously.

Kathleen nodded and tucked the pendant inside her dress.

"I love you, Kathleen," Lukald said.

Trumpets blared, and the royal wedding procession began to move forward.

People of all classes came to wish her well as the wagons rolled down the main thoroughfare of the city. Every house had people waving white flags, crying, "For Candoreth and House Dal Sundi!" Blue banners were hung from the tallest spires, and the bells at the Citadel rang in celebration. The priests at the Candoreth cathedral offered a blessing as the procession passed. Flowers and palm fronds by the thousands were tossed in her path, such that they covered the entire street in a carpet of softness. The greenery muted the marching of the soldiers and the clip, clop of horse's hooves. The blossoms, crushed under hoof and boot, scented the air with a sweet fragrance. Kathleen did not know until this day that there existed so much love and admiration for her family. She was swept up in the beauty of the scene.

"Stay warm, Katie! I love you." Kathleen heard a small shout from behind. It was her sister, Elayna, smiling broadly, waving. Kathleen blew multiple kisses to the little girl, who pretended to catch them in the air and hold them against her face. Elayna stood on her tiptoes until the wagon passed beyond her view—then Girdy lifted her up, still waving high above her head.

Kathleen tried to hide her tears from her subjects. She wiped them away as fast as they sprang forth. However, the people only cheered louder to see the emotion she displayed at leaving her home.

"They love you, Kathleen," Larissa said sincerely.

"I just want to make everything okay for them," Kathleen responded.

"You will make a difference for Candoreth and all of Sundiland," Melva said. She leaned forward and patted Kathleen's shoulder.

The wheels of the wagons, almost as tall as a man, rolled onward over the flat stones that paved the streets.

"This reminds me of my wedding day," King Lukald said.

"You mean our wedding day," Renata correct him.

"I spoke of my marriage to Kathleen's mother, Renata. She does look very much like her mother," Lukald said.

"I'm sure she does," Renata said, although she had met the king's first wife. Renata seemed ambivalent about his memories prior to their life together.

Kathleen almost felt sympathy for her stepmother Renata, hearing the words her father spoke about her mother. He never said such things about his current wife. Renata seemed more impatient than hurt by the praise her husband had for his deceased wife. She looked around at the adoring crowds, and from her response you would have thought they cheered for the queen. She waved to the crowds, enjoying the attention.

They approached the passion flower gates of the city. The heavy gates, carved with dolphins and flowers, had been wrought by her great-grandfather. The morning sun doused them in a soft light. The sounds of the crowds inside dimmed as the heaviest doors finally closed.

Many of the people of Candoreth followed the procession down the road, along the Delving river leading to the high country. Fishermen in the small boats, plying the river, waved at the gleaming serpentine procession.

Kathleen turned to Larissa and said, "I wonder if I will ever look on those gates the same way again."

"I wish I could go with you all the way to the Golden City," Lukald said to his daughter as he rode alongside her carriage on horseback. His ceremonial armor shone brightly, and Lukald had his red beard braided in two strands.

"I understand, Father. Our nation needs your strong leadership, especially in these times," Kathleen replied.

"When I was crowned king, if someone had told me I would have to watch my daughter leave for her wedding and stay behind, I might have passed the crown on to my brother."

"I will write to you, Father. And tell you all that happens," she said.

"A Daughter of the Fealty arriving in the Golden City without her parents! I'm sorry I can't do more, Kathleen," Lukald said.

The queen chimed in again.

"Candoreth is sacrificing enough to allocate the soldiers, supplies, and retinue needed for the procession."

"The soldiers are not just for show, Renata—the security situation is more serious than you realize," Lukald said.

"The Sīhalt Guardian seems to think the soldiers are just for show. The man can be full of himself at times," Kathleen said.

The Sīhalt nodded to her from a distance.

Of course he did! Kathleen shook her head.

"He heard you," Larissa said.

"He has taken his role as a protector seriously from the moment he arrived," Renata said.

"He has kept an eye on Kathleen from the beginning. Even during the matches at the arena, I caught him often looking in her direction and scanning her surroundings, looking for any danger. I think he makes her feel uneasy at times with the fierceness he displays," Larissa said.

"He makes me feel uncomfortable because he treats me like an object," Kathleen said.

"I wish I could find a man to treat me like an object," Larissa said with a smile. "He really spoke up for you last night at the feast."

"He was just doing his job," Kathleen said.

"Keep looking, Larissa, it isn't hard to find a man who treats you like an object," Renata said.

"It is true, we are few and far between!" King Lukald said proudly. He had missed the subtleties of their comments.

Queen Renata just shook her head.

Larissa placed a hand to her mouth to hide her smile.

"Yes, Your Majesty," she said.

ALONG THE DELVING

The procession traveled due west, the Delving River on the left-hand side. As they approached the village of Celm, poorly-dressed peasants gathered along the road to watch the royal carriages pass. They waved, but only half-heartedly compared to the excitement shown in Candoreth.

What a change we see in just a day's journey, thought Jared.

Jared rode ahead of the procession. They were still well inside the borders of Sundiland, but the cheer that he saw in the city of Candoreth had been replaced by difficult living. The prosperity dissipated soon after leaving the main population centers.

"When the dog is freezing, the tail goes first."

The old axiom from Adisfall, his home far to the north, came to Jared's mind. He could see the desperation on the faces of the men and women who worked the land for sustenance. It seemed the meager bounty on the ships of Candoreth these days made it less and less upriver to places like this village.

Jared accompanied the scouts that looked ahead to verify the road was safe. As he rode in the saddle on the black stallion, a woman at the crossroads of Celm offered to sell him some dried fish. She held the thing up toward him and mumbled some unin-

AUSTIN REHL

telligible price. The woman looked gaunt and poorly fed. The child that clutched at her skirts looked longingly at the meal. Jared doubted the woman or the child had eaten today.

"How much for your fish?" he asked.

The woman perked up, surprised he had given the fish a second thought.

"Three, uh, two coppers, my lord. Two coppers for a dried fish of the good river Delving," she said, eyeing his cloak. "Are you a Sīhalt, my lord?"

"Yes, good woman," he said.

Jared dismounted and pulled five coins from his purse. He placed it in her hand. "I'll pay five since you delivered it right to my path. Thank you, good woman." The child's eyes hungered as the woman exchanged the fish for money and tucked the coins safely away. Jared broke the fish in halves and passed part to the child. She pulled away in fear but still reached out to grab the portion of fish and quickly put it to her mouth.

"Tell me of the surroundings, good woman. Behind me comes the wedding procession of Princess Dal Sundi. All does not seem well here in your village. What can you share with me?"

"The king is going to marry his daughter off to the prince up in the north. I'd heard rumors that she would pass this way. Will the union make Sundiland great again? I have my doubts," she said.

"Why do the people look so weary?" Jared asked, looking down the lane toward men, dirty and exhausted.

"We can barely put food on the table for ourselves. We have taxes to pay to the king, and our crops have failed. There is word from the west that the Delathrane are raiding this season. We are barely holding on, sir."

Jared gave the other half of the fish to the little girl, who accepted it gratefully. He mounted Steed and turned back toward the main body of wagons.

"Gather the people of your village. When the wagons pass, you

178

will be provided a meal," Jared said. The woman looked at him in disbelief.

"My mother always said the Sīhalt Guardians were good. First time in my life I've spoken to one, and I'm already grateful."

"Thank the Princess Kathleen Dal Sundi," Jared said. "The bread will come from her."

Jared galloped back to carriages that rolled steadily along. He approached the one carrying Kathleen and raised his voice.

"Your Highness, a word, please," he said.

"What is it, Guardian?" the queen asked as she rode alongside the carriage.

"I wish to speak with the bride-to-be and ask her charity for the poor people of this village," he said.

"We have planned some treats to share with the locals in each of the villages we pass during the journey."

"Your Majesty, these people are in desperate circumstances. There are children on the verge of starvation. They need more than treats."

"The princess is napping. I would not have her awakened for the needs of a few urchins," Renata said.

Larissa heard the exchange and disappeared into the carriage.

Finally, a sleepy Kathleen looked out the window to find the Sīhalt Guardian riding alongside with a look of concern on his face.

"What is it?" she asked.

"We have it all in hand, Kathleen," the queen said.

"The people of this village are starving. At least open the stores of bread so they may sleep without hunger pains this night," he said.

"What do you mean? We have not scheduled a meal for the population until we reach Sagav," Kathleen said.

"Share food with your people, Your Highness. They have not benefitted from the relative peace in Candoreth. Let them remember your procession with fondness, not bitterness."

"I am the one who will decide what will be shared out. Not you, Guardian," Renata said.

"Actually, as the bride-to-be, I have a right to offer charity to any of those in the path of my procession. It has ever been thus," Kathleen said.

Queen Renata scowled.

"If you give a meal to every pauper along the way, you will run out before you make the King's Highway. You do not have enough!" she hissed.

The procession was rolling into the town now. The barren fruitless fields that surrounded the meager village proclaimed the truth in Jared's words.

"Then take a look and see for yourself," he said, pointing to the people running to the town square as the wagons approached. Their frames were gaunt and drawn, but they ran with hope in their hearts.

"They are lucky to celebrate the procession of their princess!" the queen said.

Melva, from her perch on the carriage, squinted her eyes and looked closely at the scene playing out before them. The wagons rolled closer with each moment. Captain Channing ordered the troops to widen and set a picket to keep the people away from the carriages. Still they swarmed from the woods and ramshackle houses to gather along the main road, baskets and buckets in hand, waiting with the hope that salvation might be at hand, if only for a day.

The royal carriage moved forward, and the crowd stilled. The jingle of the horses' harnesses rang louder than the voices of the crowd. All became quiet at a signal from Kathleen. The wagons stopped.

She climbed atop the high seat of the royal carriage and looked about in all directions. Her eyes fell upon the faces of families haggard by the wear of work without rest. They looked dirty and broken. The fathers looked up at her, attempting to be stoic in the face of such defeat. The women sought to calm their children, pointing to Kathleen, whispering in their ears, telling them to be patient. The old and infirm continued to make their way slowly toward the wagons on the road.

Jared watched the princess closely.

What was she thinking? he wondered.

Would she be moved with compassion, or would the concern for her planned celebrations lead her to ignore the plight of these people? He thought of the days of starvation he had passed through as a child.

Jared noticed Larissa swallowed deeply as the realization sunk in that they were witnessing the complete collapse of a village. Melva's furrowed brow told the truth that she had seen suffering before and recognized it immediately. Kathleen seemed breathless. She looked around, almost as if she had forgotten that she held it in her power to relieve the suffering of these people. Queen Renata motioned to the leaders of the military escort.

"Lieutenant, will you please remove the people from the road. We have a planned stop in Sagav."

Kathleen stood. She looked toward the Sīhalt. Their eyes met. She blinked as they looked at each other. It was as if she felt the sadness in his eyes and accepted it as her own. Jared could hear Kathleen's heartbeats increase. She felt the stress of leadership.

"You shall have bread!" she shouted in a high clear voice. "And open a cask of wine to soften it for the elderly."

A cheer rose up from the people. On her command, the quartermaster ordered the stewards to open the wagons packed with the supplies. They began passing armloads of bread to the hungry people.

Kathleen looked back toward Jared.

She vocalized the words quietly. "Thank you for waking me," she said. Jared heard her clearly.

From the seat in the saddle he inclined his head in approval, then rode back to scout the far side of Celm.

THE GLADE

Jared watched as the form of King Lukald and Queen Renata disappear into the carriage. The feast in Sagav had been meager in the face of such need in all the villages. The rain ran in rivulets from the roof of the inn as they departed.

"I don't want a trickle of hungry peasants and their families to become a flood into Candoreth. We need these people here to plant crops next year too. We can't let a crisis turn into a catastrophe," the king said.

"Pass the word on the road. We promise to send supplies to these rural areas along the river," Queen Renata said to Jared.

"Candoreth needs its own reserves, especially if the harvest this year in the high country will be meager," Kathleen noted.

"Just try to behave like a queen and give them hope," Renata said.

Kathleen nodded as the queen waved once and then turned her carriage back to Candoreth.

Jared watched closely. He paid attention to those speaking as well as those listening.

"My wedding procession is the source of their hope, and we

are not even sure how we will afford the journey to Tyath," he saw the princess say.

As the storm came down in sheets, Jared held his cloak tighter about his neck and leaned into the rain. The heavy wagon train began to make ruts in the road as the water softened the earthen surface. Those in carriages closed the windows and curtains against the weather. Progress slowed, and Jared sensed that Steed was growing as impatient as he felt. The horse snorted and kept moving his ears forward and back.

He decided to ride ahead and see what this next section of the road held. Jared used his knees to bring Steed to a gallop. The drops of rain stung his face, but he was already soaked down to his boots. Letting go of the cloak, the Guardian allowed it to stream out behind him. Passing the foremost soldiers, he called out to the officer, "What news from the scouts?"

"In this weather? No news. They are probably holed up somewhere dry in the next village."

"I will ride ahead. With clouds this thick, night will be upon us early this evening."

The trees that lined the road became a blur. Jared smiled to himself and closed his eyes—he felt his feet in the stirrups, the sword at his side bouncing in its sheath with the movement of the horse. A glade opened up beside the road, and the young Sīhalt Guardian felt limitless. He ran onward, and it was as if his soul melded with the rain, the road and the wind. For one infinitesimal moment, he felt free.

When he finally pulled on the reins, bringing Steed to a sudden halt, Jared looked westward toward the cloudy horizon. The road ran straight into the distance. He stared at it quietly.

"Are you there?" he whispered to himself, before adding in a lower whisper just one word: Seth. Was he still alive? That duty still weighed upon him. He knew the Delathranes did not often take slaves. Only the most capable, the most beautiful or strongest were given any chance to live. Among the People of the Serpent, captives were a badge of honor to the captors.

I have not forgotten you, brother. I will find you and bring you peace, he silently promised.

Jared was soon riding into the rain again. He didn't get far, looking down at Steed's flying mane, before something in his vision caused him to pull hard on the reins, bringing the great horse into a pawing slide. When he stopped, Jared called out softly to the horse. "Easy, boy. Did you see what I saw?"

Jared considered for a moment that his vision might have been predisposed to see a thing like that. He had been thinking about Seth and his captivity just a moment before.

Returning to the spot on the road, Jared dismounted and planted his boots on the wet earth. He crouched down carefully, examining the road surface now running with water. The Sīhalt reached down to touch a few blades of grass bent low. Jared wiped the water from his face, flicking it aside. He reached down and plucked one of the blades of grass. A look of suspicion passed over his face. The Sīhalt quickly climbed back into the saddle. He rode back toward the procession, gathering speed as he went.

The tracks were faint, but the signs did align with each other. The rain made it difficult for him to be sure—the smell was so faint on the grass it seemed a memory.

Am I conjuring this up on my own? he thought.

Jared shook his head. He had learned to trust his instincts in situations like this. It had saved his life a number of times. He would trust his senses.

When Jared got back to the point where he had passed the glade, the procession was there. The wagons had been arranged in lines. The cooking fires had been lit and the tents erected in neat rows like the wealthier homes in Candoreth. Servants began to unhitch the horses and tether them in a nearby pasture. Jared saw the layout of the camp was all wrong for defense. He felt a surge of anger at the foolishness in front of him. Even the sentries on duty were placed too far apart.

"What is happening? Who ordered the procession to stop?" Jared demanded. His face was full of concern and exasperation.

"I asked the captain to help us settle in for the night," Kathleen said. "We are all tired of the rain."

"Your Highness, there is a village just a few miles down the road. We should stop there," he said.

"I don't know if I can stand to see the looks of hope and desperation any more today," Kathleen said. "Besides, I don't want to upset them by arriving soaked to the bone after dark."

"The signs I have seen on the road ahead of us do not look good," the Sīhalt began.

Kathleen shook her head.

"Sundiland has been at peace for most of your lives," Jared said, observing the encampment. "The village is a much safer place than this glen."

"But we have so little to share with the village now. Our coffers are almost empty."

"We need the village right now more than they need us. If we are not going to seek shelter there, we should at least form up the wagons into a perimeter."

"They have already unhitched the horses and begun setting up camp for the evening," Kathleen observed.

"We are not safe with the procession laid out like this," he said.

"Are you afraid of an attack, Lord Sīhalt?" she asked.

Jared looked up the road and then turned back to Kathleen.

"I have seen signs of the Delathranes."

"This far eastward on the road? We haven't even gotten to Hawote. We are still in Sundiland!" she said.

He nodded. "The signs on the trail do not look fresh, but I am fairly certain of what I have seen."

Captain Channing sat nonchalantly on his bay mare a short distance away.

"What seems to be the problem, Your Highness?" he asked, bowing formally from horseback as he rode toward them.

"My Sīhalt Prime has spoken with me regarding possible danger on the road ahead. He said Delathranes have crossed the road before the next village."

"Nonsense, Your Highness. I had my scouts search well ahead of the procession. None of them spoke to me of this."

The captain turned to the Sīhalt Guardian with a look of suspicion.

"I saw tracks that resembled the way they move and ride," the Guardian said.

"Are you sure of what you saw? How deep in the mud were the tracks?" Channing asked.

"They must have passed before the rain started," he said.

"How could you possibly see tracks made on hard-packed earth that has been pounded by rain all day?" the captain pressed.

"I believe if we are not going to stay in the next village, we should form the wagons into a perimeter for safety," Jared said.

"Sīhalt, you act as if we are in the middle of the Great Plains. There hasn't been a barbarian war band east of the Great River since the battle of Dumal Wells," he said derisively. "We don't have anything to worry about."

"The Delathranes have crossed the river and killed people recently," he said with a cold tone. He struggled to remain composed—an iciness coursed through his speech, but the captain remained oblivious.

"Where? Up north? West of Tyath where the river bends, maybe, but not here, close to the borders of Hawote," the captain exclaimed.

"What would it hurt, Captain, if out of an abundance of caution we simply asked the soldiers to circle the wagons into a perimeter and double the watch?" Kathleen asked.

"Your Highness, a moment." The captain pressed the Sīhalt

Guardian. "How big do you estimate this group of Delathranes to be?" he asked.

"Two, maybe three war bands, I would guess," the Sīhalt said sharply, irritated by the captain's questioning.

"How long ago did twenty-six barbarians pass this way?" he asked incredulously.

"Three weeks, perhaps," Jared replied.

"Three weeks! You think you can read trail signs from three weeks ago? Even if you could, how would you make sense of it after the rain we've had today?" the captain asked derisively.

Jared looked at the scattered cooking fires among the tents.

"At least have the men extinguish their fires. We may be making ourselves a target," Jared said calmly, regaining his composure.

Turning to Kathleen, the captain said, "Well, Your Highness, this Guardian must be as good on the trail as he is in the arena!"

"You may not have confidence in my judgment, Captain," he said, "but please believe me when I say that there may be dangers we have not yet calculated."

"If it became necessary, we can handle a war band or two without any problem, I am sure," Channing said.

"Do you know what the barbarians do when they attack, Captain?" the Sīhalt said quietly, his voice dropping to a whisper. The captain leaned close to hear, and so did the princess.

"I have seen what they do. They wait until you are asleep, or drunk with wine, or simply resting in the shade during the midday heat. They like to ride people down, pounding their bodies into the earth or dragging them behind their ponies until the poor victims can no longer be held with a rope. They would favor a quiet evening such as this. The sentries would not even see the black arrows fly. Believe me, even one war band would be enough to cause chaos in our ranks."

"You have fought them before, Sīhalt?" Kathleen asked.

"I am familiar with their tactics," he said bitterly.

"I will order the men to form the camp up into stronger defensive positions if you wish, Your Highness, but they won't like having to venture out into the rain again," the captain said.

"They will need to man the perimeter with pikes as well," Jared said.

"Pikes! We are still within the borders of Sundiland! Are you mad, Sīhalt?" Dur Ruston said, shaking his head.

Jared watched as Kathleen considered his requests. Jared felt tired and miserably wet, but his training taught him to push aside thoughts of comfort. He wanted the princess safe, and for now she might be in danger. He could not rest until the situation changed.

"If soldiers of Sundiland cannot stand firm in the drizzle of a rainy night to protect their princess, there is no hope for this kingdom," the princess said. "Have the wagons encircle the pavilion."

The captain was offended by the seriousness with which Kathleen listened to the Sīhalt Guardian.

"Stick to your own duties, Guardian, and seek not to teach me mine," he said as he walked toward his men.

"Form up! Regiment of the procession, the good Sīhalt Guardian does not like our camp and requires that we extinguish our cooking fires, re-hitch the wagons and form a circle around the royal pavilion."

Jared heard no grumbling, but he saw the looks of men who were tired and resented the command to rearrange the camp at dusk, in the rain, after having settled in for the night.

"Will you join me in my pavilion this evening, Lord Sīhalt?" the princess asked. "We have some matters to discuss, and I would like you to be there."

"As you wish, Your Highness," he said.

BY FIRELIGHT

The leaders of the procession wrung water from their clothes, thankful for the shelter of the pavilion. The sound of the soldiers and teamsters maneuvering the wagons and carriages into a rough circle around the area could be heard outside.

"Tomorrow we should arrive in Horming," Kathleen started. The gathering consisted of the military officers, the lead servants and those tasked with provisions and meals.

"Lately, even our good quartermaster has begun to offer up resistance to my generosity," Kathleen said to the gathered group.

"I try to hide my concern, Your Highness," the rotund man said, "but our supplies are dwindling daily."

The master chef nodded his agreement with a look of grave concern.

"I did believe that the situation would improve once we made our way to the high country—unfortunately, the high country is no better off," Kathleen said.

"We barely have enough food to finish the first leg of our journey. Your Highness, we did not calculate the needs of so many along the road," the chef said.

"Clearly, no one has calculated the needs of these people for a very long time," agreed Kathleen.

"Word has begun to spread ahead of us. I have had to use more discipline in the ranks of the soldiers to keep the crowds from becoming unruly," Captain Dur Ruston said. "If these were larger towns, I'm not sure what we would do."

"Hungry people are less predictable," the Sīhalt Guardian agreed.

"What began as a wedding procession has turned into a rescue mission, I fear, my lady," Melva said.

"I had no idea it was so severe," Kathleen said. "My father has been so focused on the naval fleet keeping the shipping lanes open that he has not paid enough attention to the difficulties of the peasants westward along the Delving. Did you see all the fields laying fallow? No wonder they are starving."

"We must represent House Dal Sundi proudly when we arrive in Horming. The nation of Hawote cannot know the extent of our circumstances," the quartermaster commented. A few of the others nodded solemnly in agreement.

"However, we cannot pass the people by with our wagonloads of food. We cannot dine and drink and laugh while we know their children lie in bed at night with hunger pains!" Kathleen said.

"None of us blame you, Your Highness. We admire your charity, but you cannot fix a problem in one day that took years to create," Melva observed.

"You cannot show up for a royal procession feast with a few potatoes in a sack. The best way to help these people will be to make your way swiftly to Tyath and bind these people closer to the Empire through your marriage to Heathron," Larissa offered.

"Perhaps we may resupply in Horming City. Unlike the villages we passed though in the countryside, Horming is fairly prosperous. I'm sure we'll find better circumstances as we turn north through the Glengeld Forest," Captain Channing Dur Ruston said.

All eyes turned to Kathleen. They looked at her expectantly. Kathleen felt her face begin to flush. She felt she had done the right thing in helping her people along the road, but also felt responsible for the dire situation in which they found themselves.

"We do not have the money to resupply all our provisions," she admitted.

A collective breath was heard from those gathered in the pavilion. For three beats of Kathleen's heart, no one spoke.

"Then we are in no position to host a feast in Horming!" the quartermaster said. "What will we do?"

"We will be able to obtain meager provisions, flour, meal, the basics," Kathleen said. "We won't starve. We just do not have the means to offer more . . . appropriate fare."

"I have never served porridge at a royal wedding feast," the chef intoned. He shook his head—the idea was obviously a nightmare to him.

"Revonah, being a smaller town, will expect little from us. So if we make it through the next few days without having to host a feast in Horming, we may be able to arrive at Tyath with our shoe leather intact," Melva said.

"I may have a solution," Captain Channing spoke up. "The local lords in Horming have invited Candoreth to field a team for the Calvaris tournament."

"How is that going to help us?" Kathleen asked.

"The winning House of the tournament is treated to a feast. If we win, they pay," he explained. "They will be none the wiser regarding our financial straits."

"Would a victory in the tournament outweigh the processional duties of hosting a feast?" Kathleen asked.

Lady Larissa and most of the men in the room unanimously agreed that it would.

"They would not dream of asking us to host if we win. If we lose, though, we are on the hook for dinner and lots of drinking for all of the teams," Larissa said.

"May we decline the invitation to play?" the Sīhalt Guardian asked.

"That would be worse than offering gruel at the feast! We must play, and play to win," Lady Larissa said.

"And I am eager to play in the tournament!" Captain Channing Dur Ruston said with excitement.

Kathleen was not sure what to do.

"I am not as familiar with the game of Calvaris as you might think," she said to the gathering. "Does Candoreth have a chance of winning?"

The officers looked slightly offended by the question. They nodded vigorously in the affirmative.

"Oh yes, Your Highness, they probably did not even want to give us an invitation. We have wiped the field with these Horming devils during most of our matches."

"Go ahead and organize the team," Kathleen said.

Captain Channing grinned and swept his sodden feathered cap low toward the ground as he bowed to Kathleen.

"Thank you, Your Highness. We will play our very best for you in the field," he said.

"Just try to keep your shirt on this time," Kathleen said.

The crowd laughed. Most of them had watched the Marth match between the Guardian and the captain at Candoreth.

Kathleen saw the Sīhalt laugh briefly too, and she was glad to have brought a smile to his face.

"And we will need your Guardian if we are to win," the young captain said reluctantly, looking away from the princess.

"Captain, are you still smarting from being unhorsed?" Lady Larissa ventured.

"On the contrary, my Lady Albodris," he said, turning to Larissa and straightening. "I proudly wear the good luck charms given me by his Windstall Stallion." He traced where the prints of the horseshoes would have stamped his chest. "I just thought the

Sīhalt Guardian would not participate unless the princess asked him to do so," Channing said.

"I am here as the Prime, dear Captain," Jared said. "But if I may obtain the princess's blessing, I will join you on the field."

"Aww, he sounds like the little boy asking his mother to go out and play!" Larissa said.

The Guardian ignored Larissa and turned to Kathleen with a look of subtle indignation. There was, however, a slight smirk on his lips.

"I insist. Will you play for our team, Lord Sīhalt?" Kathleen said.

"I have some skill at Calvaris," he replied.

"Guardian! I have begun to read your feigned humility. If you admit to having 'some skill,' I imagine that you are actually quite good! What do you say we show these Horming men how to play Calvaris!" the captain said. He slapped his thigh with his hand in excitement.

A man's scream punctuated the damp evening air, startling some of those in the pavilion. Kathleen and the captain turned toward the direction of the noise. The Sīhalt Guardian was already darting outside, his whip-like sword drawn. The narrow blade caught the light of the cooking fire outside.

In the warmth of the evening air, Kathleen could see that fog had formed along the edge of the forest that surrounded the glade. The camp was suddenly alive with soldiers running to grab the pikes from the wagons.

"At arms, men!" cried Captain Dur Ruston. The soldiers scrambled out of their tents, rushing to the perimeter while trying to belt on swords and buckle breastplates in place. Kathleen ran to where a group gathered with torches lit, bending over a fallen figure. A young Candorethian soldier squirmed on the grass, grasping at the black arrow that protruded from his neck. Kathleen covered her mouth with her hand, images of Girdy lying in the sailboat flashed in her mind. Two soldiers tried to hold him steady, but his movements began to slow as they spoke in urgent voices, trying to calm the young man. The Sīhalt turned to the gathered crowd.

"The black fletching is used by the Delathranes," he said. The crowd drew back as if the arrow itself might attack them.

"I will call for Melva," Kathleen said, turning to go.

An arrow whistled by Kathleen's shoulder and struck a soldier's lowered shield.

"Extinguish the torches and shield Princess Dal Sundi! There is no more that can be done for him," the Sīhalt said, removing his fingers from the side of the soldier's neck.

"Yes, protect the princess!" Captain Dur Ruston said as he was shaken from a momentary stupor.

"It came out of nowhere. Jas wasn't even on the sentry line. The arrow sailed right over and caught him in the neck, sir, when we came out of the mess tent," one of the soldiers said.

"It's a distraction," the Guardian said, then yelled for the group to take cover and motioned for more soldiers to support the perimeter. Suddenly Kathleen could hear the sound of rapidly approaching hooves.

Men yelled for reinforcements as the crash of horses struggling to break through was accented by the war cries of the Delathranes. They jumped up on the wagons and began to attack. More arrows flew overhead, finding targets silhouetted by the firelight dancing on canvas tents and wagons.

Kathleen struggled to see when she looked out at the darkness. Her eyes had not yet adjusted to the absence of light beyond the perimeter of wagons. She heard the Sīhalt command the men to douse the flames.

"Extinguish the fires! All of them," he shouted. "They will attack again."

Kathleen could not imagine trying to fight in the darkness.

All at once the Delathranes retreated. The wounded cried out for help while those who defended the perimeter cursed the barbarians and sought for greater courage in anger.

The Sīhalt walked to Kathleen. He took her arm and said, "Walk with me." She was pulled along at a quick pace as he led her back inside the royal pavilion.

"Stay here, Your Highness. I can't risk you being harmed."

"I will not hide in a tent while my people are fighting. I will help the wounded," she said, turning to join Melva as she knelt beside a servant.

"I insist, Your Highness," he began.

"No, I *insist*, Lord Sīhalt. I *command* you to go and do your best to stop this attack. I will do the best thing I can do to help, which is to tend to the wounded. Use what skills you possess to help my people. There is no safety for me as long as my people are in danger. Defend us."

A veil of darkness seemed to pass over the Guardian's face. A distance grew in his eyes. He knelt formally and said, "Yes, Your Highness. I will stop this attack." He held an extinguished wooden torch in one hand. As he rose from a kneeling position, he took the blackened wood and rubbed it onto both sides of his hands. Dropping the torch, he now applied the soot to his face. He covered his neck and ears as well. As they stepped out into the night, the black cloak and clothing he wore blended with the foggy night. He walked with purpose toward the perimeter, climbed atop one of the supply wagons, silently unsheathed his sword, and disappeared into the night.

Kathleen stood aghast.

Have I sent him to his death? She thought.

"Where is the Guardian?" Captain Dur Ruston whispered when he got close enough to see Kathleen. "I need his advice," he said.

"I commanded him to stop the attack...and he went out there," she said, pointing out toward the darkness of the forest.

BATTLE IN THE DARKNESS

J ared's boots landed softly on the ground outside the perimeter of wagons. His fingers twitched in anticipation. He felt like a hunting mastiff released from the leash. He hungered for his prey.

The emotions Jared had kept under control since the night of Seth's disappearance resurfaced. He felt a flood of rage fill his soul, but the result was not one of trembling fury, but rather a cold and calculated intent.

Princess Kathleen, the one he was sworn to protect, had said it. There was no safety for her, as long as her procession was in danger. There was truth in her words. She had asked him to stop the attack. She had *commanded* him to do what he could.

Jared could feel the restraints he tried to rebuild in the presence of Master Tove begin to dissolve. The command of the princess was as good as a license to kill. Jared tried no to smile at the thought of more Delathranes meeting their end.

Jared sheathed his sword and removed his black dagger. He was no longer the diplomat, not simply a protector. He was a predator prowling in the darkness. His senses sharpened at the opportunity to hunt his enemy.

The killing was easy. It was the silence that was the challenge to maintain. He strove to keep each and every Delathrane from making a noise as he ended their lives. Jared used an approach from behind. Delathranes fell, one by one. The first got a knife to the throat. The second took it to the lungs as a vice-like grip closed over his mouth. The Sīhalt Guardian laid each of them softly on the wet leaves, like a father putting his sleeping children to bed, nine in all. Jared knew there were more of them. He moved like a ghost in the darkness, flowing from one spot to the next in among the trees.

The Delathrane war band had stayed in the area for weeks. Why? He thought.

Jared walked a few paces and stood still, listening. He heard the sounds within the perimeter: cries of pain from the wounded and the voice of the princess seeking to comfort them. He scanned the area. His eyes easily penetrated the darkness. The fog, however, blocked his vision as surely as a tree or stone. The mist was thick and wet. He would rely on his ears to lead him. Thankfully the rain had begun to taper off. The wet ground provided a softened surface. Few twigs would snap underfoot after a soaking rain.

Jared gripped his dagger tightly and moved over the ground silently. He placed his back against a large tree and calmed his own breathing. He listened and was rewarded with the sound of a few hushed tones.

"We should attack again," said one voice, speaking quietly in the night.

"We know what we came for. Let us ride back to the Serpent King and inform the clans," the other said.

"They will travel more slowly now. We can gather the warriors needed to head them off from Horming. If we strike them before they reach the gates, the Serpent King will be glad," a third barbarian said.

Jared eased closer. Listening as he placed one foot in front of the other, Jared slid nearer with every moment.

"We have only one war band. We will need more warriors to ensure victory," said the first.

Only one war band? Good. That leaves three more men to make a dozen, he thought.

The Sīhalt crept through the swirling mist and saw the three figures crouching in the leaves near the base of a great beech tree. He was no more than two paces from them. One wore the metal armband of a war band leader. They were young warriors, probably newly raised to war band status.

"Your arrow almost hit the princess," one warrior said. "We must not harm her. That was a direct order from the Serpent King."

Jared was surprised at this statement.

Who is the Serpent King, and why does he know of Princess Dal Sundi? Jared considered.

"Let's go now. Forget the *Handri* horses. Gather the band," the leader said to the other two as he rose to leave.

Jared acted swiftly. He pounced on one, striking him at the back of the neck with his fist. The warrior collapsed to the ground. One spun to engage him in combat and the other fled on foot. Jared flicked his dagger but missed his target. The Delathrane turned to run, calling for his comrades. Jared drew his sword and gave chase. He caught the warrior just as he made it to his pony. Jared cut both man and beast down before they could ride away. The sounds of the struggle in the darkness made the men of Candoreth call out. "Lord Sīhalt, are you okay?" the captain called. Jared turned back to the Delathrane lying in the leaves, cursing himself for letting one get away.

"I am here, Captain!" he called loudly.

Jared walked from the edge of the forest, dragging an unconscious barbarian by the scruff of his neck. Soldiers opened a space for him to pass through the perimeter. They stared in awe at the lone man covered in black emerging unharmed from the darkness.

"You may relight the fires. There will be no more attacks tonight," he said. "Stay vigilant, though," he added, pulling the Delathrane toward the royal pavilion.

"I thought I would never see you again," a soft voice said behind him.

Jared turned to see the face of Princess Kathleen Dal Sundi standing before him. She wrung her hands, still covered in blood from tending the wounded.

"Were you able to save any?" he asked.

"Yes, a couple. Some of them won't let Melva touch them," she said.

"I stopped the attack, Your Highness." He inclined his head toward her. Her eyes drifted downward, struggling to make out the form at his feet.

"You captured one of them? The rest ran away?" she asked.

"One got away. The rest are dead," he said flatly. "We need to talk to this one. Will you call for Melva?" he said.

Melva entered the pavilion, chewing purposefully. She swallowed and looked at the form slumped on the ground.

"I have never Healed a Delathrane," she intoned.

"They live and die just like the rest of us," Jared said.

"It isn't the dying I have a problem with," the old woman said.

"I need to speak with this one. I promise he will not go free," Jared said.

"I'm feeling kind of faint. You know a woman can wear herself out trying to do too much with the Gift," Melva replied.

"I just gave him strike to the neck. It shouldn't take much," Jared said.

"I can just put him out of his misery," Melva said, grabbing for the small knife she kept on a necklace around her neck. Jared put out a hand to stop her.

"He spoke of a Serpent King who is seeking the princess. I need to interrogate him," Jared explained.

Melva considered this briefly and then said, "Restrain him. Then I will wake him up."

The captain had a couple of officers tie the Delathrane warrior to the post inside the pavilion with his hands behind his back. They tied his feet to the post as well with a length of rope.

Melva placed a hand on his forehead and barked out a command. "Wake!"

The young man jolted with the force of her command and snapped alert once more. He looked around, confused for a moment. Murmurs of disapproval were heard from some of the officers in the pavilion.

"He would have murdered you in your sleep," Melva said to those with looks of disapproval. "If I am a witch, what does it matter to you that I use my powers on a demon?" The men dropped their gazes and looked askance.

Jared asked for more torches to be lit and walked in front of the prisoner. The man's eyes lit up in recognition.

"How did you escape?" he asked in a thick Delathrane accent.

Jared immediately thought of the fateful night in the encampment of King Raldric. He did not want to give any information to this barbarian.

"I have my ways, barbarian," he said guardedly.

"No one escapes from the Serpent King," he said with reverence for the name.

The light from the additional torches illuminated more of the pavilion. The prisoner looked around the room, surprised to see so many in attendance. Kathleen and Larissa watched from a safe distance while Captain Dur Ruston and Melva both seemed ready to run the man through. When the Delathrane looked back at Jared, his eyes grew wide.

"You are not him! I knew it was impossible to outsmart the Serpent King," he exclaimed.

"Who? I am not who?" Jared asked in a cold whisper.

"The slave of the Serpent King. He looks like you, only his eyes are the color of the sky," the Delathrane said.

"Which clan does your Serpent King call his own?" he said.

The prisoner raised his head and, with pride in his voice, said, "I am Tan'atta, a warrior for the invincible Serpent King, son of Clan Tisane, leader of the war band Death Spirit. My brothers will avenge my death, *Handri*." He punctuated his introduction by spitting in Jared's face. The wet saliva clung to Jared's nose, and he wiped the moisture away. The Delathrane grinned defiantly.

Jared leaned in to the face of the young Delathrane.

"Your one remaining brother fled the battle like a lamb crying for the lost udders of its mother. I wish I could have killed him too, but I needed to speak with you," Jared explained calmly, showing him the dark dagger at his waist.

"You lie, *Handri*," the young man said scornfully. "We move like the night wind—you were only lucky to have captured me, and I will not speak."

Jared motioned for the captain to approach. Leaning toward him, he spoke in a low tone so that only the captain could hear. Dur Ruston nodded gravely and motioned for two of his subordinates to join him with lit torches as he walked out of the tent. They reentered the pavilion pulling the bodies of the dead members of the war band.

The prisoner watched in horror as he realized that the Sīhalt was not lying. Ten bodies lay on the ground before him, each face frozen in the eternal silence of death.

Jared turned back to the warrior.

"Who is the Serpent King?" he asked.

"One of my brothers got away. You will find out soon enough, *Handri*." He spoke with vehemence but was clearly shocked by the pile of bodies that had been his war band.

"Tonight, perhaps?" Jared said and landed a fist deep into the prisoner's stomach, driving his full weight forward. The young warrior heaved and gasped as Jared leaned closer to him. "Who is the Serpent King?" he asked again.

"The Clans are united. We have built the Serpent and the Egg. What was lost will be regained," he said cryptically through clenched teeth.

"What Clan is he from?" Jared asked, hitting him hard again.

The man did not break, only cried out in pain.

"Why does he seek the princess?" Jared continued with a sharp elbow to the man's face. The strike left a gash along the cheek.

"Lord Sīhalt, please!" Kathleen said, a tremor in her voice. "We have gained all that we need to know. There will be no feasts or tournament in Horming for us. We leave directly for Revonah at first light." Then she left the pavilion.

"You are *Der'antha*," the young warrior said, looking at Jared.

Jared nodded. "Captain Channing," he said, "allow this prisoner to visit with your men. See if the soldiers of Candoreth are able to obtain any information from the Delathrane who killed their brothers-in-arms tonight. I have no more use for him."

"Yes, sir," the captain said. "My men will relish the chance to even the score against their enemy."

EVIL MISTRESS

The Sīhalt Guardian watched with a curious look on his face.

Kathleen tried to ignore him as she pointed to a small pile of personal belongings she had sorted from the rest.

"Yours can be no bigger than that," she said, looking at Larissa and pointing to the pile.

"You should instruct the quartermaster to leave all of the water casks behind. We can't haul that weight either," Melva said.

Larissa sighed and began reluctantly opening another trunk.

"Might I ask, Your Highness, what you are doing?" Jared said.

"You are right, we must travel fast. This is all I will be carrying."

"As the bride-to-be, you may need a larger number of personal belongings," he said.

"I can't ask my entourage to dispose of anything extra if I am not willing to do the same," Kathleen said.

She looked up at Jared and saw an approving smile on his face. She felt annoyed that his approval made her feel validated.

"Tell Captain Dur Ruston to rid the procession of all unnecessary items. If we leave immediately, we might make it to Revonah by nightfall," she said.

"If the Delathrane Clans have built a Serpent Mound, we are in grave danger. They mean it as a declaration of war, as a united people," Jared said.

"This Serpent King, is he seeking me, specifically?" she asked.

"In the forest," he said slowly, "I overheard the war band leader tell his men not to harm you because they wish to deliver you to the Serpent King, alive."

Kathleen stopped.

"Oh, dear Abbath," Melva said softly.

"Candoreth hasn't had dealings with the barbarians for many years. I could understand if you were a lady from Horming and your father had created an honor feud with the barbarians. This makes no sense," Larissa said.

"I cannot see the answer to this riddle, yet," the Guardian said.

"Someone in Tyath does not want you to arrive for your wedding day," Larissa said.

Kathleen considered this.

"What advantage would it give the Delathranes to capture me?" Kathleen said, her voice full of concern.

"They do keep slaves if they are prominent people among their enemies. Perhaps that is the reason they wish to capture you," Melva said.

"If we were not so far along in our journey, I would consider turning back," Larissa said.

"I cannot turn back to Candoreth. I cannot lock myself in my carriage and wait for reinforcements either. So much is resting on my marriage to Heathron. We must press forward," Kathleen said.

Although her face bore the exhaustion she felt from the horrors she had seen this night, she was resolute. The small gathering nodded unanimously in support.

Before the sun rose over the eastern mountains, the royal procession had already entered the realm of Namth. A trail of personal belongings, empty casks, and spare wagon parts lay strewn along the road. The soldiers marched with purpose, keeping a wary eye around every bend in the road. A sense of urgency reigned.

The town of Revonah stood at the crossroads of the Trader's Way and the King's Highway. The intersection included the Salting River and its canal boats. The procession made it safely there by nightfall, and the guests were welcomed into the town with hospitality to dress their sore muscles and empty stomachs. The people of Revonah listened intently to the story of the Delathrane attack. Although they were sympathetic to the plight of the travelers, they seemed disappointed that they were called upon to furnish a meal instead of enjoying royal favor. They were hesitant to offer any more than a night's respite to the guests.

"We can place a guard for your rearward position," the mayor offered, but Kathleen knew this was simply a courtesy. The barbarians, if they chose to attack, could easily bypass the small Revonah guard.

Kathleen thanked the local lord and graciously accepted a gift of wine and cheese for the remaining journey northward. She felt a knot of fear in her heart. They were by no means safe, and still had a long road to cover before the mountains opened up and the wagon could roll more quickly toward Tyath.

Slender, soaring stone arches allowed the wedding procession to pass under the overhanging cliff. The towpath was wide enough to accommodate six horses abreast with the riders feeling only slightly cramped.

The Sīhalt Guardian rode beside Kathleen's carriage when he was not scouting ahead or behind the procession. Since the attack, he had remained ever more at her side. She found that his frequent presence did not bother her as much now as it had in Candoreth.

"I do not like the layout of the land. I feel constricted," Kathleen said to the Guardian.

"Even close to the town, visibility is decreased with the density of the trees," he agreed.

"Could enemies hide in the ledges that protruded toward the towpath?" she asked.

"They could be anywhere. I expect that Delathrane scouts are watching us now. We need to be wary. I don't know how far the main body of their war bands are located, but the warrior that got away would have run all night to make contact with them."

Kathleen shivered and eyed the surrounding evergreens.

Large ferns and saplings grew below the understory wherever the sunlight had a chance to peek through the canopy of the steep slopes. The increased sunlight made the undergrowth even thicker. The narrow road was the perfect place for an enemy to hide. The procession held to the trail and the sheer rocks of the cliffs along the river were a protection in one way, and a danger in another. It all depended where the enemy might be.

Captain Dur Ruston rode up to Kathleen.

"I am worried about our position here," he said.

"I agree, Captain. We need to move this procession onward quickly. Even during the daylight, I don't want to get hit by an ambush while we can't even form up," she said from atop her carriage.

"Have the men march double-time. There is a widening in the road just before the Trader's Way. We'll be safer there if worse comes to worse," the Sīhalt Guardian said.

The captain saluted and rode along the line, issuing orders for increased speed.

Kathleen was glad to see that the captain would now salute the Guardian. The two men seemed to have a mutual understanding between them now. Evidently, the Sīhalt had prevailed again.

The Sīhalt Guardian rode close by.

"Anciently, a legend held that this river gorge was a place of woe," he explained. "There are old stories that spoke of the large black hand on the cliff face."

Larissa pointed to the opposite side of the river.

"There it is," she said. "The black hand of the gorge."

The sheer rock was discolored in some places where the rain water spilled over the cliff's edge to the river below. What looked like a black hand on the cliff, partially covered in vegetation, allowed water to flow between the black fingers of stone.

"The old stories say a great warrior cut off his hand and threw it over the cliff, where it clung to the wall," Jared said.

"Why did he cut off his hand?" Kathleen asked.

"He did it to spite the limb that failed him. He was in a grand duel to win his lover's heart. He lost her to another man, and in his grief, he flung his hand over the cliff, where it remains today," the Guardian explained.

"How romantic," Larissa commented, frowning as she looked at the giant stone hand.

"Men will do strange things for the women they love," Melva observed.

"We have to be careful what we ask of men—sometimes they will do exactly as we wish," Kathleen added, thinking of her own father, and then, to her surprise, the Guardian kneeling before her the previous night.

"My mother has always said it is better to be a temptress than a nag," Larissa said. "What do you say, Guardian? Would you rather a temptress or a nag?"

The silence that followed her question made Kathleen feel uncomfortable. The Sīhalt seemed so serious, and Kathleen wished Larissa wouldn't torment him like this.

"Please forgive Lady Albodris. We have been friends for many years," said Kathleen. "She may seem a tremendous flirt, or even a temptress by some, but let me assure you she is harmless."

"Only one," Jared said finally. "I've only known one temptress."

"Oh, do tell all! Does she reside in Tyath? Will we have the chance to meet her when we arrive at the capital?" asked Larissa.

"She does reside in Tyath," said Jared, "but we may meet her anywhere. She seems to follow me wherever I go."

"That is so sweet," said Larissa. "Is she a Sīhalt maiden?"

Kathleen opened her mouth to speak but found herself unable to intervene. Curiosity and a sharp twinge of some other emotion held her tongue. What kind of woman could tempt this Sīhalt?

"Where did you meet?" Kathleen asked, tucking a stray strand of hair behind her ear.

"I met her on the Great Plains on a diplomatic assignment to the Delathranes last year," said the Sīhalt.

What would turn this man's head? How desperate a creature would this woman have to be, to follow a man throughout Desnia hoping for some small reason to believe that he returned her adoration?

"So she is not a lady?" Kathleen asked.

"She's no lady," the Guardian stated.

Coming from another man, or if a wry smile had been on his lips, she might have thought he was being comical, but he said it seriously, no humor about him.

"What is her name? Is she some exotic Delathrane princess that you can't resist?" asked Larissa.

The Sīhalt's face seemed to gather storm clouds that matched the fierceness of his eyes. Kathleen saw a savagery that made her take a sharp breath inward.

"I did meet my temptress among the barbarians," he admitted. "She goes by the name of *Revenge*. I embraced her only once, and now she constantly haunts my paths."

"You did a thing you regret?" asked Kathleen.

Jared looked beyond Kathleen and Larissa, eyes focused on a dark scene from the past that neither of the girls could see. "Regret," he said, as if weighing the word. His gaze found Kathleen's face, and he blinked, coming back to the present. "Yes, I regret it more with every passing day."

Kathleen swallowed hard and wondered what burden this man carried.

"I beg your pardon, Princess. The things I speak of are not fit for the joys of a wedding procession," Jared said abruptly. He turned and left the girls looking at each other as they rode along in the carriage. They turned to Melva, and she shrugged.

Kathleen glanced at Larissa. Her friend's levity had disappeared in the face of the Guardian's solemn mood.

What haunted him? She wondered.

The handsome Sīhalt seemed too young to have experienced so much. He was just a few years older than herself. Kathleen watched Jared ride toward the front of the procession, determined to find out.

BLOOD AND SMOKE

"Shall I massage your head and neck, child?" the old maid asked.

"Oh, please do Melva, that would be nice." Kathleen shifted her position to allow the old but strong hands to work wonders with their firm touch on either side of her head. The tension she had felt from the past two days had built up, and Kathleen felt the oncoming headache that might incapacitate her for days.

"I should get some sleep. That might help," Kathleen said.

"You have been propped up and craning your neck all morning," Melva noted.

"I need to be visible for the people. They want to see a princess when we pass."

Melva lowered her tone as she always did to say something wise or inappropriate. "You have been straining, watching the Sīhalt Guardian every time he rides by. You search the horizon when he rides ahead, waiting for him to return."

"I trust him to give us good advice on the safety of the road."

Kathleen's eyes were closed, so she could not see the smile on Melva's face, but she heard it in the old woman's voice.

"He is very nice to look at."

"I'm surprised you could see anything, with your old eyes," Kathleen replied.

The old woman laughed deep in her throat. "Sometimes I don't trust these old eyes, but a woman would have to be completely blind not to notice the manly form he presents in the saddle, and I can't decide which has a finer rump, him or his stallion."

"Melva, I'm on my way to be married!" Kathleen said, a note of chastisement in her voice.

"You are on your way to a lot of things, my child," Melva said with a knowing and loving smile.

Melva had a knack for saying what others were thinking.

Kathleen felt exhausted, but she could not fall asleep. Her thoughts tumbled together, seeking to make sense of all that was transpiring so quickly. She squinted against the sunlight shining overhead. Her headache was getting worse, despite Melva's best efforts. From the open corner of her carriage she could see the high seat where Larissa remained perched and smiling, ready to wave to anyone who might see the royal procession pass. She looked like a perfect princess.

"She is enjoying this entirely too much," Kathleen said to Melva.

"What girl wouldn't want to be mistaken for a princess every now and again?" Melva said.

"Maybe Larissa will find her own prince in Tyath. The Imperial family is large."

"Larissa is a swamp panther on the prowl. She will not go hungry," Melva said.

The bed jostled and bounced along the King's Highway. This portion of the road seemed to be in disrepair. Thankfully the highways all tended to improve the closer they traveled to Tyath. Kathleen looked forward to the smooth, easy ride they would have after they passed through the Woodfiels region. Kathleen rubbed both of her temples and tried to decide just how bad this headache would get. The sound of a horse whinnying made her want to wince. Then she heard the screams of people.

Kathleen bolted up. The scream was loud and high and followed by a chorus of other voices yelling in fear. Men's voices rose in alarm, yelling for the soldiers to form up.

"Delathranes!" the old woman said, grasping her knife. As if in echo, a soldier outside the carriage bellowed, "Barbarians!"

The heavy doors of the royal carriage were torn open, and Kathleen crouched on the far side of the wagon.

Delathranes on horseback rode toward the carriage. They twirled ropes over their heads and sent the loops flying through the air to settle over the high seat of the royal carriage. Larissa scrambled to avoid being caught on top.

Everything seemed to move in slow motion for Kathleen. The carriage began to tip, as the Delathranes pulled the ropes tight. The carriage rocked to one side, seeming to pause on two wheels and then topple over. Kathleen felt a stabbing pain in one ankle where her foot had slipped out the window as the carriage toppled and bent her foot against the ground. She wrenched her ankle free and crawled out of the open window onto the ground outside.

It all happened so fast. The House Dal Sundi banner—burning. Delathranes gathered what food remained, her scattered dowry, and her female servants. Thick smoke burned her eyes. Kathleen coughed and choked, using one hand to cover her face. She tried to rub the pain out of her stinging eyes. Kathleen was appalled when she caught glimpses of her surroundings. There were so many Delathranes. This was no small barbarian raid.

Men stood around the rim of the steep, narrow pass. Their bodies were painted in tortured patterns of blue. They rolled burning piles of wood over the edge.

Kathleen only had one thought at that instant—*Where is Jared?*

In shock, she huddled under a pile of blankets, unsure of what to do next. Kathleen drew the small decorative knife she kept at her waist. She cut some strips of fabric from the blankets. She tied these around her mouth and nose to try to filter the smoke billowing in her direction. She needed to move but dared not draw the attention of the nearest attackers. She stayed low to the ground, blending in with a jumbled pile of blankets.

All about her was a scene of grim hostility. One of her newest maids screamed for help as a laughing Delathrane pulled the young girl from the carriage. There was not a soldier in sight who remained free to assist her. They all fought for their lives individually. Others lay still, having already done their utmost duty. Kathleen could her the blasts of the trumpets calling for the soldiers to form up, but the smoke and narrow layout of the valley made this impossible. Stones and arrows rained down from the cliffs above on those few soldiers that had joined ranks. They lifted their shields to ward off the attack from above.

Captain Dur Ruston raised his voice above the noise. "To the princess! For House Dal Sundi!" Kathleen thought she could see him pointing his sword in her direction, but she doubted the captain had any idea of her exact location. The distance was too great for her to run without certain captivity or death. Even as she watched, the slowly forming phalanx of soldiers in her view became obstructed by more smoke and even more barbarian warriors. Kathleen felt terrified, behind enemy lines, alone in the haze of smoke and battle. She closed her stinging eyes and bowed her head to pray for a miracle.

"Lord Abbath, save me," she cried.

She opened her eyes again just as the smoke briefly parted. To her horror, she saw the soldiers of the Dal Sundi phalanx retreating. Shields locked together, swords and spears at the ready, and they took measured steps further and further away from their princess.

The fear of being left behind overcame her terror of being found. Kathleen arose from her hiding spot. Throwing off the blankets, she waved her hand high above her head and screamed for the captain.

"I am here!" She sounded shrill to her own ears. The shouts of men locked in battle drowned out any chance she had of being heard. She closed her eyes against the stinging smoke that rolled across the battlefield. The captain of Candoreth would never hear her.

Kathleen thought of the only man she knew would hear her shout.

"Jared!" she screamed, looking around frantically. "Jared!"

LEFT BEHIND

Burning piles of wood pushed, over the steep embankments by the Delathranes, filled the air with smoke. Kathleen stumbled forward. She cowered again when through the smoke she saw the Chief Steward and his assistant stabbed repeatedly as they died splayed awkwardly against the supply wagon.

"Jared help me!" Kathleen cried out again.

The thick smoke whirled in front of her face and from the dark billows, a man emerged. He wore all black, and a cape that blended with the surrounding smoke. He held a shining blade. He too had his face covered. His eyes, though rimmed in red from the smoke, were familiar.

"Kathleen, stay close to me," he said.

She reached out to grasp his hand. The Sīhalt Guardian pulled her through the chaos. Her dress was torn, she was missing a slipper and her right ankle left a trail of blood on the ground with every step.

Through burning eyes Kathleen saw Jared let go of her hand momentarily and leap to the top of a boulder, only to launch himself forward and smash his knee into the face of an oncoming

Delathrane. Blue war paint smeared across the man's face, as Jared's knee destroyed his nose. The Sīhalt turned and used his elbow to strike the next attacker in the side of the head. The sudden blow drove the man sideways, his body now as slack as the golden chain about his neck. As the Delathrane fell to the dust, Jared stooped to pick up a loose stone. With a fist sized rock in one hand, the Sīhalt smashed the base of his next opponent's neck. The warrior fell with a sudden cry of surprise. Jared followed the blunt weapon strike with a slash to the naked chest of the Delathrane behind him.

Another warrior bellowed with a raised hammer. The barbarian sprinted forward. Kathleen was certain the maniacal warrior would crush them both. Jared deflected the strike barely to one side, and stepped in close. Jared slammed his forearm into the man's throat and followed it up with a quick thrusts of his brilliant sword. He puncturing the leather chest plate multiple times the entire depth of the body faster than a blue heron spearing fish in the water. The Delathrane's eyes widened and his hand released the hammer. Jared's movements seemed graceful, and fast as a whirlwind. The commotion of the retreating Phalanx drew the attention of the other barbarians. Jared led Kathleen forward, stepping over the bodies of the slain.

The sounds of terrified people, crazed barbarians, and steel against steel raked the forest with confusion.

The Sīhalt Guardian sprinted with Kathleen through waist-high shrubs along the road. She felt her legs could no longer move and cried out in pain with each step. Jared kept pulling on her arm, her feet spun like a windmill as he forced Kathleen to run, each step a torture of its own.

They ran until they arrived at the edge of a ravine. Without hesitation, the Sīhalt leaped with Kathleen close behind. Kathleen screamed as she landed on the opposite side. The jolt of shearing pain in her ankle made her clutch her leg, unable to stand.

As she crouched holding her shattered ankle, Kathleen heard

the approach of thundering hooves and she cowered, expecting a barbarian approaching on horseback. She could almost feel the javelin that would pierce her back, protruding through her chest. The Sīhalt leaned over her in a protective stance.

When the hooves seemed close enough to trample them, the horse let out a shrill whinny. Kathleen flung herself to the side gasping for breath. The Sīhalt Guardian stood quickly.

"It is Steed! Now we will ride." he said, and slung the pack over the saddle horn. He lifted Kathleen onto the large black stallion. Then he climbed into the saddle behind her.

Kathleen struggled not to cry out with each impact of hoof on the road. She almost lost consciousness from the pain. For a moment she was taken back along a train of memories to when she was a little red-haired girl riding with her father. His arms held her safely as she looked down and watched the sand and surf pass beneath the swift hooves of King Lukald's horse. Ringlets of her hair, wet with the spray, blew back like a storm. She leaned forward and fell asleep, a small child safe in her father's arms.

In the distance, Kathleen could hear someone calling her, snapping her out of her reverie.

"Kathleen, wake up! Drink this!" the deep, comforting male voice said to her.

Kathleen opened her eyes. She lay on a smooth boulder, the rock cupping her like a throne. She looked around. How far had they travelled? How long had she been unconscious?

"You haven't been out too long," Jared answered, as if reading her thoughts.

The Guardian knelt before her now, offering her the drink. Kathleen regained her senses and looked at the man. He was less blurry now.

"Wh… Where…?" she tried to say.

"You are weak," Jared said. "You lost some blood while we rode."

Kathleen felt a sudden breeze rush along her legs and looked at her dress. It was torn, significantly shorter now than it had been, frayed well above her knee. Instinctively, she tried to cover up by stretching her arms, but she was weary and collapsed back down to the boulder.

"I used some of the fabric to stop the bleeding. I've placed a splint."

She took the cup he offered and drank the contents slowly. It was cool and refreshing but each swallow was followed by a bitter aftertaste. She frowned.

"It's satinwood," he said, gesturing to the cup. "It will ease the pain and give you energy following an injury. I mixed it strong so you may feel some disorientation and euphoria as well."

"I think the carriage wheel fell on my ankle. Then...when we jumped that ravine..." Kathleen said, looking down at her foot, now partially bound with strips of her yellow dress.

"I will finish binding your foot, but you must avoid walking." Jared rose up on his haunches and looked around. "It'll be fine. We have Steed to carry us the rest of the way to Altrastadt."

Kathleen crinkled her nose. "Altrastadt?" she said, confused. "We have to go to Tyath, not Altrastadt. We need to rejoin the wedding procession!"

Jared looked away. "I promise to get you to the Golden City by midsummer," he said, nursing a faint graze on his knuckle – the most the Delathranes had landed on him. "We still have time. We will rest for a few days in Altrastadt first, formulate a plan, and then ride to the capital city."

"But what about my entourage?" Kathleen said. "There are requirements for the marriage contract. It won't be valid if I don't—"

"Many people in the procession were killed," the Guardian said, interrupting her. He was suddenly cold. "Those that survived were lucky to be able to defend as they could," he added, a shade of empathy softening his sternness.

Kathleen gazed out to the ravine. The scent and sound of the trickling water filled the air, but it was the image of the steward's violent death that was most keen in her mind. What if that had been her, or Jared?

"Why did they leave me behind?" she said, turning to the Guardian.

Jared looked up from his knuckle. "I believe Captain Dur Ruston believed Lady Larissa to be you. She was riding in your seat when your carriage overturned. In the smoke of battle, the soldiers formed up around Lady Larissa. They were too busy fighting for their lives to see that your bridesmaid was the one they defended," Jared said, and returned to tending to Kathleen's ankle.

Kathleen took a deep breath that shuddered with emotion.

"Is that too tight?" Jared asked as he gently but firmly wrapped Kathleen's ankle, immobilizing it.

She shook her head. "I was just thinking of Melva and the rest of them. I hope they are safe."

"They still have a good chance to get to Tyath. The soldiers of Candoreth were fighting bravely."

"We need to join them," Kathleen said, looking around at the surrounding forest. The air was still and she could no longer see any haze of smoke in the afternoon light.

"It is too dangerous to travel back the way we came, and there is no way to circle back. The mountains will not allow it. We are going to Altrastadt—perhaps we can meet up with what is left of the procession once they reach the Amaranth Plains," Jared said.

"I am sure Captain Dur Ruston has reformed the ranks. He probably realized their mistake and is waiting for me," Kathleen said.

Jared looked at Kathleen. With his head tilted to one side, he seemed to be waiting for her to be more honest with herself.

Kathleen felt challenged. She crossed her arms and straightened.

"I *command* you to take me back to the procession," she said, attempting to once again have him kneel and obey as he had in the roadside glade.

Instead he shook his head.

"My duty to protect you will not allow me to obey your command. We will be killed if we turn back."

"Then what will we do? We can't be on the road together — alone." She hesitated before saying alone, just enough for Jared to sense something in the word, something that he didn't read as fear. Was it something short of excitement, perhaps? He batted the thought away.

"Karina," he said after a while. "That will be your disguise."

"Who?" Kathleen blinked several times, trying to make sense of his meaning.

He finished tying off the ankle wraps. He leaned back and leveled his storm grey eyes at her.

"Your name will be Karina. And we need to adjust your appearance..." Jared raised his hand to her collar, tentatively at first, before, in one swift motion that Kathleen could barely see, he had torn off the embroidered insignias of House Dal Sundi.

Kathleen gave a little cry in shock.

"Why did you do that?"

Jared smiled, and then he placed the insignias in a hidden pouch beneath his cloak.

"Like I said, you need a disguise."

"But I'll never pass for a Northerner..." Kathleen scoffed, trying to see the pouch where he had placed the collar – it was exceptionally well hidden. She found this funny and giggled.

The Sīhalt Guardian stopped and looked into each of her eyes.

"I hope I didn't mix that satinwood tea too strong. We can get another dress for you in Altrastadt."

Kathleen was preoccupied with another concern, however, one that made her blush. "But I've never done this before."

"What?"

"How can I be alone in the wilderness, with a...man. Will it not raise questions?"

"From who?"

Kathleen was shaking her head. "No, I need to have someone else with us," she said, and then hushed her voice to a low whisper. "I am betrothed to Prince Heathron Dol Lassimer, and I don't even have a chaperone."

"I am your chaperone," Jared said. "A little more than a chaperone, actually." His voice trailed off.

Kathleen stared at him. "What do you mean by that?"

"I mean that in order to keep you safe, you will have to become a Sīhalt Bride." He paused before what he would say next. "I will be your groom."

"Groom!" Kathleen cried, before avoiding eye contact with the Guardian.

A hush fell over the pair for the next minute. Jared occupied himself with checking the contents of his saddle bags, then he closed them and tightened the straps.

"Do you think that will work?" Kathleen asked eventually, breaking the silence.

Jared considered the question.

"At the moment, I cannot think of a better plan. We could not pass as siblings with your Sundiland looks and mine of Adisfall, that would inspire too many questions. Now, I must wear my sword, for our protection, so the role of me as a hospitable monk is not possible." He rubbed his chin. "That leaves you with the option of assuming the role of a highway harlot, which you might be able to pull off with the short dress..."—he raised his eyebrows gently and indicated her legs with his chin as he said this—"but I prefer the Sīhalt newlyweds story."

Kathleen shot up. "I will not be disguised as a prostitute!"

Jared ignored her and continued. "The newlywed disguise would explain why we are traveling alone, and I could defend you without anyone suspecting who you really are."

Kathleen thought about this. "Okay, I agree," she said reluctantly, "but how should we explain it when we arrive?"

"Well, you will be Karina Sula," he began, "a wealthy young lady of Sundiland. You have two brothers that are ship captains, both are out at sea. Your father is a sea merchant as well. Your mother has passed away," Jared said.

"May I have a cat named Mustache?" Kathleen added, smiling. "Elayna has a cat named Mustache."

The satinwood was gaining effect.

He passed over her comment and went on.

"We met in Sundiland a few months ago. I did some negotiations for the Grand Lakes fishing guild, and during my travels as a Sīhalt Guardian, I met you, a wealthy sea merchant's daughter and fell headlong in love with you," Jared recited.

"Wow, you have really thought this through, haven't you?"

"It is part of my training to take on different identities. By adding truth to the disguise, it makes it more believable."

"You mean the part about my mother's passing?" she said. "Or have you fallen for a sea merchant's daughter?"

"I don't enjoy the ocean that much. It seems a good story that would be difficult to verify," he replied.

"The story does seem plausible, I guess," she agreed.

"That's right, we married after a whirlwind romance. Your father and brothers are now out to sea. We are on our honeymoon journeying to visit my family on the north shore of the Clearwater Sea whereupon we will make a return trip to Sundiland in the spring," he added confidently.

Kathleen nodded. "I can remember that."

"Why do you want a cat?" he asked, referring to her previous comment.

"My sister Elayna has a white kitten with a little dark fur under his nose. He looks like he has a little handlebar mustache so we call him Stache for short. But what if someone knows about

Mustache?" she asked. "Wouldn't that ruin our disguise if I use his real name?"

"Who could possibly know about this cat?" Jared asked with a look of confusion on his face. "It's just your little sister's kitten."

"I just didn't want a small detail like that to ruin our disguise, or let the cat out of the bag, so to speak."

"Did you really just say that," Jared smirked.

"What?" asked Kathleen innocently.

Jared raised his eyebrows. "That satinwood tea is working I think."

"Is that a smile I see on your lips, Lord Sīhalt?" Kathleen said.

He became serious again. "It is a good thing I only have to deliver you to Tyath, Your Highness. If I spend too much time with you, I may find myself becoming merrier."

"Thank you for saving me," Kathleen said.

"I am pleased to do my duty." Jared replied.

"It is all about duty for you, isn't it, Lord Sīhalt?" she said, "haven't you ever let your guard down in your life?"

"It has never turned out well when I did," he replied

"What will we do in Altrastadt?" Kathleen asked. "Perhaps we can tour the city?"

"We'll blend in," he said, "but we need to arrive before dark. We will ride straight through until we get to the mountains."

She found herself looking forward to riding close to the Sīhalt Guardian again. This time she rode behind him, her arms encircling his waist. His back and torso felt muscled and taut. She could feel the rise and fall of his breathing. His strength and resourcefulness was a comfort to her on the wild road, but she wondered how, in her present condition, she could ever make anyone believe she was a Sīhalt bride.

TRUTH DISGUISED

After several hours passed, the soaring stone towers Jared had seen among the mountain peaks were finally in front of them. The alpine city of Altrastadt was built into the steep rock of the mountains. The waterfalls that surrounded the city flowed down to a beautiful mountain lake in a steep valley.

Presently, Jared and Kathleen dismounted and left the road, making their way to a narrow path along the city wall.

Jared drew Steed's head into his. The horse seemed nervous, but he soon settled under the spell of Jared's whisper. After this, Jared opened a saddlebag and pulled out a stretch of coiled rope and what looked like an iron hook.

"We would be stopped and interrogated at the gates if we try to enter right now. We look so worn and bedraggled," Jared explained to Kathleen.

"I feel dirty, but I'm not even tired." It was true, her eyes were bright and filled still with energy.

"It's the satinwood," Jared said. "You will need to be inside the city, and resting, when it wears off," Jared said.

"I have always wanted to see Altrastadt. Just not like this," Kathleen said, looking down at her disheveled appearance.

"It is one of the most beautiful places in all of Desnia. In winter, when the waterfalls freeze it becomes an ice kingdom. The place is beautiful," Jared said.

"Will we be able to see any of it?" Kathleen asked.

"If all goes right with our disguise, we will be able to travel freely. However, we cannot risk anyone recognizing you. Right now, you don't look like a princess."

She let her mouth fall open in surprise, then she swatted him softly a few times in mock anger.

"My mother always said…" Kathleen began loudly.

"Shhhh…quiet!" Jared whispered, placing his hand to her lips.

"A noble lady carries her refinement within her, not by the clothing or jewelry she wears," Kathleen said in a dramatic whisper.

Jared looked at her intently and scratched his eyebrow.

"I'm going to have to take you with me," he said.

"Of course! I'm your wife, remember?" she said, aware how suddenly comfortable she felt in the role.

Jared hushed her again. He considered using a gag for Kathleen while she was under the influence of the satinwood tea he had given her, but decided against it.

At least she isn't in pain right now, he thought.

"Kathleen, I need to sneak into the city and gather some items for our disguise," he said.

"How will you get in?" Kathleen asked, still whispering, with eyes wide and wondrous like those of a child. "These walls are so high!"

"We will climb over them," Jared explained.

She looked up, craning her neck to see the top of the wall in the darkness. Watchfires flickered above, and the clip of heels and heavy boots of patrolmen walking the walls could be heard echoing into the stillness.

Kathleen appeared hesitant. "I should wait outside the walls while you climb over," she said, nodding to herself and crossing her arms.

Jared shook his head at the silliness and lifted Kathleen to her feet. "Stand right there. Don't move."

Kathleen stood and put her arms at her sides, as if she were a soldier standing at attention, and smirked—as if it were all a game.

Jared uncoiled a rope and tied it to a large metal hook. He swung the hook in small circles as he judged the closest outcropping of stonework. When the guardian released the rope and the metal hook struck true to his aim, he waited to hear if any of the Altrastadt patrol had heard it. When he was satisfied no alarm had been raised, he motioned to Kathleen.

"Climb on my back," he said. "I will carry you up."

Kathleen looked surprised, but put her arms around Jared's neck. He hoisted her up, and tied a rope around both of them.

"This is in case you fall," he explained.

"But what if you fall?"

"I won't."

And just like that, Jared began to rise like a black spider up the smooth, pale wall, holding onto the rope and digging his toes into the joints between the stones. Kathleen held on tightly. They did not pause to enjoy the splendor of a moonlit mountain night in Altrastadt.

Once they were over the wall, and safely back on the ground inside the city, Kathleen grabbed her leg. Jared could see easily, despite the darkness of the street, that Kathleen was grimacing from the broken ankle.

"It has been many hours since I gave you the satinwood tea. It will wear off soon," he said.

"A moment ago I felt fine, but now my leg is throbbing with pain."

She tried to take a step, but instead lifted the injured ankle to keep it away from the ground.

"Its effect always grows more profound just before it is gone," Jared said.

Almost in tears from the pain, Kathleen gritted her teeth.

"We are almost there. We just need to be careful. If we're quiet, we will slip through and make it to her house. Then we will be safe."

"Whose house?"

"You'll see," he said, and lifted the princess off her feet, carrying her through the quiet streets of Altrastadt.

THE DRESSMAKER AND THE JEWELER

T he shutters on all the houses and shops were closed so Kathleen was unable to see inside the place as Jared knocked gently on the door.

"Who is it?" came a voice from inside.

"I seek the hands of a Healer," Jared said quietly.

There was a pause. Then another question.

"Who sent you?" the voice inside asked.

"We come in dire need. The Windstall Hermitage will pay you for your assistance," Jared said urgently.

The latch slid back and the door opened to reveal a plump, friendly face, standing in the candle light. The woman had light brown hair and rosy cheeks, and she held a baby in her arms. "Anyone from Windstall does not need payment," she said kindly. "Come in, come in, please."

"Who is it, Cara?" a man's voice said in the hall.

"A Guardian, I believe. They need our help," the woman said in a hushed tone.

A stocky, bearded man entered. He wore thick glasses and an apron of heavy leather. He approached with a concerned smile and extended his hand toward Jared.

"Lord Sīhalt, my name is Richard. You've met my wife Cara. How may we be of service?" he asked

Jared looked to one and then the other. "Are you the Jeweler?" he asked.

"And she is the Dressmaker," Richard said, nodding to his wife.

Jared nodded and helped Kathleen to sit in the chair.

"I am on assignment for the Imperial House. This is Kathleen Dal Sundi, betrothed to Prince Heathron Dol Lassimer. We were attacked by Delathrane barbarians on the old King's Highway near Revonah. She needs to be Healed and fitted for a gown."

The couple nodded and bowed to Kathleen. "Your Highness, we have great love for the Emperor and we will do all in our power to help," Cara said. "Now, let me put this child to bed and I will do what I can to help."

Cara led the way toward a room full of fabrics and samples of beautiful dresses. The Sīhalt lifted Kathleen and carried her.

"Her ankle is severely injured," he explained.

Cara gestured toward a chair, where Jared gently placed Kathleen. The artistic expression displayed in the gowns in the room showed a true love of craft. The dresses had detailed needlework unlike any Kathleen had seen.

"Did you make all of these?" Kathleen asked.

Cara nodded. "I learned from my mother when I was very young. People love to come to Altrastadt to be married or spend their first weeks together here, so I get lots of practice," she said, looking closely at what was left of Kathleen's dress.

"We were ambushed. I was separated from my procession," Kathleen said.

Cara let out a sigh as she unwrapped the splint.

"Your Sīhalt Guardian knows what he is doing. This is the proper way to bandage an injury like this, but I have something better for you, if you are okay with being Healed."

"You are a Healer as well?" Kathleen asked.

"I was part of the last class from the Talent Academy in Tyath, before it was closed." Cara explained.

"The Luzian Church banned the training school right?" Kathleen asked as Cara gently unwrapped the bandages.

Cara nodded. "I had to leave the capital. Richard is from Altrastadt, and we thought it would be a better place to raise our family. The people here are more tolerant of someone who is Talented," Cara said, touching the bruised and swollen flesh around Kathleen's ankle. Kathleen winced.

"The Sīhalt gave me satinwood. I am not sure what I would have done without it," Kathleen explained.

"Forgive me for asking, but why did the barbarians attack your procession? You had guards, did you not?" Cara asked.

"I fear war is upon us. There were so many Delathranes, my soldiers were overwhelmed. If it had not been for my Sīhalt Guardian I would surely have been captured or worse."

"As you can see, she needs new clothing," Jared said.

Kathleen raised her palms. "Survival before propriety, I always say."

Cara looked at the dress she was wearing.

"Clearly the Guardian follows the same mantra." She examined the short hemline of Kathleen's torn dress. "I would have ripped my gown apart to bind my ankle as well. Allow us some time to work, and I will see what I can do for both the wound and the dress," Cara said.

Kneeling beside Kathleen, Cara placed her hands on the ankle.

"You may want to bite on this," she said, "but I will try to be as gentle as possible while I Heal you." Kathleen accepted the stick of soft wood and placed it between her teeth. "Okay, I'm ready," she said as she clenched. Cara closed her eyes. She began to breathe evenly, and then she hummed softly. Kathleen felt a tingle travel across her foot and up her leg. She braced herself for the pain she feared would come—instead a warmth seemed to wrap her ankle as if air were being pushed against it from all sides. She felt a muted click as the bones in her foot and ankle adjusted to their proper form.

Kathleen let out an audible breath. There was no pain. Once the bones were knitted together again, Kathleen was able to move her foot in circles without any discomfort at all. Kathleen looked at her fingernails and the ends of her red hair. Both were somewhat longer. Her ankle felt wonderful.

"It is good that your body had not done more of its own healing. That break might have been difficult to reset," Cara explained.

Kathleen stood and put her full weight on the newly Healed ankle.

"Does it feel okay?" Cara asked.

"There was no pain as you Healed me," she said, "you are truly gifted in your Talent."

Cara smile and seemed abashed.

"I get to use my Talent so rarely these days, but thank you. Now lets get your measurements and make a new gown for you," she said.

"What you don't think this would be well received in Tyath?" Kathleen said indicating the soiled and torn dress she wore.

"There's the playfulness again. I'm glad you are feeling better, Your Highness," Jared said.

"We have decided on a disguise. We will rest here in Altrastadt, hiding in plain sight. My Sīhalt Guardian will pose as my new husband. We will pretend to be enjoying our honeymoon here in Altrastadt. Hopefully we can rejoin my wedding procession before it arrives in Tyath." Kathleen explained.

"So you are going to pretend to be married?" Richard asked with his eyebrows raised.

"Can you think of a better reason for a Sīhalt Guardian to be on the road, alone with a Sundiland woman?" Jared asked.

"I see your point," Richard agreed.

"So the gown needs to be elegant but not look too lavish?" Cara asked.

"It also needs to hold up to the necessities of the road. We may yet journey though the wilds on the way to Tyath," Jared said.

"I have just the thing for a Sīhalt bride," Cara exclaimed. She retrieved a bolt of fabric that had a dazzling brightness even in the candlelight.

"This material will not pick up stains. The deepest wine will not affect it. You should be able to wear it day and night without looking the least bit sullied."

"Now that is magical," Kathleen said touching the white cloth. It shimmered as her finger moved over the surface. "Won't that bring too much attention to me?" she asked.

"Your Highness, you have auburn red hair, tanned skin dusted with freckles and bright green eyes. You already *are* a spectacle. Anyone who sees you will immediately know you are a foreigner," Cara said.

"The best you can hope for it to pass off this disguise. Once you are cleaned up, I am sure the two of you can realistically portray a Sīhalt and his exotic bride on their honeymoon year."

"I should probably not wear this then," Kathleen said as she removed the necklace her father had given her.

"Who gave you that?" Cara asked.

"This was my mother's. She was a Green Grower, but died during the Plague," Kathleen said.

"Keep it safe, but do not wear it once you arrive in Tyath," Cara said. She took measurements around Kathleen's waist and bust line, as well as around her hips.

"I haven't had measurements like these in a long time," she remarked as she worked.

"I like you just the way you are my dear." Richard spoke up. "There is now more of you to love," he said with a smile.

"Well, if I keep eating the sweet dough rolls you always make, there might as well be two of me to love."

"I love you just the same Cara. I'm so blessed to have you as the mother of our children." Richard said.

"When was your baby born?" Kathleen asked.

Cara's hands flew as she measured and cut the fabric, pinning pieces together, stitching them here and there to hold the pattern in place.

"Bjorn is our fourth child. He arrived two months ago, and his older sisters will barely give him a moment alone. I fear his feet will not touch the floor until he outweighs them."

Kathleen laughed at the image. She thought of her sister, Elayna. She felt a pang of concern, thinking of her family.

"I have to make it to Tyath," she said.

Cara stopped and gave her a serious look. "Richard and I have worked with the Sīhalt network since we were married. We have never before heard the concern among the sources like we do today. Of course I cannot share all that I hear, Your Highness, but please know, so many people are counting on you."

"We saw a lot of hardship on our way here. I hope Prince Dol Lassimer is as good as it is rumored," Kathleen agreed.

"Why don't you get some sleep while I finish this dress?" Cara said, "Your Sīhalt is standing guard with Richard—you will be safe here."

"Thank you, Cara. I am exhausted. I have not slept in two days. Your Healing did wonders for me, though I think a rest would help. Jared and I need to climb back over the wall before the dawn comes."

Cara gave Kathleen some food to eat as she lay down to rest.

"You call him Jared?" Cara asked.

"Perhaps it is the exhaustion. My Guardian said we need to make a proper approach to the gates tomorrow," Kathleen explained.

"I will wake you when I have this dress ready," Cara promised.

PERFECT FIT

"**A**re you sure this will fit me?" Kathleen held the brilliant white dress up in front of the mirror. The form appeared even more slender than their own body.

"The fabric is able to stretch. It is very forgiving. By wearing it, the material will adapt to your shape and fit even better with time," Cara said.

"I will need some help with the buttons," Kathleen said as she turned the beautiful dress around before her.

She slipped out of the soiled dress, and Cara helped her to wash with a towel and warm water. The soap was scented with lavender, and Kathleen took a moment to enjoy the feeling of being clean and rested.

Standing before the mirror, Kathleen was pleased to see that all of the cuts and bruises had Healed with Cara's administrations. Her body looked flawless.

"Do you think I should braid my hair?" Kathleen asked.

"I can do your hair and your nails. If you want to blend in at Altrastadt, you need to look your very best."

Kathleen agreed, so she wrapped herself in a soft robe Cara

handed her and sat down to allow Cara to do her work. In short order, Kathleen was transformed even further into a picture of bridal beauty.

"Is this a common style for a Sīhalt bride?" Kathleen asked.

"They may wear whatever they like, but it is traditional for them to wear the wedding gown during the time your people call the honeymoon," Cara explained.

"We only wear the wedding dress the day of the wedding and on the first anniversary," Kathleen explained.

"Sīhalt brides are expected to adopt all of the customs of their husbands, so it really doesn't matter what country you call home," Cara said.

"Do Sīhalt brides really wear a gown like this for the whole first year?"

"Traditionally, yes. The veil may or may not be worn after the ceremony. That is up to each bride. I made one for you."

Cara held up a beautiful veil.

"I'll clip it in your hair once you are dressed."

Kathleen slipped into the form-fitting dress as easily as a diver enters water. The gown easily rose to the curve of her hips, at which point Cara stopped her.

"I am supposed to put this around your waist as well," she said, and held up a silken rope of white shimmering material.

"What is that?" Kathleen asked.

"We need the disguise to be complete," Cara said. "This is a *kanatra* belt."

"Do I just tie that around my waist after I put the dress on?" she asked.

"No, you tie this on your waist first. It will be next to your skin," she said.

Kathleen paused. "Okay, but if it is under my dress, why does it matter if I wear it?"

"We do not know all the dangers that lie ahead of you. It is important that the disguise be as real as possible. A Sīhalt bride wears the *kanatra* from her wedding night, until she is first with child."

Kathleen accepted the thin silky rope.

"Do I just tie it in a bow?" she asked, holding the two ends of the *kanatra* in her hands.

"It is a special, intricate knot. I don't know how to make it. I'll have to get the Sīhalt to tie it for you," Cara said.

Kathleen looked at Cara in surprise and then down at her half-dressed appearance.

"Not yet!" Cara laughed. "Let's get the dress all the way on first. We can leave a couple of buttons on the back open. It'll be okay."

Kathleen sighed in relief.

"Thank you for helping me," she said.

Kathleen pulled the dress on with Cara's help. She turned toward the candle burning low. The panels of the dress caught the dancing light. The bodice had fine detailed embroidery that made Kathleen think of white flowering vines or lace made of tiny shells. How had Cara made this in one night? It felt comfortable, the kind of dress that made her feel more confident and beautiful than ever. When she slipped on the elegant yet durable shoes Cara had selected. They added a few inches to her height as well. Kathleen liked the way she looked.

"Your Highness, do you realize what a disguise like this entails?" Cara asked.

"It means we will have to convince everyone we are married. Do you think that is believable?" She turned and viewed her reflection.

I'd like to do my hair like this more often, she thought.

Her hair was partially lifted and pulled away from her face, revealing her smooth jawline and slender neck. A portion was allowed to fall past her shoulders. The earrings were oval-shaped white pearls that hung from a delicate silver link, and when Kathleen turned from right to left, looking in the mirror, she saw them sway gently.

"Have you ever met a Sīhalt Guardian before Jared?" Cara asked.

"Our family has a Sīhalt that has served on my father's court since before I was born. He's like a grandfather to me. I know him very well."

"We see many people pass through Altrastadt's because of its location and its fame as a place for lovers. Have you ever seen a Sīhalt during his honeymoon year?"

"No, I can't remember ever seeing a Sīhalt other than Girdy and now Jared."

The dressmaker smiled broadly and let go of Kathleen's hair. She came around and looked her in the face. She pursed her lips.

"What?" Kathleen asked. "Why are you smirking like that?"

"Have you ever been kissed?" Cara said.

"No, I...why do you ask?" Kathleen was taken aback.

"When you're in public with him, folks are going to want a mutual blessing. It's an old tradition for the people, of every class, to call out to a Sīhalt Guardian and his bride. They will say things like, 'For a prosperous future!' or 'For love!'"

"Okay...what are we supposed to say back?" Kathleen asked.

"You don't say anything, Your Highness," Cara smiled, "You kiss the groom."

Kathleen hesitated. "You mean I...you mean the Guardian and I have to ...kiss. In front of everybody!"

"It would seem very strange if you didn't. People would assume you were angry at them, or they may not believe the disguise."

"Oh, dear Abbath," Kathleen said, "he didn't tell me that!"

"I suppose he thought you knew."

"It would probably be easy for him. He's very good at acting."

Kathleen remembered the farewell feast. She could not have imagined that she would be required to kiss her Guardian.

"Then he's probably good at kissing too. It does take some emotion to do it right. The more passionate the kiss, the greater the blessing on those who see it. When you go out tomorrow morning, you will hear the people calling out to witness you and Jared kiss."

"What am I supposed to do!" Kathleen said. She covered her face to hide the deep blush on her neck and cheeks. "I'm engaged!"

"I am sure you will do fine. I just wondered if you had thought about it."

"I don't know if I want my first kiss to happen just because I am pretending to be someone else's wife," Kathleen said.

"It is all right, Your Highness. I kissed plenty of boys before I met my Richard. Practice makes perfect." Cara laughed quietly, she was clearly enjoying Kathleen's distress.

"Should I practice with him before we go out in public? I don't want to look like a fool."

"That, Your Highness, is entirely up to you. But there are spies in Altrastadt," Cara explained, "and your safety may very well rest on how well you can convince the crowds. As you said," Cara winked, "survival before propriety."

Jared knocked softly and entered the room.

"We need to leave soo…" He stopped in mid sentence. Kathleen looked over her shoulder. The man paused before approaching further. He stood with his mouth slightly open, his hands at his sides.

"Could you help us with this?" Cara asked him as she tried to hold the dress closed with one hand while she still held both ends of the silken *kanatra* cord. When he did not immediately respond, but instead stood staring, Cara spoke again.

"Lord Sīhalt," she said with a knowing smile, "what do you think of the disguise?"

Kathleen could not help but smile. The man remained speechless.

"I think you are having the desired effect," Cara said to Kathleen.

"Truly beautiful," Jared said almost reverently.

"The dress is amazing," Kathleen agreed.

"I saw the dress finished before you awoke. For all Cara's talents, it is not the fabric or thread that brings that dress to such vibrant life." He paused, as if what he was to say next was stuck in his throat. He looked away hesitantly, then leveled his eyes at her and said, "It is you who makes it the image of grace and perfection that is before me, Your Highness."

"Thank you, Lord Sīhalt," she said, turning away to hide the color that again rose in her cheeks.

"You made the *kanatra* as well?" he said in surprise.

"The disguise must be as precise as possible," Cara explained, "Will you tie it?"

Jared tied the cord in an intricate series of loops that made the *kanatra* lie flat against the hollow of her back.

I wonder if Heathron's hands will be this gentle? Kathleen wondered as she felt his fingertips brush against the small of her back.

The question made her next breath deeper, and she turned her thoughts away from that line of thinking.

Cara adjusted the clasps to allow the small knot to show at the back, proclaiming Kathleen as Jared's Sīhalt bride.

"Can you move in the dress easily?" Cara asked as she smoothed the dress at the shoulders and hips.

Kathleen took a few large steps, and bent her knees and twisted at the waist.

"I believe so," she said, satisfied.

"We should go now. Thank you so much," Jared said to both of them.

"It has been our honor," Richard said, bowing.

When Cara tried to curtsy, instead Kathleen hugged her with heartfelt gratitude. "I will not forget this," she promised.

"Get going," Cara said, wiping the corners of her eyes. "You make a beautiful bride, Your Highness."

EVERFONT INN

J ared and Kathleen found Steed where Jared had stationed
him earlier, outside the city walls. The night before, Jared
had brushed his silver-lined black travel clothes and
placed them carefully in the saddle bags. Today he wore
his finest formal attire.

The return trip was much easier for Kathleen now that she
was Healed. Jared used his senses and was able to avoid the city
night patrols. He held up a hand and stopped at intervals as they
sneaked past merchants who began their day before dawn. The
horse flicked his ears and bobbed his head when Jared and Kathleen descended the city wall.

They rode together through the gates of Altrastadt. She sat in
front of him, on the saddle. Jared held her protectively from
behind as a new husband might do. Her smell was intoxicating.
She Scented of fragrant, essential oils, and her hair smelled like
the freshness of summer rain. Her clean Scent made his heart beat
faster. He hoped she did not notice. They made a distinctive
couple, Kathleen in her brilliant white gown and Jared in the
black Sīhalt garb. Kathleen sat in the saddle with poise and seren-

ity. She needed to play the part of the Sīhalt bride and was doing admirably.

They arrived at one of the many checkpoints in the city. Altrastadt was a place of beauty and order, and the city fathers were willing to pay to ensure it remained so.

"Hello there," one of the guards said, looking them up and down. "Visiting Altrastadt for business or pleasure?"

The Sīhalt Guardian beamed a brilliant smile to the guard.

"Our business is pleasure!" he said. "Just look at my beautiful Sundiland bride." Jared smiled at Kathleen. "She has never visited the mountains. We look forward to staying a fortnight in your beautiful city."

Jared affected an easy manner. He seemed as if he had not a care in the world and was fast friends with the Altrastadt guards.

A young guard, dressed in a blue tabard, stumbled over the questions he tried to ask of the Sīhalt Guardian.

Another guard interrupted him. "Perhaps it is the fierceness in your eyes, Lord Sīhalt, or the distracting beauty of a Sundiland woman. I apologize. Enjoy your stay." He opened the small gate that diverted travelers along the checkpoint.

"That was a change from your normally somber, calculating demeanor." Kathleen said.

"Why shouldn't a man be happy while vacationing with his new bride?" he said.

"I remember the night of the Farewell Feast in Candoreth. I was delighted by your performance that night in my defense. What is your natural disposition, Lord Sīhalt? Are you the outgoing showman or a brooding warrior?"

"I am whatever you need me to be...my love," he added, as other people, within earshot, made their way alongside the powerful black stallion.

"Last night Cara said we would have to... kiss today. Is that true?" Kathleen said.

"Karina, I will do anything to keep you safe. You know that." he replied.

"I'm not pretending," Kathleen said through clenched teeth, "I didn't know that was an expectation of…our disguise."

"Only if people ask for it," Jared said.

"I don't know…what I'm doing, when it comes to that…kind of thing," Kathleen said.

"Just be as natural as possible," he whispered in her ear as he waved to a baker in the window of his shop.

"I don't want to look like a fool," she said, "I need to practice with you."

A bolt of emotional fire ran though him as they rode Steed along the central avenue until they came to the Everfont Inn.

Jared recognized the wisdom in training for a battle, a duel, or a speech. He had done it many times in his life. But the reaction he felt in his chest at Kathleen's suggestion took him by complete surprise. Why did he feel so…willing, no excited by the thought of *teaching* her to kiss? He almost broke character.

"Aerick," she said, using his fake name, "did I say something wrong?"

"No,…my love," he said, regaining his composure, "I will happily teach you whatever you would like to learn."

A waterfall bounced over rocks along one side of the inn. The windows were clean, and the lights shone out from the windows cheerfully. Jared could hear a familiar tune played by a musician troupe inside. That would provide some distraction for the guests. Jared spoke softly in Steed's ear, and the horse allowed himself to be led away by the stable boy.

"We may stay for a while, lad. Give him a measure of grain daily and fresh hay," Jared said to the lad.

"Of course, my Lord Sīhalt," the boy said, knuckling his forehead. "Anything for a Guardian, my lord."

Jared inclined his head toward the boy, who was bowing.

"And a good evening to your lady as well," the boy continued.

Jared admired how Kathleen made even a small stable boy feel honored to be in her service. She smiled, and the boy beamed.

They stepped into the common room of the Everfont Inn.

"For a prosperous future!" a young man called as soon as he saw Jared and Kathleen.

In an instant, the Sīhalt grabbed Kathleen. He slid one hand around her narrow waist and the other around the back of her neck. She let out a little "Whoop!" of surprise as he dipped her low and pressed his cheek firmly against hers. Jared made kissing noises and moved his head against hers as he mimicked a passionate kiss. Their lips never met, but the guests in the inn could not have seen from the angle of their observation. Had they doubted at all, the look on Kathleen's face and her tussled hair would have convinced them when the couple stood back upright.

The people cheered joyously and offered the young couple a seat at their tables or a free meal at their expense. Jared laughed like a man in love but insisted on taking his bride to their honeymoon suite. He carried their few belongings inside while escorting Kathleen up the steps.

"Oh my goodness!" Kathleen said as soon as their door closed. "That was unexpected." Her heart was racing.

"Forgive me, Your Highness, I did not know what else to do," he said.

"Cara was right," Kathleen said, running fingers though her hair to tame it after Jared had so passionately embraced her. "The people are enthusiastic about a Sīhalt and his bride."

"I should have warned you. I thought you knew about that custom. I just assumed with all the social interactions you would have as a princess in Candoreth…the dances."

"No… I have never been kissed." Kathleen said. It felt more comfortable to tell him than she imagined it would be. "I have been betrothed to Heathron since I was a little girl. I was saved for this purpose—an alliance. None of the young noblemen in my kingdom would ever dare to ask me to dance or try to steal a kiss.

I spent my time with servants and family, waiting for the day when I would travel to the Golden City to be married."

"This is the first time you have been alone with a man," Jared observed.

The door was closed, and he was standing close to her. Kathleen felt her temperature rise.

"Yes," Kathleen said, her voice catching as she spoke.

"Do you really want to practice...kissing?" he said. His voice was rich and deep.

Her pulse quickened. Kathleen could feel her heart pumping faster. Jared set the bags he carried on the floor beside his feet but held her gaze the entire time.

"I think it would be better for my safety if I knew what I was doing out there." Kathleen pointed to the window, overlooking the busy street, but did not turn her eyes away from Jared's face.

He took a step closer, closing the gap between them. They stood just one pace apart. This close, Kathleen could see the smallest flecks of blue in his grey eyes.

"There are many ways to kiss," he said softly, then paused and touched her arm. "Are you sure you want to do this, Kathleen?"

Kathleen licked her lips, preparing them.

"I think so." She laughed a bit nervously.

Jared touched her hair above her ear and slid his fingers down toward her neck. Kathleen wanted to simply enjoy that sensation alone, but the Guardian came even closer. He ran his hand down her arm toward her fingertips—her skin pebbled with goosebumps when his fingers finally entwined with hers. He placed his other hand just above her waist at the small of her back where the *kanatra* was tied.

"To be believable, a kiss must express your true feelings. A false kiss is worse than a slap across the face. So just like the names and histories we gave ourselves, a kiss should have at least a shadow of the truth within it, to make it more real."

"What is true about what we are about to do?" she asked, placing her hands on his chest.

Kathleen heard herself ask the question but could not believe she had said it! What kind of question was that at a moment like this?

"It is true that I will do anything to keep you safe. I would give my life for you," he said.

"I believe that," Kathleen said softly. Her pounding heart had not abated.

"It is also true that your lips look warm and soft, and I want to kiss them."

His voice was husky, and he seemed to be making an attempt to restrain himself. Kathleen smiled and saw Jared watching her mouth as she did so. It made her feel good to see that look in his eyes, watching her lips.

"My truth is that I want to be kissed," she breathed, "not just for the disguise."

Jared closed the distance between their lips as she closed her eyes. The warmth Kathleen felt flowing through her body started from that contact and spread outward. Tingling sensations danced across her skin as he lightly held her face in his hands. His lips were firm and parted more than once to let Kathleen know that he had been truthful. He did want to kiss her, very deeply.

When at last the couple pulled apart, they held each other in a warm embrace. Kathleen could feel his heartbeat as rapid as her own. To Kathleen, the splendor of the kiss was like the pleasure that came to her as she made things Grow, but the kiss was not a lonely thing—it was shared with Jared, and she did not have to hide it.

"They don't all have to be like that one," Jared said as they hugged, "but I wanted you to know what was possible."

"Did I do that convincingly enough?" Kathleen asked sincerely.

"I must admit I enjoyed our little training session here," he said.

"Is it normal to feel hungry after you kiss? I feel hungry right now."

Kathleen thought of the hunger that arose after using her Talent and wondered if a passionate kiss worked the same way.

Jared laughed. "I suppose you could work up an appetite, but you have taken my mind away from food. It is getting closer to mealtime. Are you ready to venture outside?"

"I think I can handle it now," she said with a smile.

DINNER

That afternoon they walked along the terraced roads of Altrastadt. Jared took note of the possible escape routes and where the gates and walls were located. The city of Altrastadt rightfully earned its place as a destination for lovers. The views were breathtaking across the many mountain peaks in a panoramic view. The highest ones were snowcapped.

Kathleen seemed to enjoy looking at all the shops and merchandise that made its way to the city. Jared tried to remain interested in window shopping. Although it was not an activity he would choose for himself, he found that in Kathleen's company he wanted to smile. He never recalled smiling so much, not even in his childhood. *Especially not in childhood*, he thought.

The Trader's Way ran through the middle of the city. It linked Altrastadt to the rest of the Empire, a halfway point for merchants going east or west over the mountains. That road, and a natural abundance of gemstone in the region, made the small city a center for commerce and tourism. The taxes gathered from each wagon on the Trader's Way increased the splendor of Altrastadt. Only the harsh winters and rugged terrain of the surrounding mountains kept the place from being overcrowded. The wealthy came here to play--the poor came here to work. The relatively few permanent locals made a nice living from the ebb and flow of the seasons. If you were lucky enough to inherit property in Altrastadt, you held on to it.

After all their exploring, Jared and Kathleen decided to dine at the large banquet hall adjacent to the Everfont Inn. It was perched on the rocky cliffs that faced the western valley. There was a line along the front walk, and the people talked and laughed as they waited to enter.

A few patrons cheered their arrival throughout the day, and the couple had obliged by kissing their way about town.

"We have been hiding in plain sight all day," Kathleen said.

"Rumors will soon make their way eastward on the road soon. People will hear that Princess Dal Sundi's wedding procession was attacked. We need to be part of the local scenery by then. If we make ourselves visible today as newlyweds, no one will believe that in reality, you are a Daughter of the Realm, betrothed to Prince Heathron Dol Lassimer."

In the banquet hall, a talent show was in process. Kathleen and Jared were led to a table by a cheerful waitress. "Will this do, my lord?" she asked, pointing to a round table for two. It had a tasteful small centerpiece with white flowers and a white candle burning.

"This table will do just fine. I imagine the room could get quite noisy," he said surveying the many people lining up to come in.

"It's true, my lord. We have the best food and happiest entertainment in Altrastadt here."

They sat down. And looked at each other.

"That dress suits you," Jared said sincerely. The soft white fabric seemed to grasp her body in a way that made her seem like a statue of the ancient love goddess come to life. Jared liked the way the dress fit snug across Kathleen's hips. He found himself following her movements again.

"You think so? I was surprised at how comfortable it is. I

thought it would be rigid and inflexible, like so many other dresses I've had to wear. This one bends easily and flows when I move and then falls back into perfect place when I stand still." Kathleen stood up and twirled once to show Jared what she meant. He smiled at her.

"No one would guess what we have recently endured," Kathleen said.

"Thank you for finally agreeing to the disguise. I know it was not expected," Jared said as he looked across the table.

"I hope it works and we can join back up with the procession further north," Kathleen said.

"That is my hope, but we need to spend some time here in Altrastadt and let things calm down some. There will be scouts sent in every direction, and I would rather not be out on the road for a least a few days."

"Then we might be able to see more of the city after all?" Kathleen said.

"Have you memorized your new identity?" Jared asked.

"I am Karina Sula, from Sundiland. I have two brothers that are sailors, both are out at sea. My father is a sea merchant. My mother has passed away and I have a cat named Mustache."

"Where did we meet?"

"We met in Sundiland only months ago. You did some negotiations for the Grand Lakes fishing guild, and during your travels you met a wealthy sea merchant's daughter and fell headlong for her," Kathleen recited, pointing to herself. "Now what about you?"

"My name is Aerick Cal Sīhalt. We married after a whirlwind romance. I finally gained your father's approval before he went to sea with your brothers. We are journeying to visit my extended family in the Grand Lakes region. We will make a return trip to Sundiland in the spring," he finished quietly and nodded, looking around.

"What would you like to eat this evening?" the waitress said as she approached the table. She filled crystal glasses on the table. Each was cut exquisitely,

"The crystal is beautiful," Kathleen said. "I can't believe it is being used for everyday use!" She held the glass in her hand and admired how the spiral cuts enhanced the surface.

"The pure water inside is the best part," the waitress said. "If you've never tasted Altrastadt spring water, you are in for a delight."

Kathleen sipped the water. Her eyes brightened. "It refreshes your whole mouth! Try some, Ja...uhh, Aerick," Kathleen said.

Jared winked at Kathleen and lifted the glass to his lips to taste the water. It was pure, cool and bright.

"It is just water?" he asked. "Nothing added?"

The waitress smiled and nodded.

"We have famous local greens too. Take a look at our menu. Our special this evening includes fresh yellow fish. It was caught here in the mountain streams."

"Oh, that sounds good," Kathleen said.

"Shall we both have the special tonight, Karina?" Jared asked.

Kathleen agreed.

"Enjoy some of our buttered rolls while you wait," the waitress said as she placed a basket of warm bread and butter in front of them.

"We have to take the disguise seriously," Jared said quietly. "We have to behave in a way that convinces others if we want to be safe."

"Sorry, I almost forgot. I'm not the best at pretending," she said.

Jared reached across the table and offered Kathleen his hands. She placed her hands in his.

"I am so happy to be here with you, Karina," he said.

Kathleen smiled.

"You, on the other hand, are very good at this Lord Sīhalt," she said.

A master of ceremonies took to the stage at the front. He waved his hand and spoke loudly, calling the attention of the audience. He introduced a young woman who stood by an enormous harp. She curtsied and sat and began to play softly.

Jared and Kathleen dined in comfort. The sun went down as they talked of what they had seen during the day and what the road ahead might hold. They avoided any discussion of Delathranes or the procession for fear of being overheard. Instead, they finished their meal and Kathleen laid her head on Jared's shoulder, in the candlelight, listening to the beautiful strains now of a young man playing a violin, deep and resonant.

The next performance was a soprano with a soaring, ethereal voice. She sang of what it was like to live in the mountains and look down at the world beyond. It was fitting for the location they enjoyed. After she was done singing, she simply walked back to her table and became part of the audience. Kathleen had never seen such unencumbered performances. The people in the room came to perform and be entertained as well. The room begin to fill. Wine flowed freely, but the crowd was happy, supportive of the performers, and kind.

"Let's see a Sīhalt dance!" a lady from the front suggested to the crowd, pointing at Jared and Kathleen.

"No, no, we came to watch," Jared protested humbly.

"Oh, please, favor us with the beauty that is Love and Commitment in the form of a dance," she pleaded.

"We dare not. Allow the others to perform," Jared said, starting to feel uncomfortable for Kathleen.

A man holding a lute said, "I will give up my place to see you dance."

Others nodded approval.

"Who would like to see a Sīhalt dance?" the Master of Ceremony asked the audience.

A scattered cheer rose up. Jared looked at Kathleen helplessly.

"You did say we have to take the disguise seriously," she said quietly in his ear.

The crowd grew insistent and began to chant, "Dance, dance, dance!"

The house musicians rummaged through their music sheets, looking for the proper tune, and waved the couple to the front when they had found the music for the Sīhalt wedding dance.

"All right then...since you insist," Jared said loudly, and stood with Kathleen. He wondered how it would look for a Sīhalt and his bride to fumble through the Sīhalt wedding dance. Jared didn't even know if Kathleen had ever even seen the dance. The crowd clapped happily, satisfied the pressure they put on the newlyweds was enough to get them to comply.

Jared led Kathleen to the dance floor. He noticed the flush in her cheeks as the crowd in the hall pounded tables and cheered for the newlyweds. Jared was surprised by the way she walked and curtsied in the fashion familiar to his people.

A perfect Sīhalt bride, he thought.

"Just follow my lead," he whispered closely in her ear, concerned that Kathleen would stumble in the intricate steps of the traditional Sīhalt wedding dance. He could see that she was flushed and knew that her heart was pounding harder than his. She was born in the southern lands and knew little of the world beyond the kingdom where she was raised.

DANCING

S tanding on the dance floor, Kathleen laid her hand lightly
on Jared's. She trembled with emotion. Even as a royal
princess, she got very nervous when forced to be the
center of attention. Kathleen always thought of herself as a
capable dancer—some even said she had natural talent. She could
keep time with even the fastest reels in Candoreth, but the Sīhalt
wedding dance!

She closed her eyes momentarily to recall the image of her
younger self twirling in a skirt and following the graceful turns of
a surprisingly agile, older Sīhalt. Girdy had taught her the dance
as a young girl.

Could she remember the steps? They were sweet memories.
She remembered him always presenting her with a flower as the
dance began. She opened her eyes when she felt the emotion of
her memories well up inside her. Kathleen watched as Jared
produced a small white flower.

Where did he get that? She thought.

Kathleen suddenly realized that what she thought was Sīhalt
Girdy's little way of showing her his love, was actually the tradi-

tional beginning of the Sīhalt wedding dance. She moved to accept the flower, and Jared held up a hand and she stopped. He reached up and tucked the flower in her hair. It was just as Girdy had always done!

Jared held himself with the utmost confidence, but his eyes seemed to worry.

"Just follow my lead, Karina—we might be able to convince the crowd," he said.

He assumed she knew nothing of the Sīhalt wedding dance. Why would she?

Kathleen wasn't sure she could remember it all. It was always done in fun when she and Girdy took a picnic to the islands, or whenever she was getting tired of practicing her music lessons. Girdy would spring up and say, "Princess, I have a flower for you." He would lean forward and place it in her hair and then dramatically strike a pose that made her smile with admiration. When Girdy and Melva danced, she always loved it so much and clapped loudly. "It's my turn, Girdy! It's my turn!" She would run to them and squeeze between them and place her hands in his. When she was very small, he would have her stand on his feet for the intricate steps and then twirl her so strongly that her little feet would fly around like a Wintertide spinning top.

As the music played the introduction, and Jared assumed the starting pose. His head was turned sharply to the right, the point of his shoulder in line with his partner. His right hand stretched out toward her, his left tucked formally behind his back. There was a quiet in the crowd, and the players pulled their bows soft and slow across the strings.

One, two and three.

One, two and three.

The players held time for the dancers. Establishing the tune. The drummer struck the drum head in slow rhythms.

Kathleen lowered her head and assumed the demure pose of

the Sīhalt bride. Her shoulder turned slightly away from Jared, eyes looking away. She reached toward him with a delicate hand. In that instant, the room was silent except for the music and their breathing. Then came the sound of his boots and her slippers sliding slowly apart and back together again.

Jared leaned close and whispered in her ear, "This dance was meant to evoke the back and forth of courtship, the pulling apart and drawing together of a young man and young woman as they transitioned from admiration and intrigue to respect and loyal love."

She looked at him as he pulled his head away gently and smiled. "I know," she said.

The Guardian looked confused.

The people in the crowd held their breaths. They loved to see a Sīhalt couple dance. "Agile as a Sīhalt groom," was a common phrase among the kingdom's people. "Graceful as a Sīhalt bride," was another. Jared and Kathleen gave the audience a reason to believe.

Jared held his pose, his features firm.

"Are you ready?" he said, smiling.

Kathleen grinned, but then hardened as she concentrated.

If she imitated the way Melva had always done it... Yes, that's it! she thought. She recalled the way Melva, in the courtyard in Candoreth, would take a half step away from her partner before she snapped her head back to look him directly in the eye, her chin raised confidently. Kathleen had always found the power of that move amazing, and had often practiced it later at night in her room. Like players on a stage, the dancers were supposed to express their emotions on their faces. That is what she would do now. She breathed and closed her eyes.

Jared, meanwhile, was growing more and more curious. His eyebrow rose in anticipation of what she would do next, how fluid and natural she would move. She had piqued his interest.

They walked slowly toward each other now, each step placed

carefully with the music. Just a few movements into the dance, Kathleen could see Jared's astonishment at her ease with the forms.

"You seemed surprised?" she said, a slight close-lipped smile rising prettily in the corners.

"But how have you…"

Kathleen swiftly raised a finger to his lips. "Shhh…' she said.

He gained confidence and seemed to look at her as if to ask, 'How have you managed this?'

Kathleen smiled. She would explain later. For now, with the rush of excitement in her veins, she just wanted to dance.

The polished wooden floor allowed them to slide and twist, twirl and move to the music. The crowd, at times, would be held in silence. Other times they would gasp with delight or laugh softly with the theatrics of the Sīhalt bride and groom.

Jared didn't hold the moment long enough for Kathleen, who felt the subtle push from her dance partner and responded expertly, following his lead. She rolled back out, pushing away with one hand, while hanging on with the other. Her hair fell gently like a cascade. As she turned, she extended her arm, but he ducked low, and her arm passed over his head. He rose again as she twirled back into his arms.

The crescendo of drums thumped in the hall. Kathleen used her thin veil to cover a portion of her face dramatically. They came together and apart again in movements that mimicked the chase of romance, the elation of finding true love, the heartbreak of a broken dream and the joy of its being mended. They danced the movements of lovers on a long walk. They danced the steps of admiration and joy at a kind word, a compliment, a smile from the one you love. They danced the steps of a promise kept.

Jared now moved to the dance of physical desire, of passion and expectations. Kathleen responded with movements of her own, eyes ablaze. She wanted this man. The crowd loved it.

And then all else in the room seemed to disappear, and the

emotion and physical effort were focused only on each other. The drums were their pulse, the sound of the music became their only guide to what came next.

When the music finally began to slow, Kathleen realized the crowd was silent. She was breathless. The drumbeats softened and her steps slowed. She was more often in the arms of her partner, more often gazing into his eyes. He was amazed at her ability, and she knew she would need to explain how it was all possible.

The dance, as Kathleen remembered it, had always ended with a kiss on her cheek from Girdy. What would Jared do now? Her heart raced with anticipation.

This time, however she was not dancing on the beach as a little girl. She tilted her head back, exposing her soft neck as the last of the drum beats disappeared and the strings came to rest.

Jared lifted Kathleen's face to him and kissed her gently on the lips.

She looked into his eyes and forgot herself. As she had done throughout the dance, she allowed the most natural next step to happen. She grabbed the back of his head, running her fingers through his hair, now wet with sweat, and kissed him again firmly on the mouth.

The crowd erupted in applause. Tinkling of tableware on crystal glasses made them kiss again and there were cheers from every table. The applause rang out with scattered shouts of "For the love!" and "Blessings on your life together." The people of Altrastadt stood in awe that night. Couples in the room now held hands and stood close. The dance had reminded them of the love and commitment they had for each other.

Kathleen could barely believe what had just happened. During the dance she truly felt as if she were Jared's new wife. It felt as if he truly loved her. They had carried off the disguise perfectly. No one would have guessed that they were pretending to be young lovers. Kathleen had never felt such excitement, so alive. He bowed to each side of the room while she curtsied before Jared led her by the hand from the dance floor and returned to their table.

The serving staff met them there with refreshing drinks and smiles. "My master wishes you much love in your life together, my lady Sīhalt," said a serving girl who carried a large platter of fruits and sweet breads. "Oh, thank you!" Kathleen said.

"That were the most beautiful dance I ever seen My lady. You were like an angel." The other servants nodded in agreement.

"The credit doesn't belong to me. Actually, my husband..." Kathleen hesitated, pointing to Jared. "He is the one who deserves the compliment. He leads perfectly."

The serving girls looked at Jared with the greatest approval. Kathleen thought she might even need to help a couple of the poor girls lift their jaws back into place as they seemed to have grown slack as they gazed at Jared who was now wiping the sweat from his face. He was smiling.

"That, was invigorating!" he said.

The serving girl closest to him just stared.

Setting down the platter of food, she turned to him and spoke in the common tongue: "I didn't know a man could move like that. It were a thing of beauty, I'd say! I mean, it were very handsomely, me lord. Handsome, and manly... Oh ay, and beautiful all wrapped together in a man-dance..." She trailed off, not knowing what else to say. She blushed furiously, then curtsied.

"Thank you, miss. The crowd was most encouraging."

At that moment, a couple approached Kathleen and Jared. The young Hestinian bride, was wearing a bright yellow dress that set off her ebony skin. She looked like a younger version of Queen Renata, except she smiled delightfully. The groom wore a white shirt and britches that matched his wife's gown. He had the appearance of a Hestin nobleman as well, with dark skin that shown healthy in the candlelight.

"Thank you for sharing your dance with us," the young woman said. "What a wonderful way to spend the evening. To see a Sīhalt wedding dance!

"It is our pleasure," said Jared. "My name is Aerick and this is my new bride, Karina."

"Thank you for sharing with us," the man said, inclining his head toward them.

"You have such beautiful red hair, Karina. You are from Sundiland? Most people I've met with red hair come from the southern realms."

"Thank you, I am from Sundiland. But my husband is stealing me away to the cold north for a season."

"I hear the princess of Sundiland is going to marry Prince Dol Lassimer this year. Have you ever seen her?" the noblewoman asked.

"I have, but never so close as this," Kathleen said.

"She must be the luckiest girl ever!" the Hestin woman said.

"I hope she makes it to the capital safely. It has been dangerous of late. We haven't had troubles, but we have heard the rumors," her husband said.

"I'm sure she will make it safely," Jared said. "She is traveling with a whole contingent of the Candoreth military. You know how these things are."

"We heard just this evening that her procession was attacked by Delathranes. We pray to Abboth she is safe. How long will you be staying in our fair city?" the woman asked.

"We will rest here for a time and enjoy what the mountains have to offer and then take our path northward," Jared said.

"The Trader's Way is especially beautiful. Some of the overlooks are so steep and green with trees you will want to take your time," the groom said.

"We plan to see it all," Jared agreed. "Tell me, is there any other way through the mountains that is faster when headed north, perhaps a shortcut only known to the locals?"

"There are some mining roads that lead to the western valleys, but they are overgrown, and not as beautiful as staying on the spine of the mountain," said the nobleman.

"I see. We would rather not go west anyway. We plan to visit my family in the Grand Lakes regions with my beautiful bride."

He said it with such ease as he grasped her hand and kissed the back of it. Kathleen had to admit, not for the first time, that her Sīhalt was an excellent performer.

At length the Hestin couple returned to their own table. Jared and Kathleen finally finished their dinner and left for the night, but not before many others made their way to their table to thank them again and again for the beautiful display of dancing that brought such pleasure to all those who attended.

They walked slowly, arm-in-arm back to their inn, neither wanting the evening to end.

"Let's go for a walk. The weather this evening is nice," Kathleen suggested.

Jared looked around for any sign of danger or something being amiss. The quiet of the street made him relax.

"We could walk to the crest of the Everfont," he said.

They walked arm-in-arm along the narrow cobblestone street that led upward to where the waterfall broke over the stone. The song of falling water filled the air, and a fine mist rose with it.

Kathleen finally took the flower from behind her ear where Jared had placed it.

"Where did you get this?" she asked. Twirling the stem between her fingers.

"A man must have his secrets."

"Did you *know* we would be asked to dance?"

"I knew it was a possibility."

"Thanks for the warning," she said, smiling.

"You didn't seem to need a warning. I was planning to guide you if it came to that. Where did you learn to dance like that anyway?"

"I have been dancing since I was a small child."

"Yes, but the Sīhalt wedding dance!"

"I spent a lot of time with Girdy. He would dance with me as a little girl. Melva would dance too. I remembered most of the steps."

"I'll say. I was so nervous for you at first. I thought 'I should have warned her, or not brought her here in the public eye, but you were brilliant!"

"I had a good lead." She smiled

"That was so fun." He laughed, and Kathleen joined him. He twirled her around as they walked along the moonlit street.

"I would appreciate a warning next time, though," Kathleen said.

"About the dance or the unexpected kiss?" Jared asked, smiling. "You seemed to do just fine with both."

Kathleen made a mockingly shocked look.

"How dare you, Lord Sīhalt. I was simply doing my duty. You told me to behave as naturally as possible. It seemed…natural in the moment."

They stopped walking and turned to each other.

"You truly convinced the crowd we were in love."

"I've never been in love," Kathleen said quietly.

"When I find someone to love, I hope it feels like this," he said.

"I do too," she said without hesitation.

Jared broke off their gaze, struggling against the feeling he was experiencing, and began walking again.

They walked in silence for a number of steps, still arm-in-arm, listening to the falling water.

"I picked the flower from the box at our window. Before we left the room," Jared finally said.

"I thought you said a man needs his secrets."

"I don't want any secrets between us," Jared said, his voice catching in his throat.

Kathleen remained quiet and rested her head on his shoulder

as they looked out over the moonlit mountain valleys that surrounded Altrastadt. Jared could feel her heartbeat thundering like the walls of falling water called the Everfont.

Kathleen twirled the small white flower between her fingers.

"I'll keep this forever," she said.

WEDDING GIFT

The cool mountain air made Kathleen want to draw even closer to Jared for warmth, despite the comforting brazier burning with firelight all along the rim of the overlook.

"So what is the significance of your ring?" she asked when they sat on a stone bench to admire the sound of the water on rocks.

Jared leaned back, resting his shoulders against the bench. She wondered for a moment if he might excuse himself. Instead, he looked out at the waterfall, paused to breathe deeply, and leaned in close. He looked into Kathleen's eyes with a seriousness that she appreciated. Yet Jared wore the barest of smiles as he spoke.

"Her name is Arabella. His is Tand." He looked down at his ring, then glanced up again with those storm-gray eyes. He pulled the ring off his index finger and placed it into Kathleen's open hands. "Master Tove had it made as a mourning gift when I lost them to the Delathranes." Kathleen turned the ring over in her hands and admired the intricate detail used to create flowing lines to suggest the form of a woman and a baby boy with a smile on his chubby face.

"They are beautiful," she said.

The thought that Jared might have been married struck Kathleen as a shock. The idea that this man, pretending to be her new husband, could in reality have a wife far in the western lands had never crossed her mind.

He could have a wife that was still alive...somewhere, she thought.

She wondered how much time had passed since Jared had seen his wife. Surely he would have done everything in his power to get her back. Most people did not survive a long time as a captive among the barbarians.

"When were they taken?" she asked.

"Arabella would be twenty-two, and Tand was just a baby." Jared smiled at the memory of the little one. Kathleen wanted to ask about his wife.

Does she still live? She asked herself.

"Were they taken as slaves?" she ventured aloud.

Jared shook his head.

"They were killed."

"I am sorry," she said. "You must be heartbroken."

She wanted to ask if the child's mother was Jared's wife but didn't want to seem overeager.

"I lost my brother Seth among the Delathranes that same year. He may yet live. That is why I need to find this Serpent King. If the clans are united again, my brother would be considered a prize for the king."

"We need to strengthen our borders," she said, remembering the horrors of the attacks. Jared sat nodding, concern creased along his brow. The firelight was waning. Kathleen laid her head on Jared's shoulder.

"What of the child's mother?" she asked. "A little bit ago you said something that made me believe you had never loved before..."

Jared let the question fade.

Kathleen regretted the question.

He blinked and looked directly at Kathleen. His storm-gray

eyes searching hers. He seemed to question her, wondering what would have prompted her to ask. Kathleen was hopeful, not for the first time, that the dim light hid the blush upon her cheeks.

"Arabella always said we should marry. She would not leave me or Seth alone about it. Even though our sister lost her husband the year prior to the barbarian attack, she always said the risk of love was worth the joy to be found in it," he said simply, quietly.

Kathleen exhaled quietly, cursing herself for probing too deeply.

"My sister died the same day as her child. Seth is the only family I have left."

Arabella was his sister! She realized.

"Seth and I cared for them as best we could. As Sīhalt Guardians, we are required to travel. I should have kept them closer." He touched the ring she still held in her hands. "I wear the ring to keep them always in my mind."

"You miss them."

"They are gone, but I will search for Seth once you are safely in Tyath," Jared replied.

Kathleen felt guilt at how her heart jumped in excitement to hear that Jared had never married. She should not feel this way. She was struggling to make it to the Imperial marriage with Prince Heathron waiting for her in the Golden City. She chastised herself and reminded herself that there was only one road in front of her —that of an Imperial bride.

"Jared, I feel badly about prying too much. I feel a greater sense of respect and admiration for a man, like you, who risks his own life to save others."

Jared looked down, not meeting her gaze.

"I want you to know about me," she said.

"I know all about you, Kathleen Dal Sundi," Jared said in a formal tone, his eyes squinting with the smile on his face. "I do my research when I accept a commission."

Kathleen pursed her lips.

"You think you know everything? I have a few surprises too you know." Kathleen looked up at her Sīhalt Guradian and smiled.

Their relationship seemed so real. She knew she must eventually move on to her future in the Imperial city, the wife of Prince Dol Lassimer. For now, she could pretend. Kathleen decided to make the most of it while their time in Altrastadt lasted. The dance had erased any hesitation she felt.

"So tell me, Lord Sīhalt, what *do* you know about me?" she asked.

"Your life is an open book to me." He turned with an overdone flourish and pulled his cloak across his face, hiding his mouth from onlookers. "I will trade you one for one in this game of discovery." He laughed.

"I am a good judge of people too. I know more about you than you think, Lord Sīhalt."

"Fair enough, Let's trade observations about each other. For example, you love to ride horses on the beaches of Candoreth," he said.

"That is too easy," she said.

"Let's start simple," he suggested. "Your turn."

"You have a talent for dancing."

He clasped his hands together and pressed his finger to his lips.

"You like to sail. Don't you?" he said.

Kathleen nodded.

"And you have exceptional hearing."

"What was that?" Jared said, cupping a hand to his ear.

Kathleen laughed.

"Seriously, you miss nothing I say, even when I wish you would."

"You love people, but you don't like your step-mother," Jared said.

Kathleen tilted her head and drew the corner of her mouth up.

"I'll grant you that. On the other hand, I've noticed you can see clearly even in the darkest night too."

"Your radiance makes that easy," Jared said.

"No, seriously, how do you do it? That night in the glade, you moved like it was broad daylight."

"I thought in this game we named what we had already learned of one another."

"All I really want is for us to know more about each other. Sorry about prying."

"So tell me something about yourself that most people don't know," Jared said.

Kathleen paused.

"You know the necklace I had at Cara's? It was my mother's. I inherited some of her skill. I am a Gardener, a Green Grower."

Jared nodded. "You like to eat oranges out of season." He smiled.

"I wondered if you put that together the day we met in my walled garden. Are you a really a Sensor?" she asked.

"Yes."

"Did you hear my comments after we first met in my orchard?"

"Do you mean, '…he's enough to make a girl wish she weren't betrothed'?"

"My life really is an open book to you!" She covered her mouth with her hand and held onto his strong arm with her other. "I'm embarrassed."

"We all have our gifts Kathleen. We shouldn't be ashamed of them."

Kathleen felt warmth flow over her body. The chilly air nipped her nose but her heart pounded. Her palms were warm against his as they held hands facing each other.

"So, as a Sensor, can you hear my beating heart?" she asked.

"I can hear the tremble in your breath, even when you try to hide it. I can feel your heart beating through the touch of your hand. Kathleen, I can even count your eyelashes and smell the scented lavender soap you used this morning."

Her heart pounded all the more. "That's amazing."

"You're amazing," he said.

She placed her face against his neck, and he pulled her close.

"Now you know the truth about me. I feel a burden lifted in knowing that you now know I am Talented and have not recoiled from my presence."

"Your nose is really cold too. That would be the more likely reason to recoil, in my opinion," Jared said.

"Lord Sīhalt! I would never have guessed you had such a sense of humor," Kathleen said.

"I don't find many reasons to laugh in the world I live in," Jared replied.

"I know. We live in difficult times. I wanted to use my Gift to help those poor hungry people in Celm and the other villages along the Delving River.

I wanted to walk slowly through those barren fields with my fingers outstretched, touching every stem and leaf. I might have been able to make the fields produce a bountiful harvest..."

"And yet you couldn't have done that, Kathleen," Jared said.

"Because you don't think I am strong enough?" she asked.

"You could not have revealed yourself to everyone in the wedding procession or the villages without losing their confidence in you. The last rumor we need in Tyath is that a Plant Witch is coming to marry the prince," he explained.

"I see your point, but the starving people would have accepted me as a Gardener once they saw the food."

"Until their bellies were full, then, I don't know," Jared said. "These are difficult times for those with Talents."

Jared reached into his cloak.

"I have something for you," he said.

"Richard finished it while Cara made your dress. I may not

have a chance like this to give it to you later. We have been running and hiding so much over the past weeks on the road."

Jared opened a small wooden box by sliding the lid back on the grooves cut into the rim. The lid of the box was inlaid with script reading:

For Kathleen

Inside Kathleen caught the brilliance of light reflecting back to her eye.

"I hope to travel a more refined road now that we have made it to the mountains," he said.

Jared presented the gift.

The light danced off the facets cut into the gemstone. Kathleen had never seen a diamond of this size and purity before. It was radiant.

"I had it set as a passion flower—for House Dal Sundi," he said.

Kathleen looked transfixed. She had never been given a gift of such beauty or one with such a personal touch.

She tried to resist. "I cannot accept a gift like this Jared" she murmured, "It is too beautiful."

He closed his hand on hers. He looked at her and laid a finger to his lips.

"It is part of the disguise," Jared said, "but I do not want it back when we reach the Golden City. It is one of my wedding gifts to you."

He slipped the ring on Kathleen's trembling hand.

"It's beautiful, Jared."

"I wish you a life filled with love, Kathleen Dal Sundi. I have never met a woman more deserving of it." Kathleen was unable to say another word. "I got you another gift too," he said.

"This is already too much," Kathleen replied.

"You really needed this one, though. Let me show you!" Jared said excitedly. He had the demeanor of a little boy on the morning of Winterfest.

Jared rose to his feet and pulled Kathleen along playfully.

"All right, I'm coming!" Kathleen laughed as they headed back toward the Inn.

They crossed the small courtyard to the stables. A light still burned near the front door. Jared took it from the wrought iron bracket and led Kathleen through the clean stable to a stall at the end of the barn. A beautiful dappled horse reached her gray head over the stall door and made some soft noises as she chewed on fresh hay.

"She is right here," Jared said, walking up to the next stall.

The mare whinnied softly.

"What is her name?" Kathleen said. "I can't believe you got me a horse."

"You have been an impressive Sīhalt bride, I thought I would honor a Sundiland tradition and, as a groom, give my lady a horse."

Kathleen's thoughts swirled with the significance of the gift.

"Do you know what this means in my country Jared?"

She honestly never believed she would receive a gift of a horse, especially from a man.

"In my studies, I recall it represents eternal friendship does it not?" he asked.

"That is one way to translate it. In Sundiland, a woman may only receive a horse as a gift once in her life," she explained softly, touching the horse's nose and admiring the fine form and bearing of the animal.

"If I have overstepped my bounds, I apologize," Jared began. "I don't mind you riding with me, but I thought you would need your own horse."

Kathleen pressed her finger to his lips and made him stop his explanation.

"I will call her *Sabo*," she said. "Thank you again, my Guardian."

BROKEN PROCESSION

Heathron Dol Lassimer breathed the warm air of summer deeply into his lungs. His bare hands passed over the crenelations of the embattlements. He shielded his eyes when the angle was just right to reflect the sunlight off the walls. It shimmered off his formal breastplate, a ceremonial piece that Heathron wore more for the looks it garnered than the authority it represented.

"In less than a fortnight, my bride will enter this city," he said, pleased that he had been so patient this past month.

"All is in order," Dirm agreed. The magistrate held a shade-maker to keep the sunlight off his face.

"Why don't you enjoy the sunlight while we've got it, Dirm? Lower that shade-maker and allow the sun and wind on your face!" Heathron said, leaning toward the expanse of fields beyond the walls as he shaded his eyes.

"Is that a command, Your Highness?" the sniveling magistrate asked.

The prince would have replaced him already, but the insufferable man had wormed his way into all the legal machinations and accounts of Imperial business of which he was a part. He had not yet found a replacement. Dream powder addiction or not, the man was talented at his work.

"I'll not be the scapegoat for you, Dirm, no sir!" Prince Heathron said. "A pleasure forced is no pleasure at all. Am I right?"

The magistrate wiped his nose, nodding while he did so.

"Is it your pleasure to sign for these orders in preparation for your upcoming wedding?" the magistrate asked, holding up sheets of paper that threatened to be twisted from his hand. "I would have delivered them to you in our office, Your Highness, but—"

"Nonsense, Dirm," Heathron said with a friendly wave of his hand. "The whole city is my office, and especially the natural world around us!"

"They are purchase orders for wine and meat. The remaining items on the menu are already paid, except for the desserts. I have not yet heard regarding the desserts."

"Lay them right up here," Heathron said, smacking his hand on the solid stone.

The magistrate held the pages down with a pale hand, struggling to control both documents and the shademaker against the wind that blew across the high walls of Tyath. Heathron signed them and imprinted his ring into the wax seal Dirm had prepared for each of them.

"My father is disinterested in my marriage preparations, I've noticed," Heathron observed.

"He has seen much in his days as Emperor," Dirm said.

"He cares about the security of the Empire and little else. I need to show him that this choice of mine is a good one," Heathron said.

"You still believe Sundiland was a good choice," Dirm said.

Heathron looked at the magistrate, impatience showing through.

"Kathleen Dal Sundi is a good choice! How many times do I

need to say it Dirm? I'm marrying the woman, not the kingdom," he said.

"These are political realities, Your Highness," Dirm said apologetically.

Heathron ran a hand over his jaw.

"The reality is that a man's choice in a wife, and I dare say a woman's choice in a husband, is more important than any other consideration. Has no one read our history? How many wars have been fought or thrones lost due to a lack of consideration in marriage? Where was the love in the marriage of Emperor Jadlet and Empress Evonne? We would not have fought a civil war in the second age if those two had actually loved each other! That is what keeps a man going—the love." He trailed off, looking out toward the horizon wistfully.

"I can see that you are a passionate man," Dirm said diplomatically.

"I will treat her with such kindness and respect, she will never doubt my love for her. I will shower her with gifts, if she likes them. We will have beautiful daughters and sons. I will build monuments to our love, and the bards will sing of Heathron and Kathleen for a thousand years."

"She seemed a very energetic young woman, when I last saw her in Candoreth," the magistrate said.

"She is my perfect love!" Heathron said. "I will shout for joy when I see her procession on the horizon."

Just then a sentry called out, "Banners on the horizon! A procession approaches."

Prince Heathron ran to the sentry and took the eagle glass from his hand. He scanned the horizon. The banners for House Dal Sundi tossed in the wind. The prince looked closer, squinting his eyes in disbelief.

"How is she here so early?" he wondered aloud. There were too few horses, and some of the men walked with a limp. A few wagons carried wounded people.

"What has happened?" he exclaimed.

"You must wait for the procession to approach, Your High-ness." Dirm reminded him.

"Tradition be slain! I will ride out to meet her. The summer solstice is not yet, we can go through the formalities on the appointed day," he replied.

"Call for Captain Bastion. Gather the Tower Guard," the prince commanded. The sentry turned and ran as fast as his legs would allow.

The prince began running down the stairs, using the hand rails to launch himself farther and farther down from landing to landing.

"I will follow you shortly, Your Highness," the magistrate said aloud, then smiled discreetly, rolling up the signed purchase orders.

Heathron borrowed the nearest horse he could find, untying it from the hitching post and swinging up into the saddle with ease. He rode the white mare out the southwestern gates of Tyath, his golden hair streaming behind him.

The closer he came to the Candorethian Wedding Procession the more concern grew in his heart. This was not what he expected. He had received no word of a catastrophe, but that is what he saw. The people looked haggard and there were many bloodstained bandages. The Dal Sundi flags snapped in the breeze. His eyes searched for the face of his love.

High atop one of the two wagons sat a woman fair to behold. She had a braid in her hair pinned up on one side. She held herself in a regal manner despite the terrible situation of her arrival.

Her hair was golden, like his, with only a tinge of the fiery shade he expected. Could this be Kathleen? How different she looked compared to the girl of his memories. She was beautiful, but not a freckle to be seen on her creamy white cheeks. Beside her sat a wrinkled old woman with few teeth.

That must be the Healer we were told of.

275

The people of the procession, upon seeing the crown he wore began to bow and kneel. Heathron dismounted and called out the woman on the wagon. "Fair Lady, I am Heathron Dol Lassimer, Prince of Tyath."

"Your Highness." The beautiful creature spoke, "I am Lady Larissa Albodris, daughter of Kenton Albodris and cousin to your bride." She said it with such great sadness, the prince was afraid to ask his next question.

"And the Princess Dal Sundi?" he began tentatively, a feeling of dread surrounding him.

"We were attacked, Your Highness," the old woman said.

A captain approached, his arm bound in a sling. He was disheveled and dirty. A large area of his head was matted with dried blood.

"The Delathranes nearly wiped out our entire procession. We have many wounded," he explained to Heathron.

Looking about at the men of arms, the prince furrowed his brow in disbelief.

"How can you arrive here without Kathleen?" he asked, his normal friendly demeanor slipping away as he spoke.

"Your Highness, we were ambushed. We came with all haste to ask for assistance," the captain said.

"When did this happen?" Heathron asked, his mind racing.

"We were attacked at the narrows, just past Revonah, near the junction of the Trader's Way. I will gladly lead the search for Princess Dal Sundi if you will give me reinforcements. There were at least fifty war bands. We were overwhelmed," the man said.

Heathron nodded. He knew the place well. Being close to the mountains, there were plenty of places for brigands to hide. Heathron had led a force to rid the Trader's Way of bandits a few years back. But Delathranes? Fifty war bands? This was unheard of in his lifetime.

"Was the princess alive when you last saw her?" Heathron asked the captain.

The man looked to the two women on the wagon.

"Your bride may yet be alive," said the old woman.

"I believe the Sīhalt Guardian was with her. The smoke was thick, but I saw him defending her at the end. Abbath help them," Lady Albodris said.

"No man could stand up to so many of the enemy. Not even the Sīhalt," the captain said with finality.

Captain Bastion and his guardsmen rode up, and a contingent of pikemen marched along behind them. The chief magistrate managed to arrive as well, sweating and awkward in the saddle.

Heathron turned to Jarek. "Take these people into the city. See to it that they are fed and washed. Many are wounded, as you can see."

"Yes, Your Highness," Captain Bastion said.

The chief magistrate looked at the Healer, sitting on the wagon, with a scowl.

"That one will not be entering the holy city?" he said, more of a statement than a question, pointing a thin finger in Melva's direction.

"The woman is my guest, along with the rest of this procession," Heathron said.

"But Master, she is a savage Meat Witch. I do not want to have a fight on our hands with the Luzian High Priest," the magistrate explained, his hands raised in a gesture of innocence.

"This woman saved the lives of many people here!" the Candorethian captain protested. "Without her more of my men would be dead."

"A superior military leader would not need to rely on the dark magic of a Delathrane Meat Witch to save him," Dirm said in reply. The captain bristled and might have gone for his sword were his arm not bound up in a sling with binder holding it tightly against his side.

The old woman spat in Dirm's direction. "I am no Delathrane, dream powder man."

The magistrate narrowed his eyes at her.

"She will be treated with respect," Heathron said, calming the captain but not the magistrate. "I want to interview her along with some others, before the day is done. We will mount a rescue for Princess Dal Sundi. I pray to Abboth we are not too late."

REOCCURRING DREAM

For hours Kathleen lay in the bed, looking at the ceiling of her bedchamber, waiting for fatigue to overcome the beautiful moments of the day. The presence of the Sīhalt Guardian right outside her door made her feel excited and she was glad he had locked the door.

"It is a matter of security," Jared had said.

It certainly is! she thought.

That would be one more barrier to the inappropriate temptation she felt to open that door and resume where they had left off at the end of that dance.

Just as she was beginning to drift into sleep, Kathleen gasped and sat up, shaking. Suddenly fully awake, she wondered what had startled her. Then, in the darkness of the room, she heard it again. A banging and a moan came through the door. It sounded like Jared!

She wondered if she should get out of bed or stay silent and hide. It sounded as if there was a fight in the anteroom where Jared slept. The awful thump hit her own door, and Kathleen jumped. She felt for the dagger in the darkness and slide to the far side of the bed. She heard the moaning again.

Kathleen cried out to him. "Jared, are you okay?"

The banging intensified—it sounded as if a person's face or head was hitting the door. She called out again. "Jared!"

"You will not take her, you will not take her!" Jared's angry voice slurred the words just outside.

"Oh Abbath, he needs my help!" Kathleen found herself saying. She ran to the door, unsure of how many assailants there might be. She took a deep breath to calm her nerves and grasped the dagger tightly.

Kathleen slid the bolt aside. "I'm coming, Jared," she said through the door. The thrashing had not quit. Kathleen could hear Jared gasping for breath and the pounding continued. Kathleen lifted the latch and gripped her small dagger more fiercely. She steeled herself for the attack that would be needed to save Jared. She hoped there was only one attacker. She would stab him in the neck and keep stabbing until he released Jared.

Kathleen lifted the latch and pulled the door open. The moonlight from the windows in the room showed her a scene that made her fall to her knees. Her Guardian was crouched on the floor twisted in the blankets he used for bedding. His fists were bloodied by the many times he had pounded them against the wooden floor.

"Jared!" she said. "Wake up!"

He moaned loudly again, his eyes still closed.

"You will not take her from me," Jared sobbed, still apparently asleep.

Kathleen felt some fear to approach him, but seeing this strong man in such anguish, she knelt beside him and placed her hand on his shoulder, gently shaking him.

"I'm right here, Jared. It's okay, I'm right here. You are having a nightmare," she said softly, letting the dagger slip from her grip.

The man jerked away from her touch and turned toward her, his fist drawn back to strike. Kathleen ducked and, in a panic, reached for her dagger. His eyes were open wide but not fully understanding what was before him. He held his fist back as if fighting a demon for control of his own movements.

His eyes slowly narrowed, recognition dawning as the moonlight bathed his face. His cheeks glistened with the tears that had streamed down during the dream. He looked so sad, so empty. Kathleen wanted to hold his head against her chest but refrained. She was terrified of the image he had just shown her.

"Are you okay?" she asked intensely.

"I am sorry!" he said, pulling his fist down with his other hand. "I was fighting, I was…angry," he said through deep breaths.

Jared looked at his knuckles that were bleeding on the white sheet where he had pounded them into the floor.

"You are bleeding. Come, let me bind up your hands," Kathleen said and led him into her room. She lit a wall lantern and adjusted the flame. Jared was quiet throughout.

"I am sorry I woke you," he finally said.

"I thought you were being attacked!" Kathleen said. "You had a nightmare."

Jared still looked somewhat confused.

In the firelight Kathleen saw the mangled knuckles and spreading bruises the Sīhalt had caused himself. All while he was asleep. She wrapped thin strips of cloth over his knuckles as he held his hands out in front of himself.

"How often do you have them?" Kathleen asked, trying to remain calm.

"I have them sometimes. Usually I don't wake up," he said.

"You mean you just destroy your hands and go on sleeping afterward?"

Kathleen had never heard of such a thing. It was unnerving.

"I almost stabbed you in the back when I opened the door! I thought someone was choking you," Kathleen said.

"Thanks for rescuing your Guardian," Jared said wryly. He smiled up at her with embarrassment.

Kathleen wondered what torment Jared was going through.

He held his responsibility to protect her so seriously and yet she felt some alarm at how unstable he looked, crouching like an animal, pounding his bleeding fist against the floor.

"It was more of a memory than a nightmare," Jared said softly.

"A memory? My memories don't do this to me," Kathleen said, indicating the bandaged hands.

"At least I got to see Arabella's face again," Jared said darkly.

"Tell me about your dream," Kathleen said.

"I saw my sister's son. The light from the morning sun shone softly on his face," Jared began.

Kathleen listened and thought of her own sister, Elayna, far away to the south. She sat beside him on the bed, still holding his hand. She blinked back some tears that started to form.

"My heart always softened to see him sleeping. In my dream, he woke up and stretched and started making funny singing noises. He was just a baby but already had the cutest personality. Arabella smiled, and Tand giggled when I poked his round little belly. It was perfect, until the Delathranes came."

"I miss my sister too," Kathleen said trying to show empathy.

"The good and innocent shouldn't have to suffer. They should be safe," Jared said, an edge entering his tone.

"It is the world we live in," Kathleen replied.

"The world needs to be remade, then," he said.

"We will follow the will of Abbath, I guess," Kathleen said.

Jared shook his head and looked into Kathleen's eyes.

"I'm not waiting for a miracle," Jared said. "I'll do what I can to protect the good and beautiful, and destroy the ugly and profane."

"Well then, I better go wash my face, because I'm not feeling very beautiful right now," Kathleen said, smiling.

"It would take more than a terrible night's rest to make you anything other than radiant, Your Highness," Jared said, his eyes lowered with an awkward little smile. "I am sorry for waking you."

"Just be careful as you try to remake the world, Lord Sīhalt. It may need more men like you in it," Kathleen said as Jared left the room

He inclined his head slightly in acceptance of the compliment, and closed the door again. Kathleen took a deep breath and held it for a moment. When she exhaled, she no longer had a smile. She doubted she could fall to sleep again.

COMMON ROOM

In the morning, Jared and Kathleen came downstairs. The common room of the inn smelled of savory meat and sweet baked goods. Kathleen's stomach growled with hunger. The people at breakfast looked up at them, smiled knowingly, and returned to their meals. They were the newlyweds, after all.

"Would you like to sit here?" Jared suggested, holding a chair for Kathleen.

A serving woman came right over. "Good morning. How were your rooms?" she asked.

"We slept well. Thank you," Kathleen said.

Jared's nightmare during the night had left her feeling a bit groggy from the lack of sleep, but she determined to make this day as wonderful as the last.

"What would you like for breakfast?" the serving woman asked.

Kathleen looked around the room at what could be seen on the plates of other people.

"I'll have what they are having," she said and pointed to an adjacent table.

"Oh, you'll love the the apple pastries. I'll bring you some good

eggs and forest ham too. It will help you regain your strength."
She gave an irritating wink to Kathleen.

Jared seemed not to notice the waitress.

"I'll have the same," he said without glancing her way. He was
listening to the conversation at an adjacent table. The men spoke
in earnest voices of the road they had traveled the day before.

"So as I was taking my cart from the lowlands to the hills last
week, I saw a group of Delathranes!" a burly trader said to his
comrades.

"They didn't bother you?" another asked.

"No, they were way off to the side of the pass, as if they didn't
want to be seen or heard, and they were running, and I mean
running fast. My goodness, those barbarians are fast, even
without their horses."

"Have you seen any near Altrastadt?" asked the third.

"They were headed this way, but the city walls are tall and the
guards lock the place up tight as one of my wine casks at night. It
would take more than a few war bands to cause trouble here."

"What brought them that far into the foothills?" the innkeeper
asked.

"I don't know. We must need another Dumal Wells!" The burly
man laughed, and a few others pounded their mugs on the tables
in support of the idea. "That battle broke the Delathranes. We
pushed them beyond the Great River. Maybe we need to civilize
the grasslands as well, kill them all."

The burly merchant looked around the room at those who
supported him, and his eyes fell on Jared and Kathleen.

"Speaking of the battle of Dumal Wells, we have a Sīhalt
Guardian in our midst!" he said, gesturing toward Jared.

"Are you and your brethren ready to join the rest of the good
men of the empire to cut down the dirty barbarians again?" His
voice had an edge of slurred speech. Perhaps he had been
sampling his own wares too much.

"I prefer not to consider it, friend. There are few Guardians compared to generations past. I am recently married and will devote this first year to my bride."

"Newlyweds! Well, that explains all the racket going on last night. You kept us all up!" he said, and there were snickers of agreement.

The innkeeper dried his hands off on his apron and approached the backside of the bar. "Quiet, you, I'll not have you hounding my guests. We are honored to have a Sīhalt couple spend their honeymoon in Altrastadt."

"We are paying customers too," a man said in a raspy voice, "and we've a right to a good night's sleep, or at least a little fun at the hands of those who woke us up during the middle of the night." The men at his table laughed, and Jared stared at them with cold eyes.

Kathleen laid her hand on Jared's arm. His muscles were hard and as he clenched his fists with still-bandaged knuckles.

"It's okay, Jared. Just ignore them," Kathleen said in such a soft whisper only Jared could have heard her.

Not catching the seriousness of the Sīhalt's demeanor, the merchant continued, "Enjoy the newlywed phase while it lasts!"

A round of rough laughter rose from their table and a few other smirks were visible, even on the face of the serving girl.

"That's enough," a lanky Hestin trader said from the corner, "The groom is not seeing the humor in your comments, and he is a Sīhalt, if you've never met one in person."

The three traders ignored the one in the corner and continued their jesting.

"I remember my wedding night. My wife is a Sundiland redhead like yours, a very spirited woman for sure!" said one of the smaller merchant guards, laughing. He started pounding the table rapidly to the amusement of the others.

Kathleen could see the tension in Jared's face increase, and she squeezed his arm gently, trying to defuse the situation.

Jared was across the room in a flash.

"You have gone too far," he stated simply and fiercely.

Jared moved so quickly the remaining guards were caught unaware and didn't even rise to help their comrade.

He grabbed the big man by the head and yanked him out of his chair, sending him sprawling onto the floor. Scrambled eggs and ale spilled across his clothing and beard as his plate and mug splashed their contents onto the wooden floor.

The man slipped on a piece of ham as he struggled to regain his feet. Jared kicked a leg out from underneath the man and sent him sprawling to his sizable belly once more.

Kathleen was shocked by how quickly the Sīhalt reacted with force.

"You don't need to be violent, Jared!" she said over the commotion.

Jared stopped only briefly enough to glare at Kathleen.

I used his real name! she thought.

Then the Sīhalt Guardian grabbed the man by the back of his neck, twisting his fist into the cloth that made a part of the man's shirt and vest. He grabbed the man's belt with his other hand and ran him forward without stopping until his head and body were though the large glass window at the front of the Everfont Inn. A dog outside barked excitedly at the man laying in the middle of the street, his momentum having carried him beyond the side walk. Glass tinkled as it fell from the broken window frames.

The man in the street didn't move a muscle. He lay unconscious. Jared turned back toward the table of merchant guards. The smallest one grabbed for a sturdy club, but Jared whipped his sword from his scabbard so quickly it was difficult to follow with one's eye. "I'll not have you berating my wife," he said fiercely.

The man dropped his club, and Jared sheathed his sword.

"Now hold on!" the innkeeper said.

The merchant's men scattered, wondering who would be the next target of the Sīhalt's wrath.

"That window cost me four gold crowns the last time it broke," he said.

"Here are seven gold," Jared said to the innkeeper.

"Beat one dog and the others stop barking," Jared said, gesturing to the man lying in the street.

"Well I can't say he didn't deserve it," the innkeeper agreed, counting the coins.

"What about me?" asked a merchant still sitting at a side table. "That was my man. Now I'm down a guard. He probably has a broken arm or worse. I deserve compensation."

"This man, who insulted my beautiful wife, he worked for you?" Jared asked with a cold stare.

"Well, he was more of an independent contractor. He is not one of my men per se," the merchant hedged.

"I didn't think so Master Merchant, because if that were one of your men, I'd have to talk with his boss about how he upset my new bride," Jared said.

"Oh no, we picked him up along the road--he was just accompanying my wares to Altrastadt and then his contract expired. I don't have anything to do with him," the merchant stated emphatically

"I thought not," Jared said. "Surely the rest of your men are not anything like this one."

"Indeed, Lord Sīhalt. These other men know their bounds and will respect a lady, offering apologies to any lady whose honor has been offended."

He poked the closest man in the ribs with an elbow, and the man lowered his club.

"That's right, Lord Sīhalt, we ask for forgiveness to you and your lady," the bulky man said.

A general chorus of apologies with bowing followed. Jared did not smile the entire time.

Kathleen accepted the petitions of forgiveness with a nod of her head.

"Why are you so quick to harm others?" she began and she stepped closer to Jared.

"We need to leave," he said to Kathleen.

"We have not had a chance to eat." She looked back at the delicious meal the waitress was bringing to the table.

"If Delathrane scouts are looking for us here in Altrastadt, it will not do to sit here in comfort and wait to be found. We leave now," he said emphatically. Jared took Kathleen by the arm and led her back toward their room.

LEAVING ALTRASTADT

J ared quickly laid out the map in their room and traced a path through the mountains north and then angled northwest toward the great inland sea. Kathleen looked forward to seeing the shoreline again. She had never been away so long from a sunrise or sunset over water. She realized she missed it.

However, a deep sense of dread hung over them. Perhaps the thought of braving the road again made them feel so melancholy. In truth, Kathleen knew that the beautiful time they had shared together in Altrastadt was coming to an early close. She felt a sense of urgency to savor the remaining time they had. She walked out to the balcony and looked up and down the road. Kathleen could see a beautiful vista like the one they had shared the night of their dance. The lake was as blue as the sky, almost milky in its turquoise splendor. Kathleen turned back to Jared. She had learned so much about him, and yet she had so much more to learn. Kathleen fantasized about spending the rest of the year with him here in this dream-like place nestled in the mountains. She imagined for a moment the crystal-like appearance the city must have when coved in winter's ice. She looked at Jared as he studied the maps and committed the images to memory. Jared was all seriousness now, his dark hair fell forward hiding his face. He had not a moment more to reflect and enjoy.

They got Steed and Sabo from the stables. When the saddlebags were packed, they mounted and rode out of Altrastadt. They passed the shop where Cara and Richard looked up from their work and waved a farewell. Kathleen looked at her hands holding the reins. Not a scratch remained after the Healing Cara had given her. Jared had been made whole as well.

Jared seemed lost in his own thoughts. Kathleen looked at the ring he had given her. It shone in the morning sun. She patted Sabo on the shoulder. Kathleen wondered when, if ever, she would pass this way again.

The further they traveled on the road, the more distant Jared seemed to grow.

Perhaps he is just wary out here, Kathleen thought, but the emotional wall he had retreated behind made no sense, and he kept it in place for much of their morning ride.

Is he that good at pretending? she wondered with rising irritation.

She trotted her mare even with Steed and looked at Jared as he rode, her hand shielding her eyes from the bright morning sun.

"Do you hear something?" she asked.

He shook his head and kept riding.

"Let me know if I need to be quiet, because if I need to be quiet, I will be," she said.

"I'm not sensing any danger," he said.

"Good, because you had me kind of worried. I mean, ever since you looked at the map in our room this morning and laid out our course, you kind of went back to being the serious Sīhalt Guardian. Not Jared, my friend."

He looked at her flatly, and except for the slight twinge in his brow, Kathleen would have thought he felt nothing for her at all.

"We are out of the city with its crowds that provide safety. I need to be sharp as your protector again on the road."

Katheen cocked her head and wondered if she was hearing him correctly.

"Jared," she said, an attempt to reach him emotionally. "Did any of that matter to you?" she gestured back toward the city in the distance.

"Any of what?" he asked.

"Jared I know you can tell by my voice that I am upset. You can probably hear me breathing harder because I am feeling hurt and angry right now!"

"What can I do, Kathleen?" he asked, looking around at the wilderness around them.

"Open up to me, like you did these past few days. I want to be your friend, no matter where our paths lead us," she pleaded.

"Friend?" Jared almost spat the word with incredulity. "I don't know how we will be friends after you arrive in the Golden City," he said.

Kathleen felt hurt. *Why was he pushing her away?*

"I can't imagine our paths will never cross again, even when I am married," she said.

"I am alone, Kathleen. My parents, my brothers, my sister are gone. I am alone."

"And that means you can't have friends?"

"It means I shouldn't have friends. I am not the man you think I am."

"Jared, you are confusing me."

"I am not worthy of your friendship or admiration," he said.

"You are the most inspiring man I have ever met, Jared. The world needs more men of your valor and virtue."

"The other night when I told you of my brother Seth, I said he might yet be alive."

"I remember," she said.

"He was lost to the Delathranes, but it was my fault." Jared exhaled as if he prepared to lift a great burden.

"After we buried Arabella and Tand. He tried to stop me."

Kathleen rode up next to him leaning in her saddle toward him, offering empathy. Sensing he wanted to share more, she slid from her saddle. "We should stop here, Jared," she said.

He dismounted and tied the horses to a small tree. Kathleen retrieved some cheese and dried fruit, and they ate beneath a giant beech tree—its smooth silver bark-covered branches were horizontal and enormous in girth. The leaves of the tree held the slightest tinge of yellow from the sunlight it shaded.

They leaned against a fallen branch of that tree and Kathleen urged Jared to continue.

"I was so angry and heartbroken. All I could think of was revenge."

Now we are getting somewhere, Kathleen thought.

Kathleen could see the barriers of his emotions breaking and encouraged him with a touch of her hand on his.

"We rode to the encampment of the clan called Razewell. Seth and I were greeted with angry stares and derision. They might have pulled us down from our horses if King Raldric had not called for us to be brought before him."

"Were you terrified?" she asked.

"I was numb, and cold, as I protected the flame of vengeance within my heart," he said, his eyes getting a distant stare as he recalled the memories.

"The king was there, in his big tent with his wives and best warriors. He was feasting and laughing. The whole scene assaulted my senses. The whole tent smelled of their filthy liquor, human stench, and the uncured animal hides."

Kathleen listened intently.

"Seth asked if I would leave with him and I refused. I was angry, so like a fool I tried to negotiate with an inebriated barbarian king." Jared swallowed hard. "Are you sure you want to hear all this?" he asked.

"Of course. Sometimes you just need to tell someone else about your burdens and it helps. So you tried to negotiate…" she said

"I tried, but the Delathrane king offered me a drink. The crowd in the tent laughed. The chalice that held the liquor was the upper portion of a fresh skull— that of a child," Jared continued, his voice getting quieter.

"'Do you like my new cup?' he said to me. 'Do you like my new cup?'" Jared placed his face in his hands, running his fingers through his hair. Kathleen could see that he was struggling not to cry.

"The skull still had flesh attached in spots, and I could not stop looking at it, thinking of my sister and her murdered child. The king found the look on my face comical and slapped his thigh in humor. I looked around the tent, lit by the firelight, and for the first time in my life, I saw only people I despised. I could not think of them as someone's brother or sister. There were no fathers or mothers in that darkened Delathrane dwelling, just vicious monsters. I saw them that night as monsters."

Kathleen's mind raced.

Do I really know this man?

"So what did you do?" she asked, transfixed by the story he told.

Jared's outward emotions suddenly stopped. In an unnatural way, he iced over and spoke in a distant tone, still continuing the harrowing story.

"When he offered me a drink, newly made from the attack on my sister's house, I dumped the dark liquor on the ground and stabbed the barbarian king through the heart."

Kathleen grimaced, horrified by the story of violence. She thought she saw a smile on his face as he continued.

"Seth and I fought our way out of the tent. We were attacked on all sides, fighting to survive. I lost my brother for foolish revenge,"

Kathleen did not know what to say. His lack of emotion with the details of this story made her wonder if he might be a danger to her as well.

"There was a sickly Delathrane boy. He couldn't have been more than seven years old. I turned to leave and he raised his hand against me. An upwards stoke of my sword ended him."

Kathleen appeared in complete shock.

"I am the one the barbarians call *Der'antha*. I am not worthy of your admiration," Jared explained.

"I have heard that word before. The warrior called you that the night of the first attack. What does that name mean?" Kathleen asked with barely a whisper.

"It means Dangerous Hunter," he said.

"That is it, then?" Kathleen asked, her face ashen as his whole story lay before her.

He knew he was a danger to us all! she thought.

"I waited for Seth to join me. He never did. I buried my sister and what was left of her family in the graveyard at Windstall Hermitage. I didn't want them be further desecrated by the barbarians."

"Were *you* the reason for my wedding procession being attacked?" she asked hesitantly.

Jared sat silently for five of her rapid breaths.

Finally, he spoke. "I pray to Abbath I have not brought this upon you."

She sat in stunned silence, trying to come to terms with the new understanding she had of the man with whom she traveled.

DISTANCE BETWEEN

Jared admitted his guilt with such finality and absence of remorse that Kathleen wondered how she had ever felt she knew this man. She got up from her seat beneath the tree and steadied herself with a low-hanging branch. Certainly, her father had no way of knowing this man was the Dangerous Hunter hated by the Delathranes.

"Did my father know you had a bounty on your head when you were hired to protect me?"

"He did not ask."

"Girdy didn't know. He would have told me."

"Kathleen, none of the warriors who saw me up close that night survived."

"You certainly made that clear. You even smiled about it!"

"I find no joy in killing."

"Unless it is a sick little boy living in a tent."

"He stabbed me in the leg!" Jared said, revealing a nasty scar behind his right knee. "You don't know the depravity of these people."

"I don't know you! I need some time to try to make sense of all this."

A flock of crows called in the distance, disturbed by the rising pitch of her voice.

Terrified, Kathleen tried to estimate how long it would take her to ride back to Altrastadt at a full gallop.

Perhaps I could make it there and send for help from Father, or Heathron — we are closer to the Golden City by now. she thought.

"Do not even think of riding back to Altrastadt," he said.

She glared at him.

"Are your ears so keen you can hear my thoughts too?"

"I should not have unburdened myself to you, Kathleen. I am sorry. It was unfair, and unprofessional of me."

"You may call me Your Highness or Princess Dal Sundi if you desire to be professional. We aren't pretending anymore, are we, Guardian?"

She spit his title out, amazed that she had the confidence to do so. Years of training in a royal court had taught her to rely on her social position and command of others. When she felt vulnerable, Kathleen became haughty. She climbed back into her saddle, being sure to keep the horse between herself and this dangerous man.

"Your Highness, you will not be returning to Altrastadt," he said.

Kathleen dug her heels into Sabo's side then pulled the reins to one side wheeling the horse around quickly.

The young Sīhalt warrior was on his feet in an instant and jumped the large oak branch lying on the ground. The leaves swished against his legs as he ran forward and grabbed Sabo's reins.

"I am sworn to protect you, Your Highness. I am sorry I scared you just now by sharing some of my painful story, but I can't let you go back to the city. We are being sought and we must journey northward toward the Clearwater Sea."

"I don't think I can go anywhere with you. You are a murderer!"

"Girdy has had to kill. *You* ordered me kill that night we were attacked in the glade!"

"But never a woman or a child!"

Jared, still holding the reins, lowered his head.

"I will give you some space, but we must ride that way," he said, pointing down the road.

Panic rising, Kathleen wondered how she would ever get word to her father far to the south. Here she was, so many leagues away from home, in the wilderness, on the road with the Dangerous Hunter.

I allowed him to kiss me! Kathleen felt betrayed.

"Stay away from me!" Kathleen said, turning away.

She rode her horse on the road, still in the direction they were headed. Kathleen knew Steed to be faster and stronger than Sabo. Jared could give her a twenty minute head start and still catch her well before the city wall.

He could slit my throat and leave my limp body by the road and my loudest scream would be heard by no one, she thought.

"Kathleen wait," Jared said. "It isn't safe to go on alone."

"I'd rather be alone right now. Girdy warned me about trusting you."

Jared just stared at her, not knowing what to say. A look of pain and confusion flooded his face.

"Girdy said, 'I believe he is very dangerous.' He was right about that! I can't believe I let you pretend we were married."

She nudged Sabo with one knee. The mare responded with energy. Kathleen gave her more reins, and the horse snorted with pleasure, the smooth, sloping road boosting her desire to run. Kathleen looked back to see Jared gathering their things, putting them in the saddlebags.

"I just need to think," she said out loud.

Even at over a hundred paces, with the pounding of Sabo's hooves, Kathleen knew Jared would hear her.

FALL OF A GUARDIAN

J ared allowed Kathleen to ride ahead. It worried him to be more than a few paces from her side, but he felt she deserved some time alone if she wanted it.

I revealed too much, he thought.

The bitterness of regret welled up in Jared's heart. He shook his head, thinking of how he had gone wrong.

"Girdy was right to warn her," he said to himself.

I allowed myself to indulge. I have been a fool!

"She is betrothed!" he reminded himself.

Looking ahead, Jared could see the flash of white on Sabo's hind legs. Steed tossed his head. He wanted to join the other horse.

"I know how you feel, old boy, but the girls need to be alone for now. We have done enough damage."

The horse snorted, clearing his nose with a shiver and shake.

"Okay, you're right." Jared patted Steed's neck again and said, "it's my fault, you had nothing to do with it."

I just need to be the Guardian I swore to be - nothing more. I lost focus and this has put us in danger, he thought.

They rode this way throughout the day, Kathleen riding ahead and Jared a distance behind for her privacy.

◟

Her mind wandered, feeling torn between her attraction to Jared, and the revulsion she felt at his violent behavior. She scolded herself for not keeping in mind her betrothal to Heathron and getting caught up in the pretend honeymoon she had with her Guardian.

The road was clear, and they had studied the maps before leaving Altrastadt so Kathleen did not worry too much about turning down the wrong road. They passed the few intersections and branches off the Trader's Way.

The sun reached its high point and Kathleen refused to stop. She did not want to break the silence between them yet. Instead, she reached into her saddle bags and ate some of the provisions they had prepared before leaving the inn. She looked back a number of times as the sun drifted downward, peering through the summer leaves. Although the mountain morning was crisp, the afternoon sun was warm enough to make her fold her riding cloak behind her saddle. Kathleen wished she had never heard the truth of Jared's past. She wished she could go back to the moment before he had told her of his crime.

Are there no perfect men in the world?

She knew the answer to that question.

There are only perfect moments, she thought as she looked back again.

Her fear and anger began to cool, and she wondered how he would respond as dusk approached. A part of her grew bold in wanting to have him ride at her side again. To be close to her. To feel his strength, his presence. But she had asked for space and the Sīhalt Guardian had given it to her. Surely she would be weak to fall back into his arms now?

Be strong, Kathleen, she told herself.

But did that mean she would have to find a place to rest for the night on the open road alone? In the darkness, would he not come closer again? The oncoming night seemed to melt her resistance to his presence. A headwind began to blow as well and Kathleen put her riding cloak back on as it whipped around her shoulders.

J ared watched as the princess rode ahead. He silently tried to gauge the level of her anger. At times it seemed like she had slowed her horse, perhaps to see test his honor in granting her solitude? Or perhaps as an invitation to rejoin her? He wanted nothing more than the latter.

But no, he would display his honor and remain faithful to her request. He slowed Steed to a walk and even paused to keep the distance between them, but also wondering about the best way to break the silence. He decided that he would let Kathleen be the one to restart conversation. They had a couple of days before the next town and as long as he listened for anyone else on the road, she could keep her distance. She would be safe.

After an hour, Jared watched the clouds darken. When the wind started to increase, Jared found it a bit harder to hear. He paused Steed more often and used his keen ears to listen for the creak of the wagon wheels belonging to the traders that drove their teams from high up in the mountains down into the valleys. Only experienced merchants drove the Trader Way at this time of year, because the fierce early summer storms in the mountains could endanger their cargo on the soaring paths.

As dusk approached, Jared wondered what to do. On one hand, he did not like the idea of Kathleen sleeping along the road alone. Rain would likely commence soon, and he doubted that she knew how to set up a shelter. The road curved up ahead and descended sharply. It would be much better to set up camp at the summit rather than descend halfway and brave the weather on the most exposed side of the mountain.

Up ahead, the sharp curves of the road took Kathleen out of sight. When he called out to her, she didn't answer.

She's still just angry, he thought.

"Kathleen," he yelled, his voice fighting against the increasing wind.

Jared touched his heels to Steed's side and the stallion sprang forward. A crack of thunder nearly broke Jared's eardrums. The sudden rushing wind tore the leaves from the trees, scattering them in a swirl of green in the fading light of day. As he rounded the curve, Jared saw Kathleen had dismounted. She was trying to coax Sabo back onto the narrow road. The horse was spooked and pulled hard against the reins in Kathleen's hands.

"Come, Sabo... Good girl!"

Kathleen lurched forward and her forearms caught the rocks at her feet. The mare pulled away and began running straight down the mountain.

"Wait... Sabo, come back!"

The horse leaped over the shrubs that lined the road and raised her tail as she cleared some of the smaller trees below.

Jared rode to her.

"I was pulled over the rocks!" she said, looking down at the blood dripping from her elbows. Her forearms, scrapped and bleeding, had been sacrificed trying to hold the reins of the terrified horse.

"Walk back to the summit Kathleen! I will get Sabo and meet you there," he said.

Jared rode to intercept Sabo as she whinnied and tossed her head in fear. He whistled and guided Steed alongside the running mare, grabbing for the reins but missing them the first time as the rain had made them slick. It was cold and wet. His second attempt succeeded and finally Sabo slowed to a walk as the horse breathed hard, her sides rising and falling rapidly.

"Easy girl, that's it, easy," he said softly, calming the horse and drawing her closer to lead her back up the mountain.

Jared turned his head at the same time the horses turned their ears toward the screams that came from the summit. A chill ran down Jared's spine with the realization that the scream belonged to Kathleen.

Just then, the wind's strength grew and the storm front slammed into Jared's face with the force of a hammer. He lost Sabo's reins again. His mind focused on Kathleen alone. Leaning over Steed's neck, he urged the horse back up the switchbacks of the mountain road. As fast as he rode, he dared not take the shortcut the mare had run coming down, bounding over the slippery stones and shrubs. The rain had a godly force of wind behind it now, and each droplet of water seemed to cut diagonally across the world, lashing his eyes, his face, his hands. He had difficulty seeing even with his hood thrown back. All the while the same tormenting question chanted like an incantatory curse: *Did she fall in an attempt to follow me on foot?*

When Jared reached the place he had last seen Kathleen, the trail was almost impossible to read. Swollen gullies and rivulets of water ran all around. He shielded his eyes to take a closer look. The signs were marred by the rain. Jared sprinted toward the trees on the opposite side of the road. He looked for any twig or branch that would give him a clue.

Jared didn't call out for fear of alerting an enemy, whether it be man or beast. Instead, he listened with the keen ears of a Sensor, straining for some sound beyond the wind and rain.

The isolated clump of trees told him nothing. Jared reemerged from the grove. The horse stood, bracing with his hindquarters toward the storm, head down.

I must find her!

Rarely had Jared ever found himself in a more desperate situation. He knew from the sound of that first scream that Kathleen's life depended on the decisions he would make in this moment. He closed his eyes and took a deep breath to calm himself. It was the way Master Tove had trained him. He listened...nothing.

She must have fallen.

The thought pierced him as painfully as if he had been struck by one of the white bolts of lightning that danced from the surrounding mountaintops. Jared ran across the road again, his cloak whipping in the fierce wind. He approached the sheer cliffs that ran along the downward side. Only a thin band of vegetation clung to the rocks here, where loose boulders had tumbled to the river below. The gray granite, wet with rain, looked black. In the slashing cold rain he peered over the edge of the cliff. His heart pounded as he feared to see the shattered remains of the young woman he was sworn to protect.

The dazzling flashes of lightning did not reveal a crumpled form of a princess on the rocks. He did not see Kathleen's face surrounded by a fan of wet hair and blood as he imagined.

Where is she?

Jared decided to risk a call out to her, hoping for a response. "Kathleen!" he yelled, trying to be heard above the storm.

Is that a muffled cry?

He ran a few paces to the right and called again.

"Kathleen!"

Then he heard the sound again. Like a person choking and crying against an obstacle. He moved toward the sound, trying to place it.

Perhaps she has fallen to a ledge below?

He turned to look, leaning over the edge as far as he dared. Another enormous crack of thunder boomed, and the night sky became flooded with a flash of light as bright as noonday. In that flicker of lightening, the Sīhalt Guardian saw a sight that made him reach for his sword.

Jared drew the blade in that instant. It was too late. The Delathrane barbarian, crouching in the grass, holding Kathleen with a hand across her mouth, managed to land a heavy kick on

Jared's hip. A cry was heard, and Jared was sent tumbling out over the edge of the cliff. Even as his body moved outward, into the cold open air, the Sīhalt felt relief that Kathleen yet lived.

But as he had been struck, Jared had slashed the leg of the brute before it could be withdrawn. It was the Delathrane whose cry had been heard. And now the skin and muscles lay open from his inner thigh to below the knee. Jared knew the man would not survive the wound. Arterial blood loss would loosen his grasp on Kathleen and the Delathrane would be dead in minutes.

But I shall die in seconds, he thought to himself.

Time moved slowly for Jared as gravity began its assured course. His body rotated and twisted, compensating for the sword stroke he made in mid-air. His cloak billowed in the storm, rising like the hood of a snake. Jared fell toward the rocks below.

During that fall, his thoughts bent on how he might have done better to protect Kathleen. An image of their conversation the final evening in Altrastadt came back to his mind, a vision of her turning and smiling at him while the candles illuminated the highlights in her red hair, and the way her eyes glistened as she smiled.

I was not pretending.

His thoughts coalesced around a single truth.

I do love her.

BARBARIAN SUMMIT

"W here is Povni?" Cedric said. He looked up at his sodden barbarian warriors. They looked pathetic after the rain. He could tell from the sound of hooves on the wet earth that they had captured a horse.

"He's dead," Rumner replied, "but he killed that Sīhalt too. Kicked him right over the cliff. Didn't he, Kalt?"

Cedric set down his small fingernail-cleaning knife and stood. He looked intently at the returning war band.

"Povni killed the Sīhalt?" Cedric was disappointment at the news. He wanted to be the one to end the Sīhalt Guardian's life.

He owes me that chance! he thought.

"Yeah, Povni grabbed the girl while *Der'Antha* was chasing her horse," Kant explained. "She screamed, and he came flying like an arrow back up to the top of the summit. With the stormy weather, he had trouble finding us," said Kalt.

He chuckled the way men do when they realize they have avoided death against the odds.

"What happened? Tell me exactly what happened," Cedric said slowly. He drew close and the members of the war band knew this was no time for lightheartedness. Their king towered over them and stared intently at each of them

"Where is the carcass of this Sīhalt?" the Serpent King asked. He looked at the bundle dropped over the back of the horse.

"That's the princess, and she's alive, but Povni almost choked her out when she was trying to scream, and she is still sleeping from it," Rumner explained.

"The Sīhalt," Cedric hissed. "Where is the Sīhalt?"

"I suspect he's lying on the rock down in the ravine, right beside Povni. We rolled Povni over the side too once he stopped breathing. We knew you wouldn't want one of the band lying along the road for travelers to see. Now a person would have to lean out over the cliff to see him lying down there. It is steep," Kalt said, turning his wrist and forearm to demonstrate the angle.

We had better learn to adapt quickly if we are to defeat these Handri in their own lands. By the Serpent's Egg, we will. Cedric swore to himself.

Cedric noticed the knife tucked into Kalt's waistband. Surely Povni must be dead, if Kalt had his knife. Povni had treasured that knife more than anything. If Povni had any breath in his lungs, he would kill anyone who laid a hand on it.

Cedric nodded. "You saw the Sīhalt hit the rocks?" he said, his face stern in the torchlight.

The war band leaders nodded vigorously along with their men.

"We heard him hit the rocks, and we all saw him lying there at the bottom. He wasn't moving, and it was a long way down."

"Why did you not bring his body back? You took time to bring me this horse," said Cedric, pointing to Sabo.

"We tried to bring the other horse too, but it wouldn't move, just stood there and refused to move. We tugged on the reins and then he reared up to strike us when we got close. We think that stallion must have gone crazy from the lighting. The black horse turned in circles at that spot on the summit, trying to kick my head in. I told Rumner and the others to leave it and see if he would follow the other horse."

Cedric the Serpent King stepped forward and grabbed Kalt by the shoulder, his grip so strong the hardened warrior lowered his eyes and winced.

"You *do* remember the reason for our being in these mountains, don't you Kalt?"

Kalt's tattooed face began to quiver.

"If the river… was not so swollen with rain… we would have brought him back…my king. Only we would have had to cross the raging currents at least three times on the way down to reach him among the sheer cliffs."

Cedric tightened his grip. "I do not want to hear excuses. We came here to retrieve the honor of our clans from *Der'Antha*. The debt he owes me will be paid when I drink from his skull. If his head is shattered upon the rocks I will piece it back together." He paused and looked at the Delathrane. "If it is lost, perhaps I will use your skull and pretend that it is the Sīhalt Guardian's."

Kalt shivered and nodded vigorously. Cedric leaned in close to his ear. "We will retrieve the body of this Sīhalt, you and I," he whispered, "because if we don't…"

Kalt kept nodding. "Yes, my king, of course. Yes…"

When Cedric let go of the pitiful Delathrane he turned to the rest of the war band—they stood in the clearing, staring at him, waiting.

"Watch the girl. Make sure she is alive and kept safe. She is of no use to us dead. Now gather your weapons and men. Leave the horses here, they will not go where we are going."

The full thuds of a thousand footsteps filled the misty air as the Delathrane barbarians began to run in double-file in the early morning light, climbing back to the summit with its deadly cliffs. Cedric set the pace, his leather boots padding softly on the wet road. He breathed evenly and deeply, his arms swinging in stride with his body moving forward in a run. The other warriors, both young and old, pushed themselves to keep up with their leader's remarkable pace.

ON THE ROCKS

The wind pushed Jared away from the face of the cliff. He was falling, and the rotation from the last slash of his sword had sent the Sīhalt tumbling downward in a disorienting spin. He couldn't tell which way was up or down, where the sky was, or for how much longer he would fall before crashing into the rocks below. He had only one hope.

Jared gathered, with his left hand, what he could of his Sīhalt cloak. The thin, tightly-woven black cloak was silk-soft in his hands.

Please, work for me, he thought, each word scrambling in his brain. The wind rush around his ears like the screams of horses. He was closer now, he could sense it. And then he crashed into the rocks. As soon as the first fiber of the cloak struck the wet rock it snapped into an rigid shield. The fall bent Jared into an unnatural shape. His head struck the rocks, even as his body was protected from the brunt of the landing on stone.

All of the air was driven from his lungs in one violent sigh. When his body came to rest at the bottom, the Sīhalt cloak finally softened again, settling gently over his body. The rain continued to fall, and he lay as a dead man.

SIGNS OF SURVIVAL

C edric leaned as far over the precipice as he dared. He strained to find the form of the Sīhalt Guardian on the rocks below.

"I see the blackbirds of the dead. We will go down and remove Der'Antha's head," the Serpent King said.

Cedric had played the moment over and over again in his mind since the terrible day. He had heard no sign of Der'Antha after he left their people without a king.

"I thought Der'Antha would come looking for his brother." Cedric would say to his people. "But perhaps I am mistaken. Der'Antha is cunning for sure, but the *Handri* do not really love their families like us. They have no tribes, only nations," he explained. The people nodded in ascent.

And now his search was over.

They made their way carefully down the steep slopes, turning around at times to place a hand on the sharp stones and lower themselves down a jagged step or slick boulder.

When their feet were finally on the soft green grass of the valley floor the Delathranes walked confidently toward the flock of vultures that jostled each other for access to a meal.

Vultures perched on the largest rocks along the river. Some spread their wings in the sunlight that bathed the valley. They squawked disagreeably at the men.

Cedric stopped and picked up an object from the ground. He held it up to the sunlight and the thing glinted, its shiny surface catching the light and reflecting it back into his eyes. His reflection in the shiny metal tube was stretched wide by the curve. It showed a face riven with rage.

Cedric looked at the mangled body on the ground. He sprinted to it and scattered the carrion birds. The clothing was clearly that of Povni's although the features were no longer recognizable after the vultures had done their work. Cedric ran to the river's edged and looked up trying to estimate if it were possible that the a person could have landed in the water. He decided it was not possible.

"Do you know what this is?" he asked Kalt as he stormed back to his followers.

Kalt looked confused, he squinted and got a closer look at the item.

"I have never seen one before," he said.

"Neither have I," Cedric said, his voice trembling with the difficulty with which the barbarian king restrained himself. "Neither had Povni I am sure." He continued, gesturing toward the broken body on the ground.

"What does it do?" a warrior asked.

"It proves that Der'Antha is still alive," Cedric said and lunged to grab Kalt by the throat. The man struggled to pull the grip from his neck but Cedric's strong hands held fast. The Serpent King leaned in close to Kalt and whispered, "The Sīhalt is still alive, and so are you. You will keep your skull a while longer while we hunt for his. You said Der'Antha was dead. He is not." Cedric released the man who fell to his knees and gasped for air as he crouched to protect himself and coughed loudly.

Again Cedric had the thought that perhaps he *was* chasing a spirit instead of a man.

How had he survived the fall?

"It is better this way," Cedric said, "now I will yet have my revenge." He crushed the metal tube between his fingers and crumpled it up in his hand. Then the Serpent King stuck the thing in the pouch at his waist and turned to go.

STOLEN BRIDE

"Come on, Kathleen!"

The boy stood behind her, holding out his hand impatiently. "You promised me you would show me the ocean."

The little girl with red curls smiled but buried her face deeper in her mother's skirts. Only one of her bright green eyes was visible, surrounded by a sprinkling of freckles.

Queen Annalise knelt down to her daughter's level.

"Father and I need to speak with Emperor Kade and Empress Rema." She brought out the small handkerchief once more and held it to her mouth. The cough was getting worse.

The sandy-haired boy that stood close by still held out his hand, his eyes bright with hope.

"Don't you know we are going to be married when we get older? That's what our parents are talking about," he said.

This made Kathleen shrink back in embarrassment. The princess rarely had visitors to her home in Candoreth, and she had never been told to play with a boy before.

Presently, she looked up at her mother to see if what the boy had said was true. A serene smile spread across the queen's face.

"Someday you will be married, Katie. Prince Heathron's parents want the best for him, and we want the best for you."

"Your mother is right," came a deep, rich voice. This voice belonged to King Lukald. Dressed in finery, he emerged now at the queen's side, his large hand stroking her neck. He gazed down at his daughter. "Now run along and play, Kathleen. I bet Prince Heathron would like to see your horse." He leveled his eyes at the boy, whose eyebrows rose with a short intake of breath.

Kathleen brightened at this suggestion. She turned back to the boy.

"Do you ride horses?" she asked, and the little prince laughed.

"I'm eight years old. Of course I ride! I'll show you how."

"Well I already know how to ride. Hurricane is my horse. He is really fast," Kathleen replied.

"Let's race to the stables then and see who gets to ride him first!"

Princess Kathleen considered this for a moment, then made to spring into a sprint across the courtyard. Quick on his heels, the prince darted off ahead.

Kathleen watched him go. He didn't turn back. Instead of chasing him, she was more interested in what the grown-ups were talking about. Softly, she padded across the hallway, back to grand double doors, and peered around the edge, listening.

"It's true what they say. The city of Candoreth possesses a truly amazing view. I wish we had such a warm and sunny view of the water from our home," Empress Rema sighed, leaning over the ornate railing of the viewing veranda and gazing across the stretching lands.

"The sea breeze does help to moderate the heat," Queen Annalise said.

The empress's brow hardened a little as she pursed her lips in concern. "Queen Annalise, I noticed you have a recurring cough. I thought those of us in the cold north were the only ones to suffer from such ailments. May I offer you some remedies?"

"Oh, thank you, Empress Rema, you are too kind, but this is nothing," Annalise replied, waving a dismissive hand through the air. "It came all of a sudden and I expect it will go away just as quickly." She laughed weakly, then coughed again, this time more vigorously.

"We would love to have you visit the capital. You should come to Tyath next summer," Rema said.

Analise replied with a sigh, "Oh, how dearly I would want to see the snow. I've never seen ice outside before."

"Then you must surely journey to our palace. We have lots of ice and snow. Though the sailing can be difficult in the winter."

"Yes, depending on the month of your visit, you might get snowed in with us," Emperor Kade warned. His voice, Kathleen thought, was equally as deep as her father's, King Lukald, but not quite as rich.

"Promise me you'll take me north to see the great city of Tyath," Annalise said, turning to Kathleen's father.

"I would love to see our daughter's future home," the king beamed, cupping her cheek in his hand, before turning to Emperor Kade.

"Then you must," he replied. Kathleen watched the emperor rise from the seat where he sat, drawing himself up to his full height and spreading his arms wide. "We will look forward to welcoming you to our home, our city and to the Empire. With the marriage contracts all in order, I suspect you will be visiting many times. The people of Sundiland will prosper with the union of our families," the emperor added graciously.

"Then we will proceed to carry out the first shipments of trade goods as soon as possible." King Lukald spread his palms as if in celebration as he said this.

"We are not concerned, the memorandum of understanding is completed. All that is left is for time to pass, and our son and your daughter will be married to the benefit of the Empire. May the years between now and then be prosperous!"

Kathleen watched her parents raise a glass in a toast, and then watched the parents of Prince Heathron lift theirs too.

"Here, here."

Kathleen awoke to the force of a powerful hand slap across her face.

"Wake up *Handri* girl," a young voice said.

Kathleen opened her eyes, the dizziness still making her head swim. Her mouth felt hot from the pain, and when she tried to get up, another hand landed on her face again.

"Wake up, *Handri* girl," the man said once more.

Kathleen steadied her posture and looked at the face of the Delathrane warrior leaning toward her.

The enormous barbarian's hair lay slicked back by the grease of some animal. Kathleen didn't recognize the smell of it—she was thankful that she could not name the beast from which it had come. The sides of his head were shaven. His neck was a bundle of sinew and muscle. His voice contained a strange hiss as he spoke. Kathleen saw that his tongue was split in two, like that of a snake. The wide scar on his face, lined up with the divided tongue, made the ugly visage twice as fierce.

"You are the Serpent King."

"I want you to scream," he said.

Kathleen furrowed her brow, trying to fend off a headache that threatened to dance across her forehead.

"I have a headache coming on," she said defiantly. "If I scream, it will only get worse."

"When we are ready, you will scream," he promised with an evil grin.

The barbarian tightened the leather thong that bound her wrists, and Kathleen winced as it cut deeper into her flesh. What could she do?

She shivered with fear. How would he make her scream? Kathleen determined to be brave. Barbarous people often respected the virtue of fortitude, if they valued no others.

"You ride on horseback?" the hulking man asked.

"I certainly can't walk with my ankles tied together. I might be able to ride side-saddle," she said.

"Side-saddle?" He looked confused, then looked at her and back to the saddle a few times. He seemed to finally understand. He picked her up and dumped her unceremoniously sideways across the horse's back like a blanket roll. Her wind was knocked out from the rough treatment. Kathleen struggled to breathe. She should have kept her mouth shut. They lashed her down and secured a rope to the next horse in the line.

They travelled a trail that was narrow and overgrown. Kathleen could not avoid her feet and head being dragged through the brush. Anything that protruded beyond the belly off the horse was exposed to thorns and thistles. Branches swatted her face, neck and arms. The barbarian king held the end of the rope leading the horse. He pulled her along without noticing the difference.

In the darkness of the night, she could hear the words and smell the sweat of her captors. From the sound of many feet, she knew other groups of barbarians had joined them as well. Kathleen tried to think of why a Delathrane war band would be traveling this far east across the Great River. To get to her, they had already crossed at least two borders of kingdoms within the empire. Delathranes had not been seen this far into Desnia for three generations.

Kathleen listened to see what she might learn. There must be some reason they were keeping her alive. They spoke with a thick barbarian accent, and she did not catch every word.

"Povni is dead," one of them stated.

"So is the Sīhalt?" another asked.

"Yeah, he fell to the rocks," said the first.

Upon hearing this, Kathleen felt like a blade had passed through her.

Could someone survive a fall from those heights? she thought.

"Your man, *Der'Antha*, he hit rocks hard," the barbarian said, laughing and smacking his hands together, palm against palm. Kathleen jerked back at the noise and the thought.

"He will come for me," she said quietly.

"No, *Handri* girl, he will not save you," the Serpent King said.

He spoke with such finality that Kathleen felt her hope being crushed by his certainty. She recoiled from the sound of his voice.

The barbarian warriors just laughed.

Jared could not be dead! it was unthinkable.

Kathleen tried to think back to the last moment she had seen Jared.

He had called for her. The wind had been fierce, and she had been crushed by the Delathrane as he held her so tightly along the cliff.

Kathleen had almost jumped over the edge in the moment before she was captured. A part of her wished she *had* jumped over the cliff. Being at the mercy of the barbarians might be worse than death.

Kathleen struggled for hours against the tight leather, trying to find some extra space to wriggle a hand or foot free. That left her gasping for air from the pain as the skin tore under her resistance. Finally, she lay still, allowing her head to bounce against the side of the horse as it trailed her captors.

She would not believe Jared was gone. She felt sorry for having treated him so poorly the day before. He had done all he could to save her, and she had behaved as an ungrateful child. She had to think! She had to stay alive. She had to escape.

How would Jared know which path to follow?

Where am I? she thought.

The jagged peaks of granite on either side of the trail had been tall and sharp. She knew she must calm herself and use her mind. She was not strong enough to overpower the men who held her or the cords that bound her. At times, thorny plants tore at her dress where they bent over the trail. The gown, however, seemed not to show even the slightest tear. Not so for her exposed arms. Kathleen felt a thousand small cuts where thorns and branches broke her skin. Drops of blood dripped from her fingertips and fell to the wet ground. They were traveling west. The ground sloped downward and Kathleen prayed the horse would not trip forward on the steep slope.

What did she have at her disposal? Her hands were bound

tightly. Warriors walked not far in front of her as darkness began to fall.

An idea came to her, and she began to breathe in rhythm. In for three heart beats, out for three more. In this way she was able to occupy her mind and not focus so much on her physical pain, but on her own mindfulness.

If he is alive, Jared will come for me, Kathleen was sure of it.

Kathleen realized she needed to make the trail as easy for him to follow as possible despite the cold, the sporadic rain and oncoming night. She focused on the drops of water running down her back. She felt tall grasses and weeds brushing against her, and she allowed herself to surrender to the gentleness of their leaves. Even with her eyesight taken, she could still feel the parallel veins of the grasses and the serrated edges of the broad leaf plants. They began crossing a level meadow, and she knew what she must do. Kathleen spread her fingers even as her wrists were bound and allowed the plant stems that were tall enough to pass through her fingers. She was reminded of the lesson Melva had taught her on the beach in Candoreth. She allowed her Gift to flow, but only in small amounts. She felt a tingle start at the base of her neck and roll down her shoulders to her fingertips.

She shivered with the comfort of it despite her terrifying circumstances. She would make sure Jared would have a chance of finding her. In the darkness of night, the Delathrane barbarians would not see what she had done.

MORNING GLORY

Jared rode among the boulders and trees again. The increasing light beginning to illuminate the ridges of mountains. His path was downhill.

As he rode, his mind turned back to the beautiful days in Altrastadt. His memory of the dance with Kathleen shone brightly. She had been so beautiful, so graceful. Jared tried to remember a more perfect Sīhalt bride. He had never seen one. He remembered her lips against his, the heat of her breath after the vigorous dance. If that kiss had been shared in the quiet of their own room, instead of the crowded dinner hall, Jared was certain he would have not let go of her. Instead, he would have held her like that forever.

Then another thought entered his mind. He replayed his first meeting with Prince Heathron Dol Lassimer. The man had been sincere. Jared felt his duty weigh upon him, and he cursed himself for his lack of discipline.

How can I dream of her? She is another man's betrothed.

I am sworn to deliver her safely to her husband! he berated himself.

The anger Jared felt toward the Delathranes was fanned by the truth that Kathleen was never meant to be his.

The dawn continued to advance, and Jared could see even more easily where the trail led down to an enormous field of slanted rocks. There the barbarian's trail disappeared. The solid rock held no sign of the war bands passing.

Jared dismounted and crouched down to examine the rocks. The stone field was so smooth in places even he had difficulty keeping his feet.

"I need to go on foot again, Steed," he said, and placed the reins back over the saddle horn.

The horse shook his head but walked carefully behind his master. Jared sought for any disturbed lichen or newly crushed vegetation that might adorn the solid sheet of rock. He smelled the rocks. The bands had split up. They were trying to evade him. Jared could find no sign of the passing of the Delathranes, no sign of Kathleen.

He stood back where the tail entered the stone field and looked in each direction to see if there were any possibilities he might eliminate. Jared knew the general direction but did not want to choose the wrong path back into the forest. The terrain was so rough that within a few paces, a man might not be able to easily cross over to a different path. He would be channeled down a ravine on a slope that was isolated from the rest, allowing the Delathranes to get away. They would be protected by the sheer walls of rock that rose between the many possible paths. Fearing he was losing too much time in his pursuit, Jared chose a path and began to pull Steed along behind him. He didn't get far before a feeling of dread came over him.

What if she isn't on this path? he thought.

Jared began to breathe heavily against the panic that rose in his heart. Because he was a Sensor, Jared rarely lost a trail—his skills as a tracker were unmatched. Given time, he was certain he could find the trail again, but he did not have time!

Jared examined the surface of the rock.

He then ran back and looked closely at the entrance of each

steep ravine. Loose bits of stone tumbled downward in a small avalanche.

A single red flower stood out on the rocks.

A red flower.

Rock Flox in summer?

Jared crouched down on one knee and leaned over the small flower. He touched the small petals gently with his fingers. Then he noticed the smallest fleck of blood staining the delicate stem of the plant.

Had she made this happen? A shiver ran down his spine.

"You dear, sweet girl," he found himself saying aloud.

Jared sprinted down the channel, rocks spraying out from his feet as he raced to catch up.

When he rounded the bend of rock in the narrow channel, the light of the morning sun finally illuminated the rising slopes before him. What had begun as a single flower now climbed the slopes in front of him, a blazing trail of blossoms.

Jared looked in awe. The scene before him was so naturally beautiful. Plants of all kinds were in full bloom. Trees had open flowers from the lowest branches. Shrubs were ablaze in white, red, violet and pink. The smallest wayside flowers held yellow the color of butter, and small white petals of the softest materials. Blooms that normally would have been found throughout the spring, summer and fall all presented together in a single sight of amazing beauty. Jared could have followed the trail by use of his nose alone. Gusts of wind brought the fresh scents toward him again and again.

Jared smiled through his bruised lips and looked westward to where the ribbon of flowers wound its way through the thick forest.

She must have done this under cover of darkness. Very clever, he thought.

Jared began to ride along the trail that Kathleen had made for him. He rode swiftly, not needing to second guess his direction.

She must have touched every plant she could manage as she was led along the narrow forest trail. Even as trees opened into a meadow, the grasses and broadleaf plants had put forth new shoots and held themselves in expectation of the insects and wind that carried the pollen from tree to tree and flower to flower. Jared blessed Kathleen's Green Growing abilities and continued on, knowing he was gaining ground on the barbarians. He hoped he might even catch them later in the day.

He slowed to a silent walk. The flowers on the trail had ceased. The war band must have discovered what Kathleen was doing once the morning light revealed her handiwork. Jared dismounted again and told Steed to remain in place. He crept through the trees, pausing to listen. A man standing still, no matter how much noise he might make when moving, was a danger to the Sīhalt. It would not do to go blundering into the war band camp and squander Kathleen's only chance for freedom.

Jared settled down on a hillside overlooking the hasty camp they made. He looked through a small clearing in the trees and saw a few Delathranes walking about. An enormous warrior barked orders to the others. When it was safe, Jared moved to another vantage point and tried to locate Kathleen's position. He could not see her anywhere.

Jared crept closer through the trees. While pausing to listen, he crouched down on a hillside and just caught a glimpse of radiant white fabric near one of the largest trees in the clearing. He unsheathed his slender Sīhalt sword. He smiled beneath swollen black and blue eyes.

Now I have found her!

FOREST RESCUE

She sat, head bowed, hands covering her face. She looked so graceful. If she were alone, Jared would have thought he simply stumbled upon a forest fairy in sad repose. She looked up to the sky. She appeared to be weeping—or praying. When she looked around at the surrounding forest, Jared saw the thick leather gag tied tightly across her mouth. Her feet were bound as well.

Kathleen caught sight of him. Her eyes went wide in surprise. She tried to communicate with him, moving her eyes with the smallest movement of her head. He could not make out her meaning. Placing a finger to his lips, he crept forward. Kathleen shook her head.

Jared could hear the barbarians arguing over a game of dice. He moved with the stillness of a shadow. Suddenly, a twisted rope sailed through the air, passing over his head and shoulders. Despite his gift of heightened senses, Jared was unable to avoid the lariat. The rope was yanked tight around his middle, pinning his arms suddenly to his sides. His sword's tip scraped the ground, and then he lost grip of the hilt as he struggled to get his hands between his body and the rope.

"I got him!" a barbarian yelled. Another loop quickly cinched around his torso.

Jared immediately lowered his center of gravity, bending his knees and pulling away from the hands that held the ropes. He was able to get some slack in the rope and used it to his advantage. Jared switched to a martial art style he learned from a Sīhalt Guardian in Hestin. Those people threw off the ancient chains of slavery in their homeland, and founded a free nation in Desnia. They passed down the traditions to their sons and daughters of fighting with their feet only, as a reminder that their hands had been bound. Jared had studied their ways, along with many others.

He stepped side-to-side with a back step each time, always moving. Jared could hear the rhythms in his mind that worked with this martial art. The drums and cadence in his mind set the timing of his feet. The oncoming barbarian received a heel strike to the face and dropped, unconscious on the ground. Another loop sailed overhead, then another and another. He was caught like a wild horse on the grasslands of the west. Each warrior pulled in an opposite direction and Jared was held fast by six. He finally collapsed in the struggle.

They brought him into the clearing and tied him among the trees. Jared was standing, secured by ropes running outward like the spokes of a wagon wheel. Each rope restricted his movements in each direction. Jared thought of the daggers he had hidden in his boots and among his clothes. They were useless as his arms were pinned to his side. Jared struggled to breathe—the taut ropes dug into his skin.

Kathleen looked at him. She was trying to say something, but the gag in her mouth obscured the words.

The enormous leader of the war band walked toward the Sīhalt. He was bare to the waist and walked with purpose. He stroked the stubble of his jaw and the sides of his head. He held a small knife in his hand.

"Hello again," the barbarian said, hissing the Delathrane accent. A serpent-like tongue flicked between his teeth, the gap at the center matching the vertical scar that marked his face. "I had hoped I could catch you alive. And I have." He tested the sharpness of the small knife against his thumb.

Jared did not struggle to be free. He knew the futility of that at this moment.

"We have met before?" Jared managed to say, despite the ropes that held him tightly. The man wanted him alive for some reason. Now was the time to use his mind.

"You don't remember? I am disappointed in you, Sīhalt. It was not that long ago," he said.

A smile, twisted into a grimace by the scar, spread across his ugly face.

"I have had no dealing with the Serpent King," Jared managed to say.

"Don't you remember our battle, *Der'Antha?*" the warrior said, taking a step closer to look intently at Jared's face. The Delathrane gestured for the Sīhalt sword one of the men had retrieved.

"I remember this blade." He held it up in the light. "So thin, so sharp." He placed the tip in the soil and held up his small knife. "Do you remember *my* blade Sīhalt?" he said.

Jared searched his mind for any situation that fit the barbarian's words.

"I think you have me confused with someone else," Jared said.

"I know your blue-eyed brother," the hulking Delathrane said.

Jared held the barbarian's gaze and struggled to keep himself from flinching at the news.

He must be from Clan Razewell, Jared thought.

"I waited to see if you would come to rescue him, but you did not. The *Handri* do not love one another like the Delathranes do. Who would take a job to protect a foreign woman, for money, while his brother was in the hands of the enemy?"

Jared found himself straining against the ropes despite himself.

"I was the only one to draw your blood that night," the barbarian said, almost as if he spoke to himself. "Do you carry a mark behind your knee, Sīhalt?" the Serpent King said. His lip quivered with emotion.

The events of that fateful night in the Delathrane encampment came back to Jared in a flash. He remembered the stabbing pain in his leg as he and Seth fought to leave the barbarian king's tent.

"Little Cedric," Jared said, remembering the small child he had killed. The memory stung, and a part of him was relieved with the realization that the man that stood before him was alive. Jared felt a rush of relief, the guilt of killing a child lifted from his soul. His face reflected this peace, and the barbarian king reacted.

"I am no longer 'Little Cedric'! I passed through the pain of death and more. I lived when others would have died. I will avenge my father on you, and all of the *Handri*."

Grabbing the Sīhalt by the throat, the Delathrane said, "My father offered you hospitality. You returned his kindness with murder."

Jared struggled for breath as Kathleen screamed against the leather gag in her mouth.

"First you will drink with me," the Serpent King said. He brought out a gruesome chalice like the ones Jared had seen in the hands of King Raldric. The thing had a handle made of black hair. Jared thought of Seth as the barbarian filled the skull with dark liquor, the color of Jared's bruises.

Jared coughed violently. The ropes were so tight against his body, he failed to properly inhale after the coughing. The ropes constricted like a snake crushing its prey. With wide eyes, Jared clenched his teeth. Veins stood out on his neck and forehead as he twitched involuntarily.

The Serpent King grabbed Jared by the hair and yanked his head back. Cedric forced the cup to Jared's lips. The Sīhalt fought to keep his lips closed against the barbarian's foul drink as the contents poured down the front of Jared's clothing. The Serpent

King's muscled arms crushed the cup against Jared's face, leaving gashes in his lips. Jared cried out in the struggle, and Kathleen screamed for the Serpent King to stop. The other warriors gathered close by, chanting for their leader.

They began to relieve Jared of the weapons he still carried. An impressive pile of previously secreted knives now lay at his enemy's feet. The Delathranes gathered them up, hooting their approval. They began to untie the ropes that held him.

One warrior untied Kathleen and pinned her against a tree, moving her out of the clearing, away from Jared.

"We will kill her if you try to escape, Sīhalt," the barbarian promised. Jared believed him.

"Now you get to use *my* little knife," the warrior said handing Jared the small blade.

"And I get to use *your* sword," he said, picking up the magnificent blade.

Jared's mind raced. He sensed a change in the barbarian's purposes. The man planned to kill, right here in this forest. Kathleen cried as she was held with a blade to her throat. What could Jared do with a blade no longer than his thumb? He held the child's weapon in front of himself in a defensive posture. The barbarians laughed at the sight. The Serpent King stretched himself, preparing for combat. He slapped his powerful chest.

Jared rubbed his arms and legs. He felt numb from the tightness of the ropes that had restricted blood flow. One eye failed to open all the way, and blood poured from his mangled upper lip. Jared wondered how soon the feeling would return to his lower extremities. Jared looked quickly from the Serpent King to the girl he loved. In the face of such danger, Jared only cared for Kathleen. He did not fear for his own safety. He tried to position himself within the space that separated her from the Serpent King —even while doing so, he knew that another man held a knife to Kathleen's throat.

He took a step and almost tripped when his leg gave out. He

struggled to his feet. The purple root was wearing off. A wave of nausea hit Jared. The pain washed over him like the ocean's surf. The barbarians laughed, sensing another victory was at hand.

PLANT WITCH

K athleen watched in horror. She wondered what she could do to help Jared. She shut her eyes, trying to make the living nightmare go away. The man she thought of as invincible stood bruised and bound before her. The Delathranes held the ropes in all directions, using tree trunks to bind the Sīhalt more tightly in one place. The Serpent King held the bone chalice high over his head. He shouted a battle cry to his men, and the warriors rattled weapons against shields.

The warrior that held the knife to her throat pinned her to the tree with a heavy arm across her chest. Kathleen strained against his weight and her need for more air than the leather gag allowed. Her dress was wrenched to one side, revealing the necklace tucked beneath it. The barbarian saw it and removed the knife from Kathleen's throat as he reached to take it from her.

Kathleen looked down and saw her mother's necklace about her neck. The filthy Delathrane grabbed for it with greedy fingers. Kathleen used her bound hands to try to stop him from yanking the necklace away. She bit down against the leather thong tied across her mouth. It cut deep into the corners of her cheeks. Her tongue could taste the blood. The barbarian shoved his hand into her face. He slammed her back against the tree when he was not able to rip the necklace free. Kathleen saw the sunlight hit the necklace and reflect back into her eyes.

I am a Green Grower.

The thought formed as tiny seed in her mind. In the midst of the great mountain forest, Kathleen was surrounded by enormous trees, plants that would obey her command. These giant plants towered over the humans with their petty differences.

She leaned against the smooth bark of the mature tree. Its branches were twice as thick as a man's body. The upper heights were lost in the canopy far above her head. Kathleen stopped resisting the man who guarded her. Instead she tried to breath more slowly despite the gag. She allowed her Talent to flow. Kathleen placed her hands against the bark of the tree at her back. It was ancient, easily two hundred feet tall. She could feel the life within it. She could sense the sap flowing upward and through the branches. Kathleen felt some sadness for what she was about to do. She shifted herself to the far side of the tree. Then she closed her eyes and began to concentrate. She began to infuse the tree with her own will.

The ancient hardwood responded. It began to grow, but only on the side she touched. The tree had spent its lifetime striving to grow straight and tall. Now it obeyed the soft hand of a Green Grower and allowed itself to be guided by the girl standing at its base. The upper canopy, covered in green leaves, began to move to one side. Some of the branches groaned with the shifting of the weight. Kathleen pushed her mind and will deeper into the tree. She kept her eyes closed, focused on what she was doing.

She heard some surprised shouts from the Delathrane barbarians. They yelled, wondering why the tree was disturbed by a wind that wasn't there. They would realize too late what she intended to do. The bark under her hand visibly expanded. The roots on her side of the tree roiled the ground, digging deeper as she pushed her strength into the tree. With a thunderous crack, the tree began to sway more closely toward the center of the camp.

The tree groaned deeply like a giant finally awaking from a summer slumber. Then the tree shook like the sail of a ship, snapping in the wind. The side that Kathleen encouraged to grow caused the balance of the tree to shift. It became top-heavy and swayed dangerously. Branches on the near side of the tree shot skyward. The roots expanded, lifting the rocks surrounding the tree. The warriors stood, transfixed at the noise. They moved toward Kathleen once they realized how the great branches were tilting. Kathleen kept her hand on the tree. It appeared as if she was pushing it over. The strangeness of the sight held them spellbound. The tiny frame of a girl was pushing over a giant tree. The Warriors began to scatter, yelling for their companions to clear the area. Although the tree seemed to fall in slow motion, it moved faster than the barbarians. As the great tree came crashing down, the bodies of several warriors were crushed beneath its mass. Jared dodged the falling tree, but the Serpent King was pinned to the ground by one of the large branches.

He yelled for help and tried to lift the heavy branch off of his leg. The Delathrane warriors rallied to the calls of their king, and Jared ran to retrieve his sword. He grabbed the Serpent King's forearm and slashed with the small knife. He howled and released the Sīhalt blade. Fighting the nausea, Jared ran as best he could to Kathleen's side. The warrior that guarded her he dispatched without any extra effort. The man did not appear to notice he had been struck until Jared was past him. The barbarian crumpled to his knees, a mortal wound through his lungs.

Jared cut her restraints and untied the leather that gagged her. The Sīhalt turned to defend Kathleen from more barbarians. She felt weak from the exertion she had endured at the felling of the giant tree. She watched as the Delathranes began lifting the branch free from the Serpent King. He rose like the Cursed One of the underworld, unable to die, unable to stop seeking the souls of the living. She placed her hands on another tree. Out of fear, she commanded the tree to grow. Its branches shot skyward until they ripped apart from the rest of the tree and fell toward the Delathranes.

Kathleen struggled to understand Jared's voice. She still felt afraid and knew that she must escape. Since her capture, Kathleen had eaten very little. In truth, she was hungry already, and weak. She hadn't had the stomach to eat what was offered her. Now that she was using her powers so intensely, she faced a real danger.

In the haze that was her mind, Kathleen considered what she could do. She had never used her powers to harm others. It had never crossed her mind. Melva, as a Healer, had always helped others. She had always used her powers to comfort, to mend. The idea that she might use her Talent to harm others made her recoil. Then she saw Jared's trembling hand as he struggled to maintain hold on the hilt. His feet staggered. The barbarians advanced and Kathleen placed her hand on another trunk of another tree—it erupted with an explosion of soil as the thing bent and snapped. The tree crushed more warriors, their screams raw and filled with fear. The barbarians slowed but the Serpent King would not back down.

"Surround them. The Plant Witch cannot attack in all directions at once."

Jared and Kathleen took steps of retreat deeper into the forest.

Kathleen knew that she must be free. So many people were counting on her. Kathleen began to panic. She thought of her little sister Elayna. She thought of Sam and Girdy. The people who waved to her procession as she left Candoreth had such hope in their eyes! Kathleen's safety was theirs, as well as her success. They were all counting on her. Kathleen felt faint. She thought she might lose consciousness. Her heart pounded and she felt dizzy but light on her feet. She felt airy, like a wisp of smoke.

"There are too many, Kathleen. Run!" Jared said.

FOREST PHANTOM

athleen sprinted but no longer felt her legs moving. She placed her hands on as many trunks of as many trees as she could reach. The smaller trees shot forth with bushy growth. They blocked the vision that her captors had of their escape. The larger trees, like the first she had touched, grew twisted, leaning inward, and fell, making the warriors pull back, twisted obstacles in their way.

Then Kathleen felt as if she was being lifted up by wings as she ran. Her footsteps felt light. She could only hear her rapid heart-beat—the crashing trees sounded distant. She really didn't know what direction to go. She headed north since that was the last direction they had traveled. Who was the man she journeyed with? Her husband? What was his name? She couldn't remember in the fog that clouded her mind.

Jared? Was that his name?

J ared called out to Kathleen. She was becoming faint, and he could see the shafts of light penetrating the canopy also pass through her. Areas where her shadow should have been were still lighted as she passed. Kathleen seemed to float over the ground. Like a bird winging over a forest pathway, her feet seemed not to touch the ground.

He could not keep up. All the pain from his fall the previous evening returned. The purple root tincture's effect had worn off. The pain concentrated along his spine. Jared staggered. He felt sharp stabs of pain in his side and down the back of his legs. The crushing ropes that had bound him had left their mark as well. He had neither eaten nor slept during his search for Kathleen. He worried about her stamina as well. At least she was staying ahead of him! Jared noted more distant yells of the barbarians behind them. The peaceful silence of Kathleen's movements ahead was punctuated by the crash of falling trees. He had never seen such a thing, nor considered it to be possible. He feared that Kathleen was in shock and running like a horse might, in panic — only to collapse in the end, its strength and life spent.

"Kathleen!" he called again loudly, despite the pursuing Delathranes. He could no longer hear them the distance. Jared could barely see Kathleen now as he ran on will power alone.

How does she move like this now after being a captive for days? he wondered as he ran after this beautiful young princess. Through his one good eye, Jared struggled to look at the forest floor and realized he could no longer make out her footprints in front of him. Although he could faintly see her feathery form gliding over the tumbled trees and thick decaying mat of leaves ahead, Jared did not see any disturbed twigs. Not a single pine needle was out of place. She was moving at an incredible speed and not leaving a trace of her passing now except a swollen bud on a branch here or there.

Where did she learn to move through the forest like this? What is happening to Kathleen?

A worry rose in his own heart. At the realization that she might be in more danger now, Jared screamed her name.

"Kathleen, wait for me!"

The figure in the white dress wavered and slowed. Jared fought down the pain and weariness and continued to run, striving to breathe in regular breaths, arms pumping at right angles. He dipped under overhanging limbs and timed his steps to carry him over the fallen timber in his path. Kathleen's form drew closer as he ran. Then she turned and stood in the middle of the wooded path. Her bare feet levitated off the forest floor.

One hand touched lightly on the bark of a large beech tree, while the other was raised in front of her with an open palm. It was as if she were asking him to stop, or looking down the path and seeking to hold the barbarians at bay. Her form was not sharp, but faded at the edges and as Jared slowed to walk a few steps from her, he knew Kathleen was in grave danger at that moment. Kathleen's eyes were wide and seemed to look though Jared back down the path. She whispered something to him, or herself. It was a language he had heard before but did not fully understand. He had heard it in the bubbling brook on a quiet summer night as he slept under stars. He had heard it among the rocks of an ancient altar when the winds were excited just before a storm.

Kathleen was balanced on the edge of the spiritual and physical realms. He gently reached for her. She was flawlessly beautiful in this moment. Her complexion was pale but lit with an energy of spirit that made her seem to give off her own light even as the dappled sunlight that made its way to the forest floor passed through her. Kathleen's hair was lighter too, and seemed to rise from her head in floating locks of silvery flax, the way long hair behaves underwater. Small movements of her head made them drift slowly in the air.

She continued to hold her hand up and whisper. Jared could almost make out a question.

"Have you any meat, my love? For I would journey with you further."

Jared moved slowly forward and raised his palm toward hers. He was in awe of her image before him, but wanted desperately to bring her back safely to the physical realm. He moved ever-so-slowly and spoke in a quite tone.

"Kathleen, you are weak. You must rest, and eat."

Jared reached into his pouch with his other hand and retrieved a small journey cake. He could barely feel the sensation of her palm against his. Her attachment to the mortal realm was almost gone.

Will she have the physical strength to grasp the food? he thought.

Kathleen was almost completely in spirit form. He would go along with whatever she said, if it meant saving her. He decided to try another way.

"We meet at long last my love. May I hold you close and share with you a meal?"

Kathleen paused, her hair floating out slowly from her perfect face. Jared saw the eternal spirit of Kathleen's soul. She could read the truthfulness in the words he spoke. Finally, nodding slowly, she smiled. Jared reverently ran his fingers up her arm. He circled around behind Kathleen. She now seemed to see him as she turned to look over her shoulder at him, her hair still floating in illuminated waves in the calm forest air. They stood as an angel in the arms of a wounded warrior. From behind, Jared encircled her waist as softly as he would have touched a skittish colt—he was prepared to hold on to what remained of Kathleen's mortal body —whatever it took to save her.

Jared fought down the exhilarating sensation of holding her, so close. He slide a hand upward along her torso and held the food within her reach. Kathleen looked down at it with a questioning look, as if she were remembering a distant memory.

"After we eat my love, may I rest my head upon your chest and sleep? I am so tired, but I have waited so long for you."

"I will run my fingers through your hair until your eyelids close and you are lost in dreaming," he said, reaching past her shoulder with his free hand to touch her neck.

If Jared had been in this dream himself, he would not have wanted to wake. All that was noble and beautiful about Kathleen seemed heightened and refined in this moment. Jared felt blessed to be near a creature so divine, but he needed Kathleen to come back from the brink of immortality. He gently nudged the sweet bread closer to her lips. Kathleen took a small bite, chewed and swallowed. Jared felt a flood of warmth enter Kathleen's body. He encouraged her with another small bite and watched the blush of her cheek and neck slowly deepen. He could feel her physical presence strengthen. With a few more morsels he could now feel her body pressed against him, could feel his arms around her shoulders. Kathleen looked into his eyes and slowly the light of regained recognition came back into her eyes. She was no longer the spirit of the forest, but the princess.

"Did I fall, Jared?" she asked and looked at his arms around her.

"You were faint, and I kept you from falling."

"Are we safe?" she asked, confused.

"We need to find a place to rest. I believe we will be safe."

Jared decided not to remind her at this moment of the part she had played in their escape from the barbarians.

"I was asleep?" she said, somewhat confused.

"We ran a very great distance—you are exhausted. Have some water."

"I am so hungry."

Jared gave Kathleen another journey cake, and she ate it immediately.

"Where is Steed?"

"I will call him in the morning when we can ride. Right now, we must rest."

Kathleen seemed to have no recollection of the last few hours. Without her help, Jared knew he would not have been able to escape. He had been in difficult situations before, but not to this degree. He realized he was willing to take risks for Kathleen. The odds had been stacked against him.

Kathleen knelt. Jared was pleased to see the movement among the leaves as she passed her hand back and forth on the ground in front of her. The light no longer passed through her, and her hair had settled, somewhat messy around her shoulders. He also noted that the cuts and bruises she had endured were gone. Traveling to the brink of immortality had Healed her as well.

"I am hungry, and I think if I get a little to eat and drink, I will be fine," she said.

"That sounds good. I have more food, and I hear water close by." Jared opened the oiled leather bag slung around his shoulder. Jared offered her dried fruit and journey bread. Kathleen accepted the small amount remaining. She wiped her lips and smiled. For an instant in that dappled forest light Jared caught another glimpse of the achingly beautiful immortal angel within her. He swallowed and stared at her.

"What are you thinking, Lord Sīhalt?" Kathleen asked. "You look like you have seen a ghost."

Jared dropped his gaze.

"No ghost, Kathleen, just a girl with an amazing spirit. You ran so fast I could not keep up!"

"I don't think I even looked back," she said. "I was so scared I ran until my side hurt and my lungs burned. Then I felt filled with anger." She frowned as if trying to remember something. "Then the anger went away and I felt like the wind," she said. "I felt calm and pure. It was the longest I think I have ever run." She chewed the sweet bread, then looked up at Jared. "Then you caught me before I fainted." Jared realized she did not remember the events of her danger. She did not remember calling him 'my love'. She did not remember asking him to hold her.

Will she ever remember that moment?

"Let me fetch the water for you, Your Highness."

When he came back from the spring, he handed the water to Kathleen.

"So we are back to 'Your Highness' now?"

"I am just in amazement at what you were able to do."

"Escape, you mean?"

"Do you remember using your Talent?"

"I made that tree fall?"

"You made many trees fall."

"Did I hurt anyone?"

Jared hesitated.

"They were going to kill me. You saved me."

Kathleen covered her mouth. "It crushed them. I ... killed them, and then I ran," she said, memory suddenly cascading upon her.

"I am sorry. It is a heavy burden to carry."

"Talents are for helping others, not harming them!" Kathleen cried.

"I would not have been able to win that fight without you."

Jared watched as the girl in the brilliant white dress contemplated this: her parted lips and wide eyes caught in that distant somewhere between pride at having saved the brave Guardian, and fear and disgust at shouldering the weight of knowing she had taken a life, many lives.

"I have never had to...kill before."

"If they had left us in peace, we would live in peace. Nevertheless, it is terrible to be required to kill—and live with the memories."

Jared placed a hand on her arm. She hugged him tightly.

"I am sorry for judging you. I called you a murderer, but now I think I understand a little of what you feel."

"When they took you away, were you harmed greatly, Kathleen?" he asked tenderly.

She shook her head and wiped her eyes.

"I am fine. They tied me up, but they intended to ransom me. I was not harmed greatly. You are the one who has suffered most."

She lightly touched the bruises on his face, tracing the edges that were beginning to turn a deep purple.

"I will be fine now that you are back at my side," he said. "We will find Steed in the morning."

That night they camped hidden high among the darkness of the boulders that were strewn throughout the forest. Kathleen used a bit of her new strength to grow a shelter of vines and leaves to cover them. Her eyes closed as soon as she lay down. As sleep came upon her, the Sīhalt Guardian watched her breathing slow and even. He stood guard a short distance away, wrapped in his cloak. Amidst all his bruises, pain and exhaustion, he struggled to stay awake. When he nodded off, he dreamed of holding her again in his arms and running his fingers through her hair.

RESCUE DESTROYED

edric watched as the column of proud Tyathian soldiers marched into the valley closest to the slopes of the mountains. Their banners fluttered brightly in the wind.

They must be looking for the Princess as well, he thought.

He nodded, knowing that this meant that he still had a chance to recapture *Der'Antha* and the girl. He had spent the last day and night searching for them. The Sīhalt Guardian had disappeared into the forest, but Cedric knew the way they must eventually turn.

Cedric stretched his aching leg where the tree had fallen on it. He reminded himself that he was not invincible, even if he felt like it at times. In the game of *Chendris,* often the victory went to the player that was most patient and yet willing to strike when the opening was there.

He rode out to the meadow with a small group of his warriors. With shrieks of surprise, the soldiers of Tyath quickly surrounded the Delathrane barbarians. The People of the Serpent formed a shield wall with every spear facing outward. The moment was tense, exactly what the Serpent King desired.

"You are unlawfully on Imperial lands, barbarian!" said an officer.

The Delathranes, standing shoulder to shoulder, tightened their ranks defiantly. The captain called a halt to the soldiers' advance. Their swords, however, remained drawn.

"Why are you in our lands?" the captain asked.

"All these lands you call Desnia belong to the People of the Serpent. You *Handri* are the trespassers," Cedric said with disdain.

"We are taking your little war band in for questioning," said the officer.

Cedric stepped forward, his weapon lowered. He stood without fear, his eyes leveled at the mounted captain's face.

"And what if we refuse to be taken in?" the Serpent King growled.

"It appears to me that we have won the day," the officer answered, gesturing to the ranks of soldiers surrounding the Delathranes.

"You *Handri* should learn that you cannot believe everything you see," said Cedric.

He smiled and pointed his sword at the captain. "I am calling for your death," said the Serpent King.

The captain had a look of irritation on his face.

"We don't have time for this," he muttered.

"I am calling for your death!" the Serpent King said again, more loudly, the veins beginning to stand out on his neck as he strained to maintain the officer's attention.

"Yes, yes, I hear you," the officer replied. "And I am calling for your arre—" Whatever else the Tyathian officer was going to say was cut short by the arrow with black fletching now lodged in his neck. It was followed by three more in short succession, each from a different direction. The officer fell from the saddle without another sound. The second-in-command looked around and began searching the borders of trees for archers.

"Hold the line men!" he said. "Sergeant, take a contingent of men with shields and search the tree lines." Cedric hoped he would turn his men to face outward. Then the whole line would be flanked by his men at the center.

Cedric pointed his sword at the new commanding officer.

A deep voice rumbled from his chest.

"Now I am calling for your death," he yelled.

No sooner had his sword pointed out the new commanding officer, than two more arrows sprouted from this man's neck. He had time to put the spurs to his horse before he died. As the horse galloped away, he fell from the saddle and was dragged by one foot, still caught in the stirrup. His limp body bounced across the deep grass until his horse finally stopped.

The soldiers, realizing that they had not accounted for all of the barbarians, became uneasy and began to look over their shoulders even as they tried to keep an eye on the war band gathered in front of them.

With a shout from Cedric, more barbarians ran from the trees, into the open field. Others stood up from the tall grass, no more than ten yards away. They held composite bows in their hands with black arrows nocked. The Tyathian soldiers realized that they, not the barbarians, were surrounded. Some tried to form a phalanx. A few dropped their shields and ran. Others decided to attack the war band in the hopes of eliminating the Delathrane group before being attacked by the wave of additional warriors.

Cedric climbed atop his horse. When it was clear that the Tyathian men were being slaughtered, he approached the young sergeant who still lived. The man stood breathing heavily, leaning on his sword, his feet struggling to set.

"Why are you here at the foot of the mountains, far from your Golden City?" Cedric asked him.

"We don't need to explain ourselves to filthy barbarians," the officer replied, spitting blood into the dark earth.

"I do not seek your death, only victory. Do you swear to lay aside your weapons and serve me?" Cedric offered.

"I am sworn to serve the Emperor of Tyath."

"Swear fealty to me or die," Cedric said, holding his bloody sword up before the remaining soldiers.

The man wiped sweat from his brow and held his jaw high.

"I cannot have two masters. I will serve House Dol Lassimer until the day I die."

Cedric was surprised by this comment coming from a *Handri*. He did not know that some of them would honor their words even in the face of death.

"I am *almost* of a mind to prove you correct at this moment, *Handri*," Cedric said. "Your prince is not even here to fight along your side. He is not a leader deserving of your loyalty."

"He is searching for his betrothed. He will be here soon. If you kill us, our prince will avenge this attack."

"We already captured the Dal Sundi Princess a few days back. Tell your prince he will not be married to her. She has been taken by another."

The Tyathian soldiers cried out in rage at this statement of violence toward their princess.

Cedric didn't mind if his enemies took their own meaning from his words.

"Tell your Emperor that the Serpent King has reclaimed these lands for the Delathrane people," he said.

"You will pay with your life, barbarian," the officer said through gritted teeth.

"I have already passed through death, *Handri*—it holds no fear for me," the Serpent King said, "You may return to tell Prince Dol Lassimer the sad tale of your attempted rescue. Take what few men you have left—you will need them in the coming days."

The Serpent King turned away without another word and rode his shaggy pony from the open field.

THIS MEANS WAR

Prince Heathron met the small group of ragged men making their way toward his regiment. Captain Jarek Bastion called out to the officer leading the group of men with tattered emblems of Tyath. He recognized them. The men wore uniforms that were no longer bright. The dark stains of bloodshed could be seen on each one of them. Whatever had happened, the men looked haggard and ashamed. It was unnerving to the prince. He had never seen men wearing the uniforms of Tyath defeated. Only in the illustrations of past battles did he ever see the banners of Tyath torn or soiled by dirt.

"Sergeant, where is your platoon?"

"The barbarians ambushed us around the curve of the mountain. They destroyed all the others," the officer explained.

"What of the Raven platoon?"

"They followed us into the trap. There were hidden archers and more cavalry than we could ever have stood against."

"Have you seen any sign of Princess Dal Sundi?"

"We were spared by a barbarian that calls himself the Serpent King. He wanted us to carry a message to you. The message is of the princess," he said. The soldiers in his company looked askance.

"Speak up, man! What did he say?" the prince asked impatiently.

The sergeant hesitated. "I would not like to tarnish the honor of House Dol Lassimer by speaking openly of this."

"Honor of my House be forgotten, Sergeant! What did this Delathrane say?"

The sergeant sighed. "He said the princess was captured days ago. He said she now belongs to another man."

Heathron looked like he had been punched. He doubled over slightly, trying to maintain his composure.

"Did you see her? Was she among the captives?" Prince Heathron asked.

"We saw no sign of her. We saw no captives at all."

"The Delathranes are savage," he whispered, more to himself than to the sergeant, before blinking and adding a little more loudly, "but they do not usually lie. What did the barbarian say exactly? Every word he used is important."

"He said something about reclaiming all of the lands of Desnia," replied the sergeant. "He said, 'We already captured the princess. Tell your prince he will not marry her. Tell him she has been taken by another.'"

The men of Tyath, circling the prince and the sergeant, considered silently the words they had heard. Many of them remembered the stories they had heard from their childhood. They were all too young to have fought in the great Delathrane War. And though the Plague may have reduced the strength of the Empire, the forged spirit of each man gathered on the grassy plain made up for that. The insult to their nation, their Liege and the Princess Dal Sundi made each one of the soldiers resolute in their decision.

Captain Bastion summarized their feelings when he spoke: "We will exact a heavy price on the Delathranes for the sin they committed against Prince Dol Lassimer, his bride and all of Tyath!"

"The savage vermin will pay!" a soldier spoke up.

The sergeant's gaze silenced him, and he turned his eyes back to the prince. "The force was large, Your Highness, numbering many times those we have gathered."

"We will have war, Sergeant. We will ride back to Tyath's walls and crush them. I pray that Kathleen is yet alive..." Prince Heathron said.

Captain Bastion's balled fists tightened on the reins of his horse. "We will fight to the end, Your Highness."

Heathron nodded. "First, protect the people making their way to the capital. We need to have the refugees safely inside the walls of Tyath before we make any move against the war bands. Call for the reserve reinforcements at the wall and prepare your men for battle."

The sergeant nodded and turned his horse into a gallop. Heathron, gazing into the middle distance, listened until the dull sound of its hooves faded away.

LAST RUN FOR LOVERS

They left the village of Lutain behind. The place had been deserted. Only the graceful waterwheel turning slowly in the distance lent an air of peace to the town. The smoke rising from the town square told a different story: the Delathranes were yet between them and the Golden City.

"Kathleen, will you ride in front of me?" Jared said.

"I will take the reins if you need me to?"

What little they had spoken since they escaped the Serpent King had been tinged with sadness.

Jared set his jaw. "It will be easier to protect you. I fear the mounted archers of the barbarians."

Kathleen slid from the back of the saddle. She intended to climb back up in front of him, but the Guardian surprised her with a show of strength even in his battered condition. Instead of waiting for her to place a foot in the stirrup, his lean, muscular arm reached back and pulled her swiftly and smoothly back on the horse in front of him. Kathleen turned to look at Jared but felt his arms encircle her waist. She had rested against his broad back during the day's journey, with her arms around his waist. Was it his turn now to hold her in these last moments of their journey together? She pressed gently into him, enjoying his breath on her neck.

"I'm sorry, I…" he hesitated, regretful.

"Do not say it," Kathleen responded, "just hold me."

T he Guardian held her fiercely as they rode.

Smoke rose in ghostly plumes from homes that burned along the way. At times, Kathleen could feel the heat from the smoke that rolled across their path. She imagined the families the flames had forced out, and then with greater agony, the families that hadn't escaped. Could this have been avoided? Could she be to blame for their deaths? She gazed at the charred windows, the blackened felt roofs and bare earth. The idea of so many people suffering on her behalf made her wonder if she should have ever left home. Kathleen could not see very well through the haze of smoke that rolled across the road and, to avoid the fumes, she covered her mouth and nose with the sleeve of her dress. It seemed as if the whole world was burning.

Noticing her discomfort, Jared narrowed his eyes and made a decision. "We can't stand this much longer. We have been circling for days. Every time we double back the scene is always the same, burning farms and destroyed hamlets. There are Delathranes between us and Tyath. We have to make a break for it toward the city," Jared said.

He clicked his tongue rapidly, and Steed seemed to understand.

Kathleen tried to match the movement of her body to the rhythm of the horse flowing beneath her. At a full gallop, Jared reached for the saddlebag and opened it. He pulled out three sections of a pole and neatly fastened them together. Kathleen heard a click as each piece was locked in place. He held it under one arm like a long lance, and Kathleen wondered how it would hold up to the impact of another rider if it came to that.

They rode across a portion of the Amaranth Plain. The Imperial road widened and improved—there were less potholes and felled trunks to navigate. In the distance, the Golden City emerged like a bright beacon of hope. From the small rise they could see the ancient capital city of Desnia, set like a sparkling gemstone of white on a field of emeralds. The highest towers and walls were adorned with bright flags. For miles around and far out to the Clearwater Sea, the Golden City could be seen gleaming.

Still she could not bring her heart to feel joy at ending the journey, or leaving Jared. The shining city was no longer her beacon of hope—it was a symbol of the separation she must endure—if they even survived.

"Despite all our travails, I find myself wishing this journey would not end." Jared said softly in her ear.

His deep voice sent shivers through her body.

Kathleen wanted Jared to hold her again like those peaceful days in Altrastadt. She wanted him to promise he would stay with her—always. She knew that his word would hold him when nothing else had the power to do so. It would be painful, and she already knew her wish was impossible. Even though she wanted to scream "Stop!" and tell him how much she was in love, she knew she must not.

Against her will, words formed in her mouth.

"Jared, the plain is very open and the road has very little cover." Inside she was screaming, *I love you, I love you, can't you feel my thoughts? I love you!*

"As long as no one is in front of us, Steed will out run them," came his reply.

Kathleen exhaled. Could he not see that an obstacle did stand before them! Even if they could ride openly and in leisure right up to the golden gates, her betrothed, Prince Heathron Dol Lassimer, stood before them. She considered again how she didn't even really know the man she was to marry.

Steeling herself against the emotion that she so badly wanted to express, she asked, "What of their bows and arrows?" He took the trembling in her voice for fear, and although she was afraid of the Delathrane assassins, her voice truly shook with the thought of their time growing short.

"Kathleen, I will shield you," he said.

"Jared." A sob began deep in her throat as she twisted in the saddle to look at him. "Is there no other road that you and I may take to find safety?"

J ared looked down at the beautiful face of the girl he had grown to love so swiftly. He heard the deeper meaning in her question. He saw agony rather than fear in her eyes: a reflection of his own soul. If he could have made an image of his heart's desire it would have captured the look in Kathleen's eyes at that moment.

"Our only hope of survival lies in our reaching Tyath. I cannot defend you against so many on the open Amaranth Plain. Our disguise is broken,and we are out of supplies," Jared said.

He was speaking what they both already knew to be true. Perhaps he thought to strengthen their resolve by listing the reasons they must go on, to make the last dash for the gate.

"And when we enter the city, we will be parted?" Kathleen asked.

How it hurt to consider, let alone to voice, the truth of their coming separation.

"We knew at the beginning of our journey that this would be our destination," he said.

With tears in her eyes, she looked toward the Golden City that soon would be her home.

"We just didn't know that it would hurt so much, did we, Jared?"

He looked away, scanning the distance. Unable to meet her gaze any longer. He blinked back tears and steeled himself for the dash to the cover of the city walls.

Jared first spotted the Delathrane horseman when he still had more than five hundred yards to ride for the Eastern Gate. He yelled to his horse, knowing that Steed could run faster than the Delathrane horses.

"Hold on tightly, Kathleen!" he said.

OPEN THE GATES

Chief Magistrate Dirm Upperslaw adjusted his gold threaded robes as he looked up from inside the walls of Tyath. From the grand courtyard, he saw distant smoke rising into the blue summer sky and decided to climb to the top of the tower-gate walls and take a look for himself. Once he was able to peer over the battlements, he smiled inwardly at the devastation. He shielded his eyes from the intense light of day.

Prince Heathron should have listened to his father, he thought. *This girl isn't worth the effort.*

"The barbarians are fulfilling their assignment enthusiastically," Lord Balfoest said, emerging under the bright light, his smooth footsteps too soft to be heard. He glided close to Dirm, coming to a stop at his side. The chief magistrate jumped slightly, alarmed by the sudden presence of the man.

"Yes, we wanted the girl captured, not all of the surrounding villages burned…" Dirm said. "These Delathranes do lack subtlety."

Lord Balfoest leaned in close and cleared his throat. "Be that as it may, I would gladly sacrifice a few towns if it meant we have success in the end," he whispered, covering his mouth to disguise his words. There were many guards on the walls watching the poor farmers and their families streaming toward the city. They didn't need some unfortunate citizens hearing something they shouldn't.

Dirm surveyed the crowds streaming into the capital, but there was no sign of the red-haired Dal Sundi princess, nor the arrogant Sīhalt Guardian. The fair-skinned girl would be obvious among the throngs of black-haired Tyathian farmers.

The people moved frantically within the walls, trying to make room for the continued stream of peasants that gathered into the courtyard of the Golden City.

"I plan to look out from the top of the walls. If I can make my way through the stinking crowds," Dirm said.

"They should at least respect your magisterial robes," Lord Balfoest taunted him.

"The common people irritate me. I will be glad when this Festival of Longest Day is over. I don't like the smell of the peasants — it is all too chaotic."

"We don't belong among them," Balfoest agreed. "Only the timing of this dramatic end to the royal Sundiland girl's Wedding Procession would bring me out among these crowds. I did not want to miss seeing this."

The chief magistrate rubbed his nose. If all went well today, he could lock himself inside for a week straight. The masses of wretched folk could make merry all they wanted on Mid Summer's night. He would not have to deal with any of them. The thought brought a spring to his step.

Once they had climbed another set of steps toward the very top of the wall, they emerged with a better vantage point. They could see for miles over the treetops in the distance, to the land between the city walls and the distant forest, bare of trees or buildings. From here, any enemy approaching the city would be spotted long before they reached the gates.

Dirm watched the sun make its track across the afternoon sky.

Soon it will be too late! The Sīhalt Guardian has failed, He thought. Dirm comforted himself with the Tyathian maxim, "Experience and treachery will always overcome youth and good looks."

The gates had been ordered closed as the last stragglers made their way through the internal portals. Dirm heard the City Guardsmen slide the enormous iron bar across the portals, locking it. The satisfying clunk of the heavy bar on stone made Dirm feel secure in the knowledge that he had won.

"Congratulations Chief Magistrate. You have performed admirably." Balfoest discreetly placed a small packet into hand. He recognized it immediately as a dose of dream powder. The magistrate closed his eyes to revel in the moment. Sweet victory.

Then Dirm heard murmurs from other soldiers atop the wall. Their agitation increased as they pointed to the distant tree line. Dirm hiked up his ornate robes and ran to the spot where they gathered, pointing to the trees. Dirm squinted his eyes to try to see what the commotion was about.

"Serpents and ashes!" Captain Jarek Bastion of the City Guard swore.

"Over there! Near the entrance of the old King's Highway," the Candorethian captain, Channing Dur Ruston, said, pointing.

"We have a rider coming! And he is moving fast," a guardsman said.

Dirm looked closer, shading his eyes.

It couldn't be! he thought.

In the distance he could just make out a speck of white, rising and falling, partly obscured by the smoky haze. The lone horse continued toward the city at a pace. As it swept into full view, Dirm could see that it was not one, but two people on the back of a black stallion.

The horse ran at a full gallop. Dirm could make out two people riding together. The man wearing a black cloak looked familiar…

"The Sīhalt Guardian?" Lord Balfoest asked, turning to Dirm.

"It …cannot be," Dirm said, leaning further over the walls.

In front of him, the man on the horse held a woman wearing a brilliant white dress. Her long red hair streamed to one side.

Captain Bastion swept the field glass toward the trees as he looked out over the ancient King's Highway.

"Open the gates!" the Captain Dur Ruston called.

"You will not!" Uppenslaw commanded. "He has no authority to give that command. He is a foreigner. The gates will remain closed."

Both captains, Bastion and Dur Ruston, along with all the soldiers atop the wall, turned to look at the pasty man in elegant robes.

They paused in surprise by his sudden command.

"Chief Magistrate Uppenslaw," Captain Jarek Bastion said, "I believe the black horse is being ridden by the Sīhalt Guardian who was commissioned by our prince to protect Princess Dal Sundi. Look here, sir." He passed the spyglass to Uppenslaw.

Dirm looked through the brass tube and sighted it toward the galloping horse.

"Oh, they do look desperate, don't they?" he said, wiping his nose. "But we can't be sure. It could be a ruse, a trap!"

"If it isn't?" Captain Jarek said.

"I will not leave my princess to die at the hands of the barbarians!" Captain Channing Dur Ruston said. His sword was already drawn, and he looked like he might leap from the walls if the gates were not opened immediately.

"We have been told the barbarians had her already. If you are so sure this isn't a trap, where is her entourage? Where are her banners, or even a herald? This is a ploy to get us to open the gates. The gates will stay closed unless the details of a formal wedding procession are fulfilled."

Captain Jarek Bastion looked back over the walls in desperation, biting his lip, calculating the risk.

"Emperor Dol Lassimer will have your head if you open those gates to a barbarian horde. You don't even know for sure who this is," Dirm continued. "You should shoot both of them as soon as they are in range."

A few of the archers on the walls nocked arrows.

"Hold your fire until they come closer! That is Kathleen Dal Sundi on that horse!" Captain Channing said.

The horse ran faster than Dirm had ever seen. The red hair of the woman stood out against the white dress, and the black cape flowed out from behind the man.

"It's definitely a trap, Captain. The contract stipulates she must have a retinue of at least fifty horses. I see only one," Dirm spat the words.

"I know very well the details of my responsibilities, Magistrate!" Captain Bastian said. "If the details were met, the gate would be open already."

As the stallion streaked toward the city gate, the man in the saddle raised a long pole. The wind caught the fabric attached to it and unfurled the symbol of House Dal Sundi, a passion flower on a field of white.

In a loud voice the man stood in his stirrups and yelled. His voice was faint over the pounding of hooves, but it rang clear on the wind. "I am the herald of Princess Kathleen Dal Sundi, Heiress of Candoreth!"

A cheer went up from the people who heard the Sīhalt's cry. Soldiers called to the people below telling them what they saw on the fields beyond the walls.

"These barbarians will stop at nothing to entice us. How pathetic. We will not open the gates," Dirm insisted.

"That man appears to be the Sīhalt Guardian," Bastion said, looking through the brass tube.

Suddenly the low-lying haze in the fields roiled as a horde of Delathrane horsemen galloped through the smoke. They bent their bows and released arrows at the fleeing couple.

"Open the gates!" came a call from below.

A tall young man sprinted across the courtyard and began

taking the steps to the top of the wall two and three at a time. The crowd melted away from him, and peasants bowed their heads low to the ground as he ran past. Dirm recognized Prince Heathron running toward them.

Captain Jarek Bastion called to the archers. "Take your positions!"

The iron bar slid back and the gears to open the hinges began to turn.

"You cannot do this, Your Highness!" the chief magistrate insisted.

The captain pointed out to the scene on the road below.

"She has been announced by a herald. He holds the banner of her House. Princess Dal Sundi has been announced at our gate. As far as I can see, I count at *least* fifty horses following her to the gate. I know my duty, the requirements have been met!"

"Take aim," the Captain of the City Guard commanded.

"Protect the princess!" Captain Channing yelled.

"Fire at will!" came Prince Heathron's next command.

A thick volley of arrows shot over the ramparts, arcing over the princess and guardian as they rode and descended toward the oncoming horde.

Chief Magistrate Dirm Uppenslaw grimaced in anger as the gates of the Golden City began to open again.

THE HERALD

She could not hold any tighter. Already the stalks of purple amaranth were a blur to her eyes. Kathleen tried to lean as far forward as she might, holding onto the saddle horn. She saw a black arrow pass closely.

"Dear Abbath protect us!" she prayed. Kathleen felt Jared lean even closer to her.

"Come on, Steed!" Jared yelled. "Give us your best, old friend."

The horse responded with greater effort from the urging. The large, clean-limbed horse poured all that remained of his raw power into this run to the gate. Jared gave the horse freedom of rein and leaned protectively over Kathleen, holding her with a fierceness born of desperation and love.

Then Jared stood up in the stirrups, no longer hunched over, no longer trying to make himself a small target. He lifted the silken flag aloft as they rode. Kathleen gasped. She realized what Jared intended. He called out in loud but desperate voice,

"I am the herald of Princess Kathleen Dal Sundi, Heiress of Candoreth!"

Kathleen could not contain her emotions as he unfurled the silken banner of House Dal Sundi. She let out a cry. The late afternoon breeze pulled and snapped at the passion flower banner. A cheer went up from the people on the wall. The laws were clear, and against all odds, the Sīhalt Guardian would fulfill his duty.

Steed became one streaming line from nose to tail as he stretched out his neck in rhythm with his flying hooves.

From the corner of her eye, Kathleen saw more black arrow shafts arc in the light of the late afternoon sun. The razor-sharp tip caught the sunlight briefly as it glinted and continued its path, now downward, picking up speed. Two buried themselves in the road immediately in front of them.

Why haven't the gates opened? Jared thought as a third and fourth slammed into his protective Sīhalt cloak. With the wind in her ears and the pounding of Steed's hooves, Kathleen could still hear the crackle of the cloak's fibers hardening around the arrow-heads, stopping their penetration. Another volley of arrows arched through the air, and she heard the horse scream in pain. She heard the pounding hooves and heavy breathing. A sliver of light in front of them began to widen.

"The gates…!" Kathleen said. "The gates are opening!"

Steed now seemed to be flying like a bird, or cutting through waves like one of the dolphins at the prow of her father's ships. Jared coughed and heaved as two more arrows hit him in the back.

"I can't feel my legs," he stated seriously, but he gritted his teeth.

The cloak would protect him from one or two strikes, but each additional impact struck deeper as the Sīhalt cloak lost the power to harden and clamp down on the arrows. First the arrowheads reached the depth of a coin, then a finger, and then a fist. Jared almost dropped the pole. As the silken banner flapped close to the dust, he managed to raise it again and call out to the city guards again.

Kathleen heard excited shouts and quickly turned her head and looked out over Jared's arm. Delathranes were riding hard close the gap. They had the advantage of the angle toward the Eastern Gate so that for all of Steed's effort, they gained.

It was fearful to see how these barbarians could ride at a full gallop and still be able to use their bows. Kathleen saw them gracefully pull back the arrow and release when their horses were in mid-stride—not a hoof touching the ground. In another setting, she might have appreciated the beauty of their practiced movements. Some of the Delathranes held only swords and did not bother to nock an arrow—they only rode leaning far over the neck of their mounts, yelling excitedly and holding their blades in one hand, using it to smack the hindquarters of the horse to urge them on. Some warriors held reins in their teeth and swung loops of rope, like the ones they used to capture Jared, above their heads. Kathleen knew that these barbarians would ride to the very walls of the city and not hesitate to spend their own lives in an attempt to kill them. Every rider, to a man, was painted with an emblem of the serpent and the egg.

Another arrow flew through the air. She watched with difficulty through her tear-filled eyes. Kathleen realized it was too close to avoid. Jared shifted forward to shield her. The arrow passed through his right forearm and sliced Kathleen's hand, the arrow sinking into the saddle horn leather. She saw blood, both his and hers, running down the side of her dress. The city was so close!

Now arrows began to rain down on the assassins from the walls of Tyath. Delathrane horses collapsed, screaming in pain, their riders trampled by the oncoming horde of horsemen.

Kathleen felt pain, but it was distant. She wished there was some way for her to help him this time.

"Hold on, Jared. We are almost there!"

His head wobbled from side to side.

"The gates are open!" she cried.

"I'm sorry, Kathleen."

He barely flinched as another arrow lodged in his right shoulder. He was losing consciousness. Jared's hand released the shaft of the white flag he held. The silken passion flower banner fell to the dirt and was trampled by the barbarians.

Men in shining plate armor streamed from the open city gate. They formed up, shield locked to shield, a bristle of spears protruding outward. A gap remained large enough for a single horse to run through.

Jared wobbled in the saddle as blood crested his lips. Kathleen screamed on his behalf as Steed stumbled, at a full gallop, through the gate. The princess and her Sīhalt Guardian were thrown head-first onto the hard gray flagstones in the courtyard of the crowded Golden City. They tumbled head over heels and finally came to rest in a pile of broken arrow shafts and blood.

They lay unmoving. The din of battle, as the gates closed again, did not wake them.

HEALTH FOR YEARS

Melva and Larissa pushed their way through the crowd gathered at the gates. The Sīhalt's black stallion lay on its side. Its hooves kicked the air as it tried to right itself. Melva saw Kathleen lying facedown on the flagstones. She had been thrown from the horse when it collapsed and skidded to a stop as they cleared the gates. The Sīhalt lay beside her—he coughed blood that bubbled up from his throat. Black arrows pierced his body from many angles.

The people of Tyath stood back, avoiding the dark horse that finally stood and trotted in a circle around the wounded couple. The shod hooves clattered on the stones. The stallion whinnied and shook his head in defiance at anyone who approached the Sīhalt Guardian or the princess.

Melva rushed to Kathleen's side. The horse reared up, lashing out with its hooves. The old woman courageously knelt before the beast and reached upward in a submissive posture.

"We are here to help your master," she said.

The horse quieted and stood still, breathing heavily through wet nostrils. The arrows stuck in the animal's flanks twitched as the horse shifted its weight. Others came to lead the horse away.

Melva touched Kathleen's brow. Knowing she had little time to act, she pushed a wave of Healing into her, and Kathleen responded by taking a deep breath. Her eyes remained closed.

Melva then reached down and snapped the broad tips free from the arrows that pierced the Guardian. She shoved the arrows, half-buried in flesh, all the way through in order to pull the barbed tips free. The man barely responded to her forceful treatment.

"Bring a stretcher!" Captain Jarek Bastion called from atop the wall.

Soldiers scurried to retrieve one from the gatehouse.

When Melva confirmed that the Guardian was free of the wooden arrow shafts, she ripped open his vest and shirt and placed her hands on the Sīhalt's chest. She began to chant.

"Sorcery is forbidden in the Holy City!" a Luzian priest said, stepping in front of Melva, blocking her. There was murmur of agreement from the crowd.

"I may be able to save him, but only if you allow me to work quickly, Priest. Now step aside and let me, by the grace of Abbath, try to save this man."

"Abboth has nothing to do with the witchery of the Blighted, or Talented, as you like to call yourself, woman. This man has lived his life and I am here to help his soul to pass to immortality." The priest wore a long ceremonial length of white fabric around his neck. The written characters scrawled along the length of the scarf-like material held prayers inscribed for those who soon might die.

"Praise Abboth, we must all die someday," a peasant woman spoke up from the crowd.

Dirm arrived to the chaotic scene. He used a handkerchief to mop his brow and nose. "I told Prince Heathron not to allow a barbarian Meat Witch within the walls. Not a week passes and she is already dealing in gore," the Chief Magistrate said.

The crowd swiftly parted as if an angry bull ran through it.

Melva looked up to see Prince Heathron Dol Lassimer breathing heavily.

"Step aside, Priest! Allow this woman to Heal them if she can," he said.

"Your bride is alive, Your Highness. She fell to the stones, but she lives!" Melva said.

"She has been touched by a Witch. That is why she lives," Dirm said.

"Take her to the infirmary," Heathron said. "Immediately."

"Why is she wearing a Sīhalt wedding dress? Prince Heathron, are you sure this red-haired woman is your betrothed?" asked Dirm.

"The poor thing barely survives," another said.

Prince Dol Lassimer knelt beside Kathleen. He gently lifted her hand. The intricate facets of the gemstone set in her ring caught the sunlight. It shone brighter as Heathron's face darkened. Kathleen was lifted onto the stretcher.

"It appears this maiden has already been married," the magistrate said.

"I must speak with him!" Heathron managed to say, turning desperately toward the Sīhalt.

"Your Highness, this man has already died. He is crossing the Waters of Night. It would be a sin to call him back from Abboth now," the priest insisted.

"This man has braved the dangers of the wilderness from here to Candoreth and back. He crossed mountain and vale to bring my bride to the gates of Tyath. I have questions only he can answer."

"The Witch will bring the Plague back upon us!" the priest protested.

"I will speak with him! Even if a Meat Witch must Heal him," the prince said.

"The dark magic cannot be used in the Holy City of Tyath,

under the very shadow of the Great Cathedral!" the priest said. Looking at Melva, he shook his head in warning.

"The Great Cathedral was built with the Talents. You'd know that if you knew our history," the prince said.

Melva kept her eyes closed. Chanting in a rhythm, she strained against some invisible obstacle. In a moment, the Sīhalt Guardian took a shallow breath. His eyes did not yet open, but he was no longer losing as much blood. The stubble on his face began to grow longer. She would have continued, but rough hands pulled her away.

"You will bring the Plague upon us again, woman!" a soldier said.

"Release that woman immediately," Prince Heathron commanded.

The soldier hesitated and looked to the priests for further direction. Prince Heathron drew his sword and immediately struck the insubordinate soldier down.

"Will anyone else disobey my command?"

The people stood transfixed. Their young, easy-going prince had just exercised his right to ultimate judgement. No one else spoke during that tense moment. "The Sīhalt Guardian will be Healed." Heathron nodded to Melva.

"Take the princess to the infirmary," he said. "The nurses will see to her."

The crowd murmured its disapproval of Talent usage. Most of them had lost loved ones in the Plague, and they feared the curse being brought back to the city. However, no one else spoke up in defiance of the prince.

Nurses stood by, wearing gray smocks with white aprons and hats that looked like they would fly away with the slightest breeze. Most were young girls, but the head nurse frowned at the crowd as if she had seen it all before.

Heathron knelt where Kathleen lay unconscious, cradling her head.

"She hit the stones very hard," Larissa said.

He smoothed her fiery hair. He said something soft under his breath that sounded kind and compassionate.

"Your Highness. Do not move her until we have checked her head and neck for injuries," said the nurse.

"I believe I can quickly Heal the princess," Melva said, walking toward Kathleen.

The people gathered at the scene once again murmured against the suggestion. Prince Dol Lassimer, seeing the reaction of the people, held up a hand.

"You must not touch the princess," Heathron said softly.

The head nurse addressed the Witch. "Tend to the Sīhalt. You have enough blood on your hands already."

Melva's hands were coved in blood from examining the Guardian. She wiped them on her apron. "I only managed to Heal him partially, though he may yet survive. May I have some assistance in carrying this man to a bed where I may finish my work? He has been gravely wounded."

Prince Heathron motioned for a couple of soldiers to carry the man away.

"I will accompany Kathleen to the infirmary," Larissa said as the princess was carefully loaded onto a stretcher. The head nurse, her face dark and sour, turned to her and said, "Surely, you do not expect to be allowed inside?"

"I am Lady Larissa Albodris, cousin to the princess, and the closest kin she has right now in the city. I will attend her bedside."

The nurses looked to Prince Heathron, and he nodded his consent.

The head nurse looked Melva up and down. "Surely that one isn't allowed in our House of Healing."

Melva glared at her. "If Larissa will go with the princess, I will attend to the Guardian. Now, we must hurry!"

"Just keep your cursed magic to yourself. We will not be defiled by your sorcery, Witch."

Melva ignored her, turning instead to Prince Heathron. "Your Highness, you said you would like to speak with this man. If I do not Heal him soon, he may be lost to us forever."

The prince nodded. "Do as she has requested!" the prince said.

Captain Bastion called from atop the wall. "Your Highness! The leader of the barbarians wishes to speak with you and Chief Magistrate Uppenslaw."

Heathron looked up and blinked, as if unsure how to react. He turned to the nurse and said, "I wish to know as soon as my bride or this man is conscious!"

Prince Heathron glided off through the crowd, climbing the steps to the top of the wall. He was followed by the slower pace of Chief Magistrate Dirm Uppenslaw.

The nurse began to warn the soldiers who were crouching by Jared's side, lifting him from the flagstones. "The Sīhalt Guardian has already been tainted by her touch. Keep him quarantined after the Witch is done with her work. Put him in the rooms near the stable."

The soldiers carried the Sīhalt Guardian on a stretcher the short distance to the stable rooms. He was laid on a simple bed in a stark room normally used by the servants that cared for the horses. A wooden chair was placed near a simple table. It held a wash basin and a small mirror. Overhead, a window allowed light into the chamber from above. The soldiers seemed nervous to be in the same room with Melva, especially when she intended to Heal someone. After transferring the Sīhalt Guardian to the bed, they turned to leave abruptly and took up positions outside the door.

Melva pulled the chair over to the side of the bed. The young man was breathing, but the thin rattling breaths were shallow. His eyes were closed. He remained unconscious. Only the worst of the arrow wounds had been addressed when she first laid hands on him in the courtyard.

Melva cut his vest and shirt away, revealing a torso that was punctured and bleeding in many places. The old woman removed the man's boots and unclasped the cloak still fastened around his neck. Melva turned his head from one side to the other. Then she placed her hands on his chest and sought the Talent.

She chanted softly and hummed. She took her time, feeling with her mind for the many broken areas within his body. She evaluated his heart and found it was intact, then she mended the vessels designed to allow his blood to flow. She was thankful the Guardian had been healthy and strong to begin with. Many, with similar wounds, would have been beyond her ability to Heal. After the delays in the courtyard, Melva had feared she might have been too late to save him.

Melva finally focused on the detailed work of repairing his lungs. She purged him of the clotted blood that partially blocked his airway. The Sīhalt Guardian coughed violently and finally took a deep breath.

The Red Grower followed the tissues and reconnected the large nerve that had been severed along his spine. His hands and feet twitched. Now she knit the smaller nerves and muscles that allowed the man move and stand.

She chanted a higher cadence, and the shattered elbow was repaired. The deep bruises she lifted to the surface and used her Talent to clear the black and blue stains from his skin. Melva reached out to his joints, where tendon met bone. She sought to strengthen the ligaments that had been shredded. What would have taken many years to heal naturally, the Red Grower was able to fix. She hummed softly.

"Child, I give you back the health you sacrificed to bring Kathleen safely back to me," Melva said. "But I cannot give you back the years."

Jared lay still. Sleeping quietly. Breathing peacefully. Melva poured some water in the basin and began to wash him with a cloth. She wiped away the blood and dirt on his face and hands.

When she had cleaned him thoroughly, she walked to the door and spoke to the soldiers.

"Will you bring us food? He will be hungry when he wakes. Bring fresh clothing too," she ordered one of the soldiers, who acknowledged her request and walked briskly away. The other remained on guard at the door.

Melva opened her small pouch and brought out a pair of scissors. With them, she began to carefully trim Jared's beard and hair, which had grown long in the process of Healing. He now had a few subtle streaks of gray at his temples, and it peppered his beard as well. Melva spoke to him as she worked, although the man continued to sleep.

"We can't have you looking dirty and shaggy when you see Kathleen again or go to meet the fancy folks of the city, no sir," she said. "I won't have them saying the Meat Witch reanimated a monster." She chuckled softly to herself before squinting down at him and adding, "You know, I think you may even be more handsome then when Kathleen first saw you in Candoreth."

Melva trimmed and clipped and brushed the man until his hands and feet and hair were in good order. When she lifted him from his pillow to brush the tangles from his hair, now falling past his shoulders, the Sīhalt Guardian finally began to stir.

"Kathleen!" he said, eyes still closed. "Where... Where is she?"

BARBARIANS AT THE GATE

The barbarian Serpent King stood outside the city walls. His thick arms were raised high, his giant palms planted against the gate.

"I have come to claim my kill."

The forked-tongued giant spoke in a voice all the people on the wall could hear.

Prince Heathron arrived and held up his hand to quiet the murmurs coming from his own citizens. He couldn't believe that this nightmare of a man was standing confidently at the walls of Tyath, in broad daylight.

Two of the tower guards cranked a handle to rotate the base of a Ballista, its enormous shaft tipped with iron. The bolt alone was the length of a man. The Delathrane shields would not withstand such a weapon.

"Be gone, or you will die at these walls," Heathron said. He wanted to show his people the barbarians were not to be feared.

"Give me the Sīhalt Guardian, the one we call *Der'Antha*. That will be enough payment for me," the warrior insisted in the same threatening tone. "I know that we have struck him with our arrows."

"We will give you the blade," Captain Channing Dur Ruston said, glaring down at him. "He was riding with the daughter of my king!"

"I want the Sīhalt Guardian who rides the great black horse. Throw him back to me. He is of no use to you now. I am sure he is dying in the courtyard at this moment. Buy yourselves some time, *Handri*, and throw his corpse to me."

"Who are you that I should deal with you?" Prince Heathron asked.

"I am Cedric, the son of Raldric of Clan Razewell. I am the Serpent King."

"You attacked my bride and her Guardian. You destroyed the peaceful wedding procession."

"I did all of this at your bidding."

Heathron looked toward Dirm, a question on his face.

Dirm shrugged his shoulders. "These barbarians are insane. He speaks madness."

Lord Balfoest made his way past the soldiers manning the wall and eased himself close to Dirm. He shook the silver-trimmed cuffs he wore to clear them of the handrail that led to the embattlements.

"What is going on here?" he asked in his voice that sounded like tearing silk.

"Will you give me the Sīhalt Guardian to avoid war?" the Serpent King bellowed.

"If the Sīhalt does not survive, I will burn his corpse and give him a burial by sky. The man has done his duty," Prince Heathron said.

"Can you believe the audacity of such a man, Your Highness?" Lord Balfoest said. "Have your men fire upon him at once. End this insult to the dignity of the Golden City."

"With an enemy such as this, war is the only answer," Dirm agreed.

Captain Bastion nodded. "Very well. My men are ready to fire on your command, Your Highness," he said.

"He owes me a great debt," the barbarian growled.

"He may already be dead, savage," Heathron replied.

"Then I would have his skull."

"I only promise to give you … fire!" Heathron said.

The soldiers manning the ballista reacted to the sudden command. The great bolt streaked toward the Serpent King. Warriors around him dove for safety, but he stood still. Holding his sword upward in a show of defiance. The tip of the weapon struck the earth at the feet of the man, barely missing him. The shaft threw dirt into the air. It sank deep into the ground at a steep angle. The Serpent King laughed. He took two steps, balancing himself upon the ballista bolt that had buried half its length into the earth. He climbed up to the highest point of the wooden shaft. The wood bent slightly as he walked up. The barbarian flexed his legs and jammed down with his feet. A loud crack was heard, and then the ballista shaft broke under his weight.

The Delathrane warriors cheered and rattled their blades against their shields. A few shot arrows back toward the tops of the walls.

"Your weapons will not stop us. We will destroy the Golden City," the Serpent King said loudly.

He pointed again with his sword.

"I swear to you that these walls will be torn down, stone by stone. I saw it in a vision. The People of the Serpent will run through your streets when the great shining walls no longer stand." Again the warriors yelled exultantly.

"We are the rightful heirs to these lands," the Serpent King spat.

"Our fathers fought and died to establish this Empire. We will do the same as needed to defend it," Heathron said.

"Your dead fathers are not welcome to rest in this ground. If you wish to join them, you may fling your dead out to sea. Your God could not save you when the Sickness of the land swept your cities, and yet our people were unharmed. The land you call Desnia is not yours. She is rejecting you."

The muscles rippled in his arms as the Delathrane gestured to his men.

"Knock over the *Handri* death stones," he said to his warriors. The men threw ropes over headstones of nearby graves and toppled them to the ground by pulling with horses. They kicked over the sacred symbols of Abboth's Eternal circle that marked the resting places of Tyathians who had died.

The men on the walls were angry. They surged forward and yelled for the barbarians to cease their desecration. The Tyathian military was livid and knocked more arrows to shoot down from the walls. The Delathranes hooted and mocked them, knowing the large trebuchets mounted on the city walls were ill-positioned to hit an enemy at such close range.

A heaviness now hung in the air. The people waited to hear what would come next.

"You have denied me justice," the Serpent King called out.

"Justice will be served in due time, Delathrane. Prepare your wretched nation for war! We will draw the sword, burn the scabbard, and not sheath the blade until the Serpent Mounds that pollute the western lands are level with the Amaranth Plain!" Heathron said.

The giant barbarian roared his agreement for war and leaped upon his horse. He galloped in a swift loop, gathering the warriors that remained and leading them from the field until they finally disappeared along the western horizon.

UNCOVERED

At the infirmary, the nurses began to work.
They laid Kathleen on the bed, and the head nurse raised each eyelid while focusing a beam of reflected sunlight into the eye.

"Hmmm," the large woman said as she examined the pupils.

"Strip her," the head nurse said without an ounce of compassion.

"She will need to be bathed. She is filthy."

"How is this dress so immaculate?" one of the nurses asked.

She ran her hand along the sleeve of the brilliantly white gown.

"This is a dress fit for the Empress," Larissa agreed.

"That is a wedding dress. The poor girl probably thought she would dance right into Tyath and marry our prince the same day. How pathetic," the head nurse said.

"Princess Dal Sundi has more decency than fifteen noble ladies of Tyath combined. She deserves your respect, even if she is unconscious," Larissa said indignantly.

"Touchy, touchy!" the head nurse replied. She looked satisfied that she had offended Larissa.

"I guess I should expect it from you," Larissa said. "All the Luzian devotees I have ever met are smug."

The nurse huffed but continued her examination. She turned Kathleen on her side and unbuttoned the dress.

"What is this?" one of the nurses said, holding the necklace with its pendant. Her eyes widened and she dropped the thing like a poisonous snake as she recognized the symbol of the Talented.

"It's true? She is a witch too!" the nurse said to her superior.

"No, she is Prince Heathron's betrothed, and she is in need of care," Larissa said adamantly.

"Abboth save us!" the head nurse said as she removed the dress, pulling it down over Kathleen's shoulders and down her back. The nurse stopped when she got the dress past Kathleen's hips. There, the white silken rope accented the soft skin of Kathleen's waist. The *kanatra* was tied in the same intricate knot that Jared had woven that night in the dressmaker's shop in Altrastadt.

"This cannot be," the nurse said. She looked up at the surprised face of Larissa.

"This woman is married. She has been claimed. The knot has been tied. Are you sure this girl is betrothed to Prince Dol Lassimer?"

"There must be an explanation. This is Kathleen DeLunt Dal Sundi," Larissa said half-aloud, looking in astonishment at the slender cord. "I last saw her a few weeks ago when we were attacked on the King's Highway outside Revonah."

"She came to the city today, alone, with her Sīhalt Guardian," the nurse said.

"He was hired by the prince to protect her."

"Well maybe he took his job a little too seriously," one of the nurses uttered under her breath. This was followed by a titter of laughter among the group that heard it.

"Young people have been known to make foolish choices. She is still unconscious, but the prince must be informed," said the head nurse.

"I can try to wake her," Larissa offered.

"It probably won't matter now," the nurse said.

She looked at the necklace lying on the floor.

"How unfortunate. Sterilize the room. I don't think that girl will be with us long."

Larissa shook Kathleen by the shoulder. "Wake up, Katie! Oh, Katie, you need to wake up."

One of the youngest nurses, with brown hair and soft eyes, handed Larissa a bottle of clear liquid.

"Make her smell this. It might help," she said.

The older nurses gave the kind girl a scowl, but she just smiled at Larissa.

"I really want to know what happened," she stated simply.

Larissa waved the uncorked bottle beneath Kathleen's nose, but the princess did not stir. She shook Kathleen more vigorously.

"Katie," Larissa said urgently, "you really need to wake up."

NEW MAN

He opened his eyes as if waking from a dream. Passing his hands across his face, he looked around the small room and then at Melva.

"Where is she?" Jared said.

"Hush now, child. Kathleen will be fine. You brought her safely to Tyath."

Jared, relaxing a little, looked down at his naked chest and touched the scars that were scattered across his torso. He remembered the arrows sticking out like the quills of a porcupine.

"You… you Healed me?" Jared extended his arm and examined the elbow that had been smashed against the rocks during his fall. He bent his arm a few times and smiled, like a child waking from a sweet dream.

"Is my horse okay?" he asked.

"That horse will be fine. It takes more than a feather in his rump and a tumble at the gate to take down a Windstall stallion. You presented a challenge, young man." Melva laughed. "I thought we had lost you."

"You did lose me! I mean, I remember watching you work. My

soul stood in the corner of this very room and watched you work. I saw you Heal my body."

Jared looked at his arm again, amazed that it was real. He had the elation of a man given a second chance.

"Miracles happen every day," Melva said.

Jared got up from the bed and walked to the spot. He turned around, realization settling on his face.

"It took you a long time to bring me back," he whispered playfully.

Melva narrowed her eyes. "But I did bring you back, Guardian." The tightness in her face melted into a smile. "It was the right thing to do."

Jared thanked her with his eyes and then walked slowly toward the mirror.

"I might have never walked again," he said, examining himself from different angles. Then he turned to her, suddenly aware of something—some prospect that caused him discomfort. "How many years, Melva?" he asked. "How many years did this Healing take from me?"

"It is good that you were a young man," she said. "Not that you are old now, it is all relative to an ancient woman like myself, but I'd say fifteen years. The spine was not easy to mend."

Jared grasped the mirror and looked closer at his reflection. The muscles in his neck, shoulders and chest were firm and toned, but when he looked at the face, he saw a man that reminded him of his father. The face looked more weathered. Jared touched the lines that radiated out from the corners of his eyes. The small furrows in the skin wrinkled deeper when he changed his expression. He noted gray hair mixed with the black of his neatly trimmed beard. He saw small streaks of gray along his hairline at his temples. Jared passed his hands along his jaw and over his chin.

"I am no longer young," he said.

"You are more of a man, I'd say. The Luzian priests wanted to let you die. You should know that Prince Heathron insisted that I Heal you." The old woman smiled.

"Prince Heathron is an honorable man," Jared said, hesitating. His eyes filled with a mist then, faraway and sad. He blinked and looked up after a few moments. "I must go to him at once."

"There's no need to rush, child. You have just been brought back to the living. Rest. I'm sure the prince will be along shortly."

Jared did feel dizzy. He returned to the bed and sat on the edge of it, next to Melva. He tried to make sense of all that had happened in the past few hours. What would Kathleen think of him now? Should he leave now to travel back to Master Tove? He had done his duty to accompany Kathleen to Tyath. Now what?

"Where is my sword? I would like to get dressed," the Sīhalt Guardian said.

"It is in the corner with the rest of your things. Your clothing needs to be mended and washed. First you must eat. You must be starving after being Healed. One of the soldiers has gone for some food."

Just then the sound of boots on the flagstones approached.

Jared listened to the footsteps growing heavier. His instincts told him this was no welcoming party. "You said that someone went to get food?" He raised an eyebrow and glanced at his sword as the sound of at least ten pairs of feet halted outside.

The wooden door swung open, and Prince Heathron Dol Lassimer stood with sword drawn. He was surround by members of the Tyathian Guard.

"Captain Bastion," the prince said. "Arrest this man and chain him in the dungeon."

INQUEST

The long tolling of the bells in the Great Cathedral rang out across the Amaranth Plain. Jared blinked into the darkness, straining his eyes to make out something, anything. He could see little. And what little light there was in the damp-smelling room was faint—it drifted in through a little barred window cut out high up in the stone wall. Somewhere distant, muffled, he could hear the slow, constant drip of water. There, in the darkness, he thought how he could have escaped the soldiers that came to take him. He could have killed them all, even without his sword—it would have been so easy. This, however, was a different story. Now he felt the heavy manacles around his ankles and wrists, and the rock used to secure his chains was as thick as Jared was tall. There was no escaping from this. Whatever fate awaited him, he was powerless to stop it.

Kathleen!

The thought of her filled his mind. Melva said she was safe. He assumed the Imperial family of the Golden City would not wait to have the prince fulfill the marriage contract. Maybe they would do it while he was still in chains?

Just then, the bells rang loud, and Jared could hear distant shouts of excitement from the crowds outside. The city seemed to be full of life. Prince Heathron and Kathleen would be walking down the white steps of the Cathedral, hand-in-hand. The thought of the scene was more painful to him than the arrows that had pierced him.

"Wish we were out there today," a voiced croaked in the dark recesses of the dungeon, followed by the clinking of chains.

Jared turned and saw a skeletal figure sitting on the floor, chains attached to each leg. The man was partially clothed in rags, he could see. He made out a scraggly beard, a sunken face from which ancient eyes peered out of a thousand wrinkles, and long, bony hands resting on his knees. He looked older than dust.

"Today is Wedding Day," his old, cracked voice muttered slowly. "The streets will be flowing with ale. There will be bread and meat for everyone in Tyath. Everyone but us—we don't count." The old prisoner's voice was tormented, longing.

"Yes, I know," Jared said, his head bowed. "Prince Heathron is getting married."

"I should begin by asking the obvious question…" The old man shifted up a little, straightening against the wall what little he could of his stooped back. When he was comfortable, he let out a sigh. "What stupid thing did you do to get yourself thrown in here on Wedding Day?" the old man asked.

Jared didn't answer for many seconds. "I don't know for sure," he said quietly. "I got too close to the Imperial bride, I think. I didn't do my duty."

"Close?" The old man leaned forward into the light a little to understand, and suddenly every nook and wrinkle of his face was illuminated.

"I sort of married her," Jared muttered.

The old man's face blinked in confusion at first, then his toothless grin was drawn wide as he cackled with wild laughter. "Yes…that would do it!" cried the old man, slapping his thigh and throwing his head back. "I hope it was worth it."

"She was worth every moment," Jared whispered, more to himself than to the old man.

There was nothing he could do. He had lost Kathleen. He tried to comfort himself with the fact she was alive and safe. Jared knew that he would never have the chance to walk again with her, alone in a garden, or admire the beauty of a mountain sunset walking arm-in-arm with her as they had done in Altrastadt. They would never again ride together on horseback, her arms holding him tightly. Jared remembered the kiss they had shared after the dance. Even though it had been an act, a way to convince the crowd of their disguise, it had felt real to him.

"A woman can be a dangerous temptation. Make a man fall in love when he shouldn't," the old man said finally, drying the tears from his eyes.

"She loved me too," Jared said, half to himself.

But the Empire stands between us now.

Suddenly, both prisoners became alert at the familiar sound of boots pounding the floor, approaching along the stone corridor.

"This ain't likely to be good!" said the dusty old prisoner.

Keys worked in the heavy metal door. There was a high creak, and then men with torches entered the room—the last of them was Prince Heathron Dol Lassimer.

He stepped in calmly, looking around at the prison, before leveling his eyes at Jared. "Leave us," he said, addressing the guards. "I will speak to the Sīhalt Guardian alone."

There was a shuffle of boots and clinking armor as the guards moved back out to the hallway.

"What about me, Your Highness? I'm still here," the poor prisoner croaked, his voice as creaky as the prison door.

Heathron looked at the old man in the torchlight.

"Who is this prisoner and why is he here?" Heathron said, aiming the question at the guards lined patiently outside but never taking his eyes from the prisoner.

There was some mumbling and finally a hesitant answer.

"He has been here since I was assigned this duty seventeen years ago, Your Highness. We don't have any records for him. He was here when I was assigned. I never asked his name," the guard said haltingly.

The old man, bowing while still seated on the stone floor, said, "My name is Maxwell."

Prince Heathron raised his eyebrows. "Oh... Well, what was your crime, old man?" he asked.

The prisoner chuckled. "Your Highness, honestly, I've been here so long I can't remember myself," he admitted. "My mind is like a moth-eaten brocade: it still functions, but there's a few holes in it!" He slapped his thigh again and began to cackle.

"He's mad," one of the guards whispered.

"Well, today you are free." Heathron smiled and motioned for the guards to remove the prisoner.

The old man got up. "What are you going to do with him?" He jerked a thumb at Jared. "Is he going to die today?"

"He must stand trial for treason against the Empire. He will take the stand in the Imperial court as soon as the festivities are over," Heathron said.

"Is that all? I thought he was going to die today, and if he was going to die today, I was going to offer him company. After all the time I've spent in here, I'd hate to see a man die alone. It's terrible being alone. You start to argue with yourself. I'd be willing to wait until tomorrow for my freedom if you were going to kill him all alone."

"I assure you, his life is quite safe for today," Heathron said. "When he is executed, it will be done before the entire city. He won't be alone."

"In that case, I'll take my leave," Maxwell said with a smile that folded his bottom lip entirely too far over his top.

"Thank you for the thought," Jared said. "Have a mug of ale for me, will you?" The scrawny figure knuckled his forehead and bobbed toward the door. He gave one more gap-toothed smile and ducked into the hallway, a guard leading him to freedom. Jared watched this play out before him, and he felt somewhat amused until Prince Heathron closed the door.

"Aren't you supposed to be at a wedding?" Jared asked, glancing at the small barred window where the festive sounds of the city could be heard.

"Why did you commit treason against the Empire?" Heathron asked, walking closer to Jared.

Jared gazed up at this man, the man to whom Kathleen was promised. His whole body was tense, his eyes smoldered and his jaw was set.

"I did my duty. Did I not deliver the princess as agreed?"

In a swift movement, Prince Heathron drew back his fist and slammed it into Jared's stomach.

"You should not have taken advantage of her youth and naivety. You will stand trial for treason," he said. His nostrils were flared, and he breathed heavily.

The Sīhalt Guardian absorbed the blow, doubled forward, and grunted.

The prince exhaled and leaned close to speak into Jared's ear.

"Lord Sīhalt, your life depends on the answers you have for my questions. I am trying to make sense of what has happened. I should be at the cathedral right now. Instead, my half-brother is being married today."

Not married! The prince could have struck him a thousand times and no amount of pain would have extinguished the relief at those words. "Not married..." he said aloud this time, as if by speaking it the words would secure its truth.

"What?" the prince asked.

"Nothing... I said, where is Kathleen?" Jared asked.

The prince straightened. "Princess Dal Sundi is at this moment unconscious, being tended to by the nurses. She suffered a fall from your horse as you rode through the gate, if you don't remember."

Jared felt a wave of concern for Kathleen, swiftly followed by that critical voice in his head.

Don't be foolish. This means nothing. She will never be yours.

"Will she be okay?" Jared asked. "Melva can Heal her if—"

"The zealots of the Luzian church are gaining power, and they forbid her to be Healed by the old woman," Heathron interrupted impatiently. He was pacing the floor now. "They have the force of the people behind them. As if that were not enough of a mess, my bride-to-be arrived, for all the world to see, wearing a Talent necklace, your wedding ring and a *kanatra!*"

Now Jared understood why he was imprisoned.

"The barbarians said she had been captured. They said she was taken. Is that true?"

"I tried to keep her safe," Jared said. "She was captured by the barbarians for a short time. I rescued her."

Prince Heathron knelt down in front of the Guardian. He clamped a hand around his chin and lifted it to meet his.

"Where did she get the wedding gown?" Heathron said.

"The dress was a disguise," Jared explained.

"A very convincing one, I'll say!" the prince exclaimed.

"I was honorable with her," Jared growled.

"Why didn't you rejoin the procession after the attack?"

"We were overrun. There were too many Delathranes between us and the main body of the procession. I had to find another way."

"So you went to Altrastadt?"

"We hid in plain sight—pretending to be a newly wedded couple there."

"Did you give her the ring she wears?"

"I did. It was part of the disguise. I thought she might change it to her right hand and keep it as a gift once she arrived in Tyath."

"When you were in Altrastadt, you had no other servants with you?"

Jared could hear the question that remained unasked. His frustration rose as he followed the line of questioning by the prince.

"We stayed in separate rooms. We barely survived our travels on the open road together, Your Highness. Does it really matter whether I slept in the antechamber at an inn? I needed to be close to her, to keep her safe."

The prince seemed to consider this, uncertain if he believed the explanation.

"Did you tie the *kanatra* about her waist?"

Jared hesitated, wondering how he might explain.

"I wanted to keep her safe. I believed there were spies who would inform the Delathranes. I wanted the disguise to be as true as possible."

"Did you tie the knot!" Prince Heathron shouted, his voice echoing down the stone hall of the dungeon. He clearly understood the significance of the Sīhalt tradition.

"I did," Jared admitted.

"Please tell me there was at least someone who can verify your story," Heathron said, his voice trembling.

Jared looked the prince in the eye.

"There is a dressmaker in Altrastadt by the name of Cara. If you can speak with her, she and her husband can verify that what I say is true. They saw me tie the knot for her in an honorable fashion. The woman made the dress the princess wears," Jared said.

Prince Heathron stood up and looked toward the dark ceiling.

"I believe I have heard enough," he said. "I will go to speak with Princess Dal Sundi."

The heavy door slammed shut. Footsteps faded away, and the darkness of the dungeon returned. Only the distant sound of cheering crowds in the streets above offered any variety to the drip drip drip of water—somewhere.

TRUTH REVEALED

"The prince will see you now. You may enter," the servant said. He was thin and straight-backed, and he wore that obedient expression that all servants possess as if it was drawn on them. The man closed the door behind Kathleen as she entered the room alone. It was high and wide—in fact, the ceiling was so high Kathleen thought her father's whole castle could have fit inside. Though she remained straight, her head still, her eyes took everything in. The colorful glass in the windows of the enormous space depicted scenes of victory from the history books of the Golden City. The sunlight poured in. It reflected from the floor, made from stone similar to that of the walls. It seemed to gather and then share the sunlight inside the room. Because of this, no torches were lit—the room did not need them—and stippling the path ahead was a stand along one wall, and on it rows of scented herbs burned, infusing the air.

Kathleen wore a green gown with trim of white and gold, and her red hair had been curled and partially plaited to reveal her slender neck. In this light, the deep scratches could be seen on her hands and face. Her face was an irregular pattern of swollen bruises on one side. Kathleen wore a bandage on her arm where the arrow had pierced it.

Softly she stepped closer to the throne. The sequined slippers she wore matched the fabric of her new dress, and they made no sound as she ruffled painfully forward. The color was fitting, she thought.

I am a Grower. I cannot change that he knows that now.

Despite her fear, and despite not knowing if it would invite punishment, Kathleen decided to wear her mother's Talent necklace again. The truth was now revealed. She wore the necklace outside her dress where Heathron could see it. Heathron Dol Lassimer held her in his hand. He could do what he wanted with her future. She was at his mercy now. Kathleen swallowed as she traversed the long aisle toward where he sat on the Imperial throne.

Continuing to walk as steadily as she could—one foot in front of the other—she finally came to a stop before the raised throne. Kathleen looked up at the man she was to marry. He sat with a simple crown above his brow. The shining silver metal held his sandy blond hair smooth to his head. Prince Heathron wore a maroon brocaded jacket with a short stiff collar. The cut of the velvet fabric mimicked his sharp jawline. Kathleen remembered wondering if he would be as handsome as the painting. She decided the artist had not done the man justice.

She bowed before him. The floor was cold under her palms, and once down she found it hard to will herself to stand up. Her breath was short, her heart thudding. This was not the way she had pictured meeting him.

"Kathleen," he said, breaking the silence with a rich, regal voice. Kathleen sensed the prince rise, and then she heard him softly descend the stairs. His smooth leather boots barely made a whisper on the steps. Her heart thudded harder. He was standing before her now, and with great effort she raised her head, and they locked eyes. The prince was looking so deeply into hers it was as if he were looking into her soul. But they were pained eyes, suspicious eyes. He was not smiling.

"Your Highness," Kathleen muttered, her voice weak. Then she curtsied.

"Welcome to Tyath," the prince said, and a little awkwardly he spread his arms and drew his handsome face into a smile. His lip twitched for just a moment.

"Yesterday was a difficult day," Kathleen said, touching the horrible bruises on the side of her face.

"It was. But that was yesterday. And today is the Wedding Day," Heathron stated matter-of-factly.

"I am glad to have arrived in time." Kathleen lowered her eyes.

"Are you?" he asked.

The sharpness she could hear in his voice made her scramble to gather her thoughts. She had displeased him already. Beginning your life with someone who already found you unpleasant was no way to live.

"Why would you ask that, Your Highness?" she said, trying to make her voice a little louder, harder.

He turned his back to her and raised a hand tentatively to his cheek, then shook his head. "I am not sure…" he began to say, then paused and looked up at the ceiling, "I'm not sure, Kathleen, if we can be married."

Kathleen blinked. "You're not sure?"

Prince Heathron turned and looked at her now, his eyes hard, face chiseled—he looked the same, and yet so different from how she remembered him as a child.

"I cannot change what I am," Kathleen added, emboldened by her silence. Despite this, her voice still trembled.

"You are not ashamed? I believed in love, Kathleen! Now you have betrayed me. What did I do to deserve this?"

Kathleen began to understand what angered the prince. "But this was no choice of mine, Your Highness. If you think it gives me joy to see your pain, you are mistaken."

"Were you forced, then? Against your will to marry the guardian and wear the *kanatru* about your waist?" Heathron said, his voice catching in his throat.

Kathleen touched the necklace at her throat.

"Your Highness, I thought you spoke of me being what is called a Gardener, or a Green Grower. I am Talented, I admit it. I did not reveal that to you in our correspondence," she said.

"Some in this city would call a woman such as yourself a Plant Witch."

Kathleen held his gaze as tears welled in her eyes.

"But a Talent is no deterrent to my love. I assumed all along you might have the gift, since your mother was Talented."

Kathleen dropped her gaze to the floor.

Heathron reached out and placed his hand on her chin and gently lifted her eyes back towards his.

"The ring you wear on your hand isn't the one I gave you. I need to know the truth. I want to hear what happened before I condemn a man to death," the prince said earnestly.

Kathleen sucked in a breath. The words came out in a tumult.

"I will tell you everything. Jared is innocent. It was only part of a disguise. The Delathranes attacked and I was separated from the procession..."

The prince held up his hand, and Kathleen stopped speaking.

"Jared?" Heathron said. "You call him by his given name?"

"It is not like that, Your Highness. I left Candoreth with a willingness to spend my life with you. We were attacked multiple times, and the Sīhalt did the best he could to protect me."

Heathron nodded and tapped his chin with his finger, resting an elbow on his knuckles. He rose up to the throne once more and lowered himself into it. "I am listening," he said.

Kathleen went on to recount the details of the journey from Candoreth to Tyath. She recounted the first time the Delathranes had attacked and looked specifically for her. She described the fall Jared survived and her abduction by the Serpent King.

Throughout it all Heathron nodded and listened. At times he stopped and asked for details. He listened gravely.

"And then we made the dash for the gates. I thought we would die."

Kathleen finished and waited for Heathron to speak.

The handsome prince pursed his lips in thought.

"I have dreamt of this day since we were children," he said. "I have loved you, or at least the idea of you, for as long as I can remember."

Kathleen let out a small laugh at the confession.

The prince continued. "I take my promises seriously, and I have held myself to the oath I swore to you as a boy."

"I remember," Kathleen said, her eyes growing moist.

Heathron looked up at the beautiful expanse of the ceiling, and then back at Kathleen.

"Did you save yourself for me?" he asked seriously.

"I have," she replied.

"Do you love him?"

The question took Kathleen by surprise. She had answered it for herself only days ago, but to be asked right here in front of her future husband, she stammered for a reply.

"We… we went through a lot together."

"Kathleen, we cannot be married—not today," Heathron said.

Relief and worry filled her heart. Kathleen felt relieved that she would not enter into a marriage when her heart was held by another, but fear for her nation came crashing down upon her. Tears sprang to her eyes.

"I'm sorry," she said.

"I believe all that you have said. I am prepared to wait longer if I must. You see, I don't just want your willingness to marry me. I want your desire."

Kathleen shook with difficulty to control her emotions as she cried. After all she had been though, all she had sacrificed, she still could not protect her family or her people. She had failed.

"I know you worry about Sundiland. You never struck me as a girl taken by riches. It isn't the wealth you want, is it?" Heathron asked.

Kathleen wiped away tears and shook her head.

"I am prepared to protect your home city of Candoreth, but you must remain as my guest here in this city. Perhaps with more time together, we may become not only friends, but find the love we both seek."

Kathleen nodded, not knowing what else she might do.

"I will stay here," she agreed.

"I fear a great war is upon us," the prince said gravely. "The Delathrane barbarians have disappeared from our borders—for now. They departed as soon as you made it within the city walls. Still, it would not be wise to send you home anytime soon. I will send our navy to assist your father in the defense of Candoreth from the pirates. Along with military support, we will send food. I heard of your difficulties on the road."

A flood of gratitude swept over Kathleen. Despite herself, she rushed forward and threw her arms around Prince Heathron, hugging him tightly.

Heathron stood awkwardly for a moment. "We in the north are not as familiar with each other as you are in the South," he said, but finally returned Kathleen's embrace.

"Thank you so much, Your Highness, but why would you defend Candoreth if we are not even to be married?" Kathleen asked.

"You have kept your portion of our agreement. Although the journey was dangerous, here you are, standing before me on the appointed day. Even if the methods required for your arrival were ones that I was not prepared for, you have kept your promise. I will keep mine as well."

"I heard the Guardian was arrested. Will you release him?" Kathleen asked.

Heathron paused for a moment, and Kathleen could see him

harden a little at the name. He breathed out heavily through his nose. "He is currently being held in confinement. He stands accused of treason against the Empire. If he is innocent, he must leave Tyath. That is the best I can do."

"May I see him before he leaves?"

"You should avoid being seen with him," Heathron said.

"He risked his life for me, and I have not been able to even thank him," Kathleen pleaded.

"That was the risk he accepted when I hired him. Nevertheless, you may visit him if that is your desire."

"Thank you, Your Highness." Kathleen turned to leave, eager to make her way to Jared.

"One more thing I must request of you as you remain as my guest here in Tyath," the prince said.

Kathleen stopped and turned around. "What is that?" she asked.

"Would you call me Heathron?"

Kathleen nodded again, wiping tears from her eyes. She was smiling, and she felt a great deal of relief.

"Thank you, Heathron."

HEALING PAIN

The people of Tyath were elated that the summer solstice had finally arrived. The Imperial Wedding Day would go ahead as planned with all the attendant feasts and celebrations. More soldiers stood ready on the walls of Tyath, but the barbarian threat had disappeared like the smoke of their sudden attack.

Emperor Kade Dol Lassimer spoke to his people. He encouraged them to make merry and refuse to allow the Golden City to be held hostage by what he called the "ignorant barbarians from across the river." The Midsummer's Day festivals were as loud and colorful as they had ever been.

Presently, Kathleen ran through the crowds, moving fluidly in her green dress as she made her way toward the stables. She was told that she might find Jared there, and, afraid she might miss him, her long delicate neck ached from craning it at every angle to see her Guardian rider anytime a horse passed. She could not find him in the throng of people that crowded the streets.

Kathleen ran down a tiled hallway, the arch high enough to allow mounted men to pass. She looked into each stall, hoping to find Steed.

"Boy!" She called to a stablehand at the end of the hall. "The Sīhalt Guardian—where did he go?"

The boy, dressed in rags with dirt on his cheeks, looked back and said, "Is he the man that rides that black devil? That horse nearly took my arm off when I put some salve on his wound! Some gratitude that is!"

Kathleen marched to the boy. "I haven't time. Where is he?" she asked desperately.

"Over at the stablehand rooms, my lady. He's right beside his horse's stall. He's the only man that can care for that beast." He pointed to the end of the next row.

Kathleen looked and saw Steed's head nodding over the gate of a distant stall. She could barely keep herself from sprinting like a foolish milkmaid to the open door beside it.

"Be careful not to slip in here, my lady. That is a fine dress you are wearing!" the boy called out behind her.

Kathleen came to touch Steed on the nose, and he nuzzled her hand and flicked his ears forward in response. She noticed that he had been saddled, and a scabbard and blanket roll had been placed upon his back.

"I guess you deserve my thanks as well, Steed," she said, drawing his head in closer and stroking his neck.

The horse bobbed his head twice as if he understood.

Next, Kathleen walked into the room as quietly as she could. Jared's back was turned to her, and he was bending over to put on the clean shirt. He looked stronger now, and there were scars scattered across his back. Those wounds had almost taken his life, she thought. Jared slid one arm into a sleeve, still not noticing her. Kathleen stood watching.

"Now it's your turn to sneak up on me, I see," he said, but his voice was deeper and had a rougher sound than she remembered.

As he turned around, he slid his other arm into the shirt. The white linen hung open, and Kathleen's eyes danced across his exposed chest before stopping at those storm-gray eyes.

He stood with hands open, arms at his side. Vulnerable. She could not hide the shock on her face at the change the Healing had wrought. Her hand covered her mouth. It was as if her Sīhalt Guardian had taken a long voyage to a distant land and returned today, older and more profound.

He stood with the same posture that was so familiar to her, one of a man ready for instant action, but graceful like a song. His hair was streaked with gray at his temples, and his closely trimmed bread was both salt and pepper. His visage was that of a man both rugged and refined. Kathleen was speechless.

She fought down an urge to run into his arms. Her heart pounded, and she knew that he could read her every emotion. She didn't care.

"I heard you didn't get married," he said.

Was that a smile she saw on his lips?

She shook her head.

"I'm older," he said, arching his eyebrows and holding his hands in front of himself. It was almost an apology.

"You are alive!" Kathleen finally said, feeling the relief of that truth.

"And free. Thanks to you, I suppose," he replied.

"Melva Healed you, but they wouldn't let her touch me." Kathleen gestured to her face.

"Purple is a good color on you," he said, and smiled with a smile that touched his eyes.

"They said I hit my head on the stones. I remember you holding on to me as we clattered through the gate. Thank you, Jared," Kathleen said, shaking her head and blinking back the tears.

"I did not want to let go," he said in that deep tone. There was that faintest smile again.

Kathleen swallowed and leaned forward, rocking up to her tiptoes, but took no further step forward. She didn't dare. He stood fixed where he was as well, unwilling or unable to close the gap between them.

"How long will you stay?" she asked, hoping he might say forever.

"I am leaving right now. I must report to Master Tove. He promised me if I brought you safely to the Golden City, I would be allowed to search for Seth."

"I see..." she said, and opened her mouth to say something more but closed it again.

Jared raised an eyebrow. "You are hesitant. What is it you want to say?"

Katheleen was fidgeting slightly, rubbing her arms, gazing into the corner of the room. Then she came out with it, terrified about what answer would return, but relieved to have finally released it.

"Is that the only reason you agreed to be my Guardian?" Kathleen asked. "So you could have permission to go into the wild searching for Seth?"

Jared seemed to consider this. "I had no idea what I was getting into," he began. "Anyway, Prince Dol Lassimer was kind enough to allow me to keep my head. I shouldn't push my luck."

It was these last words that struck a blow to Kathleen the most. What she would say next, she knew she would have to summon the strength to keep her voice strong.

"And who will protect me when you are gone?" she asked. It came out as a whisper.

"Kathleen, you belong here now. You are safe. You are protected by these strong walls. The prince said you would reside here as a guest for this year. I heard he even said he would send food to Candoreth."

"He does seem kind," Kathleen said. Jared nodded.

"You are strong, Kathleen." He smiled kindly, stepping forward now so that he stood but an arm's length away from her. He raised her chin. "Give yourself the year to consider what lies before you. I plan to return to find out what you have decided," he said.

"I have already decided," she said, tears spilling onto her cheeks. "I want to be with you!"

Jared took a step closer to her and stroked a stray red curl back behind her ear. "You have changed so much since beginning our journey from Candoreth," he said softly. "And so have I."

Kathleen studied the lines on his face, the gray flecks of his hair, and understood what he meant. Still, if anything the color of his eyes was even more intense than she had remembered.

He continued, "But the Empire is protecting Candoreth, and all the people you love, in the hope that the marriage will take place. I will not be the one who destroys that."

"For a man who didn't want to be my Guardian in the first place, you sure did a good job of it," she said, tears finally falling down her cheeks. She wiped them away with a brush of her hand. "I love you," she said.

"You need time to consider all the implications. Try to enjoy this year in Tyath."

"I know my heart, Jared."

"I do not doubt it. When I am free of commitments, then we might be together."

"But you could die out there."

Jared shook his head. "I will return. If you still want me, give me a sign I will understand."

"A sign? But…what sign?" she asked, shaking her head, feeling the hot touch of more tears streaming down her cheeks.

"If you decide to move on and marry Heathron, I will bless the memory of our time together. Perhaps, in a year, I will watch your wedding from a distant perch as you walk up the steps of the Great Cathedral. You would never have to see me again," he said.

"Don't taunt me," she said, biting her lip against her smile and wiping her eyes again.

"For weeks you were mine," he said. "At least it felt that way during the moments we were together."

He gathered up the last of his items and finished buttoning his shirt. The Sīhalt Guardian threw his cloak across his shoulders and closed the silver clasp about his neck.

"I can be yours forever," Kathleen said.

Jared dropped his pack and swept Kathleen into his arms. Holding her against his chest. She took a deep breath, holding his scent, wishing for just a few more moments together.

"I hope that is true, Sunshine Bride," he said, then he released the embrace and mounted the black horse.

"I will come looking for a sign, Kathleen," he said.

"I promise," she whispered through her tears.

Kathleen watched him ride away, out the gleaming city gates, to the Amaranth Plains beyond.

The End of Book One

AUTHOR'S PROMISE

I hope you loved the story! Help me succeed in creating this series and leave a review online. Social proof is powerful.

In **Guardian of the Golden City**, *Book Two of the Sīhalt Series*, we will continue the adventure with Jared in his quest to find Seth, and Kathleen as she forms new friendships in a hostile city. It will be exciting! Book Two is coming along nicely. I plan to publish it in May 2019.

Go to my website AustinRehl.com and I'll give you the earliest updates as well as material related to the Lands of Desnia.

All the Best,

Austin Rehl

P.S. My email is austin@austinrehl.com.

ABOUT THE AUTHOR

Austin Rehl lives in beautiful Marietta, Ohio with his wonderful wife and six talented children. He is a practicing dentist, and also enjoys working on his farm, hunting in the woods, and spending time with friends and family.

Austin considers himself a romantic, a poet, and now a debut novelist. He enjoys reading and writing fantasy and sci-fi. Go to austinrehl.com to stay in touch.

Made in the USA
Monee, IL
05 April 2021

63596607R00233